PRAISE FOR
THE TUMBLING TURNER SISTERS

"This novel of love, grit, and the everlasting strength of family perfectly encapsulates the social mores and pressures of the early twentieth century. The Turner sisters dare to dream big—don't miss this page-turner!"

> —Sara Gruen, #1 *New York Times* bestselling author of
> *Water for Elephants*

"Filled with energetic prose and colorful characters—you won't soon forget the Turner girls!"

> —Christina Baker Kline, #1 *New York Times* bestselling author of
> *Orphan Train*

"Book clubs are sure to fall for *The Tumbling Turner Sisters*. Through this band of charming young women—and their stage mother, of course—Juliette Fay delivers the history, mystery, and prejudice of vaudeville in a story that is ultimately about the possibility of practice making something perfect (or perfect enough, anyway), the benefits of humor and ambition, and the redemptive power of love."

> —Meg Waite Clayton, *New York Times* bestselling author of
> *The Race for Paris*

"Lovable, memorable characters propel this heartwarming story, which makes you laugh while it makes you think, then sticks with you long after the last vibrant page is savored."

> —Lynn Cullen, bestselling author of
> *Twain's End* and *Mrs. Poe*

"Like the fabulous days of vaudeville itself, at once funny and poignant and memorable. These four sisters are endearing and entertaining, and book clubs are going to lap this one up—as will readers of historical fiction everywhere."

—M. J. Rose, *New York Times* bestselling author of
The Secret Language of Stones

"The Turner sisters come tumbling out of this terrific story, full of life, passion, and trouble. Forced into a life in vaudeville, the four young girls and their mother push the boundaries of propriety to achieve their dreams in a world that doesn't often allow women to have dreams. Gert and Winnie shine as each, in her own way, fights for her right to be who she is. A great piece of historical fiction that rings true one hundred years later."

—B. A. Shapiro, *New York Times* bestselling author of
The Muralist and *The Art Forger*

"Evoking the entrepreneurial, madcap era of vaudeville, Juliette Fay immerses us in the trials, joys, and dangers of four young women, whose bid for success is as uproarious and heartbreaking as the time in which they lived."

—C. W. Gortner, bestselling author of
Mademoiselle Chanel

"*The Tumbling Turner Sisters* explores vaudeville with stunning humanity and sharp humor. Juliette Fay's novel of sisters forced by their ultimate stage mother into this show business world of fanciful facade hiding cutthroat innards reveals America—from Jim Crow laws to skirting prohibition. Like *Little Women*, these four sisters, facing loss and poverty, reveal a family with an unbreakable core of fortitude and love."

—Randy Susan Meyers, bestselling author of
Accidents of Marriage

"As colorful as its vaudeville setting, *The Tumbling Turner Sisters* made me laugh, cry, and clap my hands with delight as I cheered on these four lovable and spunky sisters. A bighearted tale of adventure."

—Ann Mah, author of
Mastering the Art of French Eating

"Packed with lively characters and charming detail, Juliette Fay's thoughtful prose sheds light on an almost forgotten part of entertainment history."

—Allie Larkin, bestselling author of
Stay and *Why Can't I Be You*

"*The Tumbling Turner Sisters* takes you on a wild ride through the glory days of vaudeville, following Winnie and Gert as they hit the gritty floorboards of backwater theaters, pick themselves up, and strive again toward laughter-filled heights. The prose is riveting as the sisters carry their family out of poverty in a time of racially charged political turmoil. Through Juliette Fay's multilayered characters, I feel the sisters' entanglements and passions as if they were my own."

—E. B. Moore, author of
An Unseemly Wife and *Stones in the Road*

"An absorbing and heartfelt tale of four sisters in desperate contortions to keep their family aloft. I loved this slice of theatrical history, and Fay's meticulous research brings to life the vivid playhouses and costumed performers—ingénues and divas, swindlers and sots. I stayed awake far too late wondering whether the girls would come in for a safe landing."

—Nichole Bernier, author of
The Unfinished Work of Elizabeth D.

"Readers who delight in books set around the 1920s or feature the theater will adore Fay's spunky coming-of-age tale. Told in the alternating voices of two of the four sisters, this wonderfully evocative story charms readers. The delightful quotes from famous vaudeville performers, along with colorful details of life on the stage, are a testament to Fay's meticulous research. The pace is as rapid as their tumbling, and the appealing characters add to the enjoyment readers will feel from a story with gumption."

—*RT Book Reviews* (in a 4-star review)

"With humor, affection, ambition, and a talent for weaving in history, Fay brings the world of 1910s vaudeville vividly to life through the travails of the tenacious Turner family."

—*Publishers Weekly*

THE
TUMBLING
TURNER SISTERS

JULIETTE FAY

GALLERY BOOKS

New York London Toronto Sydney New Delhi

G

Gallery Books
An Imprint of Simon & Schuster, Inc.
1230 Avenue of the Americas
New York, NY 10020

First Gallery Books trade paperback edition January 2017

GALLERY BOOKS and colophon are registered trademarks of Simon & Schuster, Inc.

For information about special discounts for bulk purchases, please contact Simon & Schuster Special Sales at 1-866-506-1949 or business@ simonandschuster.com.

The Simon & Schuster Speakers Bureau can bring authors to your live event. For more information or to book an event contact the Simon & Schuster Speakers Bureau at 1-866-248-3049 or visit our website at www.simonspeakers.com.

Manufactured in the United States of America

10 9 8 7 6 5 4 3

The Library of Congress has cataloged the hardcover edition as follows:
Names: Fay, Juliette, author.
Title: The Tumbling Turner sisters / Juliette Fay.
Description: First Gallery Books hardcover edition. | New York : Gallery Books, 2016.
Identifiers: LCCN 2015039001
Subjects: | BISAC: FICTION / Historical. | FICTION / Coming of Age. | FICTION / General. | GSAFD: Bildungsromans.
Classification: LCC PS3606.A95 T86 2016 | DDC 813/.6—dc23 LC record available at http://lccn.loc.gov/2015039001

ISBN 978-1-5011-4534-6
ISBN 978-1-5011-3447-0 (hardcover)
ISBN 978-1-5011-3448-7 (ebook)

FOR BRIANNA, LIAM, NICK, AND QUINN,
WITH GREAT LOVE,

AND FOR FRED DELORME AND
MARGARET DELORME DACEY,

NOW DANCING IN THE HEAVENS
WITH STARS FOR THEIR FOOTLIGHTS.

Vaudeville was the major source of entertainment in America from the 1880s through the 1920s. A vaudeville show was comprised of between seven and fifteen separate unconnected acts—anything from juggling to short plays, comedy routines to performing animals, edifying lectures to singalongs. Even small towns often had vaudeville theatres, and larger cities might have upward of five. In 1914, there were approximately fifty vaudeville venues in New York City alone.

Full-length plays, often referred to as "legitimate" theatre, tended to be more expensive and highbrow. Burlesque was generally considered too risqué for women and children. Other forms of mass entertainment were still in their infancy: movies were black-and-white, and silent; "talkies" (movies with synchronized sound) weren't commonplace until the late 1920s; and the first radio broadcasts didn't begin until 1920. Until then, if you wanted to be entertained, you went to a live show.

For most of America, that meant vaudeville.

CHAPTER

1

WINNIE

Everything I know I learned in vaudeville.
—James Cagney, singer, dancer, and actor

Nothing good comes from a knock in the middle of the night.

The windows rattled in their casings as someone banged on the front door. I roused myself from sleep, thinking that between the banging and the cold, the glass would surely break. As it turned out, mere broken glass would've been a blessing.

I heard Mother's thumping footsteps in her bedroom below, through the kitchen, and across the living room, and I scurried downstairs to meet her, followed by my older sisters, Gert and Nell. Mother was at the front window, her back hunched against the cold, the few threads of silver in her hair made eerily iridescent by the streetlamp. She peered through the curtains she'd made from cut-rate lace. They did nothing to keep in the heat, but she said they gussied up the place, and the occasional hole in the pattern made it easier to peek through if you didn't want someone to know you were watching.

She stood motionless, like a rabbit after the snap of a twig, trying to determine whether the door should be opened or, as was sometimes the case in our neighborhood, a chair wedged under the knob. "Nobody there," she whispered to us without turning.

"Where's Dad?" Nell asked, wrapping her thin arms around her.

"He went out. Got his temper all twisted up about Prohibition."

"His *temper*?" Gert's tone conveyed the skepticism we all felt.

Dad was the most placid man we knew. Yet his voice did take on a slightly brittle edge at the mention of the rapidly approaching Prohibition Act. He didn't tend toward drunkenness himself, nor to public consumption in rowdy beer halls, preferring to sit home with his Blatz beer and sip quietly in the midst of his own rowdy family. He could not understand why Congress had taken this away from all the well-meaning souls whose lives were speckled with hardships of every variety, and who just wanted to enjoy the gentle lulling effect of a libation or two in the evening.

Prohibition was passed on January 16, 1919, and the next day the *Binghamton Press* in Upstate New York, where we lived, had extra-large-type headlines:

U.S. IS VOTED BONE-DRY

Though it would not go into effect for another year, once he saw that headline, Dad had been even quieter than usual.

That tar-black night, Mother opened the front door with the three of us, now joined by our youngest sister, Kit, crowding behind her. What we saw, we'd never seen before.

Dad leaned against the doorjamb, blinking slowly, a wobbly half smile on his lips. Blood seeped from crooked gashes on his right hand, bone visible at two of his knuckles. His fingers were bent at unnatural angles as if they'd been smashed under the heel of a boot.

He stumbled through the open door, and Mother lurched forward to catch him. With uncharacteristic care, she half guided, half carried him to a kitchen chair. Kit brought a pot of warm soapy water and a rag, and I dabbed at the jagged, pulpy wounds to get the grit out.

Then Mother's temper set in, and her hands balled into fists at her hips. "What in the name of holy hell happened to you! Can't you go out and tie one on like any other man without disaster striking?"

Dad seemed as surprised as we all were at the state of his hand. "There was a fight . . ."

"Frank Turner, when have you *ever*, in all your born days, gotten into a fight?"

"Wasn't me. Coupla guys at the tavern," he slurred, shaking his head mournfully. "Tried to stop it . . ."

Mother's face twisted in disgust. "Of all the stupid—"

Gert cut her off, ice-blue eyes flashing with annoyance. "It doesn't matter how it happened, Mother," she muttered. "It only matters that it can be fixed."

Mother hustled Dad and me through the dark streets toward Our Lady of Lourdes Hospital, our breath pluming like frozen feathers into the air, and I practically had to skip to keep up. I had an after-school job as a nurse's aide in the Lourdes maternity ward; Mother brought me along in case my experience or connections, lowly as they were, might come in handy.

They did not. I recognized a nurse in the Emergency Department, but she didn't have a reciprocal response. Without my uniform, she likely mistook me for a child, as my small stature often prompted people to do.

As for experience, I could have discussed any number of baby delivery procedures (having shut my mouth and listened carefully in the nurses' break room as often as I could justify my presence there), but thankfully broken bones and torn tendons were not issues we generally faced on the maternity ward.

The Emergency Department halls were quiet, save for the murmurs of worried family members or nurses checking vitals, white curtains billowing with their comings and goings. The place smelled strongly of carbolic, and I knew some poor nurse's aide like myself had recently cleaned up a mess of some kind. I looked down at my hands, dry and cracked around the knuckles. At seventeen years old, I had already scrubbed away a lifetime's worth of bodily events.

We were ushered behind one of those curtains, and the doctor, an elderly fellow with a tentacular bush of gray hair, applied shots of Novocain to numb Dad's hand. He then began the lengthy task of stitching up all that damage. The old doctor's fingers trembled as he stabbed the needle under the skin and tugged it out on the other side, the stitches growing increasingly more uneven. Though I was a poor seamstress, I had the absurd notion to offer to help. Dad lay on the gurney with his eyes closed. Mother always went gray as old bedclothes at the sight of a pinprick, so she'd stayed in the waiting room. I was the sole witness to the doctor's skill slowly wilting like a dying flower.

After he'd bandaged up Dad's hand, the old doctor said, "Now say your prayers that the nerve damage isn't too bad, and there's a reasonable chance he might recover full use."

This was the one moment when I did prove useful. I asked, "What are the chances that he *won't* recover full use?"

The doctor blinked at me once or twice as if just now noticing my presence. "Well, I suppose there's a reasonable chance of that, too."

The sun was just beginning to lick up through the treetops in the Floral Park Cemetery as we walked home. Mother was quiet, but her fury pulsed like aftershocks from an earthquake. Father, now sober enough to suffer both the physical pain and the mental anguish caused by what he'd done, was also mute. For myself, I vacillated between the childish belief that things couldn't possibly be as bad as they seemed, and the adult knowledge that they could hardly be any worse.

Mother suddenly turned on Dad. "You're a *boot stitcher*, for godsake!" she hissed.

My father worked at the Endicott-Johnson shoe factory. He spent each day with a large metal needle in one hand, wrenching it through stiff soles and thick leather uppers grasped in the other. I'll make it plain: there is no such thing as a one-handed boot stitcher. In fact, in a shoe factory, there is no manual labor that can be done by a man with a crushed dominant hand.

When we opened the front door, my sisters were crowded into the kitchen. Nell poured coffee from the percolator. Kit sat at the gate-leg table eating a soft-boiled egg; Gert ironed her shirtwaist. To their credit, no one gasped when they saw Dad's hand wrapped up like a mummy.

Then Dad spoke. "I . . . I'm sorry . . . ," he stammered, eyes damp with remorse. My throat clenched in sympathy. Nell bit at the inside of her lip, Gert's nostrils flared, and Kit inhaled a childish little sniffle.

Mother let her hand rest on Dad's shoulder, perhaps in acceptance of his apology, or perhaps it was simply to steady herself. After
a moment, she gave him a little push toward their room behind the
kitchen. "Go on and get some rest," she said, her voice hoarse with
exhaustion.

She dropped onto one of the mismatched chairs and Nell put a
mug of hot coffee in front of her. Mother took a sip, and we waited—for
the solution to this seemingly insurmountable problem, or for her to
howl like a wounded animal and throw her mug against the wall.

I don't believe I would have been truly surprised by almost anything she could have said or done in that moment. She could have told
us she was selling our father into indentured servitude to pay the bills,
and I wouldn't have been truly shocked.

She stared menacingly at the frost lacing the kitchen window, and
we could almost see the schemes she silently conjured as they took
shape and then were cast aside. Mother is a force, sometimes for our
betterment, sometimes for retribution, and sometimes simply for her
own entertainment. We waited, barely breathing, for her word.

Her expression shifted almost imperceptibly, from desperation to
determination. What she said was this:

"Be ready to work on the act when you get home from school. And
I mean *work*."

That was unexpected.

CHAPTER

2

GERT

If opportunity doesn't knock, build a door.
—Milton Berle, comedian and actor

The act.

It was Mother's idea, and so of course I hated it. At first.

It was one of the few things we Turner girls had in common: no desire to perform. We were never the types to twirl around or sing as we hung the washing. Honestly, I don't even hum.

Mother, on the other hand, had always wanted to be onstage. Her grand plans for stardom had been tut-tutted away by her parents, then she got married quickly—*very* quickly—and had Nell right away. She made her bed, is all I'll say about that.

"Gert, the way you turn heads, you'd be the star of any show," she'd whisper in my ear. Of course, there was no money for dance or voice lessons, so she didn't have the means to bully us into it, which she certainly would've done, given the dough. Lord knows Dad couldn't have stopped her. Then again, Teddy Roosevelt and the Rough Riders probably couldn't have, either.

I'll give her this: she always had her nose to the wind, sniffing out ways to improve our station in life. Once it was aprons fashioned like a cigarette girl's outfit in a swanky dinner theatre. She sewed them in black satin, with cinched waists and darts to make plenty of room at the bosom. We hawked them door to door, wearing them as we went. "Like models," she said.

I had the most success when a husband answered the door. I'd slide a hand down over my hip and say, "Wouldn't you like to come home to your wife cooking dinner in this?" He'd fork over the dollar, barely remembering to ask for change, and I'd beat a quick exit to the sidewalk, taking care to pinch the boredom from my cheeks before I rang the next fellow's bell.

"Gert's my top seller," Mother announced one night, trying to stir up sisterly competition.

"No surprise," Kit had muttered. She was thirteen years old and almost six feet tall, so her figure didn't exactly lend itself to fashion sales. With her longish face, big brown eyes, and unruly brown mane, she looked like a baby giraffe.

As for Winnie, I nearly laughed out loud when Mother found her with a stack of unsold aprons behind a tree, reading a mouse-nibbled copy of *Anne of Green Gables*.

"What are you doing with that old book?" Mother snapped. "You've read it so many times it's a wonder there's still ink on the pages!"

"That's all right, Mother," I said. "Winnie wasn't selling many anyhow. She doesn't have enough up front to advertise their best feature." Seventeen years old and she was still the size of an underfed fifth-grader. Her face had a childish sweetness, but her green eyes always seemed to be squinting at something—a book, her homework, or *me* when she didn't get my humor.

Mother let her be after that, but did I get any thanks from Winnie? Not a whisper.

Aprons were going like hotcakes (thanks mainly to my sales strategy) until the president of the St. James Ladies' Guild accused Mother of trying to turn Johnson City into one big cathouse. Sales slowed to a dribble. Murderous as a jilted bride, Mother shoved the yards of black satin she'd bought up into the attic. It sat there bunched like a panther ready to strike.

The idea for the sister act came to her like a brick through the window in September 1918. Of course it didn't include our oldest sister, Nell. She was married and living in an apartment the size of a hatbox a couple of blocks away, honorably discharged from Mother's army of foot soldiers. To clinch her escape, she'd just given birth to a fat baby boy who, if he wasn't sleeping or nursing, was bawling his brains out. Somehow he was beautiful, though, I suppose simply because he was ours.

A vaudeville act, for cripes' sake. How I rolled my eyes at that.

"What do you think?" Mother whispered as a three-girl tap-dancing act shuffle-hop-stepped their way across the stage. "You could learn that, easy as pie."

We were at the Stone Opera House in Binghamton, in plush velvet front-row seats for once instead of in the gallery up by the rafters, which smelled of workingman's sweat and cheap pomade. We loved vaudeville—who didn't?—but we didn't always have the two bits to go. Once Mother had her bright idea, we ate less and went more often. It was research, she said. Stealing was more like it.

The tap dancers belted out a whiny version of "Frankfurter Sandwiches" and tried not to maul one another with their metal-tipped shoes. "You know I can't carry a tune," I said.

"Winnie's voice isn't bad," Mother countered. "You could sing quietly."

I crossed my arms. "Maybe I won't sing at all." I saw Winnie shift in her seat.

"They look kind of ridiculous," she said to Kit, and Kit nodded.

And that's how it was. Clearly they would rely on me to be the brightest, shiniest star of our little three-girl galaxy. *Well, if I'm to shoulder the weight,* I thought, *it better be something less embarrassing than singing stupid songs about cheap food.*

Mother huffed and glared back up at the stage.

The next act was a fat woman in a black dress the size of a deflated hot air balloon. She'd taught six white rats to do tricks.

For a finale they scuttled up through her dress and out the sleeves to perch on her arms. She shimmied, and they all stood up on their hindquarters. Then one of the rats fell off—now I see it was a gag—and ran full tilt to the edge of the stage toward us. Thinking I was about to have vermin clawing up my shirtwaist, I screamed so loud I could've knocked the glass windscreen out of every car within four blocks. The audience roared with laughter, the rat ran back to its mistress, and she curtsied without losing a single rodent.

Mother glanced at us, eyebrow raised. Shameless, I tell you.

"Absolutely not!" I said. Mother, of course, looked to Winnie for reinforcement, because she never defied her.

"How would you actually train rats?" Winnie asked. "It seems like it might take a while."

I suppose it did the trick, because Mother sighed and sat back in her seat. But it wasn't exactly a show of sisterly support, either. Winnie could never just say no and let the chips fall as they might. She always had some high-minded reason why, and it made me look like a tantrum-throwing child by comparison.

The next act was a regurgitator. Bloated and barrel-chested, the man swallowed things—a goldfish or a hard-boiled egg, shell and all—and then heaved them back up. When the egg came up, his assistant rinsed it in water, cracked the shell, and ate it to prove it was real. When the fish came up, it went right into a bowl of water and darted crookedly around its little glass prison.

Thankfully, Mother didn't even glance over after the regurgitator. Sometimes I wondered exactly how far she would go to make us a success, but apparently upchucking household items was a step too far. On that day, at least. On another day, she might've found it perfectly reasonable. Fickle as young love, our mother.

She never wavered about Dad, though, always poking at him to do better at the factory. "Your damned paycheck is a mortifying pittance!" she'd rail.

"It's enough, Ethel," he'd say. Then he'd lean as close to the dented metal horn of his phonograph as humanly possible without actually climbing into the thing. All he wanted was his house warm, his beer cold, and his phonograph needle sharp so he could play his Enrico Caruso records at a volume just above what Mother could bear. By which I mean in any way audible.

I couldn't always judge Mother as harshly as I fully meant to, though. After all, it was a question I asked myself every day. What was I willing to do to have a bigger, better life—to avoid my mother's lot, captive in a boring little town, scraping for every mouthful?

I'd been planning my escape as long as I could remember. What wouldn't I do to be free?

The next night was Friday, and I worked my usual closing shift at J. J. Wiley's Pub and Cafe.

"Thirsty?" said Roy, the bartender, and slid over a glass of Coca-Cola as we waited for the last customers to toddle on home.

"Thanks." I took a sip and leaned on the bar, looking out over the dining room. I set the glass back down. "It's missing something." The glass was lifted from my hand. When it returned, I took another sip. There it was, a splash of rum. I turned to Roy and smiled.

He was twenty-eight, and it was a relief to smile at a man old enough not to blush over a silly facial expression. There were a lot of things I liked about Roy. He worked hard, saving up for a restaurant of his own one day. His good looks were subtle: medium height, not overly muscular, but with a strong jaw and powerful hands. A good kisser, too.

"Someday, Gert," he would whisper against my cheek when we necked. "Someday."

I liked a man who could wait, who didn't try and paw his way to what he wanted. We'd been quietly seeing each other for six months, and finally his wait had been over. He'd been as gentle as such things can be, I suppose. Afterward, I'd smiled sweetly and reassured him it was nice. But honestly, I just didn't get the appeal.

Roy was a very happy man, and now "someday" meant something else entirely. Something more public, and more permanent.

But I wasn't so sure about that.

I'll admit being a restaurant owner's wife was a step up, but in some way, wasn't it all the same? Working hard, day in and day out, stuck in the same place with more or less the same people?

"With your looks and charm," he'd say, "you'll be the perfect restaurant hostess, Gert."

I could be good at a lot of things, I thought.

And I'd barely begun to imagine them all.

CHAPTER
3

WINNIE

You are all you will ever have for certain.
—June Havoc, actress and dancer

We first saw the boy acrobats in September 1918. I remember because school had begun, and I was worried that I wouldn't get all of my advanced math homework done.

"*Advanced* math," Gert had sneered. "As if slaving over *regular old* math isn't odd enough."

I didn't dignify it with a response. She could flunk out and end up a washerwoman, for all I cared. Except it was Gert. She'd probably end up marrying Douglas Fairbanks. (That is, if his high-flying career ever brought him to Johnson City, New York, which I found dubious in the extreme.)

We were up in the gallery again, as Mother had finally realized that front-row seats equaled bare cupboards. The seats were wooden and the floor was scattered with cigarette and cigar butts. But we didn't mind so much. It was still a thrill to be in a fancy theatre, even if most of the fancy was far below us.

Our oldest sister, Nell, was with us that night. She had grown increasingly anxious as she waited for her husband, Harry, to return home from the Great War, and we didn't like to leave her alone too long. The anxiety mirrored the depth of her love and longing, which was understandable given its object.

Harry was a sandy-haired boy we'd all had a crush on at one time or another, he was just that universally lovable. Funny when you wanted to laugh, serious as a priest when you needed advice, he didn't have much in the way of answers so much as an appearance of deep interest in the questions. He made me feel fascinating, not like some quirky girl who thinks too much.

As Harry's return drew closer, we began collecting Nell and the baby on our way home from school, so she could sit at our house and be distracted by the comforting reliability of our family's contentiousness. It had been sad enough for her to bring Harry's son into the world without him near—even worse to know he was dodging bullets and mustard gas somewhere in the midst of the greatest war of all time. Her worry could not be contained for long within the four walls of her tiny apartment, and she preferred to be with us. Baby Harry napped among the nightgowns in the bottom drawer of Gert's dresser, when he wasn't exercising his lungs from colic.

The evening we saw the acrobats, Nell had laid him to sleep, leaving Dad to listen for his cry. Dad didn't mind. He'd just turn up the volume on his phonograph and walk the squalling baby around the living room, as he'd done with us when we were little.

There were four young men in the acrobat troupe, all dressed in black tights and red satin tops. One had thighs and a neck the girth of a telephone pole. He served as the foundation for the amazing acts of strength and agility, casually flipping another man up and into the air or over his shoulder. Two were of middling size, while the last was small and lithe. He was the ball with which they played, curling his head tightly into his bent knees as they tossed him around the stage. I stared in wonder, imagining how exhilarating it must feel to sail through the air like that. As a tiny girl I had always loved when Dad had swung me around, grasping one ankle and wrist, while the rest of me pretended to fly.

For the finale, the strong one lifted the medium-sized men onto his shoulders, the two gripping each other as they stood, outer legs extended. The opera house piano player banged out a staccato rhythm, notes climbing steadily higher to match the ascent of the acrobats. The small one climbed like a monkey up the tree of his comrades, and in a feat of true daring and skill, tightrope-walked back and forth across the clasped hands of the middle two. Then he faced the audience and held his arms outstretched, and the piano banged out a full-throated *ta-da!*

We were becoming attuned to the range of audience reaction: groans, boos, and extended trips to the lavatories; listless, tepid clapping; respectable applause; and finally booming ovations accompanied by hoots and cheers. The rafters practically shook for these acrobat boys as the audience clapped and stomped their approval.

I glanced to Gert, knowing her veto would carry the day. At the same moment, she glanced to me and raised an eyebrow in question.

Oh yes, I thought with a quick nod, *absolutely yes!*

Mother leaned toward Gert and me. "Think how that would go over with girls in pretty costumes."

At eighteen, Gert was built like a roller coaster: all curves, and just as exciting, if men's wolfish looks were any indication. Her blue gemstone eyes flashed as she considered those outfits—the satiny snugness, the brevity. Oh how her womanly features would shine.

"You'd be perfect as the small one," she said to me. "And Kit would be the strong one at the bottom."

And you would be the pretty one in the center of it all, I thought. *As usual.*

After school the next day, I trod my well-worn path to the Johnson City Public Library and asked Miss Sneeden, the librarian, where I might find a book on acrobatics.

"My goodness, Winnie," she said with a little smile. "That's quite a departure from your usual fare."

"Yes . . . well," I stammered. "It's good to broaden one's horizons."

My horizons were approaching the width of the Adirondacks, I giggled to myself, as I pored through tomes on gymnastics, tumbling and acrobatics, studying scantily clad athletes in wondrous feats of coordination. I chose two books that seemed to be the most instructive.

"Where've you been?" whined Kit when I arrived home. "I had to do your chores *and* mine!" But when I showed her the books, she sat right down on the floor to page through them.

"Books? You've got to be kidding," Gert muttered as she peered over Kit's shoulder, but she studied the pictures just as intently.

The next day, we began our first faltering steps toward becoming the Tumbling Turner Sisters. We started with simple childish moves in our tiny backyard, our muscles seeming somehow to remember the hours we'd spent as little girls practicing handstands, cartwheels, and somersaults. We returned to the books again and again for instruction and inspiration.

"Look at Kit," Mother said as our youngest sister cartwheeled over and over around the backyard. "Maybe *she'll* be our star."

Gert stiffened, then affected a careless shrug. "Maybe."

Oh, Gertie, I thought, stifling a grin, *she's playing you like a piano.*

Gert had always been the most coordinated of the three of us—and the most tenacious. She soon taught herself to handspring, flipping over from a handstand and, with one of us "spotting" her with an arm under her back, as the books indicated, nudging her back to her feet. Neither Kit nor I could manage it, and I worried that Gert's natural competitiveness would be satisfied and she'd get bored. Happily, this was not to be the case.

"Come on, now, no time for rest," she chided us, pushing a golden lock off her sweaty cheek. "We've got to learn that leapfrogging thing." This involved running up behind the first girl, jumping up and pushing off her shoulders, while she ducked down just enough to allow the leap. Then that second girl stood still while the third girl performed two leaps over the first two. The first girl would then become the leaper, and so on.

It was impossible to do in our calf-length skirts, so we took them off and practiced in our drawers between the sheets on the clothesline, lest we be spotted by a nosy neighbor. Even then it was hard. We weren't always ladylike, yelling things like "Son of a gun!" and "Get your darn armpit out of my face!"

Day after day, we practiced, adding the simpler stunts from the book. We were terrible at first, but Mother's prodding and Gert's ambition inspired a level of perseverance that produced results. After six weeks, we had an act of five minutes in duration. It was far from smooth, but at least we knew what it was supposed to look like if it were ever to be performed by *real* acrobats.

The whole effort stalled out in October of that year, 1918, a particularly somber time for the world. I guess it's safe to say that at any given moment it's a somber time for somebody. In 1906, there was that big earthquake out in San Francisco, and that put everyone in a fright. The rest of the country had a sympathy response, of course—there but for the grace of God goes my own city—but then the whole thing passed from consciousness relatively quickly. Of course, I was only two at the time, so it didn't pass through my consciousness at all.

The fall of 1918 was different. There wasn't a corner of the world that hadn't felt the doubled and tripled efforts of Death's collection department. The Spanish flu launched its worldwide attack, carrying off somewhere on the order of fifty million souls, many of them young and healthy. The Great War caused the death or wounding of another thirty-seven million. It was hard to fathom, and I wondered if God might just have become fed up with the lot of us.

We Turners were surprised by our own uncharacteristic good luck. None of us had caught the Spanish flu, and Nell's husband, Harry, had survived the war, despite the terrifying atrocities of mustard gas and trench warfare. We felt uncommonly blessed.

Nell received word that he would return in mid-October, and from then on, she refused to leave her little apartment even for a walk in the crisp fall air. "I just want his homecoming to be perfect," she insisted. "He's been in a *war*, for goodness' sake. Living in filthy trenches with only rations to eat, men blown to bits right in front of him. Is it so much to ask that his loving wife is here to greet him?"

Kit, Gert, and I took turns running her errands, keeping her company, and begging her to relax. It was my turn that day.

We sat on the sofa, two-month-old Harry Jr. snoozing in her lap, his tiny baby snores like the purr of a content kitten. Nell started in on one of her repetitive habits. "Won't he just love the baby?" she asked. It was her personal incantation, as if that one phrase uttered at least five times a day would bring her husband home safe.

I forced a smile. "I can't wait to see the look on his face."

There was a knock at the door and we both jumped up, Nell jostling the baby so he woke squalling. "Oh!" Nell panted. She handed him to me, then took him back. Handed him over again, smoothed her disheveled hair to no noticeable effect, then took him again.

"Should I leave?" I whispered frantically, my heart pounding with excitement.

"No! Yes! No!" She jiggled the baby wildly and his bawling quieted to a confused, slightly dizzy blubbering. "Well, maybe after a minute."

She hurried to the door and opened it wide, her body expanding with breath to issue the happiest possible welcome to her beloved and long-awaited husband, and to proudly introduce him to his son.

A man in uniform stood on the doorstep.

It was not Harry. And the uniform was not military.

"Oh . . . ," Nell said, deflating in bewilderment. "Are you . . . are you lost?"

He was young, the skin on his face an angry pink color from the newness of shaving. Or possibly it was the shame of knowing his job involved being the wrongest possible person to knock on anyone's door.

"Mrs. Herkimer?" he said.

"Yes?"

He handed her the telegram. That's when I knew for sure. Dread crashed into me like a bomber shot out of the sky.

"Thank you," she said, searching the pocket of her skirt for a coin to give him.

"That's okay, ma'am. No need." He glanced to me, then quickly retreated.

Nell stood at the door, the whimpering baby on her hip, the telegram in her hand.

I knew she knew. She had to know.

But I also knew that she was trying mightily *not* to know, to elongate those last few moments of her life before she would know for deadly certain that she was now a twenty-two-year-old widow.

"Take the baby," she whispered.

I got hold of him just before she crumpled to her knees.

Harry had died of Spanish flu on the train home. Two days later Nell received a letter dated from the week before. "The next time you hear from me, it will be with my own voice, sweetheart!" he wrote. He'd made it through the war without a scratch. "Not so much as a bug bite!"

A happy letter never made a family cry so hard in the history of the world. In a way, he'd belonged to all of us, and we all wept at the loss, our hearts breaking anew with every smile from baby Harry. Even Gert.

Nell gave up the little apartment on Floral Avenue. She couldn't afford it, and couldn't stand to be there alone anyway. She moved back in with us, back to sharing a small, slope-ceilinged room with Gert, back to life as one of the Turner girls. Her escape had been short-lived.

In November baby Harry's colic seemed to get worse, not better, and his sobbing made it harder to keep our own in check. Nell could barely stand it for more than a few minutes, so the rest of us passed him around like a game of eeny, meeny, miny, moe. Even a saint can only hold a squalling baby for so long, never mind a brokenhearted one.

December 25, 1918, went right by as if it were any other day. Dad never got around to hauling in a tree, and no one asked why not. There were no gifts except a toy or two for the baby, and these were handed over unwrapped, almost apologetically. The poor child's first Christmas should have been brimming with joy and excitement—our very own live infant with whom to celebrate the birth of Mary's Child, the Christian world's collective baby.

But it was just too sad. And that's all.

CHAPTER
4

GERT

It takes 20 years to make an overnight success.
—Eddie Cantor, singer, comedian, and minstrel

I spent New Year's Eve with Roy, but not out putting on the ritz or anything. We worked the late shift at J. J. Wiley's, then we drove down to Quaker Lake with a bottle of hooch and watched the sun come up.

It's 1919, I thought as the sky grew pink. *A brand-new year. And it damned well better be an improvement over the last one.*

Three weeks later, as we waited for Mother, Winnie, and Dad to get back from the hospital with his mangled hand, I watched the sky go from gray to pink again, and thought what an idiot I'd been even to hope for better days.

After Mother made her pronouncement about resurrecting the act, Winnie, Kit, and I went to school, since we couldn't think of what else to do. School, of all the useless things.

Dad went to work to tell them he wouldn't be back for a while. And that was that.

No money—even less than the no money we were used to. I figured we'd all end up at the cigar factory, working twelve-hour shifts, coming home smelling like dead weeds. Of course Mother would've had us laying railroad track with the Chinese before letting us work in a factory. After the Binghamton Clothing Factory fire, she thought every mill was a haystack waiting for a lit match. All those poor dead girls. I was fourteen at the time, and knew three girls with older sisters who'd never made it out. There were so many dead they'd held the funeral service in the Stone Opera House.

"Nell should get a job," I said as we walked home from school that afternoon.

"She's nursing," said Winnie. "How's she going to feed the baby and work all day?"

"Well, we've all got part-time jobs except her. And she's got two mouths to feed, not just one." I'll admit I was never one to coat a sour subject like a candy apple.

"He's five months old, for goodness' sake! All he eats is a little mashed banana and oatmeal. And how can you talk about him that way? He's not just hers—he's ours."

"Yes, well, what's *our* baby going to eat when we're all living at the Broome County Poor Farm, I'd like to know!"

When we got home, Mother sat at her usual perch on the end of the sofa, her mending laid out like the train of a ball gown. She took in odd sewing jobs, and I wondered who in our neighborhood even owned a black satin gown, much less one that had been worn so often it needed fixing.

"What's all this?" I said.

"Costumes," Mother replied, teeth clenched onto a couple of straight pins.

Winnie looked at me; I looked at the fabric. It was from the aprons that had ruffled the prissy feathers of the Ladies' Guild. Mother took the pins out of her mouth. "Nell's out back trying to straighten out her cartwheel. Go help her."

"Where's the baby?"

"Dad's giving his cradle a rock upstairs." Her lip flattened. "You only need one hand for that."

It was warm for January (by which I mean above freezing) and we worked all afternoon in the yard, cooking up ways to add Nell to the act. We hadn't practiced for three full months, since Harry died, and at first we could barely remember the act, much less perform it without crumpling to the ground every other minute. I never had so many bruises in all my life.

Nell was surprisingly good at splits, which the rest of us hadn't yet conquered. Maybe it was because she'd gotten so thin that her muscles didn't pull as tight anymore. She could do a full side split without trying too hard. We put that right into the act, of course.

We tried to teach her our leapfrog routine, but she didn't clear Kit's head and fell face-first into the brown grass. When she picked herself up, the front of her blouse was damp where her bosoms had leaked. Right on cue, a squawk rose from the upstairs bedroom.

"Little bloodhound can probably smell his dinner," I muttered. Winnie shot me a look, virtue wrapped around her like an old lady's shawl, as usual.

Nell limped toward the house, and Winnie helped her up the steps to the back door. "Are you sure you want to keep at it?" she asked. "No one would fault you for bowing out."

"Mother says there's a purse to be won at the Kalurah Talent Show, and I want to help if I can. I have to do something. I have no husband to pay my way anymore."

I'll admit, it got to me. She'd found her way to her brand of bliss, and through no fault of her own, she was suddenly more miserable than she'd ever been in her life.

I never want to feel like that, I thought. *Not for the life of me.*

"Stop lollygagging!" Mother called from the window. "You've got to get that jump right, or we'll be the butt of every joke in Broome County."

We practiced every free moment. When the snow flew we dragged the sofa and old wing-back chair out onto the front porch and took over the living room. Dad had to sit on the edge of his bed and hold the phonograph on his lap to listen to it at night.

There was a lot of crying, which was irritating. But I suppose it wasn't all about the bumps and twisted ankles. The whole thing was such a roll of the dice. We might win a purse or two at local talent and variety shows, but there was just as much chance that we wouldn't make a plug nickel. Then we'd be broke *and* bruised.

The costumes Mother made were scandalous. They had little cap sleeves, low rounded necklines, and fluttering skirts that fell only to our knees. We couldn't wear corsets under them, either. Every lace and bone poked out like a shadow corset in satin, and we snickered at the tawdriness of it. Kit's looked good, though—at thirteen, she didn't wear a corset yet, and the snug fabric held everything in place just fine.

"I'll add extra lining at the bosom," said Mother. "And no one better gain a pound."

It really improved the act—suddenly we could bend and twirl with freedom. Besides, it felt secretly delicious to be rid of the vise-grip corset that squeezed every rib so I could barely take a full breath, and have only the soft fabric against my skin.

The next week, we rode the trolley to Endicott, our scant costumes hidden under long coats. The Kalurah Shriners' Temple was a huge building of blond brick, with a half-circle drive and three sets of glass double doors. We couldn't figure out where to go at first, and asked a man with a high brimless hat made of stiff red felt. *Kalurah* was embroidered above a curved sword and the face of the sphinx. A ridiculous yellow tassel bobbed from the top.

"Performers, I assume?" he said.

Pride bloomed in my chest. We'd worked hard to turn ourselves from schoolgirls (or in Nell's case, a mother) into sparkling entertainers. For eight minutes—with Nell, the act had several new stunts—we would put on quite a show. We were performers, all right.

But the man's look wasn't admiring. It was haughty. Well-bred young women didn't wear skimpy costumes and prance around with their legs covered only in flesh-toned tights for all the world to see. I'd been on the business end of disapproving looks before, of course. Girls who turn men's heads always are. But this was a new flavor of damnation I hadn't tasted before.

When the show began, we waited backstage, fidgety with nerves.

Winnie did her weird little tapping thing, pecking at the knuckles of one hand with the fingertips of the other. Nell bit her cuticles and Kit shifted back and forth on her feet. I crossed my arms so tight that my hands started to tingle. To distract ourselves, we watched a tiny girl dressed as a ballerina practice prancing on the tips of her toes, as her mother hissed at her to spin faster and kick higher

"My, isn't she cute," Mother said, nodding to the little girl's mother.

The other woman put on a snooty face. "She's more than cute. She's *talented*."

Mother's eyes went steely. "She's certainly good at following orders, I'll give her that."

The woman turned her back on Mother and steered her little puppet to another corner of the backstage. Mother gave her own haughty smile and murmured to us, "We all want that big purse. It's war." She didn't seem to notice that Nell flinched at the word.

We kept to ourselves after that, and focused on the competition. A pair of jugglers tossed everything from cleavers to Wedgwood china between them. A ventriloquist threw his voice into a dummy of President Taft, telling jokes that were stale as week-old bread. The country had been through so much since 1912 it was hard to remember what had been funny back then.

Finally, the master of ceremonies announced, "The Tumbling Turner Sisters!" and I felt my stomach clench. It was our first real performance—maybe our last, if we flopped.

Our act began with Nell cartwheeling onto the stage, skirt flying through the air. I followed with handsprings and landed next to her, hands on hips. Then Kit trudged onstage lugging a large suitcase in her downstage hand, which we'd rigged with an internal latch. When Kit set the suitcase down, Winnie undid the latch, the lid flew open, and she rolled out onto the stage, landing with one knee down, arms outstretched.

Someday if I live to be very old and my mind starts to go, I might forget the stories of my life, maybe even the names of my sisters. But to my last breath, I will remember the wave of applause that crashed at our feet in those first few moments onstage.

We're a hit, I thought, *and we haven't even begun!*

It wasn't a perfect performance, though. Kit didn't crouch low enough during the leapfrog bit, and Nell once again went sprawling. For our finale, Kit held her legs wide, knees bent, while Nell and I balanced on her thighs. Then Winnie climbed up and was supposed to stand on Kit's shoulders. She must've gotten scared or some fool thing, because I could feel her tremble. Instead of standing she knelt.

"Get up," I hissed, stage smile frozen to my lips. "Stand *up*."

But she just put her hands in the air, the signal for the stunt's finish, then slid off the back. We all bounded to our places in order of height, held hands, and curtsied. To our shocked delight, the audience clapped and clapped. At the judges' table, four men in silly red fezzes smiled and nodded. My heart pounded. Would we place in the top three acts and take home a purse?

"Curtsy again!" I whispered, and the others obeyed. We kept our hands clenched tightly as we trotted offstage, as if we might float away without the others for ballast. Backstage we grinned like fools, mouths covered by sweaty palms to keep the other acts from seeing how giddy we were. Even Nell smiled.

The next act was a boy whose tap dancing was so sloppy the audience barely bothered to clap. Then an older woman with bosoms like loaded saddle bags sang "Bicycle Built for Two" as if it were tragic opera. *You'll look sweet upon the seat* sounded like a plea, as if the words *or I'll die of consumption* would come next.

"Nothing to worry about there," Mother whispered.

At the end of the show, the judges put their heads together, yellow tassels dangling in one another's faces, and we were all herded onstage to learn our fate. The master of ceremonies, a fat man with wobbling jowls, gripped a card in his hand. "Ladies and gentlemen, let's have another ovation for all of these highly talented performers, in thanks for the evening of joy and merriment they have so graciously provided!" The audience gave a forced round of applause.

Oh, get on with it, I thought.

"Each and every one of these men, women, and children has performed charmingly, and should consider themselves honorably mentioned here at the Kalurah Temple Amateur Talent Night. However, only three acts have been selected for the highest honors of third, second, and first place, with corresponding purses of five, fifteen, and twenty-five dollars, respectively."

Twenty-five dollars. That would cover almost a month's rent. The Turner sisters' hands gripped one another, strung together like human Christmas lights.

"Achieving the honor of third place . . ." He paused dramatically, and it was all I could do not to take off my slipper and throw it at him. ". . . Betty Ann Bartholemew, our little ballerina!"

Betty Ann's mother let out a shriek and hurried forward with the toddler slung over her shoulder, thumb in mouth, tiny feet dangling back and forth, as her mother stuck her chin out triumphantly. I couldn't help but think the poor tyke had years of misery ahead of her, with such a harpy for a mother.

"Our second-place honor goes to . . . the Juggling Stephanacci Brothers!"

As they shuffled forward to accept their purse, Mother whispered giddily, "That's it, we've won! They were the only real competition."

"And now, for our highest and most prestigious honor, bestowed upon the contestant with the greatest talent of all those gathered here . . ."

Kit gave a little squeal and took a step forward.

". . . our own Mrs. Beryl Jorgenson, wife of brother Shriner Karl Jorgenson, who gave such a stupendous performance of 'Bicycle Built for Two'! Mrs. Jorgenson," rumbled the master of ceremonies, "won't you do us the kindness of reprising your song?"

I thought the roof of the temple might just crack open with the gust of hot air she blew, singing *"Daisy, Daisy, give me your answer, do . . ."* The crowd began to sing along, and it was then that I noticed how many silly red hats there were in that audience. *"I'm half crazy, all for the love of you!"*

I'm half crazy, I thought. *And I'll go completely mad if I stay here one more minute.*

Performers began to slip away, and we followed the unhappy

herd to the dressing rooms to get our things, and right out the door to the street. As we all stewed on the rent money we hadn't made, the only sound was an occasional sniffle from Kit. At thirteen, a girl just isn't prepared for the kind of unfairness this world is ready to hand out every single day of the week.

We were just sitting down to a skimpy dinner the next night when there was a knock at the door.

"Morty Birnbaum!" said the small man, his voice scratchy and insistent. He stuck out his hand and pressed a business card on my mother. "Boy, are you all hard to find! I had to go through all the Turners in Johnson City. You got a lotta cousins?"

Mother blinked at him, dumbfounded, and that's not a common occurrence.

"You're the Tumbling Turners, am I right? You'd better be, because you're the last address on my list." He leaned his big nose around her and into the house. "That's a lotta girls you got there. Yep. This must be the place." He eyed the empty living room, and the kitchen table set for dinner. "Ah, now look, don't let me keep you from your supper. I'll just wait outside on the porch till you're done. I notice you've got some comfortable-looking furniture out there."

Mother glanced down at the business card in her hand, then passed it quickly to me. "Oh, Mr. Birnbaum, we can't have that. Of course you'll join us!" She cut her eyes to Kit and muttered, "Set another place, and get your father away from that phonograph!"

I looked down at his card. Morton G. Birnbaum Talent Agency, it said, and below it, Morton G. Birnbaum, President. There was an address in New York—on Broadway!

"How long are you in town, Mr. Birnbaum?" I asked brightly, taking the hat from his hand and the coat from his back.

"Oh, it all depends. Especially in *this* business!" He let out a harsh little barking laugh. The way he slouched, I wondered if he'd have a humpback when he was old. Unless he was old already. It was hard to tell. He was short and balding, with muddy-colored wisps of hair pomaded over the top, and his brown suit certainly hadn't seen a good pressing anytime in the recent past.

Our dinner was patties made from lima beans, eggs, and bread crumbs sautéed in bacon grease. Mother was mortified, but Mr. Birnbaum didn't seem to mind. When he wasn't talking he was hoisting forkload after forkload into his thin-lipped mouth.

"So, it's like this," he said between bites. "I travel around, I see an act with potential—like I saw you girls at the Kalurah—I offer my services. You don't want my services? No problem. There's always another act that does. And there's no guarantees, you understand. I get you a tryout at a small-time theatre to see how you do. If the manager likes you, we build from there."

"What would it pay?" asked Mother, and I cringed. She didn't see life as a chess match. She saw it as a shootout, and always tried to be the quickest draw.

Birnbaum sucked some beans out of his teeth and chewed a little more. I thought I caught a shadow of a smile behind all that chomping. "Well, now, Mrs. Turner, that remains to be seen. Your girls bring down the house, the sky's the limit. They fall flat—hah! no pun intended—it's back to the salt mines for all of us."

Not you, I thought. *Just the Tumbling Turners.*

"Do you honestly think we're good enough?" I asked him.

He eyed me to see if I wanted a straight answer or a fluffy one. He guessed right. "Good? No. Your tumbling ain't exactly a fireworks show. Good *enough*? Well, that's another story. Pretty girls in short skirts sells, even if you're up there laying bricks. That's what I'm banking on—that, and you girls picking up some new tricks along the way."

If we hired him, he would get to work right away, looking for a tryout. This was a half week of continuous shows from eleven in the morning to eleven at night. "There are other acts, of course. You'll probably only perform five or six times a day. How long's your act—about ten minutes? That's like getting paid for only an hour of work!" He'd let us know what the wage was when he cut the deal. "I get ten percent of your take, so believe me, I am highly motivated to get you the best possible dough. You can count on that."

When he left, we had no idea where he was going—the fancy Arlington Hotel or to sleep in his car, we hadn't a clue. But he'd be back in the morning for our answer, he said, after he made a few more "house calls."

Mother nearly tackled him at the mention of that, but I fended her off, smiled my highest-voltage smile, and said, "We'll look forward to rendezvousing with you in the morning."

For a man whose color palette only went from brown to gray, it was hard to miss the blush in his cheeks. But it was gone as quickly as it came, and so was he.

"*Rendezvousing*?" Winnie said with a smirk. "Are we French now?"

"We're whatever gets the job done," I said flatly. Birnbaum had changed everything. In my mind, the act went from just another one of Mother's half-baked schemes to a whole new world of possibility. I didn't plan to squander it.

"What about school?" said Kit. "If it's a half week, we'll have to miss at least a day." Her eyes brightened. "Maybe three!"

Suddenly Dad spoke up. "I'm not sure about this. He could be one of those shysters you hear about. He talks very fast for a man who appears out of nowhere with no guarantees."

"No guarantees," Mother said dryly. "Why, it sounds just like the institution of marriage."

CHAPTER
5

WINNIE

*It wasn't a career that I was after. It was just that I wanted a
life that didn't mean spending most of it at the cookstove and
the kitchen sink.*
—Sophie Tucker, singer

When Mr. Birnbaum explained the tryout, my heart sank. Missing
three days of school wasn't so bad; I could make up the work. But
what if there were more engagements? Mother's goal had always been
vaudeville, but I'd never actually thought it would happen. Oh, we
might win some purses, enough to tide us over until Dad could go back
to work. But if we began to travel, and I didn't finish high school, I'd
never make it to college. And yet, if I didn't make a boodle somehow, I
wouldn't get there anyway.

College. It was my deepest, darkest secret. Assuming I could convince my parents to let me go—an assumption so vast that if it were
to fall off a cliff into the ocean, it would cause a tidal wave of his-
toric proportion—the answer would still have been no because of
the money. Cornell, the college of my dreams, would cost two hundred dollars. Per year. And that's without factoring in luxuries such as
room, board, and books. In 1919, I was a junior in high school, and
figured I had a year to come up with a plan. Or to stumble upon a
bag of gold coins.

I couldn't sleep that night, my mind revolving on a carousel of unanswerable questions.

Could we wait until summer so we could finish the school year, at least?

But what if Mr. Birnbaum goes on his way, and we never get another chance?

What if Dad's hand never gets better and this becomes our only source of income?

Kit snored beside me in the double bed we shared, probably sweet-dreaming about three days off from being teased about her height. I slipped out of our room and across the hall, hoping Nell was up with little Harry, and she'd help me untangle my snaking thoughts. But she was fast asleep, the baby content in his cradle.

From the other bed, Gert glared. *What are you doing?* she mouthed.

Desperate to talk to someone—even Gert—I whispered, "Are you worried about all this business?"

"No." It was a lie. She was just annoyed with me for asking.

"Don't you want to graduate?" I said. "You've only got half a year left."

"No."

"Why not?"

"Because I want a *life*, Winnie, a chance for something different. You're not planning to hang around and marry some shoemaker, either, so don't act like you are."

"How do *you* know?" I'd certainly never confided in her—we didn't even like each other.

She didn't dignify this with a response, only said, "You think Birnbaum's on the level?"

"Hard to say. I've never met anyone like him. You?"

"Oh, I've met plenty like him. They offer you something, but it's only so they can get a payout themselves. At least he doesn't hide it."

I ruminated on this a moment. "Gert? I don't want to do it. I just want to stay in school."

In the blue-gray light I saw her eyes flash with fury. "Then you'll never get out of here, and you'll ruin it for the rest of us, too!" She rolled over and turned her back on me.

The next morning Mr. Birnbaum returned with a contract, and Mother, Nell, and Gert signed it. Because Kit and I were minors, our signatures weren't required. In fact, no one even asked our opinion on the matter. The entire course of my life changed without a single word of discussion.

It had been almost two weeks since Dad's accident. Mother wouldn't take him to get the stitches out; she said he could damn well go by himself. She was disgusted with him for imperiling our family over a bar fight, certainly, yet she tied his shoes and buttoned his buttons, even undid his belt when he needed to use the bathroom. He never said a word of thanks. But then, Dad rarely said a word of anything if he wasn't spoken to first.

Besides, with her squeamish nature, it was no surprise she wouldn't accompany him to the hospital. I had been the one to change his dressings, and I'll admit the first look at all those black threads crisscrossing his fingers bloated with pus made me wince. But you get used to these things. At least I did.

I knew what infection could do. Sometimes a woman who'd had a cesarean section would return to the hospital with red streaks up her belly, especially if she had no mother or sister to help her. One woman came in with an infected wound and a husband with a gash on his head. He'd tried to help, took one look, and fainted to the floor. The nurses snickered about that for weeks.

I took Dad to Lourdes Hospital myself. I told him that I wanted to see the stitches come out, but I doubted they'd let me go in with him. "They'll think I'm too young or squeamish, but I'm not."

When the nurse called his name, Dad took my hand and strode toward her. She was plump and plain, gripping his chart as if it'd been her best reason to get up that morning. A plain girl with a good figure gets along okay in this world; so does a plump girl with shiny hair and bright eyes, or some similar attractive combination. Both plain and plump can be a difficult hand of cards to play.

"Your little girl will have to wait outside." Her voice rang with officiousness.

"She's seventeen," Dad said with as much firmness as he possessed, which is to say, not very much. "I get real anxious, and I might go a little haywire. She'll help me stay calm."

The nurse shook her head. "I'm afraid that runs contrary to every rule—"

Dad began to breathe quickly. "Oh dear . . . ," he panted. "Oh my . . . " He mopped his brow, though there wasn't a bead of sweat on it.

"Now, now . . . ," the nurse stammered. "All right, she can come."

He gave my hand a little squeeze, and I had to hold myself back from kissing his cheek.

The doctor was pleased with the state of Dad's wounds. "I see you've been keeping them clean and well dressed," he said.

"I have my Winnie to thank for that." Dad patted my arm with his good left hand.

The doctor gave me a nod. "You might consider a career in nursing, if you can't find a man to marry you."

Standing beside him, the nurse's face remained placid, but pink splotches arose on her neck. There was no ring on her finger, and I guessed that people were starting to call her an old maid behind her back. I also guessed that she was acutely aware of this possibility. I had a sudden inclination to pinch that doctor quite hard.

When the doctor finished snipping at the black threads, my father's hand seemed to have tiny railroad tracks running every which way, and his index finger was bowed crookedly toward the others. He couldn't even make a fist. The doctor said he might still regain almost full use of his fingers, though his hand strength would never be the same. I was grateful for the doctor's thoroughness and encouragement. But I still disliked him for the way he shamed that nurse.

I suppose I felt a bit of worry, as well as indignation. I was small and slight, though not entirely without physical merit. I didn't have Gert's curves or citrus blond hair, but my nose was straight and my light brown hair curled enough not to look like a broom. Gert herself had once pronounced my green eyes "pretty, especially if you like the look of an empty bottle of ale."

Everyone likes to think they might be appealing to someone, some-where, and hopes that person has all of his mental faculties, most of his teeth, and might even be kind and lovable, too. I had yet to find any evidence that this person existed for me, and I had my doubts about it. What did I have to offer, after all? I wasn't beautiful or coy, and my vocabulary alone was enough to make most boys scratch the backs of their necks and eventually turn to talk to someone else.

"Dad?" I said as we walked home. "How did you know you wanted to marry Mother?"

A glimmer of a smile peeked out from his normally stoic expres-sion. I couldn't tell if it was happy or sad. Then he sighed. "Well, you know, I grew up in a pretty quiet place."

He'd told us about it when we girls had demanded stories of his boyhood. He was raised outside of Theresa, New York, in the far north of the state, which is to say (in the kindest possible terms) off the beaten path. His family's farm never did that well, but mostly faltered along like a drunken monk—solemnly, with devotion, but without any actual direction in mind.

"We Turners were a pretty quiet bunch," he went on. "It was silence within stillness, and I guess I needed to find some noise. So I moved to Albany and met your mother. She was . . . well, maybe the word for her is boisterous." It occurred to me that his choice of mate was the only truly complicated thing he'd ever done, and its repercussions were many.

"And why . . . um, well, why do you think she . . . um . . ."

He chuckled at my stammering. "Why did she marry me? Well, I suppose it started with your grandparents. They were very strict, never let the leash out. And your Mother . . . well, she needs a long leash, doesn't she? Room to speak her mind, and have ideas. I give her that." He raised his chin a little. "I have always given her that."

Before I could question him further, he asked, "So, how's the act com-ing along? Think you've got a chance of performing at a real theatre?"

As we'd seen at the Kalurah Talent Show, being good wasn't always the definitive factor. "I suppose we have as much of a chance as any," I said, trying to sound more hopeful than I truly felt.

"That's right," he said, brightening a little. "You've been practicing so hard, and you all look so pretty. Mr. Birnbaum's bound to find you something. He's just got to."

I saw the worry pinching around his eyes. "Are we going to be all right, Dad?"

"Oh, we're just fine, honey," he said. His tone was high but his face remained doubtful. "February's rent is sitting right in our bank account."

"And March?"

"Well, March is a long way off, isn't it? Anything can happen. Anything at all."

"Good news!" Mr. Birnbaum told us two days later, dropping by the house just after we'd gotten home from school. "I got you a half-week tryout. You're the dumb act at Earlville, come Monday."

Dumb act? We shot surreptitious glances at one another.

"It's not dumb like stupid. It's dumb like you don't talk." His gaze shifted from person to person, searching for comprehension. "You know, so folks taking their seats don't miss anything."

"Won't they be missing our act?" Kit asked.

"Now look," he said, "opener isn't so bad. It's better than chaser, at least."

Kit pondered this a moment. "Chaser?"

He sighed, straining for patience. "The last act on the bill is the worst one—it chases people out so the stagehands can get the theatre ready for the next show. The chaser sees the backs of people's heads as they leave. We call that 'playing to the haircuts.' But don't worry, that'll never be you girls."

An act whose sole purpose was to make the audience leave? I certainly hoped it would never be us.

"Now listen," Birnbaum went on. "John Castleberry's the manager at the Earlville Opera House. He's a tough customer, so keep your yaps shut, and don't be late to rehearsal."

We'd be paid forty dollars for those three days in Earlville—about three weeks' wages for our father at the shoe factory.

We felt as if we'd struck gold.

CHAPTER
6

GERT

Your audience gives you everything you need. They tell you.
There is no director who can direct you like an audience.
—Fanny Brice, comedian and singer

Forty dollars! Mother sent Dad to the butcher for a beef shank and kidney to make a pie. Having the cash for real meat—even a cheap cut—made us feel like Rockefellers, and the luxury of it tasted even better than the meal itself. Except to Kit, of course, who made damned sure there were no leftovers.

Earlville was sixty miles away. "We'll have to stay in a hotel," I said as we sat around the dinner table, feeling leisurely for the first time in forever. We guessed the cost would be about a dollar a night per room, and we'd need two rooms for three nights. That was six dollars right there. Add on train fare, meals, and Birnbaum's ten percent, and suddenly our forty dollars was more like twenty-five. Still, it was big money for the Turners.

"I'll have to bring the baby," said Nell.

"Now, Nell," Mother said. "We just can't take him. With all his crying, he'll get us thrown out. And besides, you don't want him mixing with stage people—who knows what kinds of germs they pick up, hanging around dusty theatres, carousing till all hours."

"But, Mother," Nell said, voice trembling. "He's nursing."

"He's six months now. He can drink cow's milk like the rest of us. And Dad'll take good care of him." She cut her eyes toward our father. "What else has he got to do?"

Nell clutched little Harry to her like he might vanish and hurried upstairs. I went up later to get my sweater and heard her crying. I crossed to the other bedroom and took Winnie's sweater instead, so poor Nell could sob in private. I'd never want anyone to see me cry.

Earlville is a flyspeck of a town, and the Opera House only holds about four hundred. It was pretty, I suppose—four stories of brick with little crisscrossed transoms above the windows—but we didn't have time to stop and admire the architecture. We were late, and practically sprinted into the theatre only to find rehearsal in full swing.

Onstage, a man in a clown costume bent over at the waist while his little dog jumped through a hoop he made with his arms. When the heavy theatre door banged shut behind us, he turned toward the sound, and the dog slammed into the side of his face. The dog yelped, the clown bellowed, "Goddamn it, Rover!" and a man in the front row stood up. That last item was the worst part.

John Castleberry had a head the size of a bread box. It must have created a sort of megaphone effect, because when he boomed out, "What in the hell?" I felt the floorboards quiver.

Mother hurried forward panting, "Mr. Castleberry, our deepest apologies! That Erie Railroad ought to have its trains melted for scrap, for all the service it provides! We—"

Castleberry's tree-limb-sized arm flew out, pointing at us. "Actors come in the stage door! They do not ever—*ever*—enter through the theatre doors."

We slunk back outside, around to the alley at the back of the building, and went in through a battered wooden door. There were no dressing rooms, so the backstage area was crowded with trunks and props and people packed into every corner.

A man in a long-tailed tuxedo rubbed black polish onto his shoes, while his partner in a pale blue ball gown painted on gobs of heavy black eyeliner. I wondered if it took effort to blink. Mother saw this and beckoned us over for a recoating of makeup. "Will someone call us out to the stage?" I asked as she dusted my cheek with a cloud of rouge.

"How am I to know?" Mother muttered back. "I'm just as new at this as you are, Gert."

We were the last to rehearse, and when I did my handsprings out onto the stage, I stared straight into the huge bread-box face of Mr. Castleberry, standing in the front row. He was scowling, but in the three beats I stood there with my arms outstretched, his face softened into something that looked like, with a little sunlight and water, it might grow into a smile someday.

We didn't make any mistakes, I'll say that for us. After our curtsy we hustled offstage, panting with relief. Well, some of us were and some of us weren't. Nell's cheeks were sopping with tears. "I miss Harry," she whispered through her silent sobs.

"Oh no," said Mother. "No, no! Don't think of the baby or your milk will let down—you'll ruin your costume!"

"I can't help it," Nell whimpered. "I miss him so."

"Turn around quick," said Mother. "Girls, hold up your coats."

We curtained Nell off from the rest of the performers, and she took down the top of her costume. Mother gave her a scarf to hold against her leaking bosoms while she cried.

I stood there, arms high, creating a coat-and-human screen to hide Nell and her sorrow from the world, and wondered what it must feel like to love another person so much that your body takes up the job of loving, too, without your consent.

Then I realized she'd said, "I miss Harry." We always called the baby *little* Harry. We called his father . . . well, we didn't call him anything at all. We didn't speak of him; it was the only way to train your mind away from rebreaking your heart every moment of the day.

Winnie shot me a look that said, *This is never going to work.*

Finally, Nell quieted and pulled her costume back up. Kit scavenged a couple of stools for us to sit on. The stage manager tacked the order of acts to the board beside his office, and I walked toward the gaggle of actors jostling to see the lineup. Birnbaum had said that while we might be offered a particular spot, it could change without notice, based on the rehearsal, but also because of staging. Managers wanted rapid-fire timing, and would switch things up so there were no lulls in the program. Your spot was never your spot until the moment you walked onstage.

"There are no guarantees in life," Birnbaum had warned us. "And in vaudeville, even fewer."

I kept my chin high as I walked back to Mother and the girls. I didn't want the other acts to see how bad I felt. When I reached our little circle, I murmured one word.

"Chaser."

As we waited for the first real show of our vaudeville career to begin, Winnie pulled me aside. "What are we going to do about Nell?" she whispered.

"Tell her to quit blubbering?" I said, only half kidding.

"Gert, for goodness' sake! She'll fall to pieces completely if we don't do something."

"Like what, genius?"

"Like . . . like tell Mother to go home and get the baby."

I laughed out loud. "Are you out of your mind?"

"Fine." She narrowed her bottle-green eyes at me. "If the act fails, and we get sent home to clean bedpans and serve sandwiches for the rest of our lives, don't blame me."

I never hated that little smarty-pants more than when she was right. "Fine," I said. "You tell Mother."

"And you back me up when she refuses."

But Mother didn't fight us. In fact, she'd already thought of it. "We can't have her ending up in a straitjacket," she murmured. "The act will suffer, and God knows we don't have the money for a sanitarium." She hoped to be back with the baby before the theatre closed that night.

"You could sleep at home and come back tomorrow morning," Winnie suggested.

"And miss the end of our first day in vaudeville?" said Mother. "Not on your life."

After she left, the theatre manager, Mr. Castleberry, came backstage, a well-gnawed cigar sticking out of his huge face. He gave us an up-and-down look and said, "Those your costumes?"

No, I thought, *we just walk around like this because we're hoping to be brought up on indecency charges.*

"Is there a problem?" I asked.

"They're a mite short, is all, especially when you jump around and they fly up in the air. This ain't New York City, ladies. Earlville is good, simple churchgoing folks."

His glare shifted from our legs to the couple behind us. "Delorme and Delorme?"

"That's us," said the man with the tuxedo. He was somewhere in his late twenties, tall and thin, with dark wavy hair that fought the brilliantine he'd applied to tame it. His face was that earnest type, the kind that makes you think he'd never lied to his mother, not even once. His partner, the woman with the blue ball gown, was another sort altogether. As she leaned against him and squinted away from the bright stage lights, I guessed she'd told her share of fibs.

Castleberry frowned. "She all right?

"Just a little tired," Fred said quickly. "I'll get her some coffee and she'll perk right up."

Castleberry stormed off to bother some other act, and the young man stuck out a hand to Kit, who happened to be closest. "Fred Delorme," he said with a friendly grin.

"We're the Tumbling Turners!" She pumped his hand like water might come out of his elbow. "You're the dance-and-patter team, right?"

"That's right." He glanced to his partner. "April, say hello."

"So very nice to meet you," she said, and sat down on their trunk with a thump. She must've had quite a night for herself.

Waiting for the show to start, we wandered around, sizing up the small theatre. Notices were stuck to the stage manager's board: ads for lodging, train schedules, and a sheet of house rules with a list of forbidden words and phrases, like *son of a gun*, *hully gee*, and *slob*.

This is what passes for cursing around here? I thought. I'd heard worse waiting tables at J. J. Wiley's. I'd heard worse from my own mother, for cripes' sake.

The last line on the notice read, *This is a respectable house, with women and children in attendance. We brook no so-called blue material.*

"What's blue material?" Kit asked.

Fred Delorme chimed in. "It's big-time lingo for salty language," he said. "If you use it, you'll get a note warning you not to try it again or you'll be kicked off the circuit, and might never work big time again. Apparently it comes in a blue envelope." He gave a little chuckle. "I doubt they write a note and put it in a fancy-colored envelope around here. Earlville is strictly silo circuit—farms and fields. They'll just show you the door, and that'll be that."

Our act was mute, so we were in no danger of blurting out "hully gee!" We did have a respectability problem, though.

"Do you think our costumes are too short?" I asked Fred.

His cheeks went pink. "Why, no. They seem just fine to me. I've seen shorter." He let out a bashful cough. "Onstage, I mean." He backed away and headed for the stage door. "Well, I guess I'd better round up some coffee before the curtain goes up . . ."

The worst spot on the program did have one advantage. We could watch the other acts and see how the lineup worked. As Birnbaum predicted, the opening "dumb" act was a juggler, so people didn't have to worry that they were missing a punch line as they squeezed around one another to find their seats. The second act is called the deuce, and it was Fred and April Delorme. They danced and told jokes, and this made the audience settle in and pay attention. Then came a novelty act of a Spanish dancer in swirling skirts, her partner clacking little wooden disks in his fingers. The last act before intermission was a hefty soprano who belted out tired old tunes and led a singalong of "Take Me Out to the Ball Game." She was a little off-key, but it was the high point of the first half of the show, leaving the audience wanting more.

After intermission, the second half began with another dumb act, two people in black mime outfits who pretended to ride bicycles and have a picnic. It was silly, but it was better than the old juggler, who dropped things and pretended it was on purpose. Next came a magician who did tricks like pulling a full-sized cane from his breast pocket (from the wings, I could hear the pieces clicking into place as it telescoped out). For his finale, he sipped lamp oil and breathed fire like a dragon.

Then, in the next-to-closing spot, came the headliner, supposedly the best of all the entertainers on the bill, and the highest paid. Even we knew that every vaudevillian's dream was to headline. This turned out to be the clown with the dog.

Then it was our turn to chase the audience out, a sorry start to our career, to say the least. But honestly, the other acts weren't so fantastic; in fact, some were truly terrible. The juggler was booed, and the clown couldn't get his little pooch to do half his tricks. It gave me a sympathy pain in my stomach. For the dog, not the clown.

Kit whispered, "He should have the dog jump into the side of his head, like he did when we first came in. Now that was funny." She mimed getting hit in the face and the cockeyed expression he'd made, then snarled, "Goddamn it, Rover!"

We put our hands over our mouths to muffle our laughter. But it was like giggling in church—the more you tried to be serious, the more your shoulders shook.

"One minute and you're on." The stage manager was stumped when he saw us cracking up. "The guy's not that good," he muttered, which made us laugh all the more. Even Nell smiled.

Our makeup ran, and Nell pulled a handkerchief out of her bosom to wipe our streaks, which got us chuckling again. I got into position, excited and slightly terrified for our first paid performance. If we didn't do well, Mr. Castleberry might fire us and that would be the end of it. I didn't have time to worry, though. In another minute, we were onstage.

The Tumbling Turner Sisters never gave such a giggling performance as we did on our first paid job. Some of those haircuts did walk up the aisles to leave, but many stayed to see the silliest girl acrobat troupe this side of the Susquehanna River. For the finale, as I clung to Kit's shoulder, I whispered, "Make the hit-by-a-dog face." When she did, the audience burst out laughing, and clapped hard when we curtsied.

Our first turn as vaudevillians was a thrill, and I was only sorry to have to wait two hours before I could go back onstage and do it all over again.

After each performance we worked out what had gone over and what had fallen flat. We'd practiced so many times, but it was a whole other ball of wax to perform with a theatre full of people reacting to every move. To do that five times in a day was worth a hundred practices.

Kit's silly faces were a hit, and she came up with different expressions for each point in the act. We made a face when something didn't go right, so the audience would think it was a gag. I saw that I could flirt with the audience, like you would with any boy, and I'd widen my eyes at a difficult stunt or wink after I did a flip. I even blew a kiss to a catcaller way up in the gallery—there was a lot of guffawing and foot stomping after that.

Mother made it back for the last show, and she stood in the wings with the sleeping baby in her arms, grinning like a madwoman at all the applause.

As the stagehands hurried to shut down the theatre and head home for the night, Mr. Castleberry stopped us. "You're on first tomorrow," he'd growled.

"First?" Mother said, stunned.

"Yeah, first. As in *not last*. But if you're late, you're out altogether, you get me?"

We tried to be casual about it as we lugged our bags down the darkened street, picking our way around chunks of frozen slush. But once we were about a block away Kit let out a whoop and we laughed like we'd gone completely off our rockers. Opening act! Our first day and we were already coming up in the world.

We headed to the Fayette Hotel, listed on the stage manager's board with the catchphrase "We Cater to Theatricals!" Once we got there I wondered why we'd hurried. The building had paint peeling off the clapboards and a hedgerow that had practically taken over the yard. It was about as worn out as I felt after twelve long hours at the theatre.

Just then the headlining comedian with the dog, an older fellow with red hair that stuck out from the sides of his head, walked out the front door. "Coming or going?" he said. "And if it's going, don't bother, because there's nowhere else to go!"

He introduced himself as Roscoe McSorley, then took a bag from Mother and another from Nell, and walked us up the steps. "A few of us are heading over to the diner on Main Street. Hope you'll join us." He twitched his bushy eyebrows at Mother in a rakish way.

A girl doesn't think of her mother as being of any real interest to other people. She's "my mother," emphasis on *my*, with no real usefulness beyond her motherhood. It never occurred to me that the forty-one-year-old woman who'd spent the better part of her life scrubbing floors and ordering my sisters and me around might actually appeal to someone. She was old and sturdy. The light from the bare front porch bulb made her crow's-feet seem deep as dry riverbeds.

"Well, we'll see," she said with a coy smile.

We'll see? I wanted to yell. *We are dead-dog tired. We are going to bed!*

Mother didn't seem tired, though. If anything, there was a happy little glow about her, the type of thing people respond to without even knowing. The notion of our mother as attractive made me shudder.

Inside, the craggy old owner of the Fayette Hotel made us pay six dollars for the full three nights up front. "I've been left short by you people too many times," she complained.

"Your advertisement says you cater to theatricals," I pointed out.

"And I do," the woman snapped. "But not by choice."

Our rooms had two twin beds each. Mother, Nell, and the baby took one; this left Kit, Winnie, and me to the other. Kit was too big to share, so Winnie and I had to sleep head to foot on a mattress with a body-shaped dip down the middle. We kept sliding into each other, which annoyed me no end. Winnie annoyed me enough as it was.

I tried to distract myself by thinking about Roy, his devilish smile, his big plans.

But plans of my own were starting to sprout like dandelions—plans that didn't necessarily include Roy. I never would've thought I'd like performing, and it was hard work, all right. But it was also different. Completely different from anything I'd known before. I liked getting on a train and just . . . going.

When I'd told Roy about our tryout in Earlville, at first he thought it was a gag. Then he saw I was serious, and he recovered quickly, I'll give him that.

"That's a swell little jaunt," he said. "Sounds like fun."

"It's not fun," I told him. "It's work."

But it was fun, too, as it turned out. More fun than a boring old restaurant, that's for sure.

My mind drifted to Fred and April Delorme. I figured they'd be lucky to last till the end of the year together. I was impressed that Fred didn't flirt more; April would never have noticed in her state. I wondered how many marriages were really and truly happy. My own parents didn't seem terribly thrilled, but I saw couples who appeared not to mind it so much. Like a bag full of cats, the idea of marriage never seemed to keep a permanent shape, so I was wary to go blindly down the aisle to my possible doom.

That bed was a tool of torture. There was no possible position that could keep Winnie and me from rolling into each other, her sharp little elbows in my ribs, her toes in my hair.

"It's like sleeping in a frankfurter roll!" I tossed off the blanket and stood up.

"Where are you going?" I don't know why she felt the need to whisper. Kit was snoring so loudly it would've taken cannon fire to wake her.

"I'm going to that diner," I said, "and I'm not coming back until I'm too tired to care where I sleep."

"You shouldn't go alone. What if . . ."

"What if what?"

"What if there's someone out there with bad intentions?"

She had a point. "Get up."

"Me?" she squeaked. "I can't protect you!"

"Two against one is always better," I said, "even if one of the two is you."

We put on our coats and scarves. I opened the doorknob slowly and we slipped out.

"Girls?" We froze, then turned around.

Standing in the hallway was Mother.

CHAPTER
7

WINNIE

Always carry a flagon of whiskey in case of snakebite,
and furthermore always carry a small snake.
—W. C. Fields, comedian and actor

I could have put my foot down and refused to go to the diner, even threatened to tell Mother. But I'd learned the hard way that going toe-to-toe with Gert could have unexpected consequences. One of your boots might go missing just long enough to make you late for school. Oatmeal might be accidentally spilled on your homework. These days she had the perfect opportunity for revenge: she could drop me onstage and make it seem like a sight gag.

To be honest, a part of me was intrigued about the diner. Did all the performers go? What did they talk about? Maybe we could learn something useful. But first we had to get past Mother.

"What on earth!" she hissed. "And where do you think you're sneaking off to?"

Gert leveled her gaze. "The same place you're going, with your coat all buttoned up and your hair freshly pinned."

"Absolutely not! That is not the kind of thing that young women . . . it is far too late—"

"Mother, it's research," I cut in. "Gert and I just thought we could learn something about the business, and maybe that would help us to . . . um . . . be more successful . . ."

Mother squinted at us suspiciously. "Well, that's the very reason I'm going, as a matter of fact," she said. "Just to pick up hints and tips. And then to come right back." She turned on her heel and walked down the hall, and since she had not forbidden us, we followed.

"Research," Gert muttered in my ear. "That's rich."

The three of us trudged through the icy streets, boots crunching loudly under a sky busy with stars. When Mother opened the door, the warmth of the overheated diner enveloped us. It smelled of strong coffee and toasted bread, a scent that must have clung to the vinyl booths. Two square tables had been pushed together under the central light in the room, an overturned bowl-shaped fixture with the bulb hanging down like a small sun in the solar system of the diner. Around the table slumped the performers: McSorley, Fred and April Delorme, even the magician who'd ended his act with a fire-breathing stunt.

"The Turners!" Fred called out, and they all raised whatever they had—cups of coffee, glasses of root beer, even a bowl of soup. They pulled up chairs for us—McSorley was quick to tug a chair over next to him for Mother—while Gert and I interspersed among the rest.

April Delorme took a dented flask from her coat pocket and put it to her lips, where blood-red lipstick had smudged and seeped into tiny cracks.

Fred sat to my right, and I heard him mutter, "Not so much tonight, will you?"

Her look could've frozen molten lava. "Who wants to join me?" she called out. "Never say I don't share!" She handed the flask to Fred, who took a hesitant, embarrassed swig. He started to hand it to me, and I reached out instinctively for something extended to me.

Then he balked. "Say, what's the idea? You're too young for this!"

"I'm seventeen," I said, head high for an extra half inch. "Want to check my birth certificate?"

This brought on a burst of laughter around the table, except from Mother, who was too busy giggling at Mr. McSorley's little jokes to notice that I was about to imbibe alcohol.

"Sure, kid," Fred said, grinning. "As if you and every other underage performer doesn't have a fake to show the Gerrymen."

I'd read about Gerrymen. They were from the New York Society for the Prevention of Cruelty to Children. Its leader, one Elbridge Gerry, was obsessed with child actors, calling them "slaves of the stage." But the law said once you were sixteen, you could perform without interference from these so-called do-gooders.

"I don't need a fake," I insisted, "because I'm *actually seventeen*." And with that, I took the flask and downed a sizable gulp.

It's a strange and unaccountable thing that a liquid poured in your mouth can seem as if it has seeped into your eyes, ears, and nose, as well. It felt like they'd been dowsed in lamp oil and ignited, and if I'd ever been keen to learn fire breathing, it was quelled right then and there. I put the back of my hand to my mouth and coughed as my lungs tried to expel the dragon. Though my eyes watered, I forced a wide smile. The group erupted in laughter again, clapping or raising their mugs. Gert rolled her eyes at my inexperience.

"How'd that feel?" asked Fred.

"Just fine." My voice sounded scorched, even to me.

"Care for another?"

"I don't want to take more than my share." I passed it to the fire-breathing magician, who had enough sense to send it on to the next person without partaking. He nibbled at dry toast to soak up the lamp oil that had trickled down his throat during his act.

Tired and slowed by the effects of the alcohol, I only listened as they all compared notes on towns ("More chickens than people"), theatre managers ("He could show Kaiser Wilhelm a trick or two"), and agents ("I'm pretty sure he presses his suits by sleeping in them").

They shared hints on makeup removal: if you couldn't afford cold cream, you could use Crisco, which didn't work quite as well as pig lard, but smelled better. Apparently it was cheap pig lard that had inspired the term *ham*, meaning a poor-quality performer. They counseled one another on improving their acts ("Don't come in so fast after the line about the scarecrow on a diet—you're stepping on the laugh"). And they heckled one another good-naturedly.

The fire breather, who'd been trying in vain to flirt with Gert, complained that he hadn't had a date in six months. McSorley said, "Well, that's because kissing you is like sucking on a lamp wick. Girls are worried they'll burst into flames—and not from ardor, my friend, not from ardor!"

His bushy eyebrows flew up in fascination at Mother's every word. "Now why aren't you part of the act?" he asked. "You could pass for another sister any day of the week!"

"Oh, now, you," she said, giving his arm a playful tap. "It's sweet of you to say, but those days are gone for me." He asked about her time on the stage and she didn't lie, exactly, but it was a honeyed-up form of the truth as I knew it.

"Well, I had a little song-and-dance act, back before I got married." She neglected to mention that she'd never performed anywhere except her high school talent show, the county fair, and for us when we were little. "I like to think I had an Eva Tanguay kind of appeal."

I could almost agree with her there: Eva Tanguay wasn't a great beauty, and couldn't sing or dance very well. In fact, she ran around the stage like the cops were chasing her. But unlike Mother, Eva Tanguay was the Queen of Vaudeville, the headliner and the highest paid. *Variety* said she was making upward of thirty-five hundred dollars a week, for goodness' sake!

McSorley's overgrown eyebrows went up again. "My, my!"

Mother sighed. "But I never made it. My career was cut short by motherhood."

I slid my eyes to Gert, and she caught my gaze as she took a card from the deck the magician fire breather held out to her. *Career*, she mouthed, and we shared a secret grin.

Mother gave McSorley a brave, soldier-on kind of smile. "But seeing my girls up there entertaining, giving such joy to others, it makes all my sacrifices worthwhile."

When the diner closed, we all trudged back to the hotel, laughing and shushing one another as we climbed the creaking porch steps. McSorley took Mother's hand. Mother tugged it away, but she gave him a quick lit-up smile as she left him on the landing.

"Would she ever?" I whispered to Gert.

Gert's lip curled in disgust. "I don't want to think about it, and neither should you."

But I couldn't help thinking about it as I clung to the side of the mattress trying not to slide into Gert's feet, which were disturbingly close to my neck. Mother was not one to navigate the middle ground between the peaks and valleys of her emotions.

I remember once Gert had gotten in trouble for back-talking to her teacher, and had to stay after school to write "I will not give disrespectful responses to my elders" one hundred times on the blackboard. When I came home and told Mother, she was furious that Gert would not be available to do her chores. She marched right down to the school, and Gert said Mother gave that teacher a rather large and loud piece of her mind. *She* would be the one to punish a misbehaving child, not some twenty-three-year-old stranger! Then she laced into Gert all the way home for causing trouble. By the time they arrived, they were chortling over the teacher's quivering lip as Mother had lambasted her.

Mother indulged her happier emotions just as impulsively, and I wondered what repercussions might result, now that she was finally among performers, basking in the refracted limelight, if not the stage itself.

To distract myself I turned my mind to the diner, and the easy camaraderie of the vaudevillians. They'd never met before rehearsal that morning, and yet they'd quickly banded together to trade tips and information, to laugh and make friends they'd likely never see again. This seemed most important if you were a solo act, but I imagined that even a twosome or a small troupe might welcome new faces after so much time with the same few people.

As if to punctuate that thought, I heard Fred and April Delorme in the next room, his voice a low, aggravated rumble, hers loose and high-pitched, a word or phrase drifting through the horsehair plaster: ". . . if I *feel* like it . . . *slave* driver . . . gimme that *back*!"

Fred's voice rose to the level of comprehension only once. ". . . *ruin our chances*!"

It went quiet then, except for a squeak or two I assumed to be bedsprings.

Distracted, I'd missed the moment when Gert had slid into our bed's craterous middle. I took my pillow, tugged off one of the blankets and rolled myself into a little nest on the floor. Angled into a sliver of moonlight, I opened Homer's *Odyssey* to the section that my English teacher, Miss Cartery, had assigned. Even if I were out of school, even if I were in the throes of a hallucinatory fever, she knew me well enough to know I would read.

Earlville was a lovely little town in the daylight, what little of the town and the daylight we were privy to. Exhausted, we slept until ten, crawled bleary-eyed from lumpy beds, splashed our faces, and sponged our shadowed parts. Dressed in our costumes, we scurried downstairs for a breakfast of scrambled eggs cooked to tire rubber. Baby Harry was handed from lap to lap so Nell could pick at her food, while the proprietress eyed our short satin dresses and thick makeup with distaste. We hustled through the snowdrifts to the theatre, eager to take up our spot as openers.

Unfortunately, the audiences were not nearly so excited.

"What are we doing wrong?" Kit asked after our third performance where the applause was so weak we could practically hear individual pairs of hands. After each show, we adjusted the timing, added a roll or cut a jump. But the few bits that seemed to work with one group fell flat with the next.

"Somebody call the undertaker," muttered McSorley, the headlining comedian. "It's a goddamn morgue out there." At least it wasn't just us.

Mother seemed uncommonly happy, though, as she came and went from the stage door with the regularity of a train conductor, bringing in food, removing the baby when he squawked, and running errands for the other performers, getting them a cup of coffee, sodium bicarbonate for an upset stomach, or new stockings when the old pair had run itself into zebra stripes. They responded with the kind of gushing adoration that show business people are known for, though there was clear sincerity beneath the thank-yous and aren't-you-just-the-dearest.

"You girls are very lucky to have such a kind, generous mother," said the soprano, whom Mother had coddled and sweet-talked from one poorly received performance to the next. Happier than I'd ever known her to be, Ethel Turner basked in the attention she'd so rarely experienced as a mere wife and mother.

The audiences in Earlville did not improve. The few who showed up were what McSorley called "hand sitters." On the third day, just before the show opened, I saw him peeking through the curtains. "What are you looking at?" I whispered.

"I'm counting heads."

"What for?"

"To see how many of us are gonna get paid."

"But we have a contract!"

McSorley turned his world-weary eye on me and gave my head a pat. "Right," he said.

His words portended the future. On Wednesday night, after the final performance, we all gathered outside Mr. Castleberry's office for our payout, as cigar smoke wafted from under the warped wooden door. McSorley, who had established himself as the leader of our temporary little band, banged on the door. "Come on, now, Castleberry. We've worked some long hours and we want to get paid and hit the trail."

Castleberry opened the door, cigar clamped in his teeth like a piece of leather to bite down on during a painful procedure. He handed out envelopes, which were snatched up and inspected. Since ours contained the fewest bills, Mother was the first to finish counting.

"Why, there's only thirty dollars in here—our contract was for forty!"

Angry words erupted as each performer realized how much they'd been shorted. I noticed several of the stagehands nearby, each unaccountably holding a heavy prop, broomstick, or board.

Mr. Castleberry raised his frying-pan-sized hands. "You didn't bring the crowds, so I don't have it to give you. I cut you all by twenty-five percent. I'm a fair man, see?"

Fred Delorme's voice rose up. "That's not right. We worked hard and did our part. It's *your* job to fill the house. You didn't short your own salary, did you?"

"That's right! How much do you get paid?" others chimed in.

Castleberry crossed his arms. "Delorme, you might work hard, but your act's a joke. That partner of yours looks like she's sleepwalking. You got what you earned, and if I hear one more word, I'll smear your name to every manager from here to Buffalo." His glare shifted from one performer to the next. "And that goes for the rest of you, too."

Thirty dollars. Of that, three would go to Mr. Birnbaum for his 10 percent, and another sixteen had gone to food, lodging, and train fare for the five of us. Eleven dollars was all we had to show for eighteen performances and countless bruises to our bodies and egos.

On March 1, 1919, the rent and utilities were paid with the money we'd earned performing. But the bank account was completely empty. Worry hung in the air like sulfur from a lit match.

Mother tried to reach Mr. Birnbaum at his New York office, using Mrs. Califano's phone next door, but his secretary said he was on the road and she would give him the message. A week went by and we heard nothing. Mother called a second time. On her third humiliating trip to beg the use of the phone, Mother came home muttering that it was her last call. It was too much to suffer the secretary's apathy, Mrs. Califano's disapproval, and the horrible spicy smell of that tomato gravy that was always bubbling on her stove.

One night after a tin of beans and some mashed turnips for dinner, Mother suddenly shouted, "At least you're not going to bed hungry!" as if someone had complained, which of course no one had done.

"Not *yet*!" Kit yelled back, and burst into tears.

And if some of us weren't going to bed hungry, it was only because others of us were. Dad had taken a scant spoonful of beans, and Nell took none at all, only nibbled at the turnips.

Late that night after the others had gone to bed, I sat in the living room with Dad. The old Victrola was at its lowest possible volume, and he closed his eyes to listen, probably trying to distract himself from the rumbling of his stomach. I curled close to absorb what little heat I could through his winter coat. "Dad," I murmured, slipping my fingers gently around his damaged hand. "You need to eat. Food gives you strength to heal."

"A man's job is to feed his family, Winnie. I don't deserve even a bread crust."

"It's not your fault, Dad."

"It *is* my fault. All of it." He shook his head in self-disgust. "I'd rob the Binghamton Savings for you girls if I could get away with it. But I'd make a mighty poor bank robber—probably land in jail. Then you'd all be even more ashamed of me than you already are."

"No one's ashamed of you, Dad! We just have to hold on until something works out."

He gazed down at me. "Darling girl. I was hoping I might somehow save up enough to send you to college—I know how much you love school." His eyes went glassy with sorrow. "Now I can't even feed you. In a few weeks there might not be a roof over your head."

Eviction. It was the unspoken sword of Damocles now dangling by the thinnest of threads over our family. I had begged extra shifts on the maternity ward from Head Nurse Farquar, a stout woman sometimes mistaken for being in imminent need of labor and delivery services herself. She had eyed me suspiciously. "Why this sudden desire to empty more bedpans?"

Miscalculating her capacity for empathy, I said, "My father's been injured and can't work. We need the money."

"Your misfortune does not automatically create an increased need for your services."

Dr. Lodge stood near the nurses' desk reviewing a patient's chart, her unadorned fingers flipping expediently through the pages. She was known to be an intimidating presence on the ward and gave terrifyingly clipped responses when someone failed to perform to her exacting standards. The nurses loved to speculate on the reasons for her unmarried state, and wondered how she could be so good at diagnosis and delivery when she'd never suffered childbirth herself (though they never posed questions of this sort about the male doctors). Despite her terse manner, Dr. Lodge was the one most likely to notice my presence as I snuck into rounds, and the least likely to shoo me away.

"Nurse Farquar," she said without even glancing up. "I've observed a distinct decrease in the speed at which bedding is being changed."

"Yes, Doctor." Scowling and muttering about "ladies with big britches," Nurse Farquar conceded to adding a shift to my schedule. It wasn't anywhere near enough to make the rent, but it might put an extra bowl or two of soup in our bellies.

"Dad," I said now. "How did you know I wanted to go to college?"

"You're an unusual girl, Winnie," he sighed. "You're meant for unusual things."

CHAPTER
8

GERT

We had a hunger for something more important than fame. Food.
—George Burns, comedian, actor, and producer

Dad was officially fired. He'd been friends with Al the foreman since they'd both started in the coal room, and Al had held Dad's spot on the line as long as he could. Dad said the poor man had a tear in his eye when he said he'd had to replace Dad. It was just like Dad to feel sorrier for Al than for himself.

I didn't feel one bit sorry for Al. I felt sorry for our rumbling stomachs and chattering teeth in our freezing cold house!

I stopped carrying my little pochette to J. J. Wiley's, the one I'd filched out of the lost and found at school. I started hauling Mother's cracked old leather handbag instead. It was bigger, and I needed room for the uneaten rolls and baked potatoes I snatched before the busboys could get them. One day I even got a whole sardine sandwich that hadn't been touched, but I had to get off the trolley and eat it before I got home. The smell was making people cast their eyes around and wrinkle their noses. Besides, I was starving.

A week into March, and still no word from Birnbaum.

"Roy," I said as we stood looking at the new bear exhibit at Ross Park, watching those poor confused animals try and figure out how they'd gotten into this mess. "If I asked for a loan, would you give it to me?"

"Why, sure, sweetheart," he said, grinning a little too widely for my taste. "What've you got your eye on? A new hat?"

That smile. Like he was all too happy to have me in his debt.

I smiled back. "Yes, but I'm not quite sure about the color yet. I'll let you know when I decide for sure."

"Dinner!" Mother called. I'd smuggled two fat potatoes home, and now she served them on a platter like filet mignon. The only other dish was a small bowl of peas.

Kit eyes gleamed like she was under a love spell. "Where's the butter?"

"We're out," Mother said coldly.

Kit turned to me. "You couldn't have stolen some butter, too?"

"Why, you little brat!"

Dad shook his head. "Now, Gert. That's not—"

"It's not what?" I said. "I'll tell you what it's not! It's not grateful! I risk my job to bring home something—*anything*—for us to eat, and the Queen of Sheba here wants butter! Well, I'm sorry, but it's a damn sight more than anyone else here has done to feed this family!"

Mother slapped me. Full force. Right across the face. It stung like hell, but I didn't give her the satisfaction of showing it. I couldn't help reeling back from the blow, though. My chair tipped over and slammed to the floor like a gun going off. The baby began to wail. Kit started to cry. A few tears leaked out of Nell, too, but that was nothing new.

With all the ruckus, we almost didn't hear the knock at the door.

Winnie went to answer it, and before we saw who it was we heard her gasp.

"Mr. Birnbaum!" she said. "My goodness it's nice to see you!" She opened the door only about a foot, her little body shielding the Turner family insane asylum from view. I picked up the chair, Kit ran a sleeve under her snotty nose, and Nell took the screeching baby upstairs.

"Nice to see you, too," he said. "How about inviting me in? It's a mite cold out here."

Pleasantries were exchanged all around, as if everything was just the bee's knees.

"You all right?" he said when he shook my hand. "You're looking a little flushed." He eyed my reddened cheek, and then he must have noticed that the other was its usual pale color, because he didn't wait for an answer.

He did his *didn't-mean-to-interrupt-your-dinner* routine, but of course we pulled up a chair, completely mortified at what little we had to offer. At least he didn't take quite so long to get down to business. "So I've got some news."

In the second it took him to inhale half a breath, I thought Mother might leap across the table and grab him by those brown lapels. To be honest, I might have helped her.

"I was able to book you for nine weeks."

We looked around at one another afraid to speak for fear of shrieking. *Nine weeks!*

"Now, it's still small-time," he warned. "It ain't The Palace."

"The Palace?" Kit squealed. "We could play in *England*?"

"Not *Buckingham* Palace," he said. "The Palace Theatre in New York City. On a little street called Broadway—maybe you heard of it?" He shook his head. "Little girl, if you ever play there, you don't play for the queen. You *are* the queen. Vaudeville royalty.

"Now listen," he went on. "Most of these places are more like the palace stables, so set your expectations. On the upside, I only booked Upstate New York theatres, so it's all short jumps—you'll never be more than a couple hours' ride from the next place. Also, the money'll be better."

"How much better?" Mother asked, almost panting.

"I was able to negotiate a hundred a week, most places. Some a little more, some a little less."

It was almost ten times what Dad made stitching those stupid shoes!

"Sounds perfectly reasonable," I said quickly, before any of them could do something embarrassing, like hug him or cry. But even I couldn't keep the grin from my face.

Birnbaum smiled. "That's my favorite part of the job, naming the number and getting a happy reaction." His face returned to its usual scowl. "You'll have expenses," he warned. "Hotels, meals, train fare, freight. It all adds up, so don't be rubes about the dough."

"Freight?" Winnie asked. "What are we shipping?"

"Your trunks, of course. Costumes, props, clothes, and such—enough for nine weeks."

We didn't own trunks, and only had a couple of sets of clothes each. Silence fell on the table. Dad lowered his head, face crimson with poor man's shame. Birnbaum's eyes cut to the dinner plates we'd all but licked clean, and then to my father.

"Course you'll need an advance to get started," he said. "Only the Vanderbilts have that kind of gear lying around." He slid his wallet from the breast pocket of his suit jacket and opened it under the table. His hand came up with a twenty-dollar bill. Mother reached for it with a hungry smile.

Mother withdrew us from school for the rest of the year, though our nine-week run would only go till mid-May. "Why go through the bother of reregistering?" she said. "Besides, Mr. Birnbaum might have more work for us by then. No need to fib twice." The "fib" was that Dad had work in Wellsville, about 130 miles west, and the whole family was going. In fact, Dad was the only one who *wouldn't* be going, because Mother didn't want to pay his train fare. Or that's the reason she gave us—I had a right mind to wonder if she didn't like the idea of a bit more freedom, rather than playing the dutiful wife.

Dad picked up two secondhand trunks from a pawnbroker, and Mother brought the last bolt of black satin to make us a second set of costumes. Just the sight of those packed trunks sitting in the living room made me feel like dancing a jig.

On Monday, March 17, we stood on the platform at the Binghamton depot, the train hissing and grumbling. Dad hugged each of us, ran his hand over little Harry's head, adjusted Kit's hat, and said almost nothing.

He pecked Mother's cheek and held her shoulders for a moment — I think he would've liked to embrace her, but not in front of us girls. Mother took his lapels in her hands and stared at him for a moment, as if there were some sort of silent communication between them. Then she patted his chest and headed up the short stairs to the train car without a backward glance.

"It won't be that long, Dad," I heard Winnie murmur. "And now there's nothing to worry about." She gave him an extra hug before we all boarded.

From the window by our seats, we could see him standing, a single still figure, everyone bustling around him. The whistle blew; he raised his good hand. I had a strange moment of sadness, seeing him all alone. I wished I had given him an extra hug, too.

There was a lurch, and we were moving, picking up speed, leaving all we knew behind.

That train couldn't carry me away fast enough.

Lord, those damned trunks were heavy. It should've been a short walk from the Wellsville Depot to the Babcock Theatre, but it took five times forever. The stupid trunks had straps on either end; Nell and Kit carried one while Winnie and I hauled the other. We kept stopping to switch our aching red hands.

"You're going too fast!" Winnie whined.

"Your legs are too short," I snapped. "You need a pair of stilts so you can keep up."

"Wouldn't stilts slow her down?" Kit asked.

Honestly, if my hands hadn't been full, I would've pinched them both good and hard.

The Babcock was a brick-front building cheek by jowl with the stores on either side. The stage door was to the left of the theatre doors,

which had huge circular windows. It was dark in the long hallway that
led backstage, and I was startled nearly to death when a deep voice
said, "Can I give a hand with that trunk?"

"What in the world . . . ?" Mother said.

As our eyes adjusted, a figure loomed. White collar and cuffs, white
spats over his shoes, even the white of his teeth when he spoke. But the
rest of him still hadn't come quite clear.

"No disrespect, ma'am," he said quickly. "Just trying to be helpful."

"Well . . . all right," I said.

"You can let it down. I can carry the whole load." Suddenly, the
trunk and the man were gone.

"Who was that?" demanded Mother.

"Must be a stagehand," I said.

We made our way down the hall toward the backstage. The man
had set the first trunk down and returned for the other. His skin was
the color of maple syrup, and almost as shiny-smooth. His hair was
short and slicked down with a touch of pomade, but it had little ripples
and you could tell it would be tightly curled if he grew it out. He was
tall and muscular, with long legs built for speed, and shoulders as broad
as a bookshelf.

"Tippety Tap Jones," he said, flicking his gaze down after making
contact with mine. He didn't hold out his hand to shake.

He lifted the other trunk away from Nell and Kit, his arms wrapping easily around the girth of it. But it was clear he was no stagehand.
His smart black double-breasted suit was neatly pressed, though it
had seen some wear. The Negroes I'd seen around Johnson City were
poor and wore workers' clothing, and you didn't often see a Negro performer unless you went to one of the all-colored shows. For a moment,
we didn't know what to make of it.

Mother went off to find the stage manager, and Kit went with her.
Nell took the baby and sat down on one of the trunks to unwrap him
from all his coverings.

"Where are you on the bill?" I asked the colored man, trying not
to sound too interested. Because I *was* interested. There was something
about his quietness that made me want to make him talk so I could

figure him out a little better. It doesn't usually take me more than five minutes of conversation to accomplish that with any man.

"Oh, I can fit in anywhere, wherever they like to put me."

That was no kind of answer. "Well, your agent must have told you something," I pressed.

For the first time his gaze held mine. I saw his wariness, as if he was wondering what kind of trouble I'd be. But there was toughness, too. A sense that he'd faced worse than the likes of me.

His gazed flicked away again. "Agents," he said mildly. "They like to give the good news. Doesn't always turn out like that. I'd rather just wait and see."

"We're the Turners," Winnie said in that bright, goody-goody way she has that goes right up my spine. "We usually open, but like you said, there's no guarantee."

"Is that right?" He smiled kindly at her, thinking she was young, of course. "And what kind of act do you do?"

"We're acrobats," I said quickly to take control of things so I could complete my mission. "My three sisters and me."

"You don't say. Well, I'm sure you're mighty entertaining." He nodded and moved away. There was a huge trunk in the farthest, darkest corner of the backstage area. It lay lengthwise and had four wheels sticking out on one side. He sat down on it, opened a copy of the entertainment magazine *Variety*, and, despite the dimness, began to read.

Mr. Kress, the theatre manager, was a little man with a tightly curled mustache and a pocket watch that he clutched like a loaded gun. "I run an *orderly house*," he said, stalking around, an angry rooster in a disappointing henhouse. "There must not be more than *ten seconds* between acts. An act that begins after eleven seconds is *tardy*. Audiences get bored, and a boring show *will not sell*."

The act with the pigeons that pecked out songs on a set of bells couldn't get the birds back into their cage fast enough, which made it hard for the xylophone quartet to get all their instruments onstage in under ten seconds. Mr. Kress stamped his silly heel against the floor-boards and screamed out, *"Too much time, too much time!"*

Tippety Tap Jones was the last to rehearse. When the curtain opened, he was standing beside a small wooden table with sturdy legs. I wondered where on earth he'd dragged it from. Nearby was a mysterious low contraption: a rectangular board that lay flat on the floor, and another board attached on one end that tipped upward, so the whole thing made a sideways V. He had one hand on the table, and he leaned into this arm as he stood, one foot crossed jauntily in front of the other. The band struck up a fun ragtime tune, and he sprang into action.

I'd never seen anything like it before. His feet moved so fast they seemed to blur, but the tapping was sharp as firecrackers. He flew around the table, fingertips touching then pushing off, spinning, tapping, then he'd lean on the table, legs swinging high into the air, heels clicking. It was wild looking and tightly controlled, all at the same time.

This was only the warm-up, though, because after a few minutes he tapped backward from the table then sprinted toward it, springing off the contraption on the floor and leaping onto the table. It was so amazing I almost clapped!

He tapped complicated patterns around the tabletop. A few times he looked like he might fall right off it, but he never did. He just kept smiling, white teeth gleaming out from his full brown lips. He finished by leaping off the table and sliding down into a split on the floor.

During any show, the backstage area hums with performers getting their props ready or chatting quietly with one another. The rapt silence after Mr. Jones's performance was so loud it might as well have been applause.

Since he was last to rehearse, it generally meant he'd close, unless the manager changed his mind about the lineup. Every person in that theatre, from the lowliest stagehand to the headliner—a female impersonator who did Annie Oakley and Sarah Bernhardt—must have seen that Tippety Tap Jones was no closer.

Kress called out to him. "Jones! Jones, come out here this *instant*!"

He emerged from behind the curtain. "Yes, sir?"

"Your timing is excellent. Even with the table and springboard to set up, *very* impressive."

"Thank you, sir!"

"But next time, don't forget your cork."

He meant the burnt end of a cork that performers use to blacken their faces. A white performer pretending to be colored would also whiten around his mouth to make his lips more obvious. Then he'd sing coon songs like "Massa's in de Cold, Cold Ground," or have some sort of silly slapstick routine with another player. Colored performers black up, too, especially if they have light skin.

"Uh, well sir, I don't generally wear the cork," Mr. Jones said.

Kress scowled at him. "Why not? All the Negro acts black up."

"I figure the audience is looking at my feet. They don't pay no never-mind to my face."

"Be that as it may, you'll wear cork here."

Mr. Jones eyed the tips of his toes and said quietly, "I prefer not to, sir."

"What's that?"

"I said"—Mr. Jones looked up—"I prefer not to. Sir."

Good Lord, I thought. *He's bold.*

The small man narrowed his eyes. "Well I suppose I can't *make* you do it. I'm not going to go backstage and cork you *myself*." He snapped his watch shut and tucked it into his vest pocket. "Besides, you're clos-ing. No one's going to see you anyway."

Mr. Jones walked offstage toward us, face calm, but his shoulders were stiff as a cross. I couldn't take my eyes off him, wondering how he'd learned to act so humble and still get his way.

Nell was beside me, holding the baby as he gnawed on his fist. "I don't believe we've been properly introduced," she said. "I'm Nell Her-kimer, one of the Tumbling Turner Sisters."

"Tippety Tap Jones. How do you do, Mizz Herkimer."

"Please call me Nell." She gave a little smile. "It's vaudeville, after all."

"It sure is, isn't it?" His shoulders seemed to relax a bit. "I'm Tip."

"This is my mother, Mrs. Turner, and my sisters, Kit, Gert, and Winnie."

"Pleased to make your acquaintance, ladies." He nodded and smiled. "Well, I suppose I'd better round up my props before I end up with eleven seconds." And he strode off.

"What was all that about?" Mother demanded.

"He's the best performer of all of us," said Nell. "And his face is just fine the way it is."

"Why, Nell!" Mother was taken aback. I'll admit I was a bit surprised myself. We weren't used to strong opinions from our sweetest sister. But before Mother could interrogate her, little Harry began to whine, probably hungry, tired, or both, and we knew we'd better hurry to get some food before the show went up.

"Has this crowd been drinking?" the female impersonator asked. He was a sight, all made up with rouge, lipstick, and eyeliner, wig resting on his skirt-clad lap as he smoked a pipe.

It was a good question. The daytime Wellsville audiences had been terrific, but at night they acted like we were the latest Ziegfeld Follies show. A stagehand answered, "It's the Sinclair Oil Refinery workers, ma'am . . . uh, sir. They're generally just happy not to be working."

They went absolutely wild for Tip. We saw it each performance: the headliner would finish singing in his falsetto, pull off his wig to show the crowd he was a man, and then take his bows. People would start to get up and leave, but then the curtain would pull back to reveal Tip and his lightning feet, and they'd sit back down. It was the only act I bothered to watch after I'd seen them all once or twice.

During the other acts we'd sit around backstage, talking softly or even dozing on each other's shoulders. Tip kept to himself, off in the corner on his huge trunk, reading *Variety*. He didn't nap. In fact, I had the strange sense that even behind that magazine, he knew exactly what was going on in the room.

Mother had brought a sheet to use as a screen so Nell could nurse the baby or we could adjust our costumes. It was my turn to hold it, and Winnie sat next to Nell on the trunk as she cradled little Harry for his evening meal.

But something had been niggling at me since the dustup between Tip and Mr. Kress. "What's your point about the cork, Nell?" I whispered. "Why do you care?"

She sat the baby up for a burp, then tucked him over her shoulder and patted his back. "I got a letter from Harry once," she said softly. "His unit fought alongside a regiment called the Harlem Hellfighters. They were from New York, like us, one of the only colored regiments allowed to actually fight. He said they were some of the bravest men he ever saw."

We glanced over at Tip. He didn't look like much of a fighter, with his spats, pressed suit, and slicked hair. Still, I somehow got the feeling he could be fierce if he needed to be.

"What's that got to do with blacking up?" I said.

"Oh, Gert, think about it," Nell whispered wearily. "What if someone started telling you that you had to wear a certain makeup, or live in a particular place . . . or just be scared all the time even though you're one of the bravest girls I know?"

I'd never even considered such a thing.

Nell sighed. "All I know is, if Harry were here . . ." She set her mouth to steady herself against the forbidden fantasy of Harry's existence. "If Harry were here, he'd be kind."

The hotel room I shared with Kit and Winnie had a trundle bed under one of the twins, so we each had a mattress to ourselves. I was so tired I thought I'd fall asleep before I'd even pulled the covers over me, but as the other two began to breathe slower and heavier, I lay there annoyed at my own wakefulness.

That look on Roy's face.

I never actually *said* I'd marry him. I just never said I wouldn't. And when I told him I was leaving for nine weeks, he acted as if I were abandoning him on the Western Front with no supplies or ammunition. It's Binghamton, for cripes' sake — he'll be fine.

"I should put my foot down," he'd said.

Put his foot down! As if I was already his wife—or worse, his disobedient child.

"I already have a controlling mother," I said. "I don't need another."

Oh, the fight. And that was the end. Truly.

I should've felt worse, I know I should've . . . But I was relieved. Him and his foot—imagine being stuck with that for the rest of your life!

I got bored of thinking about Roy, and how bad I should feel. But I still couldn't sleep. Then, like a brass tack to a magnet, my drowsy brain kept sliding toward Tip—wondering how he'd come to be the only colored man in a white show, how he'd learned to dance like that, and where he was staying. Our hotel was whites only, of course. He hid behind his stupid magazine like it was the Great Wall of China, and yet he wasn't shy or timid. He stood right up to that walking watch fob Kress.

So why wouldn't he have a simple conversation with me?

At the theatre the next morning, I was done being ignored. Before Tip arrived, I pulled an old chair over toward his trunk—not right up next to it, but close enough. "Bring that stool over here," I told Winnie.

"Why?"

That girl can never just do something without a whole scientific explanation.

"Well, I can't talk to him alone," I said. "People will take notice."

"What people?"

Most of the other acts had dressing rooms behind the stage. The only other performers who didn't were the couple with the bell-pecking pigeons, and they spent most of their time either cooing to the birds or bickering with each other in a foreign language I couldn't place. Tip hadn't been given a dressing room, either, of course.

Still, people take notice. Of everything. Unless, of course, you're small and quiet, like Winnie, and you're generally the noticer, not the notice-ee.

"Just *sit*," I said, and she dragged the stool over.

Tip came down the hallway at just that moment with a rucksack on his back, suit covered by a threadbare overcoat, pants tucked into galoshes. He nodded to Mother putting the finishing touches on Kit's makeup. "Morning, Mizz Turner." Nell was tucking the baby in for a nap in a cardboard box she'd padded with blankets. "Morning, Mizz Herkimer," he whispered.

When Tip saw Winnie and me sitting near his trunk, he slowed for a second. Then without making eye contact, he said, "Morning, ladies," and laid his coat across the trunk. He sat down, tugged off his galoshes, and fished his tap shoes out of the rucksack.

The stage manager hustled in. "Jones, Mr. Kress says you're the deuce today."

Second! Tip would come on right after us.

"Pepper's Pigeons . . ." The stage manager didn't even look at the couple with the birds. "Chaser." Then he hustled right back out again.

There was a flurry of angry foreign sounds between the bird people, then the birds got into the act, fluttering around the cage. The couple immediately stopped sniping and started cooing. For a moment, I felt sorry for them, in the way you feel sorry for the slowest boy on the basketball team. But my sympathy was short-lived. After all, if you're slow, whose fault is that?

"Congratulations," I said to Tip.

He shrugged. "Least I'll get to bed a little earlier." But you could tell he was happy.

We went on, and then Tip went on, and then we had about two hours before a new audience arrived and we had to perform again.

"Where'd you learn to dance like that?" I asked him offhandedly, after he'd collapsed onto his trunk, wiping beads of sweat from his forehead with a handkerchief.

"On the road," he said. A cloudy answer, mostly made of air.

"The road taught you?" I said dryly. "Must have been some road."

"Well, now." He gave up a little chuckle. "It wasn't the road itself, as much as the people on it. My aunt and uncle. They've been on the road most of their born days."

"Your parents didn't mind you going off with relatives like that?"

"Didn't mind at all. Weren't alive to mind."

The fresh news of an old misfortune is a tricky thing. You don't know how much it still stings. "Sorry for their loss," I said carefully.

"Thank you," he said. "I only knew my father, so the other wasn't quite as grievous."

Kit had wandered over and nudged her way onto Winnie's chair with her. "How'd he pass?" she asked. It was rude, but I hoped Tip would answer.

He didn't say anything at first, just stared off as if remembering.

"Unpleasantly," he said finally, and picked up his copy of *Variety*.

CHAPTER
9

WINNIE

Everything is copacetic.

—Bill "Bojangles" Robinson, dancer and actor

The last show of the night was stupendous! The audience practically came in clapping, and every act made them cheer. After Tip's performance, the whole place erupted like Mount Vesuvius, but it was the colored section up in the gallery that made the most noise. They whistled and stomped, and their applause went on a little longer than the rest.

Tip came offstage grinning so widely we could see the pink of his gums. His joy was instantly contagious, and we smiled right along with him, and then shooed him back out onto the boards to take another bow. The applause crested again, and he raised a hand, gazing briefly to the upper reaches of the theatre, and bowed once more.

He came off shaking his head in happy wonder. The next act was the xylophone quartet, and they shot him angry looks as they scrambled onstage with their unwieldy instruments. I could understand their displeasure—Tip was an awfully hard act to follow—but I hoped that in their hearts they were a little bit happy for him, too.

"You slayed them!" Kit whispered to Tip. "You blew the roof off!"

Kit was picking up vaudeville jargon faster than any of us, and we burst out laughing at the sound of it. The stage manager scowled at our noisiness from his post on the opposite stage wing.

"I gotta buy a postcard," Tip whispered. "My aunt will lay an egg when she hears!"

"Where are they now?" Kit asked.

"Only the Good Lord and TOBA knows," he said. "I'll just send it to their hometown post office, and they'll pick it up one of these months." He saw our blank looks and said, "You never heard of TOBA? Well, I guess you wouldn't. It's the Theatre Owners Booking Association, the colored circuit down south. Chitlin' Circuit, we call it." He gave a dry little smirk. "Call it some other things, too."

He sat down on his trunk and started unbuttoning the white spats that covered the ankles of his tap shoes. I felt disappointed that we had finally gotten him to talk a little and the momentum might now be lost. But there was little to do but pack up and head to the hotel. We followed him out, and he turned left in the direction of the refinery.

As we turned in the opposite direction, Kit asked, "Where do you think he's staying?"

Nell gave her a sideways look. "Somewhere they allow Negroes."

The next day, everyone was in a chipper mood, anticipating another grand reception from the good people of Wellsville. I should say, everyone except Mr. and Mrs. Pepper (which seemed unlikely to be their real name). They were as sullen as ever.

The mood shifted dramatically, however, after the stage manager trotted over and said, "Jones, you're back to closing. Peppers, you're second. Mr. Kress's orders."

"But why?" I blurted out.

"Too much noise from the crow's nest last night." The man's eyes remained trained on his notes. "Mr. Kress says he doesn't want the place turning into some sort of colored free-for-all." He glanced up quickly in Tip's direction, gave a brief apologetic shrug, and hurried off to the other wing of the stage to assume his post.

The Peppers exchanged smug looks and retired to their little corner of bird paradise. The rest of us stood there stunned.

"It's not right," said Nell. "You deserve the deuce, Tip."

"He deserves to headline!" said Gert. "That fat old female impersonator doesn't hold a candle. If I have to listen to him squawk out the 'I Don't Care' song one more time, I'm going to scream back that I don't care, either."

Mother said, "Now, girls, Mr. Kress is the manager and we can't get on the wrong side of him. Besides, not every type of audience understands that in polite society you can't just—"

"Mother!" Gert said sharply, and we all fell silent in its wake.

Finally it was Tip who spoke. "Ladies, I thank you for your kindness. All I want is a chance. That's why I came up here, for a chance to be seen by all kinds of folks and maybe even make it into the big time one day. That was never going to happen on the colored circuit, and I'm just happy to get a spot—any spot. So as long as I'm still on the bill, I'm all right with it."

Well, you shouldn't be, I thought. But what good would righteous fury do him? No good at all. In fact, it could cause him far more trouble than anything.

If there was any small upside to Tip's demotion, it was that he seemed to feel a bit more free to talk with us. What harm could it do, after all—he was already in the worst spot on the bill.

"How come your trunk's so big?" Kit wanted to know, bouncing little Harry on her knee like a pot full of popcorn.

"So it fits my springboard and table," he said. "They fold up, you know."

We did not know, and he showed us how the table legs were hinged, and the springboard had a stick of wood wedged into a notch between the two boards at the attached end, which created the spring. When the piece was taken out, the boards lay flat. He kept his clothes in a rucksack inside the trunk, and carried them to and from whatever lodging he could find. "Some towns have a nice colored section, with restaurants and small hotels. Some just have a bad neighborhood. It's better to leave the trunk and props locked up in the theatre at night so no one takes a notion to carry them off."

"Where did you get the idea for them?" I asked. "I've never seen anything like it."

"Oh, I can't claim to have invented it. Lot of tappers use some kind of platform in case they play somewhere low rent. Grange hall or something where there's sawdust on the floor, or even hay. Can't hear the tapping if the boards aren't cleared."

He wanted to know how we'd gotten into the business, and Mother rewrote history—or at least changed the adjectives—saying we'd always been keen to perform, and Nell made the foursome complete by coming back into the fold after Harry's death. "He was a fine young man, full of promise," Mother bragged. "And he was friendly with Negroes on the battlefield, too!"

Nell looked away, and I put a hand out to press her knee, both for comfort about poor Harry, and commiseration over Mother's grandiosity.

Tip took her pronouncement in stride, merely commenting, "You don't say." I imagine he'd heard white people assert their lack of prejudice before, and I wondered what it must be like to know it was often only true when such open-mindedness was convenient.

"How old were you when you learned to tap like that?" asked Kit.

"I was about eight when I went to live with my aunt and uncle. They started me right off with bottle caps between my toes. Best way to learn, barefoot so you can feel everything. Plus it saved money on shoes. When I was good enough, they added me into their act."

"Is that how you got your name?"

"That's right. Given name's Hezekiah, but my uncle's not much on the Bible, and he said it was an askin'-for-a-beatin' kind of name." Tip chuckled. "He might've been right—I didn't keep it long enough to find out."

And so we passed a pleasant day, trading stories, stopping only to perform.

That night I had dreams of flying. This wasn't unusual for me, since I spent a good deal more time in midair than most people. But these particular dreams were of running and leaping higher than I ever had before, vaulting to dizzying heights.

The next morning, I asked Tip to show me how his springboard worked. We went into the dim hallway, where there was room to run and bounce. The first few times I went sprawling when I landed, but with Tip giving me pointers, I quickly learned both to control the height of my bounce and to anticipate how to place my feet when I came down. We soon worked out a simple but impressive move: I vaulted from the springboard, flew through the air, and dove into my sisters' waiting arms.

Gert used it to perfect her no-handed cartwheel, legs winging up, head suspended precariously a few feet from the floor until she twisted and landed on her feet. The first few times she tried it, the momentum was too forceful, and she went careening past her desired landing point and crashed to the floor, but Gert being Gert, she persevered.

"Fearless," commented Tip, nodding appreciatively, his dark eyes taking her in.

I saw her pause, and the barest blush rise to her cheeks. Knowing my sister, I doubt if any assessment could have pleased her more. Tip had unwittingly struck the perfect chord.

The next vault she attempted had a rather calamitous ending: she crashed right into Tip and they both fell to the floor. Mr. Pepper was carrying his birdcage out to the back alley to clean it, and was just in time to see the two of them sprawled together, arms and legs a tangle, and he tut-tutted at the impropriety of it.

Tip jumped up like a jack-in-the-box. "I'm sorry, Mizz Gert, I'm so sorry," he implored.

"It was my fault." Her cheeks were red even through her makeup. Embarrassed, she smiled a little too hard as she waved his apologies away. "Besides, you don't practice a tumbling act without a lot worse falls than that."

His concern was understandable. A white woman in a horizontal position with a colored man was far beyond what most people found acceptable, no matter how innocently they'd come to be there. "You sure you're all right?" he said. "I didn't mean for—"

"Of course you didn't." She ironed her face into composure "Now, let me ask you—where can we get one of these springboards? It's perfect for our act."

"I made it myself from scrap wood. I could make you one. I could do that easy." He was still jittery, and my heart went out to him.

Mother gave him the money, and he went to the lumberyard down the street for the supplies. I think he was just happy to get away from us. Spending all day with a flock of white women can be a bit much for any man, but the color of Tip's skin made it far more complicated.

He came back with a paper sack of hardware and a couple of boards that were smaller than his own. "Y'all don't weigh that much," he said. "And I thought a smaller rig would fit better into your trunks. Then I got to thinking about those trunks of yours, and how much easier it would be if they had wheels like mine. So I picked up a couple of sets. I can return them if you aren't inclined, though," he added quickly.

We were delighted at the idea, and went the few blocks to the hotel to retrieve our trunks. Tip had tools with him in case the need for repair arose, and he set to work right away. We were even able to use the newly made springboard during our last performance of the evening.

As I flew through the air, I heard a little gasp go up from the crowd, and they applauded loudly when I landed in my sisters' arms. I felt terribly grateful to Tip. I had never had a Negro for a friend before, and he proved to be as thoughtful and generous as anyone I knew.

Everything was going so well.

Perhaps a little too well, in some people's estimation.

CHAPTER

10

GERT

*Being a star has made it possible for me to get insulted in
places where the average Negro could never hope to go and
get insulted.*
—Sammy Davis Jr., singer, dancer, and actor

I had no intention to launch into him like that. I'm almost certain of it. But when it happened, and he caught me up in his arms, twisting as we barreled downward so that his back hit the floor instead of mine, a rush of excitement swept through me the likes of which I'd never felt before. God help me, but the memory of landing on his broad chest is still a secret thrill.

And I pay for that thrill every time I think of it, with the guilt of what happened next.

We were dawdling—or I was anyway—after our last performance of the night. I just wanted a few more moments to talk with him, to see his eye catch mine as we chuckled over some silly thing or another.

Fearless. If any man had ever even noticed that about me before, they'd certainly never complimented me on it. I got "doll" or "knockout." The occasional "live wire." Roy just loved how hardworking I was. (Course he did. He'd pegged me for an employee as well as a wife.)

I was so caught up in enjoying Tip's company that I paid no attention to the stupid bird people and how the husband disappeared for a while after their act.

Just then that pompous windbag Kress came backstage. "Mr. Jones." His tone made us all snap our eyes toward him, wondering what on earth had put a twist in his knickers this time.

"Mr. Jones, it's come to my attention that you have not been conducting yourself with moral *steadfastness*." His glare suddenly took in my sisters and me. "*All* performers are expected to comport themselves with *decency*. Mr. Jones, I'm afraid I'll have to dismiss you due to improper behavior. Your contract will be terminated after your final performance this evening."

Tip's face went wide with shock, but then he buckled it down into firmness, and said, "Pardon me, Mr. Kress, but there hasn't been . . . improper behavior. I've been a gentleman —"

Kress let out a little scoff, as if a man like Tip could never hope to be in such a category.

My fists curled at my sides. "He didn't do anything except keep me from breaking my neck! If you want to blame someone, blame me!" Tip's eyes met mine, and the gratitude in his gaze swept through me like a wave of warmth.

Kress warned, "You are *pressing your luck*, Miss Turner." I suddenly felt Nell's hand on my arm, squeezing more tightly than I would've thought possible from someone so thin.

He aimed himself back at Tip. "Jones, I have no interest in discussing your dubious social status. See me after the show and I'll pay you for the days you worked. This is *unreasonably* generous on my part, but as an upstanding member of the business community, I won't have it be said that I shorted anyone in my employ." He raised his finger at Tip. "Assuming, of course, there are no further acts of indecency before the completion of your final performance."

"I'll leave now."

"What's that?" Kress demanded.

Tip pulled himself to his full height, eyes boring straight into that weasel. "I said, I will leave now."

"Oh, no you won't, boy," snapped Kress. "There's a show to put on, and you'll leave when I tell you to."

A cold little smile flitted across Tip's face, a look so menacing it nearly scared the daylights out of me. "I am *no one's* boy. And I will come and go as I please."

My God, it was the bravest thing I'd ever seen. He had called me fearless, but my courage was nothing compared to his. His beauty nearly blinded me.

He turned then and began loading his few possessions into his trunk.

"I won't pay you," warned Kress, his voice growing whiny as it dawned on him he was losing a battle that was so clearly stacked in his favor.

Tip hauled the trunk up onto its wheels and tossed the rucksack onto his shoulder. "I wouldn't take it anyway." He nodded to us and strode down the hallway and out the door.

CHAPTER
11

W I N N I E

Be awful nice to 'em goin' up,
because you're gonna meet 'em all comin' down.
—Jimmy Durante, comedian and actor

We walked back to the hotel in stunned silence.

In our room, Kit suddenly blurted, "I just don't understand what Tip did wrong!"

"Nothing," snarled Gert. "He did nothing wrong, so just shut up about it."

We got into our beds, and in the darkened quiet, the anger and confusion we all felt seemed to bounce off the walls around us. Gert was in such a state I didn't dare provoke her by speaking. I wonder if she got a wink of sleep. I know I didn't.

With lead in our hearts, we trudged back to the theatre the next morning. I suppose each of us wondered what we might have done to save Tip from being fired. Gert had tried, but it was clear that Kress's narrow mind had been made up well before he'd come backstage. He hadn't even witnessed the so-called "act of indecency" himself.

But someone else had.

The Peppers had been absent during Kress's tirade, spending longer than usual behind the theatre, purportedly cleaning their pigeons' cage, a chore that had been performed by Mr. Pepper alone in previous days. It hadn't occurred to us that they might be involved in some way. Now, their newly cheery faces suddenly made clear the source of Mr. Kress's misinformation.

"It was him," Gert hissed, wild-eyed. "The man. He saw me fall into Tip, and reported it like it was Tip's fault!"

"I hope this won't hurt our reputation with other managers," Mother fussed. "It doesn't seem right that we should be associated—"

"Mother!" snapped Gert. She turned on the Peppers. "You! You got him fired!"

They only lifted their shoulders innocently, as if they couldn't understand her.

"I know you speak English, so don't pretend—"

"Gert," said Nell quietly. "It won't bring him back."

She knew all too well that no amount of fury or sorrow could magically return a man to where he ought to be, once he'd been lost.

Onstage our smiles never dimmed. But when I vaulted from the springboard Tip had made with his own hands, I felt terrible. From our friendship with him, we had gained a wonderful new skill that would improve our chances of success. As a direct result of that very same friendship, he had been fired.

When we finished, the Peppers took the stage with their stinky pigeons, and the pecking of that insipid "You Made Me Love You" made me want to scream.

"I'm going for a walk," I told the others, and strode quickly for the stage door. North Main was busy with afternoon shoppers, and I suddenly felt as if I might cry. The pure unfairness of it; the vicious use of a person's position in life—a circumstance of birth he had no control over—to make a failure of him; a good, kind, talented man laid low by lies.

I turned down a side street as furious tears began to roll. Between the garish makeup and the tears, two women who passed me on the sidewalk stared, and I ducked into an alley that led to the back of the theatre and had myself a good sob. When the back door to the theatre opened, I shrank up against the building, hoping no one would notice me in my disheveled state.

It was Mr. Pepper, hauling the birdcage out to clean it. As he reached in, the birds began to peck at him, and he muttered threateningly at them in a language I never could discern. I wondered if the birds were ever allowed out of their cage when they weren't performing. *No*, I thought. *They're just captives to those horrible Peppers, or whatever their real name is.*

Suddenly, Mr. Pepper cried out and wrenched his arm from the cage; blood welled from his hand. He hurried back into the theatre, I suppose to get a cloth to stop the bleeding.

The cage door was unlatched, but the pigeons didn't seem to realize that all they had to do was nudge it open. *Come on!* I thought hard at them. *Just give it a push!*

I am not proud of what I did next. But neither am I sufficiently sorry.

I merely gave the door the nudge that the pigeons would have given, had they known; had they not been captives for so long that they failed to recognize freedom when it beckoned.

Still, they stayed in that cage. *Dumb birds*, I thought. *Now you'll never be free.*

I went back out to the street and entered the theatre through the stage door. When I arrived backstage, my sisters saw the state of my face, and they gathered round, giving pats and kind words. Mother sighed and sat me down to fix my makeup. From the corner of my eye, I saw Mrs. Pepper wrap a cloth around Mr. Pepper's hand; she gave him a stern directive and he left.

In a moment he was back, face as pale as fog. He held the cage in his arms, and now it contained just one lone pigeon.

Dumb bird.

Saturday was our last performance in Wellsville, and we felt no sorrow at parting. Mother collected our earnings of a hundred dollars. Between the money we owed Mr. Birnbaum, train fare, our hotel rooms, and meals, we were down to about forty dollars, which Mother stashed in some mysterious place. I wondered when, if ever, I'd be able to claim my part of our earnings for my college fund.

On Sunday morning, on our way to the train station, I mailed a postcard home.

> Dear Dad: We are having a fine time. The audiences are appreciative and we have added a springboard to our act! Thinking of you.

No use worrying him with the low points, I figured. He had enough of his own.

The ride to Cuba was quiet and subdued, and I opened the battered copy of *Little Women* I'd found wedged under a coil of old curtain rope back in Wellsville. The stagehands had assured me that whoever had stashed it there was long gone by now. I'd read it before, but it hadn't caught my imagination enough for multiple readings.

Beggars can't be choosers, I told myself now, though I needed no reminding.

It's about four sisters and their mother fending for themselves while their father is off at war. The March girls: all different, but all so full of "moral steadfastness" (as Mr. Kress would say) that in the first chapter alone, they give away their Christmas breakfast and spend their last pennies on gifts for their mother. It was too sweet for my sour mood, and I closed it up again.

Cuba, New York, was even smaller than Wellsville. "I had to put some fillers in," Birnbaum had told us. "Otherwise you'd be cooling your heels for a week, paying for a hotel and meals and not making any dough." He'd warned us that the theatres would be "more or less small-time. Some are medium-time, some are more like small-small-time." Cuba was clearly in the latter category.

We stepped down off the train and waited for the porter to unload our trunks. I watched with envy as several passengers received warm greetings from those who'd come to collect them. "Safely home!" cried an older woman as she clutched a young man whom I guessed to be her son, and I couldn't help but think of Harry's mother. There had been no live child to hug and fuss over when his train had pulled into Binghamton.

Off to the side I saw a little girl standing with a man who didn't seem old enough to be her father. A brother perhaps, gauging from their similar features: dark hair that snuck out from under his tweed cap and the soft brim of her green felt hat; dark brown eyes gazing at the train they now waited to board. He stood straight as a streetlamp, hand firmly grasping hers.

I noticed a little smudge of orange pancake makeup by his ear, and eyeliner clinging to her lids. *Performers*, I thought, and took a step toward them to ask if they'd just played the Palmer Opera House, as we were about to do. His gaze took me in, and an unexpected jolt of anticipation hit me when those large brown eyes lit on mine.

"Joe, they're boarding," said the little girl suddenly, and tugged at his hand.

"Winnie, don't dawdle!" said Mother at almost exactly the same time.

He turned toward the huffing train; I turned to see my family heading up the street without me. I looked back and watched the two of them climb the steps. The whistle blew, and the great metal wheels groaned forward, leaving me unaccountably sad for the loss.

CHAPTER
12

GERT

Many a bum show has been saved by the flag.
—George M. Cohan, singer, dancer, and songwriter

I did not want to think about Tip.

He wasn't thinking about me, I told myself, so why should I bother?

If I did think about him (and I couldn't seem to stop), I only allowed myself to stew on the way he'd been treated. I daydreamed that he'd soon be a star, headlining at The Palace, like Bill Bojangles Robinson, and that idiot Kress would be shown up for firing him. Maybe Kress himself would be fired, and he'd end up penniless, shivering in a pig barn like a fugitive.

I imagined the Babcock Theatre going up in flames. I tried to imagine that there were no people in it when it burned to the ground, but occasionally the Peppers were there, locked in their own birdcage and unable to save themselves. Tragedies do happen.

The Palmer Opera House in Cuba should've been called the Palmer Spare Bedroom—it was up an entire flight of stairs, above some stores. But that wasn't the only surprise.

"Where are the seats?" Mother demanded to know as we groaned, hoisting our trunks up the stairwell behind her.

"Well now, that's an ingenious thing," said Mr. Keller, the theatre manager, a man with a permanent grin on his face. "The Opera House doubles as a dance hall, rec hall, even a basketball court! I bet you never played in a basketball court, now have you?"

"No," said Mother dryly. "I can assure you we never have."

"Where do the musicians sit?" Kit asked.

"We've got a three-piece orchestra—a piano player, a piano, and a stool!" He guffawed as if this were a hilarious joke, and pointed to the upright piano in front of the small stage. None of us laughed.

If there was any doubt about Cuba's small-small-time-ness, the other performers made it crystal clear. They were all pleased as punch to find themselves in such a grand "opera house." While we'd been shocked that the seats weren't bolted to the floor, the man with the iron-jaw act said it was the first place he'd played with real chairs instead of wooden benches.

With only seven acts, rehearsal didn't take long. Mr. Keller found every last one, even the painfully off-tempo clog dancers, to be just delightful. "What a wonderful show we'll give them, won't we? Now let me see about the lineup. Hmm . . ." He took a pad of paper from his vest pocket and a pencil from behind his ear. "Okay, we'll go contortionist, clog dancers, magician, iron jaw, then intermission, then the Tumbling Turners, Sissy Salloway and her banjo man, and we'll close with Billy the Cowboy Yodeler. How's that? Everyone okay with that?"

Mother and the girls and I looked at one another. We had the opening spot after intermission—a promotion. At least there was one small upside to small-small time.

The cowboy yodeler in the closing spot looked stunned. "I'm in it? I made the show?"

"Yes, son, you did!" said Mr. Keller. "I think you may be the best chaser we ever had!"

The boy let out a whoop, and we hid our smirks behind our hands.

The basketball court layout had one advantage: before the chairs were set up each day we could practice our springboard stunts without crashing into the ceiling or walls. "Can't we do something about that tired old leapfrog stunt?" said Kit. So we worked it out that Nell would jump over me, then we'd put our hands on our knees and Kit would jump over us, then Winnie would use the springboard to vault over all three. It was a big improvement.

The audience seemed to agree, but it was hard to know if they were actually impressed or just relieved to have something better to watch than the clumsy cloggers and the contortionist who couldn't do much more than a few backbends and put one leg up behind his neck, which was damned unsightly. That's a view no one wants.

Sissy Salloway was the headliner, and her voice had a whine like metal on metal. Her partner, Clay, was a stone-faced old guy who played the banjo as if he were pulling weeds, a chore he'd gotten so used to he didn't even seem to notice he was doing it. Miss Sissy's face made up for it, though—she had a whole brass band of expressions, mouth stretching wide as a bucket as she massacred "You're a Grand Old Flag." What's worse, she strode around the stage in a funny little walk-skip that made her flesh jiggle under her calico blouse.

"Is she wearing a corset?" Winnie whispered to me as we watched.

"With everything flying around loose like that? What do you think?"

We gossiped about Miss Sissy's underwear for the duration of her act, and came to the conclusion that she wore only a brassiere and drawers, and that while a thinner, smaller-busted woman might have been able to pull it off, she was definitely not in that category.

"You'd be fine without a corset, though," I told Winnie. "Why bother with all those laces and hooks if you don't have to?" After that Winnie stuck her nose in her book, but with that scowl on her face, I can't imagine she was enjoying it much.

Little Harry was eight months old and starting to pull himself up on the sides of his cardboard box-bassinet. If you didn't catch him, he'd spill himself over and land squalling face-first on the floor.

"Why, he's ready for a good crawl," said Miss Sissy of the under-performing undergarments. She and Mother liked to sit backstage and lie to each other about their younger years. If Miss Sissy's stories were even half as spit-shined as Mother's, the two of them could've written an entire book of fairy tales together.

"All my girls were early crawlers," said Mother. "You can see that from their natural physical grace. My Kit crawled at two months! Of course she was born the size of a toddler, so if she'd come out tap dancing, it should've been no surprise."

"My Darnell was not an ounce shy of fourteen pounds when he was born, and I let him have a few tiny bites of meat from my supper plate that very day!" Miss Sissy cackled.

They could've fed the hungry for miles around with those fish stories. But I suppose listening to them was better than wondering about Tip and where he was now. God, the place was just so boring, and I needed distraction. It came soon enough, care of Sissy Salloway, of course.

On Wednesday, the afternoon show was full of mothers passing a rainy few hours with their fidgety children. We did our second-half opener and headed for the wings. Miss Sissy took the stage as we went off, but this time she had a prop in her fleshy arms: baby Harry.

"What on earth?" Nell said.

"Just you wait," Mother said, grinning.

"Now, ladies and gentlemen—but mostly ladies," Sissy bellowed. "I'm sure you loved the last act just as much as I did. What you don't know is that the oldest girl, Mrs. Nell Turner Herkimer, lost her husband in the Great War."

A sigh went up, an "ohhhh" of sympathy, and I heard the air go out of Nell, like a bike tire hitting a nail. She had never wanted pity, I'll give her that. But bored mothers and tired old ladies do love a sad story, and Sissy had put Nell's squarely on the menu.

"This is her son, Harry Junior. Poor thing never even met his pa, but look at him, happy as a lark." He was actually bug-eyed with fear at being kidnapped by a stranger. "Little fella needs a safe place to toddle around while his mama puts on a terrific show for you. So if any of you have a baby play yard you're not using anymore, just drop it on by the theatre here, and we'll make sure she gets it." There was a round of applause and heads nodding, taking up their marching orders. Sissy smiled, lapping up every last clap of admiration for her gesture. Then she said, "Nell, honey, could you come take your boy? I've got a show to put on."

Nell froze. Mother gave her a push. "No!" Nell hissed. "I'm not going out there so they can gawk at the poor widow!"

"You go out there right now," Mother snapped. "Miss Sissy just did you a whopping big favor, and you are not going to disrespect her."

"I never asked for it!"

"Go!" Mother pushed her again, and she headed for the baby. But Sissy didn't give him over right away, and Nell had to stand there while the audience rose to their feet, clapping out their hopes for a happier future—and yes, their pity. Nell gave a quick nod, grabbed little Harry, and ran offstage. When she got to the wings, she held the baby out for someone—anyone—to take him. I was closest and got a hand on him. She ran to the darkest corner of the backstage and put a hand over her eyes, her shoulders shaking.

"Mother, that was awful," Winnie said. "You can't just surprise her like that."

"She'll be grateful when she has a new play yard for that baby," sniffed Mother.

"And why couldn't we simply buy one?" I said. "We have money now."

"Now, you listen to me." Mother's glare shot into all of us. "We are not spending one penny we don't have to. Nine weeks may be all we get, and your father's hand may never heal up. Do you want to quit school and work menial jobs, or marry any man who'll put a roof over your head, like . . . like . . ."

Like you? I thought.

"Like some pauper? I'm trying to give you choices and chances. So no, Gert. We cannot just *buy* anything. Not now, and not anytime soon." She crossed her arms and stared out at Miss Sissy, crooning like the scrape of a dragging axle, as if it were the most beautiful sound on earth.

• • • •

Billy the Cowboy Yodeler followed me around till I was about ready to slap him. "Let me hold that sweater for you, Gert," he'd say, or "Can I run out and get you a soda pop? You must be awful thirsty after all those fantastical stunts!"

He wasn't bad looking, and back home I would have let him do things for me just for sport. But I was not in a sporting mood. In fact, I don't even know what kind of mood I was in.

Once he tried to take the springboard from my hands as I carried it up to the stage. "There's no need," I insisted, wrenching it away from him.

"Oh, but your hands are so lovely. I wouldn't want you to get a callus."

"Well, your hands are lovely, too," I shot over my shoulder. "Especially for a *cowboy*."

"He's persistent," I heard Winnie snicker to Kit.

"Like a bad rash," said Kit, and they giggled into their hands.

I might have giggled, too, if I hadn't been the one suffering the skin condition.

After our last performance each evening, Mother insisted on waiting for Sissy to walk back to the Bradley Hotel, where all the acts stayed. Sissy would dilly and dally, and before we knew it, Billy had closed the show and he'd hurry up to walk with us, too.

"Beautiful night," Billy said Thursday as we headed out. His leather chaps were stiff and clean, and they made an annoying flapping sound against his thighs as he walked.

"I hadn't noticed," I said.

"Well, that means you need more time to appreciate it. Why don't we take a little stroll?"

"My legs are tired from performing. Just like your voice must be tired from all that . . . what is that girlish singing called again?"

"Aww, Gert. Let's take a walk and I'll explain all about it."

He nearly wore me out with his cajoling. There's nothing a boy wants more than a girl he can't have. I had been that girl so many times for so many boys, it wasn't even fun anymore.

The Bradley was more like a house than a hotel, and I felt as if I were sleeping in someone's bedroom rather than a room for rent. There were two twin beds as usual, but the clerk brought in a little cot, which Winnie took without a word of protest. Kit couldn't have fit, and I was having none of it. She knew it was a battle she would lose.

As tired as I was, I couldn't seem to settle down, and lay there blinking up at the ceiling.

"That Billy doesn't give up, does he?" murmured Winnie.

"Turning him down gives me something to do, at least."

"He's handsome. You could turn down worse," she said. "Think he's a real cowboy?"

"He's from Rhode Island," I said. "And he's only handsome if you like that sort of look."

"What look?"

"That pretend he-man look. It's all out front. Nothing to wonder about."

Winnie was quiet then, but it was a loud sort of quiet, as if some new inkling had shocked her into silence. I felt the fine hairs on my arms stand up. She had just figured out who I wondered about, and it wasn't Billy.

"Just go to sleep!" I hissed, and she didn't say another word.

The next morning, six baby play yards were lined up at the theatre. There were also eight bags of baby clothes, and a dresser painted with a cow jumping over the moon. It had a lumpy back and a too-long nose that made it look like a camel with udders.

"What am I supposed to do?" Nell asked. "We can't possibly take all these things."

Mother and Sissy were already inspecting the lode like miners panning for gold nuggets. "Take the best and leave the rest," said Sissy. "Or better yet—sell it!"

Even Mother balked at this. "Why, Sissy, I don't think people would take kindly to our selling off things they've given over for free."

"I suppose you're right. Folks might look askance. I know! You could bring it with you to the next town and sell it there. No one would be the wiser." Mother paused to consider this.

"I won't take any of it at all, if that's what you plan to do," Nell said quietly.

In the end, she kept a small fold-up play yard and a half dozen toddler outfits. The rest was donated to the Cuba First Baptist Church for their charitable outreach.

"Say thank you to Miss Sissy," Mother whispered at Nell.

Sissy was fingering a fine little jacket and matching hat that were far too small for Harry.

"Thank you for your help, Miss Sissy," Nell said, her jaw tight. "You certainly are someone who sees a need and takes things into her own hands."

"You are so very welcome," Sissy gushed. "And you're right about me. The world leaves the timid by the side of the road, I always say." She squinted over at her half-dead banjo player. "Don't I always say that, Clay? About being timid?"

He nodded blankly.

"There you have it!" she cackled. "I might be unconventional, but I get the job done by hook or by crook!"

On Saturday, I overheard Sissy say, "Now, Ethel, I need some advice." (Shocking, since Sissy thought she knew everything about everything.) "I'm trying to decide what to do with my pay when Mr. Keller hands it out tonight. Should I mail it home or keep it in my grouch bag?"

"What's a grouch bag?" said Mother.

"Oh, you know."

"No, I admit I don't."

"You never heard of a grouch bag?"

"Sissy, if I knew what it was, I'd certainly say so!"

"It's a little pouch you carry under your clothes." She patted her chest and gave a sly grin. "Close to your heart, if you take my meaning."

"Ohhhh!" Mother laughed. "You keep all your money with you?"

"Well, I do keep some in my room, don't you?"

"Yes, I do."

"But I'm not sure if my hiding spot is any good." Miss Sissy hung her head for shame at the poor location of her secret stash. "I stuff it under the mattress."

"Why, Sissy, that's the first place they'd look!"

"What do you suggest?"

Mother glanced around. I aimed an innocent gaze at Billy, who grinned like I'd agreed to go steady, but my ears were pricked up like a hunting dog's. I was disappointed when Mother leaned even closer to Sissy, and I couldn't hear a thing.

"Smart thinking!" replied Sissy. "I knew I was right to choose you for a friend." The conversation turned to the proper way to sew a grouch bag, and Sissy had the upper hand there, so Mother's time as the know-it-all came to an end.

That night, after Mr. Keller handed out the week's pay, we all walked back to the Bradley, and Billy tagged along after me as usual. "Won't you go for one little stroll with me?" he pleaded.

I surprised myself by agreeing. I suppose I was tired of feeling irritable, and thought spending a little time with a handsome, admiring man might improve my mood.

No such luck.

As the others went into the hotel, we continued down the darkened street. He finally mustered up the courage to take my hand, which I allowed, though it might as well have been an oven mitt for all the romance it kindled in me. And of course, once he'd achieved that lofty goal, he thought he should reach for the brass ring and kiss me. I tried to relax and enjoy it, but he was all wet lips and tongue, and I felt like I was being slurped by a yodeling cow.

"Stop," I said, and wrenched away from his licking and groping.

He grabbed my shoulders to pull me in. "I just have to kiss you, sweetheart," he moaned.

"But I don't want you to." As if it wasn't completely obvious!

He gave a sly little grin and said, "Oh, I think you do."

"No, I truly don't. I'm going back."

I turned out of his grasp, but he wrenched me back around to face him. "I hope you're not teasing me," he warned. "I don't like girls who tease."

"I don't care what you like, now let me go!"

He slammed his slobbery face against mine and stuck his fat cow's tongue into my mouth, so I couldn't even scream. He shoved me backward, out of the starlight and into the shadow of a hedge, his fingers digging into my skin.

A girl can always manage. She can sweet-talk and outsmart and generally have her way. She can do anything she pleases . . . until it gets physical. I couldn't overpower him or outrun him. But I could trick him. I went loose for a moment, and let him kiss me, trying not to gag.

In a few minutes, which seemed like an hour-long descent into hell's outhouse, he came up for air. "That's right," he moaned. "I knew you'd come around."

"I did, but now let's walk some more."

"I don't want to walk," he growled. "I want to neck."

"Billy, Billy," I cooed, turning on my most candied smile. "Don't be like that, honey." It confused him, and I took his arm, all fake cozy, and walked quickly toward the light of a little restaurant up the street. "Let's get something to drink!" I said, and he shuffled along beside me, stupidly hoping his chances would somehow improve.

Luck was with me. Dutch's Sandwich Barn was full of people—*my* people.

"Hey, Gert!" Kit called out. "How'd you know where to find us?"

I dropped Billy's sweaty hand and walked quickly into the crowd. "What's the occasion?"

Mother had her arm hooked in Sissy's as if they'd been best girl-friends since the dawn of time. "Our dear Sissy insisted we all go out and have some fun together after six days of working hard. She convinced everyone except her own partner!"

"He's an old poop." Sissy made a pouty face. "No fun at all, which is why I love you people so much!"

Even Nell was there, cradling the sleeping baby inside her coat. I wedged a chair right between her and Kit, while Billy went up to the counter to get us a couple of bottles of Moxie.

"I'm surprised to see you here," I murmured to Nell.

"I'm surprised, too, but Mother said I owed it to Sissy for getting all those baby things." Nell shook her head. "I won't mind when we're free of her good intentions."

Nell kept to herself more and more, avoiding everyone but us. I had half a notion that maybe that awful Sissy had done us a good turn after all, by making Nell socialize.

The contortionist was sitting on the other side of her. He looked down at Harry snoring his little baby snores in her arms. "You know," he said, "I used to have trouble sleeping. I'd lie there all night staring up at the ceiling."

Nell blinked at him for a second, unused to casual conversation. "Well, I . . . I'm sure that was frustrating," she stammered.

"It was. I told my doctor, I said, 'Doc, I haven't slept in weeks.' He gave me a prescription and said, 'This'll make you sleep like a baby.'"

"Did it work?" said Nell.

"Absolutely. Now every night I suck my thumb, wet the bed, and wake up every two hours crying for my mama!"

His eyes lit up at having hit the punch line so well, and Nell couldn't help but laugh, her body shaking with something other than sobs for once.

"You should try your hand at comedy," she told him.

It certainly would be less embarrassing for everyone involved, I thought, remembering his legs all twisted up, exposing bumps and bulges no one needs to see.

On the other side of me, Kit chatted with the iron-jaw man. He hooked one finger into the side of his cheek so she could study his molars. Then he stood up, pulled a ladder-back chair away from the table, and said, "Bet you can't." Before we knew it, she had locked her teeth onto the chair's top rung and lifted it, hands out behind her like chicken wings.

Mother and I yelled over each other: "Kit, no! Put that down! You'll break a tooth!"

She lowered the chair to the floor and curtsied as the other performers clapped. Mother gave Nell, Winnie, and me a time-to-go look, and we stood and reached for our coats.

Billy said, "Aw, Gert, don't leave!"

I tipped my head toward Mother and gave an apologetic shrug, playing the obedient daughter. If he'd known me better, he would've seen how far-fetched that was.

"You can't go so soon!" Sissy cried. "The evening's not half over!"

"It is for us, Sissy dear," said Mother. "We'll see you in the morning for breakfast. We can say our good-byes then."

But we couldn't. And Sissy knew that.

"Who's been in here? Who's been in my room?" I recognized Billy's whine right away and tugged the covers up over my ears. "My money's gone! Someone stole all my money!"

A prickle ran through me, and my eyes flew open.

"Gert, do you hear that?" Winnie whispered.

"Course I do. The whole town can hear it." We put our coats on over our nightdresses and went out to the hallway.

The manager was speaking in quiet tones with Billy. Was he sure he hadn't put it someplace else? Was he positive of how much he'd had? There were no locks on the room doors, but the manager made a point of saying he always bolted the place up after the night clerk came in.

"My father gave me five hundred dollars when I set out, and I haven't touched a penny of it. I've kept it in a silver money clip in my trunk for the last month, and they're both *gone*, I tell you!"

Winnie and I exchanged glances. Apparently Billy the Cowboy Yodeler was actually William the Rich Boy Whiner.

Mother opened her door, and from the look on her face the thief hadn't been satisfied with Billy's cash and money clip. Another door opened, the husband and wife cloggers. "We've been robbed!" Soon almost everyone was in the hallway, claiming to have lost money.

"Where's Sissy?" Mother turned on the hotel manager. "*Where is Miss Salloway?*"

"She and her gentleman friend left real late last night," he said, wary of the wild look on Mother's face. "Said her next show was a sleeper jump and she had to catch the late train."

It didn't take long to figure it out. Clay had ransacked the rooms while we were all at Dutch's Sandwich Barn with Sissy. Then when everyone was snug in bed, they'd snuck out.

"How much did she get?" Nell asked Mother.

Mother's face was ashen. She'd practically put our money right in Sissy's grouch bag herself. "I only have a few dollars in change from what I brought to the restaurant last night."

The Bradley Hotel manager had insisted all the acts pay up as soon as they'd come in from the theatre the night before. "I've had more than one theatre type skip out," he'd told Mother. "Or drink it away by Sunday morning." At least we didn't owe any money.

We packed up and headed to the train station along with everyone else. We had enough to get us to our next show in Fredonia, but where we would stay, how we would eat, we didn't know.

The husband-and-wife clog dancers decided to go home. "We're too old for this kind of monkey business," the wife said. "I just hope our son can take us in."

As we stood on the train platform, Billy came over to say good-bye. I nearly turned my back on him, but then an idea came to me. "Oh, Billy," I simpered, taking his arm and pulling him away from the others. "Are you going to be all right?"

We talked until the train whistle blew, and then before he could kiss me I ran straight up the steps onto the train, as if parting were like losing a limb.

"What was all that billing and cooing about?" Winnie asked as we settled into our seats.

"It was about saying thank you. Which is what you'll be saying to me in a minute." I opened my hand to show off a ten-dollar bill. "He still had his pay in his pocket because of that little stroll we took. He realized that if I hadn't been willing to go, he'd have gotten completely cleaned out like the rest of us."

"And you *helped* him to realize it," she said, grinning.

"Well, sometimes a person just needs a friend to shed some light."

"You're brilliant!" Mother cried, reaching for the cash.

I held on to that bill. It was my money—they had no idea what I'd been through to earn it.

Mother's glare was double-barreled. Her outstretched hand hung in the air like a threat.

I blinked, and she snatched the bill from me. Then she pulled out a square of black satin and a spool of thread with a needle tucked into it.

"What's that?" Kit asked.

"I'm making a grouch bag," she said. "I'm told it's the best way to keep your money out of other people's pockets."

CHAPTER 13

WINNIE

I believe in the idea of the rainbow.
And I've spent my entire life trying to get over it.
—Judy Garland, singer and actress

Fredonia was a bustling little town, unbowed by the fact that the wind blew in near gale-like force off Lake Erie, nearly tearing our coats off. Mother asked a railroad officer where we might find a hotel. His eyes were shaded by the stiff brim of his cap, but I could see them dart from the secondhand trunks to our well-worn boots. "You might find the Rus Urban on West Main to be to your liking," he said.

The rooms at the Rus Urban Hotel were small and smelled of must, and the only two available had one double bed each. It was decided that Kit would sleep with Mother in one room, while Gert, Nell, Little Harry, and I shared the other.

"There's barely room to turn around," said Gert. "We'll have to stand on the bed to change our clothes!"

"I'm sorry the baby's things take up so much room." Nell's words were so faint they seemed to float off into thin air. I could see her slipping away into one of her silences.

"We're just glad we get the two of you to ourselves this week," I said. "Aren't we, Gert?"

"Oh, we're happy for the trade." Gert was hanging clothes from nails someone had banged into the wall. "No one snores like Kit—she practically has a locomotive in her nose."

The baby sat on the bed, grabbing up handfuls of graying sheets and stuffing them into his mouth. "Oh, Harry, no!" Nell picked him up. "You're slobbering all over the bedclothes."

"He just wants something to chew on with those new teeth he's got coming in," I said. "Right, Harry-boy?" I took the baby from her and jiggled him around until he squealed happily.

Nell sat on the bed and stared out the window. I put a hand on her shoulder. I didn't know what else to do. She reached up and patted it. I suspect she didn't know what else to do, either.

At a modest little tavern with a hand-painted sign, Mother announced that she'd decided not to call Morty Birnbaum and ask for another loan. "It makes us look foolish," she said, "like rubes who don't know how to take care of ourselves." I couldn't help notice the use of the word *us* instead of the more truthful *me*. We'd have to make do with Gert's ten dollars until we got paid in a week.

The cabbage soup in Nell's bowl lay only a quarter of an inch below the level at which it had been served. The baby fussed and gnawed at his fist, but she didn't seem to notice, only gazed off vacantly.

"Let me take him so you can eat," I told her. I reached for Harry, and his little arms went immediately around my neck.

"Thanks," said Nell. "Looks like he's happier with you anyway."

"I don't think he loves anyone in the world more than his mama," I assured her.

Nell didn't answer, only took a spoonful of the broth. Half an hour later when we got up to leave, the bowl was still almost full. Kit slurped it down in a couple of gulps.

"Katherine Turner!" Mother hissed, her eyes darting right and left to see if any of the other patrons had caught Kit's transgression.

"I'm hungry," Kit muttered back. "Why waste it?"

The Fredonia Opera House had a great crystal chandelier that hung from the ceiling, and a horseshoe-shaped balcony gleaming with wood carvings. The plush red velvet stage curtains were framed by a pressed-metal proscenium arch twice as high as the one in Cuba.

The performers were twice as grand looking, too. There was a family purportedly named the Chinese Chungs, a mother and two daughters, who wiggled around in elaborate Oriental costumes. Their heavy eyeliner trailed off dramatically toward their temples, which, to my mind, put their Chinese-ness squarely into question. There was a man with four trained dogs, from a pony-sized Great Dane to a hairless little dog that rode in his coat pocket. Kit leaned toward me and whispered, "It's the dog version of us," and we snickered until Gert pinched Kit, and Kit said, "*Ow!*" and Mother shushed us.

The other performers were a mime troupe, a string quartet that played ragtime, a mismatched pair of older comedians named Case and Wheeler, and a vampy singer with long, black, Theda Bara hair and even more eye makeup than the Chungs.

"We're closing," Kit whispered.

"How do you know?" I asked.

"Look at this place. And look at the other acts. They're flashier."

I cut my eyes to Gert, hoping she would tell Kit to stop being ridiculous, and maybe pinch her again. Gert just crossed her arms tightly over her chest in that way she did when she was nervous. Which made me nervous. I started tapping the knuckles of my left hand like I do when I worry, playing a little flesh-toned keyboard.

The theatre manager, Mr. Barnes, had hair parted in a razor-straight line down the middle of his head, spackled to either side by pomade. He announced the lineup, studying his notes through pince-nez glasses that clung to the bridge of his nose as if they were afraid to invoke his wrath by falling off. Kit's assertion had been accurate—we were closing. But since we'd make more money as chaser in Fredonia than we had as second opener in Cuba, it wasn't that hard to take.

"There are six dressing rooms below stage," he said smoothly, peering over his glasses at the eight acts before him. "Two acts will have to prepare themselves backstage."

That's us, I thought, and wondered who else would share the area with us.

Apparently it was to be Case and Wheeler, the comic duo. "Now hold on there," said the tall, thin comedian, Mr. Case, after Mr. Barnes had finished his announcements. "We're the deuce. We should get the dressing room."

"Case, is it?" said Mr. Barnes with a look of dubious disdain. "Well, Mr. *Case*, we're going to be gentlemen and let the ladies have a dressing room."

"That's not how it goes," insisted Mr. Case. "It's by—"

"It's by my authority that anyone has a contract at all." Barnes's face was placid and his tone was light, but derision seeped like gutter water from his words.

"Nat," said Mr. Wheeler, Case's short, round partner. "Natty, let it go. Don't ask for tsuris."

Mr. Barnes gave a perfunctory little nod, a pretense at being polite, and strode off.

"Schmuck," muttered Mr. Case.

Mr. Wheeler gave his partner's back a little slap, and the two of them headed backstage.

"Schmuck?" said Kit. "What's that?"

"I don't know," I said, "but I'm pretty sure it isn't complimentary."

We settled onto various stools that had been left backstage. Mr. Wheeler opened a newspaper with boxy squiggles in neat rows, *The Jewish Daily Forward* on the masthead. His legs were short, so his feet—like mine—didn't reach the ground. He hooked his heels into the top bar of his stool. Mr. Case, sitting closest to us, stretched out his long legs and crossed his ankles, his short boots revealing socks that could have used a good darning. He put out his hand, and Mr. Wheeler gave him a section of the paper without even looking up. The two men, so opposite in form, cocked their papers identically in front of them.

Nell's stool was closest to Mr. Case, and she sat with Harry, who, after a little patting and coaxing, offered up a fantastic belch. Mr. Case looked up from his paper.

"My goodness, Harry," Nell fretted. "Not so loud."

Mr. Case smiled. "An admirable achievement! Every man needs to let some air from his belly when he's had a good meal." He leaned a little closer, studying the baby. "How old?"

"He's just eight months."

"Such a big healthy boy! You must be eating well, too, if your baby is so nice and fat."

She was barely eating at all, and shame rose like a fever on her face. She lowered her eyes and stammered, "I . . . well . . ."

"Ach, I'm so stupid. A lady doesn't boast about how much she eats. Let's just say you're taking good care of him, and leave it at that." He offered his hand to shake. "Nathan Klippfisch."

She shook it, looking as confused as I felt. "I thought you were Mr. Case."

"I am either the fourth or fifth Case, I can never remember which. The act started so long ago, back then it might have been Noah and the whale!" He laughed and slapped his thigh.

"You're not really Case and Wheeler?" I asked.

"No, no. You know how it is in vaudeville. Somebody gets married, or comes into some money, or can't take the life anymore—they quit. What's his partner going to do? Start over when he's already built a reputation? That's crazy! He gets a new partner and keeps the old name." He cocked a thumb toward Mr. Wheeler. "I picked up Benny Weisberg here six or eight years ago."

"Nine," said Mr. Weisberg from behind his paper. "But who's counting?"

"How can you say it was nine?" Mr. Klippfisch gave us a knowing look and shook his head. "It wasn't nine."

Mr. Weisberg laid his newspaper on his lap. "I can say it was nine because it *was* nine. I was with the Castleman Brothers at Keith's in Boston. That's where we met."

"It is not. If you were in the big time with the Castlemans, why would you leave?"

"On account of the bruises."

"You left because of the bruises? Who leaves because of bruises?"

"Me, that's who. It was a knockabout routine, and I was the shortest, and I wasn't a Castleman, so they knocked me about. I had enough."

"But Keith's is big-time!"

"This I know. You know how I know? Because I was there!" He snapped up his paper.

Mr. Klippfisch shrugged. "He could be right. My memory's not always so good." He gave a sly little smile and raised his finger in the air. "But even if I was dead, I would still remember our act, and that's what matters!"

Mr. Klippfisch—Nat, as he insisted we call him—wanted to know all about what had prompted such a nice family of lovely, well-brought-up young ladies to enter this crazy business, and entertained us with stories of growing up on the Lower East Side of Manhattan.

"I left school after the fifth grade," he said. "I tried bootblacking, but it was so boring. All these muckety-mucks over on Wall Street had nothing to say except, '*You missed my heel*,' or, '*Why should I give you two cents when that other kid'll do it for a penny?*'"

"That's not very much money," said Nell. Harry was sitting in his new play yard, chewing on a little red celluloid horse that we'd found in one of the donation bags back in Cuba.

"I knew there was something else I didn't like about it! Thank you for reminding me, darling girl."

He had been married once, but his wife got lonely while he was on the road. "She wrote me long letters, half of which I never received because I had left for the next town before they arrived. I wrote her short letters with jokes. She said my jokes made her cry in the end, because she couldn't remember the sound of my voice anymore and imagine the way I would tell them."

Nell's face went pale and she looked away. Nat stopped talking and gazed at her, perhaps guessing her unfortunate marital status from her reaction. He waited for a few moments, and then he said, "There's no pain greater than the pain of missing. To me, my wife was a hero. I understood when she needed to put the pain away and carry on with her life. In fact, I loved her so much, I was glad for her."

There was a message for Nell in his words, and she glanced up at him.

He gave her a look of fatherly kindness and said, "Any man who truly loves a woman would be."

CHAPTER
14

GERT

All my life I have been happiest when the folks watching me
said to each other, "Look at the poor dope, will ya?"
—Buster Keaton, actor, acrobat, and comedian

That guy wormed his way into Nell's confidence so fast I could almost have admired his skill, if she weren't my sister. As a waitress, I'd seen older men smooth-talk younger women a hundred times (in addition to the hundred times it's been tried on me). If the state of his overcoat was any indication, he had nothing to offer. But he had charm and soft words aimed right at a poor widow's heart. Oh, I had my eye on him, all right.

I may not have trusted them, but even I had to admit their act was pretty funny. For their bit, they got all dolled up in bushy blond wigs and tacky suit jackets. Nat's was too short, and his wrists stuck out like long hot dogs from short buns. Benny's was too large. The cuffs were rolled at the wrists, and the front panels flapped around his big belly.

The act went like this: the two men galumphed onstage and greeted each other. Benny clapped Nat on the back. "Well, Sven, aren't you glad you come to New York to spend your vaccination?" He did it in a heavy Swedish accent. The audience chuckled at his mistake.

"Yah, sure, Ingemar," said Nat. "It's very magnesium here!"

"Have you got any money?" asked Benny.

Nat pulled the pocket linings out of his trousers. "No, I'm busted."

Benny nodded with concern. "I see. Well, tell me this. Are you thirsty?"

"No, Ingemar, not a bit."

"Good, good," said Benny. "You see, I've only got five pennies and I'm dying for a glass of beer. Now, it wouldn't look nice for both of us to go into the bar here, and one of us drink, and the other gets nothing. So when we go inside, I say to you: 'What you going to have?' And you say, in sort of a careless way, 'Ooooh, I don't care for it.' Then I will have some beer, and when we walk out the bartender won't know we only had enough money for one drink. Understand?"

Nat shook his head no, but said, "Yah, sure."

Benny patted Nat's lapel. "Good. Now, let's practice. When we get inside, I'll say, 'What are you gonna have?' And what do you say?"

Nat thought for a moment, then grinned foolishly. "I say, 'Ooooh, I don't care for it.'"

"Yah, yah! That's perfect. Except . . . except . . ." Benny frowned. "See, something tells me you're not gonna do this right. Let's practice again. Now, what you gonna have?"

Nat flung his arms out sideways. "I don't want a ting."

Benny cocked his head to one side. "Aw, go on, have something."

"Oh, no, no, no." Nat wagged his head back and forth.

"Take something small."

Nat shrugged. "Well, all right, I'll take a small bottle."

The audience laughed, and the men waited so the next line could be heard.

"What! Small bottle!" Benny threw his hands into the air. "With my poor five cents?"

"Well, why do you wanna coax me for?"

"I wasn't coaxing. I was only making a bluff!"

"Why don't you say, 'What you gonna have?' and I don't have it?"

Benny shook his finger up at Nat. "I'll say anything I like—it's my five cents! All you gotta say is: 'Ooooh, I don't care for it.' Now. Pay attention. What you gonna have?"

"Ooooh, I don't care for it."

"Aw, go on, take something."

Nat shrugged. "Well, I'll take a cigar."

Still tickled by Nat's last mistake, the audience laughed even harder at this one.

"What! A cigar?" Benny turned to the audience, arms outstretched, inviting them to join in his frustration, then back to Nat. "You want to burn up my five cents?"

"Why? Do I gotta give up smokin' now, too?"

Benny clenched his hands in front of his chest. "Sven, please, I beg of you, do me a favor: use your brain. Remember, you don't drink, and you don't smoke! Now, we go in."

They walked arm in arm into the pretend bar.

Benny turned to Nat. "Sven, my good friend, would you like to have a drink?"

Nat nodded enthusiastically. "Ooooh, yah, Ingemar, I don't care if I do!"

The laughter was hearty and Benny threw his hat on the floor. "You're supposed to say, 'Ooooh, I don't care to'! You said you weren't thirsty! How come you asked for a drink?"

Nat smiled innocently out at the audience. "All that talking and practicing . . . it gave me a thirst that would sink a ship!"

The audience exploded with applause and laughter, cheering the two silly Swedes. They took their bows and trotted offstage. As they collapsed back onto their stools, Kit asked, "How'd you learn to talk like that?"

"Oh, we played the Orpheum circuit out west a couple times," said Nat.

"Four times," corrected Benny, dabbing at his forehead with a handkerchief.

"Lot of Swedes in the Midwest, and we're good at picking up voices," said Nat. "We used to do German accents, but then the war came, and let's just say not everyone found it funny anymore. Some guys in Baltimore thought we were real Germans, and that was not funny at *all*."

"What did you do?" asked Winnie.

Benny shook his head. "We told them we weren't German. And they said, '*Well, what are you then?*' We were idiots, that's what we were, because we told them the truth. '*We're Jews!*' we said, like that would get us out of the soup kettle."

"*Feh*," said Nat. "Barbarians."

"It's like the Rus Urban Hotel," said Benny. "Used to be called the Germania. They changed the name because no one would stay there, which is silly. Plenty of good German Americans. Plenty who fought in the war on the American side, against their own homeland." He shrugged. "But still, people get angry, and they need someplace to aim it. Swedes, though—who could hate a Swede? They're so quiet and hardworking, it'd be like hating a shovel."

Nat grinned. "And who could hate a shovel?"

My sisters laughed, even Nell. Those old guys were charmers, all right.

Mother got up to get us some sandwiches, and asked Nat and Benny if she could pick anything up for them, as she had done for performers at the other towns we played.

"It's too much to ask," Benny said, folding his newspaper on his lap.

"I don't mind at all," she said. "I always run out and get things for the other acts."

"You're an angel." He put on a gallant tone. "An angel should not tire herself with other people's errands."

Oh, Mother ate that right up. "I'm just going around the corner to the drugstore."

His round face fell. "The drugstore?"

"You don't like the sandwiches there?"

"I don't mean to be difficult," he said. "It's just, well, there's a reason they call it a drugstore and not a sandwich store. There's a little place a few blocks down, very reasonable. They slice the corned beef *very thin*"—he pressed his thick fingers together to show just how thin—"and the rye bread is so fresh."

Nat shrugged. "It's no Katz's, but this isn't New York."

We looked at one another; weren't we in the state of New York, where we'd been stuck our whole lives?

Nat explained, "By New York, I mean the city. You know, the *real* New York. And Katz's is the best deli on the planet." These two definitely had strong feelings about sandwiches.

When Mother returned, she handed Nat and Benny their supper, thick slabs of brown bread speckled with seeds, bursting with juicy pink meat. Ours were the same fifteen-cent cheese and white bread we'd been eating since we'd gone on the road.

"You didn't like the food at the deli?" said Benny, sounding offended.

"Oh, it looked fine," said Mother. "We're just watching our pennies."

"Because that's all we have," Kit muttered. "Pennies."

"*Katherine*," Mother warned.

Nat looked at Nell's pale sandwich, then up at her, his eyes asking a silent question.

"We were robbed," Nell said quietly. "We'll be all right when we get paid at the end of the week."

He handed her half of his sandwich.

"No, no," she said, embarrassed. "I'm fine with this. Honestly, I like cheese."

"Look at me. Now look at Benny," he said, hooking a thumb toward his partner. "I'm the skinny guy! If I start gaining weight, the gag doesn't go over so well." He held out the sandwich half. "For the good of the act, please, I'm begging you—take it."

She took it. And she ate it.

Even I had to admit it was a miracle.

CHAPTER
15

WINNIE

When you take a joke away from Milton Berle, it's not stealing, it's repossessing.

—Jack Benny, comedian and actor

I saw a strange and unlikely friendship bloom that day between Nell and Nat. From then on, while the rest of us watched the other acts, played with little Harry, read, sewed, or dozed, Nell and Nat sat on their stools talking quietly to each other, rising only to perform. I tried to concentrate on *Little Women*, but my ear kept perking to the sound of Nell's laugh, or to Nat slapping his thigh when he made a point.

Gert didn't like it. "Not one bit," she muttered as we stood in the wings, watching the sultry Theda Bara copycat wind her arms seductively above her head. "Nell's a young widow, and he's too old for—" Gert's lip curled in disgust.

"I don't think that's what he's after," I said.

"No? Well, what's he after then?"

"I don't know. He seems to just . . . like her for her own self. Maybe she reminds him of his wife, and he wants to do a kindness to make up for how he left her alone."

Gert shook her head and muttered, "You're even younger than you look."

•   •   •

Uncharacteristically, Mother dozed off several times during the day, her needle half threaded into a seam of one of the new costumes she was making. By evening her face was flushed. I put a hand to Mother's forehead, which was quite warm. "I think you may have a fever starting," I said. "I'll go and get the sandwiches and I'll pick up some aspirin, too."

"Pardon me," said the generally taciturn Benny, "but I would consider it a favor if you would allow me to procure the evening's meal."

"Oh no, that's all right . . . thank you, but . . . ," we all chimed in. We were well aware of his distaste for the drugstore's offerings, and we couldn't afford those meaty deli sandwiches.

"Now, let's see." He tapped his chin. "Five sandwiches and a bottle of aspirin. You'll give me eighty cents, and I'll do the legwork."

"I don't think I'll be eating," Mother murmured weakly. "A cup of tea perhaps . . ."

"Sixty-five cents, then." Benny got up to leave. Mother turned away in modesty to tug the little black satin grouch bag from out of the neck of her shirtwaist, but he kept walking.

"Mr. Weisberg!" I called after him, but he appeared not to hear me.

"I guess it's our treat," said Nat, with an overly innocent shrug.

Gert narrowed her eyes at me, a *see-what-I-told-you* look. "'*My treat,*'" she murmured into my ear. "That's when you know you're in trouble."

But Nell beamed at Nat with an openness I hadn't seen in months. She seemed simply happy for his kindness, without a worry for what it might mean, or what he might want in return.

When Benny came back, he had a bulging brown paper sack with sandwiches on thick bread, and we had to hold them with napkins to keep the juice from dripping onto our costumes. Gert took a dollar from the grouch purse on Mother's lap and held it out to Benny. "These sandwiches must have cost much more than fifteen cents each," she said.

"I negotiated a deal," he said, waving her off. "A volume discount. Believe me, all those sandwiches on one order is a lot for that little shop. He was happy to do it."

"Nevertheless," insisted Gert, still holding out the money.

Benny's face went firm. "You're a smart girl," he said. "I can see that. Very shrewd. But you haven't been in this business long. Natty and me, we've been in it for lifetimes. It's like a war. A soldier helps another soldier because that's the way of war, not because he'll get a payback. He may not even *live* to see a payback.

"You may never see us again. Maybe you'll quit the business. Maybe we will. Maybe we'll both be so successful that we'll headline wherever we go and never be on the same bill. It doesn't matter. Vaudevillians help other vaudevillians because it's the only way we can get by sometimes. And besides, whether you're in the business or not, it's the only way to live."

He nodded as if there was now an understanding between them. "Eat your sandwich," he said, and went back to his stool. He hadn't shamed her, merely corrected her, and she accepted it. For the moment it seemed to calm the turmoil she'd been fighting since Wellsville.

Our calm did not last long, however. Mother's headache and fever worsened, and she went back to the Rus Urban to try and get some sleep.

"Would you mind keeping an eye on the baby while we're onstage?" Nell asked Nat. "If he gets noisy, just give him his red horse. That always makes him quiet down."

"Of course! The little *boychik* and I will get along just fine." He gave the baby a big, wide-mouthed smile. "Won't we, *bubeleh*?" Harry grinned back up at him from the play yard.

Nell and Gert spun onto the stage in their cartwheels and handsprings, and Kit followed with me in the suitcase. Invariably, audiences loved the surprise of seeing me tumble out onto the boards. Nat called it our "insurance"—a part of the act that always went over. But as the audience clapped and cheered, I heard another noise from the wings, a baby's irritable squawk.

Harry's cries escalated, and we were all distracted. In our second-to-last stunt Kit vaulted over Nell, Gert, and me, all of us pretending fear at the prospect. As Kit flew through the air, Gert put her hands to her cheeks in wide-blue-eyed fright, and I was to jump into Nell's arms and stick my thumb in my mouth. Audiences always loved the silliness of it.

But this time, as Kit flew through the air, Harry let out a wail. Nell turned instinctively toward him, and I leapt into . . . nothing. Her arms weren't there to catch me so I went sprawling.

After our finale, Nell bolted offstage. Nat was dancing little Harry around singing a foreign-sounding lullaby. Nell took him into her arms and asked, "What happened?"

"He was happy!" said Nat. "Then he just puckered up his little face and cried."

"What is it, Harry?" She wiped the baby's teary cheeks. "Oh, he's so warm!"

"Take him to the hotel," said Gert. "We can't have him crying during performances."

Nell tucked the baby into her coat and left through the stage door.

"There are stunts we can only do with all four of us," said Kit. "The act will run short!"

Nat and Benny looked at each other. "They could—" said Benny.

"We don't even use half of—"

They turned to us. "We can help you fill out the act," said Nat. "Piece of cake."

"I have a big problem," I said, nodding emphatically to the audience during our next performance.

"You do?" Gert put a hand to her face in surprise.

"What's the problem?" Kit leaned toward me with exaggerated concern.

"Well, I went to the doctor yesterday."

"You weren't feeling well?" prompted Kit.

"I was feeling terrible, but the doctor diagnosed my problem right away."

Gert held her hands palm up before her. "What did he say?"

"He said I have a bad case of snew."

"A bad case of snew?" said Kit, scratching her head.

"Yes, it's terrible."

Kit and Gert exchanged puzzled looks, then said in unison, "What's snew?"

My face lit up with a toothy smile. "Nothing! What's new with you?"

The audience ate it up. Our stunts were decidedly less exciting, but the combination of tumbling and joke telling seemed to please everyone.

"I could kvell!" crowed Nat after we hustled offstage to the enthusiastic applause. "I'm bursting with pride for you girls!"

"Are you sure it's okay that we stole your bit?" I asked.

"If it's not okay," said Benny, "we have a big problem, because we stole it from someone else, who stole it from someone before that. Stealing is like breathing in vaudeville. You could hold your breath . . . but then you'd die."

"And then you'd have to go dig ditches for a living!" Nat said, and everyone laughed.

Everyone, that is, except the bespectacled Mr. Barnes. After the show, he condescended to join us backstage. "Where is the fourth Turner sister?" he asked with deceptive calm.

"Mother is ill," said Gert. "Our sister went back to the hotel to take care of her." I had to admire her quick thinking. Most theatre managers barely tolerated having a baby backstage.

"I contracted for four Turner sisters," Mr. Barnes said pointedly. "It appears I'm being cheated out of twenty-five percent of the contract."

"The audience didn't feel cheated," said Nat. "The girls slayed them with the patter!"

"I'll thank you to keep your hooked nose out of this," Mr. Barnes snapped. "You two has-beens can be replaced anytime."

Nat's kind face went murderous. "Why, you—"

"*Nathan*," Benny interjected. "A word, please."

Nat stood his ground, eyeing Mr. Barnes for another beat. Benny murmured something in Yiddish, and Nat turned away. Mr. Barnes turned his gaze back to the three of us. "Four Tumbling Turners," he said with reptilian coolness. "Four. Or I'll reduce your pay accordingly."

"Dirty gonif," muttered Nat as we plodded back to the Rus Urban Hotel.

I looked at Benny. "Thief," he translated.

"Who's your agent?" Nat asked. "He should know about this."

"Morton Birnbaum," I said.

Benny and Nat exchanged glances. "Nice man," said Benny with a little shrug.

"But what?" said Gert.

"But he's no fool. He's not going to put his reputation on the line for a break-in act."

When we said good night and went upstairs, we found Mother coughing in one room, and Nell walking the wailing baby back and forth across the other. She barely seemed to hear him, her face disturbingly blank. Her sadness had been worrisome enough. Now I feared for her sanity.

"Where are we going to sleep?" murmured Kit.

"What are you worried about?" snapped Gert. "You could sleep on your head in a hailstorm."

"All right, then where are *you* going to sleep?" Kit retorted.

"Another room will only be a dollar," I said, "and it'll be worth it to get a little rest."

Kit was dispatched to see if there was one available. Thanks to all the gods of vaudeville, there was. Gert said she would take the next three hours with the baby, while the rest of us slept.

"I should stay with him," said Nell weakly.

"You can't." I explained that we needed her to be able to perform the next day, and recounted a much tamer version of Mr. Barnes's ultimatum.

Nell, Kit, and I tried to get some sleep in the double bed, but Kit's sharp elbows kept migrating across her half into Nell's and my half. "I'm putting her on the floor," I said. Worn to a frazzle, Nell only said, "Oh, we shouldn't," and then helped me lower Kit onto the dusty braided rug beside the bed, covering her with our coats. Finally we slept.

It felt like moments later that the door was opening. "It's 3 a.m.," whispered Gert. "Your turn." She handed me the snuffling baby and slipped into bed beside Nell.

In the other room, he slumped meekly in my arms, tricking me into thinking that I could lie down on the bed with him. But as soon as I sat on the edge, he wailed as if I'd pinched him. We would walk. Harry would have it no other way.

It seemed like miles. The muscles in my face began to droop, and then almost to melt, and a little voice in my brain said, *You could close your eyes for a moment. No one would know.*

Well, Harry and I knew. It became quite clear when I walked into the wall and nearly dropped him. He sent up a fresh scream, and I was chastened into wakefulness by my own folly. Singing helped to steady my sleep-starved brain, and I gave him my mediocre renditions of "Take Me Out to the Ball Game," "Baby Face," and "I'm Just a Bird in a Gilded Cage" over and over until I could no longer stand the sound of them. I started to slump again and decided to talk instead.

"What are we doing here, Harry?" I murmured. "We should be home with Grandpa, not dragging you around to drafty old theatres. But we wouldn't have a place to go home to if we didn't find a way to pay the rent." Back and forth, back and forth we went. "Also, did I tell you I want to go to college? It isn't just for boys from hoity-toity families; young ladies go, too. Okay, not many. And mostly they study homemaking or music, and size up the crowd for passable husbands. That's what I'm told anyway. I've never seen for myself."

"Maybe I could be a teacher like Miss Cartery. Have I told you about her?" Apparently I hadn't.

I didn't like Miss Cartery at first. She had that new teacher's manic desire to prove that by force of enthusiasm alone she could inspire even the most simpleminded among us to suddenly feel an unquenchable need to devour Chaucer. A month later, when we all still had more or less the same level of holy love for books that we'd started with, she got desperate.

"She was calling on me too much," I told Harry as he rubbed his damp face into the soft spot beneath my collarbone. "Don't you hate it when teachers do that?"

Of all the names I'd been called in my life—and like any child, there had been many—teacher's pet was the one that burrowed its horned head under my skin the deepest. I had a strict policy to raise my hand only once per class. Maybe twice if I just couldn't restrain myself. Miss Cartery would ask a weighty question, and if no hand rose, she'd call on me. Even worse, sometimes she'd call on me when other hands were raised and mine lay firmly in my lap.

Yet, as annoyed as I was, there was something so admirable about Miss Cartery. I had a feeling she might understand my predicament, so I lingered one day after school and promised to offer one good answer per class if she'd refrain from calling on me unless my hand was raised.

She laughed and said, "I wish I'd worked out such a wise policy when I was your age." After that, I stayed after school occasionally, pretending to need extra help, but really just for the purpose of talking with such an educated person.

Harry quieted, lulled by the murmur of my voice. His eyelids drooped, his breathing slowed. I lowered myself onto the side of the bed to give my throbbing legs a moment of rest . . .

"*Maaaa!*" A pitiful little wail. Up I went. Searching for subject matter, I talked about Dr. Lodge from the maternity ward. "She may be the smartest person I've ever met. Can you imagine going to four years of college and then medical school, too?" I shifted him for the hundredth time to the opposite hip. "I'd be a fool even to dream of such a thing."

At that point I felt a fool to dream that he might ever sleep, but he did. I felt his body slacken into unconsciousness, and soon heard his wet snores. I sat. It was heaven.

By the time the door opened, I had crept my way by inches until I was propped against the headboard. I had expected Kit—her turn was next—but Nell came instead, brown curls matted, narrow form stooped by fatigue and worry. "How is he?" she whispered.

"Cooler," I mouthed, apprehensive that even a whisper would wake him.

Slowly Nell lowered herself onto the bed so as not to jostle us. "I can take him," she said.

"Not on your life." I gave her a teasing smile, but her face remained pinched in anxiety.

"I feel terrible putting you all through this."

"Nell . . ." My weary brain could barely assemble the words to make my point. "We love him. He's a gift you've given us. Of course we want to comfort him when he's sick or sad."

My words brought tears to her eyes, and at first I thought they might be from relief, even happiness. But what she said frightened me.

"I don't think I'm a very good mother."

"How can you say that?" The baby startled and almost woke at my harsh whisper.

"I . . . I take care of him." Tears rolled in a sudden burst down her face. "But I don't . . . feel anything. It's as if I'm just watching after him until his real mother arrives."

"Oh, Nell." Sadness clutched at my chest, and I hoped the baby wouldn't sense it.

"Sometimes I think . . . I think I should give him to someone who can truly love him, not just feed and clothe and bathe him."

"No!"

"He should know love, Winnie. I've known love, and it was the most wonderful thing. I want him to have that, too. He deserves a mother who can feel and give all the love in her heart."

"It's just that you're still sad," I said weakly.

"Yes," she said. "And I don't know . . . I can't be sure . . . if that will ever change."

As devastating as it had been when Harry died, this was worse. This was his death rippled into an endless ocean of sorrow. I reached for her hand and squeezed it. "We're all here, Nell. We love you and the baby, and we can hold you together until you feel better."

The harsh lines of suffering around her eyes loosened just a little. "That's what Natty says. He says our family is the soft ground I've fallen onto. 'You fell off a cliff,' he says, 'but you haven't fallen onto rocks.' "

"That's exactly right," I whispered.

"He says joy will find me again." She pressed the back of her hand against her cheek to dab at the wetness. "I can't quite believe that, but Natty seems certain."

"He's old!" I said. "He knows about these things!"

"Winnie, he's fifty-two."

"See!"

In the comforting light of Nat's prediction, a tentative calm settled over us. "Nell, is being on the road too much?" I asked. "Would you be happier at home with Dad?"

"And give up the act?" she said, startled.

"We could manage, if it would be better for you."

I could never have predicted her answer. "Oh no," she said. "I love the act. For those few moments when I'm performing, my life is just me—no before, when I was a wife; no after, now that I'm a widow. It's just me and my muscles and what I can do with them. There's something to that, Winnie. What you have when you're just you."

CHAPTER 16

GERT

It takes courage to make a fool of yourself.
—Charlie Chaplin, actor, comedian, and filmmaker

"Leave him here with me." The next morning, Mother's voice was as weak as a teabag that's been dunked in too many cups of hot water.

"I couldn't," insisted Nell. "You're so sick yourself."

"And how do you suppose I managed when you four were little and I took ill?" Mother snapped. "Do you think the fairies came and cared for you?"

Bone-tired and stumbling against the wind, we barely made it to the theatre on time.

"How is he?" Nat asked, dropping his newspaper to the floor.

"Still warm," said Nell. "But he's sleeping. Mother's looking after him."

"Good," said Benny. "Now let's get to work."

They'd lost some sleep themselves, as it turned out, up late adding parts for Nell into the joke sketches, and the last of my suspicions sank beneath a wave of gratitude. People don't give you something for nothing. Except occasionally when, for no apparent reason, they just do.

Actually, with Nell back, I thought we should just do the act like we had before, but when I said as much, Kit nearly bit my head off!

"The act's a million times better with the comedy," she insisted. "Can't you see that?"

We didn't have much time before the show, and we were so tired, memorizing lines didn't come easy. Benny and Nat gave Nell and me a new sketch. It was supposed to go like this:

NELL: "Did you hear our brother broke both his legs yesterday?"
ME: "Oh no! How did it happen?"
NELL: "On the job."
ME: "But he's a window washer. How could he break his legs?"
NELL: "He stepped back to admire his work!"

But instead, Nell said, "He . . . um . . . he likes his work!"

It made no sense at all, and the audience knew it.

"*Boo!*" from the cheap seats up in the gallery. "Go back to the farm!" Even worse, "*Moo!*" We'd absolutely lost them.

We bumbled through the rest of the act, and Winnie got dropped a lot. At the end, the applause was so feeble it was a mercy that it only lasted a few seconds. Nat and Benny were on after us, and they gave us quick little shoulder pats as they rushed by to the stage. Kit burst into tears, holding her coat to her face to muffle the sound. Nell just stared.

We're going to get fired, I thought as I watched the stage, trying to absorb their skill through my eyeballs. Winnie hobbled over, bruises no doubt rising on her backside. Kit and Nell came to stand with us, too. It was Nat and Benny we waited for, after all, like children at their front gates, waiting for daddies to return from work. Nat and Benny, our vaudeville fathers.

The applause was deafening compared to the limp patting of palms we'd suffered. As they skip-walked offstage, their eyes were on us, calculating the damage.

"*Vey ist mir!*" said Benny. "Such faces! Have you never been booed before?"

"Of course not!" I nearly shouted.

A strange smile passed between the two men. "Never booed," said Benny, shaking his head. "Natty, these poor children."

"It's okay," Nat replied. "That's all fixed now."

Winnie said, "You act like it's a good thing!"

"Of course it is, Winneleh," said Nat. "How else will you become true vaudevillians, if you don't have practice in handling all the misery this life has to offer? Next time will be easier."

"It will be easier," Benny said with a sly smile, "because you'll know how to boo back!" He took off his coat and draped it across his stool. "Now, for instance, the mooing? That's so old it's boring. And easy to handle. You say, *I see the cows have gotten up into the gallery again. Could someone please hit them with a stick? They're too senseless to find their own way out.*'"

Nat flicked Benny with the back of his hand. "The last time I saw a mouth like yours, it had a hook in it!" He stuck his pinky inside his cheek and pulled like a hooked fish.

It was probably the most useful education I've ever had. Nat and Benny made it fun, and I half wished we'd get booed again so we could try it out. They also helped us practice our sketches, so our next turn on the boards was much less humiliating.

Afterward, Benny insisted on getting the sandwiches, and refused to take a nickel. "If you eat every bite," he said as he handed out the thick parcels, "that will be my repayment."

Then he turned to Winnie. "Winneleh, the girl of a thousand bruises, I remember what it's like to get knocked around, and it almost made me quit the business. So I brought you a little present." He reached into the pocket of his frayed overcoat and took out a blue rubber pouch with a wide metal screw cap. "An ice bag," he said. "To heal all the bumps this life hands out."

Her eyes went so wide the thing could have been a diamond. Suddenly she threw her arms around his neck and hugged him. When she finally let go, he put his thick old hands to her cheeks. "*Zei gezunt,*" he whispered. "Be well, little Winneleh. And try not to need it so much!"

On Friday, we got a letter from Dad, posted to the Fredonia Opera House. It was dated March 31, so that snotty Barnes had obviously let it sit in his office for a couple of days before he'd bothered to give it to us. Mother was still at the hotel with little Harry, so I opened it myself. Dad's penmanship was shaky, and we knew right away his hand was no better than when we'd left him. For a quiet man, he wrote pages and pages, describing the changing seasons, and how the crocuses were peeking up through the few patches of dirt that had no snow. He must have been awfully bored to write such a rambling letter. I felt sorry for him.

I also missed him! A girl shouldn't be so surprised at missing the man who'd loved and provided for her all her life, but I was. Maybe it was because I was now with Mother all day long, with no calming influence to temper her. Dad was a little bit like a lump of coal, I realized. You don't really take much notice of it until your house is cold.

Finally he got around to why he was writing in the first place.

Tomorrow it will be April 1, April Fool's Day as it is called. I hope there will be no pranks played on you. In fact, I wonder if you're playing a prank on me by not sending the rent money until the last minute.

It was now April 4. In all the distraction of the past few days, we'd forgotten why we'd gotten into vaudeville in the first place: rent money.

After our next performance, I went to the drugstore to call him. There was a pay phone in a small wooden booth at the back. I lifted the candlestick receiver from the hook and waited for the Hello Girl to come on the line. "How may I connect your call?" she asked.

"Long distance, please."

She asked for the number and I gave her our neighbor Mrs. Califano's and said, "I have an urgent call for Mr. Frank Turner."

There was some clicking followed by silence. Then I heard Mrs. Califano's voice. "Yes, hello!" she screamed into the phone, as if the sound had to carry to Fredonia on the wind.

"Urgent call for Mr. Frank Turner." The operator sounded bored. I suppose she heard people using the word *urgent* and screaming through the phone lines all day long.

"Frank Turner!" screeched Mrs. Califano. "He lives next door! Urgent you say? It'll take me just a moment!"

"Please deposit thirty-five cents for three minutes," the operator said. I put coins into the slots at the top of the pay phone, hoping old Mrs. Califano didn't use up my three minutes just tottering across the lawn to our house. Impatient, my eyes lit on the shelf closest to me: there was a line of hair tonics in fancy bottles named for Nazimova, the sultry Russian silent film star. On the shelf below were the less glamorous products: Walnutta the Hair Stain, and a product "for promoting the growth of hair" called Baldine, which is a terrible name. What balding person would want *that* mocking him from the bathroom shelf?

There were jars of Compound Honey and Tar for bronchial afflictions, Milk of Magnesia laxative, and Carter's Little Liver Pills for dizziness, biliousness, torpid liver, constipation, and sallow skin. For a mere nineteen cents a bottle, it practically claimed to save you from drowning.

On the end of the shelf was a stack of Johnson's first aid manuals. It had small type at the bottom: With the Compliments of the Roemer Drug Company. It was free, so I took it.

"Hello?" Finally!

"Dad, it's Gert."

"Is everything all right?"

"Yes, but—"

"Oh, that's a relief! I was so worried. I didn't know if—"

"Dad, I don't have much time left on the call. We got your letter, and we don't have the rent money yet. We were robbed back in Cuba—"

"Robbed!"

"Yes, but not at gunpoint or anything. Someone snuck into our hotel room while we were out. Anyway, Dad, we won't have any money until we get paid on Saturday, and then it will be Monday before the banks open and Mother can wire it."

"The rent will be a week late by then. Ah, nuts!" It was the only time I ever remember hearing my father saying anything remotely like a curse.

"I'm sorry, Dad."

"No, no, Gert. Don't you worry, I'll come up with something to tell the landlord. How are you girls? Everything going all right?"

The Hello Girl broke in. "Please deposit thirty-five cents for the next three minutes."

"I have to run, Dad." Actually, our next performance wasn't for another half hour; I just didn't have any more money.

"All right—give everyone my regards!"

"Okay, Dad. Take care of your—" The crackling on the wire stopped, and I knew we'd been cut off. I stayed in the little wooden booth for a moment longer, holding the candlestick receiver to my ear, imagining he was still on the other end. Our dear lump of coal.

Back at the theatre, I handed Winnie the first aid manual. She asked more questions than a homicide detective. Where'd you get it, how much was it, why are you giving it to me?

"It was free, and you like all that medical nonsense," I said. "You don't expect *me* to read it, do you?" You'd think I'd never done anything for her simply out of the goodness of my heart.

On Saturday, Mother insisted on getting out of bed. We begged her to stay at the hotel, but she marched herself and little Harry to the theatre just before our first performance. "I'd be fit as a fiddle by now if I'd gotten more rest," she said, handing Harry off to Nell. "A baby can sleep any damned time he pleases, but I couldn't doze off when he was awake, now could I?"

It hit Nell like a slap, and we all sent her sympathy looks, though I can't say any of us were too surprised. It was just Mother sounding off as she always did, especially without Dad around to tone her down. She'd been bored to death sitting in that cramped hotel room, missing out on the excitement of a busy vaudeville show.

But Nat got protective of his "darling girl," pulled himself to his full height, and said, "The baby's poor mother was working hard, making money for the family!"

Mother knew this, of course, but she sure wasn't going to let a stranger tell her what she could and couldn't say to her own daughters.

"Taking care of a sick baby is the hardest work there is," she snapped. "It's certainly harder than parading around in silly costumes and telling tired old jokes. But I don't expect an ancient bachelor like you to understand. "

"Mother, please!" said Nell. "Nat and Benny have been such a help to us."

"And who was a help to me, while I lay coughing myself blue, soothing a squalling baby, tell me that? No one, that's who."

"Pardon my frankness, Mrs. Turner—" Benny began.

"I will not pardon it! You two has-beens should mind your own business."

Benny took a breath that filled him like a beach ball, and it was obvious that a lecture was about to gust from his lungs.

"*Benny*," Kit suddenly whispered. "Don't ask for tsuris!"

Benny blinked at her, taken off guard. Then he let out a slow, angry breath.

Mother shot us a confused look. Winnie gave the translation. "Trouble."

It was Nat's face that caught my notice. He did his best to keep his face stern, but I could see the pride that crinkled around his eyes at our new language skills.

Nat and Benny, the best childless fathers I ever met.

While Mother fussed about finishing the new costumes, and Nat and Benny hid behind their newspapers, we girls practiced harder than ever. And when we tumbled onstage like tornados, the audience loved every bit of it, laughing like a pack of crazy people at the snew sketch. When I asked Nell how a window washer could break his legs, I felt my pulse pause.

"He stepped back to admire his work!" she called out, her voice stronger than we'd heard in weeks. The audience laughed and clapped, and we had to hold our positions to keep from stepping on the applause, as Benny taught us.

"Timing," he'd said. "It's everything."

And it is.

When we finally got offstage to the sound of booming applause, Mother was standing there in the wings with the baby in her arms, face wide with surprise. "Well, my goodness," she murmured. Our mother isn't one for grand gestures of approval. (In fact, she isn't even one for small gestures of the kind.) But the look on her face.

Kit was the first to reach her and throw her long arms around Mother's neck, practically suffocating the poor woman. Then Nell and Winnie got in on it, and what was I going to do, stand there twiddling my thumbs?

After the last show that week, Mr. Barnes came backstage to hand out the pay. As he gave Mother our envelope he said stiffly, "I've deducted ten dollars for the night you shorted me on performers."

Mother stepped up very close to him like she was just about to bite his chin. "Oh, no you don't," she snarled. "I've had this flimflam pulled on me before, and it is never going to happen again. The Tumbling Turner Sisters *tumbled* every single time we were contracted for. In fact," she said, poking him in the breastbone, "with the new comedy skits, the act you got by the end was even better than the act you hired. So, you hand over that ten dollars right this goddamned minute, or I will make it my *life's work* to make sure you never get another decent act in this fancy hellhole again!"

I saw Nat and Benny exchange a glance, eyebrows raised in admiration.

Sweat broke out on Barnes's upper lip, and the pince-nez fell right off his nose. It was all I could do not to break out laughing. Maybe Mother could have been a vaudevillian after all, if she'd set her sights on acting instead of dancing.

Barnes took a ten-dollar bill off the wad in his pocket and held it out for her. She took it with a dainty smile and tucked it right into her grouch bag.

Nat and Benny headed to the train station straight from the theatre. They had a sleeper jump to their next show in Van Wert, Ohio. We all walked out together, and Winnie gave Nat our address in case he thought to send a postcard, but I knew it was just as likely that we'd never know what became of them. I was surprised at the pinch of sadness I felt.

"Watch your timing," Benny reminded us.

"And don't let the theatre managers push you around," said Nat.

Benny wagged a finger at us, then pointed to Winnie. "Don't drop her so much."

"Eat, little *mameleh*," Nat murmured to Nell. "You need your strength for this life."

"Be generous with the other performers," said Benny. "The world loves a mensch."

"We will . . . Thank you . . . Thank you so much . . ."

Nell was teary and she held little Harry tight as they turned and walked toward the train depot, their figures growing smaller as they trudged down the empty sidewalk.

"*Zei gezunt!*" Kit called out after them. "Be well!"

Nat elbowed Benny, and they turned around, smiles so big we could make them out through the darkness. "*Zei gezunt!*" Benny called. "Be well, you Tumbling Turners, be well!"

CHAPTER
17

WINNIE

Outside of a dog, a book is a man's best friend.
Inside of a dog it's too dark to read.
—Groucho Marx, comedian and actor

The next morning, the train clattered north beside Lake Erie to Buffalo. The car we rode in was almost full and we had to separate. Kit, Nell, and Mother sat at one end, while Gert and I squeezed into a seat with two other girls at the other end. In fact, the whole car seemed to be filled with young women around the age of twenty.

"Where you headed?" asked one of the two who shared our bench. I could see the remains of heavy black liner around her eyes and dark red lipstick at the edges of her mouth.

"Lyons," said Gert.

The girl squinted in disgust. "What's in *Lyons*, for godsake?"

"The Ohmann Theatre," I said, and was about to ask if they were in vaudeville, too, but she cut me off.

"Sounds legitimate," she said suspiciously. Legitimate theatre meant plays, not variety.

"Oh no," I said. "It's not that fancy. Just vaudeville. Are you—"

"Oh, *vaudeville*," she said and nudged the girl next to her. "They're *vaudeville*."

The other girl rolled her eyes. "Well, ain't that grand."

Gert and I cast glances at each other. "What kind of shows do you do?" asked Gert.

"Burlesque." She stuck her chin out, daring us to comment. "It's a twenty-girl revue. Adele's the featured girl." She cocked her head toward her neighbor. "Best legs, best shake."

I didn't know what to say. Congratulations?

"And we're not playing *Lyons*, for godsake," she added, and the featured girl laughed.

The next stop was Buffalo, and they got up to leave. "Best of luck," I said.

"Best of luck to *you*," she said, and nudged the featured girl. They tittered as they tugged their bags out from under the seat.

When they left, I said to Gert, "What's with them?"

"Jealous," she said with a smirk. "They don't have any talent, so they have to take their clothes off for applause. Just be glad you're going to *Lyons*, for godsake."

With the train car now nearly empty, Mother, Kit, and Nell joined Gert and me. I started reading *Johnson's First Aid Manual, Eighth Edition*, which Gert had given me. I was especially fascinated by the section titled "Bleeding from Special Parts." It had color pictures of how to stanch blood flow in various locations from head to toe.

"What on earth are you reading?" Mother sat next to me and glanced over at the pictures of blood running down arms and legs. "And what happened to *Little Women*?"

I wanted to love *Little Women*, I truly did—and not just because it was, until recently, my only option beyond discarded newspapers and the occasional *Good Housekeeping* magazine. "I don't know," I said to Mother. "It's just . . . well, they never actually *go* anywhere." It seemed boring, especially now that I had descriptions of blood stanching, fracture splinting, and burn dressing to occupy me.

Mother leaned close to get a better look at a picture with the caption:

Fig. 15. Flexion of the leg to arrest bleeding of the thigh. A stick or knotted cloth placed in the groin and the leg bent double back upon the abdomen and fastened with a bandage.

"I'm not sure this is appropriate for a young girl, Winnie," she said, peering at the next page with a map of multiple arterial wounds.

"It's no worse than the hospital, Mother. In fact, it's tame by comparison. And maybe this kind of knowledge could be useful."

Mother rested her head against the back of the leather seat and closed her eyes. "If you ever find me with a wound in my thigh, please just let me be. I'd rather die from blood loss than be trussed up like a Christmas turkey with a stick wedged in my groin."

Lyons, New York, is nestled in the patchwork of verdant farmland between Rochester and Syracuse. We got off and rolled our trunks toward town, crossing a short bridge over the Erie Canal. Looking over the railing, we could see the packed dirt of the old trails, where mules or horses once tugged the barges along the canal. Now most of the boats had engines of some kind, and the acrid smell of coal smoke and oil drifted upward toward us. However, this was soon laced with a brisk odor that became stronger as we headed into the town itself.

"What *is* that?" asked Kit, sniffing to try and place it.

"It's minty, I think," said Nell. "Smells a little like Colgate's tooth powder."

"Lyons must have the cleanest teeth and freshest breath in New York," I giggled.

We came to Water Street, which ran along the north side of the canal, and it bustled with workers from the various loading docks, warehouses, and way stations for barges delivering goods on their way from one end of Upstate New York to the other.

"Can you point us in the direction of the Ohmann Theatre?" Gert asked a man in coveralls blotched with grease.

He smiled shyly at her, revealing teeth the color of mushrooms. "Why sure, miss. It's just on Williams Street. Turn right at the Congress Hall, and go up a couple blocks."

The Congress Hall Hotel was a large four-story affair. The first two floors had wide sweeping verandas with arched columns; the top floors had little gabled windows looking out toward the canal. The ceilings were low on those levels, which we discovered when Mother strode into the lobby and booked two rooms.

"Mother, I'm sure we can find something a little more reasonable elsewhere," said Nell.

"Who knows what we'll find in this little backwater town. Some tinder box just ready for a lit match," said Mother. We unpacked and headed to the theatre, passing a lovely little park with a crisscross of walking paths lined with benches.

Mr. Burt Ohmann was the theatre's owner and manager, and it was clear that he ran it as his own personal fiefdom. And yet, despite his gruffness, I sensed an evenhandedness. As performers arrived for the Monday morning rehearsal, he greeted us all with equal disinterest.

We stood onstage waiting for rehearsal to begin, and my gaze caught on a strangely familiar face. At first I couldn't place where I'd seen him, and then it came to me. The Cuba train station. It was the young man with the brown eyes who'd held the little girl's hand!

He stood wearing a black suit, white shirt, and gray bow tie. He and the little girl—his sister, I was fairly certain—both seemed nervous. Her eager eyes darted everywhere, taking in the other performers, the stage, and the lighting in the fly space above. Her brother's eyes were hooded with wariness. And a sort of melancholy. Yes, that was there, too, and it tugged at me in the most peculiar way. I wanted to reassure him. *Don't worry*, I wanted to say. *It all looks a little crazy, but it's just vaudeville. You'll get used to it.* As if I'd been riding the rails from theatre to theatre all my life!

"Okay, let's get started," Mr. Ohmann said, waving his cigar in some indiscriminate direction. "Go on back and Albert here will call each act out when we want you."

The little girl looked over at me. "Where should we go?" she murmured.

"Just backstage," I told her. "Here, follow us."

Waiting for your first performance at a new theatre is the most nerve-racking part of vaudeville, and it never failed to make me tap my knuckles nearly black and blue. It didn't help when Gert murmured in my ear, "By the way, you might want to lay off the cheese sandwiches, you're getting harder to catch."

This took me aback. I'd noticed my costume feeling a little snug, but I didn't think anyone else had. In the past, I'd always hoped to be bigger, to have curves like Gert or even Nell before she got too thin. Now, for the first time in my life I was worried I might grow.

Albert, the stage manager, called, "Tumbling Turner Sisters! You're up next." Despite my dismay over Gert's comment, we performed well. I'm sure we had Nat and Benny to thank for that. As I trotted offstage, I noticed the brother and sister waiting in the wings for their turn. The young man was studying me.

"Dainty Little Lucy!" called Albert. "You're up!"

They looked at each other, and he raised an eyebrow. She had a lacy shawl wrapped around her shoulders and she twisted the ends with her fingers for a moment, and then nodded.

"Good luck," I said, quickly adding, "I mean, break a leg!"

His face registered an uneasy surprise.

"No, it's a good thing." I offered a little smile to show it was meant with kind intentions.

He smiled back. Oh, that smile. It nearly took my breath away. So unexpected coming from such a stoic expression. "Then I'll try to break them both," he murmured. He had the slightest whisper of an accent, so faint it was hard to tell if he might be foreign, or just from some distant American city.

A piano was wheeled out onto the boards, and Lucy spread her shawl over it, smoothing it with her small hands. Her brother sat down on the piano bench, his long fingers hovering over the keyboard. She tugged at the sleeves of her little white dress and adjusted the wide pink sash around her narrow waist. Suddenly her face lit up, eyes like saucers, lips pursed adorably into a little O. He began to play a popular, bouncy tune. Dainty Little Lucy sang out:

Everybody loves a baby, that's why I'm in love with you,
Pretty baby, pretty baby.

And I'd like to be your sister, brother, dad, and mother, too,
Pretty baby, pretty baby.

Her voice was surprisingly strong, and she had quite a repertoire of expressions and gestures—smiles, pouts, finger wagging, shoulder hugging. This girl was a natural. She sang several more songs: "By the Light of the Silvery Moon," "Red Rose Rag," and "Meet Me in St. Louis."

There was a point, just before the last song, where she looked back at her brother, and from the wings I could see the look of pleading she gave. Almost imperceptibly he shook his head, then launched into "In the Good Old Summertime," and the interchange was effectively ended.

In the good old summertime, in the good old summertime,
Strolling through the shady lanes, with your baby mine;
You hold her hand and she holds yours,
and that's a very good sign,
That she's your tootsey wootsey in the good old summertime.

At the end she performed a charming curtsy, while he bowed beside her. She held his hand and skipped along as they headed offstage, then dropped it when they reached the wings.

"I'd give you crutches," I joked, "but I think you two need wheelchairs."

Their smiles were grateful and virtually identical. I reached out a hand and said, "I'm Winnie Turner."

"Lucy Cole," the girl chirped, giving my hand a pump.

I glanced up at her brother, just the briefest flicker of eye contact to see if he might shake my hand as well. He looked down at me with those sad molasses-brown eyes, and I felt a strange connection, as if I could somehow feel his sorrow in my own heart. I wondered what had befallen him, and if I might be able to help.

"I'm Joe. Very nice to meet you, Winnie," he said, taking my hand. "Though I think I may have seen you before—at the Cuba train depot?"

"Yes, that was me." I was delighted that such a brief moment weeks before had made an impression on him, too.

Mr. Ohmann called us all out to the stage. "First of all, I don't believe in openers and chasers. You people didn't travel as many miles as you did to get ignored while folks clamor around taking their seats. We open with a flicker, we close with a flicker." We all looked at one another in surprise, happy that movies would take up the worst spots on the program.

"Second thing. We have four dressing rooms. Those will go to the last four acts on the bill. Third thing. Lyons is a lovely town, and it smells far better than most human habitats, as you may have noticed. However, despite this generally convivial state of affairs, we do not suffer from an excess of population from which to draw audiences. In my experience, three performances are quite sufficient. Also, it gets me home to Mrs. Ohmann at a reasonable hour."

Most of the acts were happy for the lightened load, but the preening tenor was worried his voice might suffer from the cold as he traveled to and from his hotel between shows. "My vocal chords are delicate instruments," he said, thick fingers held protectively at his neck.

Mr. Ohmann took a puff of his cigar and blew it out. "Then I suggest you wear a scarf."

"What's he worried about?" whispered Kit. "It's not even that cold out." The weather had finally turned springlike, and without the fierce lakeshore wind, it seemed downright balmy.

"He's just trying to establish himself as star of the show," murmured Gert. "Practicing to be a spoiled big-time headliner."

Kit smirked. "He can be the king of the monkeys." One of the acts involved two trained orangutans that did tricks, pretending to play the violin and banging on a set of drums, while their trainer played the banjo. They were dressed like a boy and girl—him in knickers and a cap, her in a flouncy blue dress, with lipstick that she repeatedly licked off. The trainer, a tall, older man named Jackie O'Sullivan, had to keep reapplying it, which was quite a sight.

Mr. Ohmann, we soon learned, simply ignored anyone who made the slightest fuss, and so the complaining tenor was left to stand there with his small face soured like old milk.

"I don't quite have the lineup yet," Mr. Ohmann said. "I'm waiting to see if one more act is coming. He's a disappointment act, though, so it's only fair to give him a little extra time."

"If he's so disappointing," I whispered, "why is he getting a break for being late?"

"*He's* not a disappointment," Kit snickered in my ear. "It's a disappointment *act*. It means the act who was supposed to be here didn't show up, and he's filling in."

At that moment, the stage door opened behind us and everyone turned toward the sound. Gert saw him first and let out an involuntary gasp.

It was Tippety Tap Jones.

CHAPTER
18

GERT

*I don't care what you say about me, as long as you say
something about me, and as long as you spell my name right.*
—George M. Cohan, singer, dancer, and songwriter

Tip.

My heart began to pound so hard it felt like it might knock
right out of my chest. *Stop that!* I said to myself, but it went right on
pounding. You think your heart belongs to you, and you can order it
around, but you can't. You belong to *it*.

"Sorry to be late, sir!" said Tip, making straight for the front of the
stage, dragging his huge wheeled trunk behind him. He was breathing
hard, as if he'd run right up the street, and he didn't notice me at first.
"Train was slow. Cows on the track, I believe, sir."

"No trouble at all, Mr. Jones," said Ohmann. "I saw you at the
Pratt over in Albion a while back. I know what you can do."

"Thank you, sir," said Tip. From behind him, I saw his back expand
with a deep breath, and then return to its usual broad state, shoulders
squared like a soldier awaiting inspection.

Mr. Ohmann listed the first half of the show, pointing his stub of
a cigar at each act. "After the opening movie, we'll have Willie 'Watermelon' Lee." The man's white skin was smeared with cork, except for

his mouth, which was covered in white greasepaint. A big ragged top hat sank down to his ears. His pants were too short and had three blue patches sewn cockeyed, as if by a half-drunk five-year-old. For his act, he squawked out coon songs and danced around with a crooked walking stick.

"He can't even sing," said Kit. "That getup does the act for him."

We'd seen coon shouters before, of course. Lots of vaudeville shows had some kind of blackface minstrel act. But when I saw Tip cut his eyes toward Lee, the difference between them struck me. Tip in his neatly kept suit, polished shoes, and spotless white spats, well mannered and hardworking. Lee in his ridiculous outfit, playing the stupid, lazy Negro. I wondered if Tip was thinking, *That's not me, and it's no one I know.* That's what I would've been thinking.

Mr. Ohmann poked his cigar around some more, and the next spot went to Dainty Little Lucy. "The last spot before intermission is the Tumbling Turner Sisters," he said. It was quite a promotion. It meant we were good enough to whet the audience's appetite for the second half.

"Dressing room," whispered Kit. "We get a dressing room!"

You would have thought my mother and sisters had just been handed diamond tiaras instead of the chance to sit in a tiny room for a week. I'll admit I was happy, too. But that happiness was a sort of pleasant background music to the thrill of seeing Tip again.

Mr. Ohmann said Tip would open after intermission, then Earl Grayson the tenor, and finally Mike and Mary the orangutans would headline before the show closed with another short film. Grayson got pouty. His small head was swabbed with pomaded black hair. He was about Tip's height, but most of his pounds sat on his lower half rather than his chest and shoulders. The man was the shape of a teardrop.

"Excuse me, Mr. Ohmann. Mr. Ohmann!"

Ohmann's face went flat with forced patience. "Yes, Mr. Grayson."

"My agent told me I'd be headlining."

"I'm sure your agent told you the bill is set at the discretion of the manager. If he didn't, you might want to consider hiring a new agent."

"I headline everywhere I go! I've never been in any other spot."

"Well, then this will be a nice change of pace for you." Ohmann waved his cigar around at the lot of us standing onstage. "Shows are at one, four, and eight o'clock. Do not, under any circumstances, be late."

Mother and Kit scampered like jackrabbits back toward the dressing room with Winnie and Nell, holding little Harry, not too far behind. Albert, the stage manager, pointed to the farthest door. "You ladies are in the sleeper jump," he said.

"Why's it called the sleeper jump?" asked Kit.

"Because it's so far away you practically need an overnight train to get there."

The sleeper jump could wait, as far as I was concerned, and I slowed my pace, pretending interest in the other rooms I passed, hoping Tip would catch up. The first was the size of a small bedroom, with a threadbare love seat on one side, a scratched kidney-shaped dressing table and chair on the other. Jackie O'Sullivan and his orangutans got this one. O'Sullivan was a handsome older man, wearing his hat at a jaunty angle, and swaggering along with a shiny black wooden cane. Maybe he just wanted to make sure people could tell him apart from his monkeys.

Each room was a little smaller and shabbier than the last. The tenor's had a tired old wing-back chair instead of a love seat. Tip's had a couple of mismatched ladder-back chairs. And ours? Well, it was practically the size of a coat closet. There was one rickety Windsor chair in the corner with a Hotchkiss peppermint oil crate in front as a footstool, and the mirror was so speckled with tarnish it was impossible to see your entire face at one time. The one thing I'll say for our closet: it was just big enough for little Harry's play yard to be wedged in at the back.

"At least when he takes a nap he won't be woken by a cymbal crash," said Nell.

"We'll do just fine back here, won't we, Harry?" Mother said, and the baby grinned, two new teeth sprouting from his lower gums. I wondered how much time Mother would actually spend in the cramped space, away from the company of the performers.

The room was so crowded with people and furniture it was easy to slip back out into the hallway and down a few feet to Tip's dressing room next door. He was unpacking that huge trunk of his, and it was like watching a giant set up in a doll's house.

"How've you been?" I asked calmly, my voice a lie to cover the thumping in my chest.

He glanced up at me, catching my gaze and holding it for a moment, taking its measure.

"I've been all right," he said, and turned back to his unpacking. "How've all the Tumbling Turners been?"

"Oh, just fine." I leaned against the doorjamb. "Except for when we got robbed."

His eyes flicked back up to mine. "Robbed?"

"In Cuba."

Full lips gave up the tiniest little doubtful smile. "*Cuba* Cuba?"

"Cuba, New York, of course. Is there any other Cuba?"

He grinned. "Oh, Cuba, *New York*. Why didn't you say so?"

"Well, it's so big-time, I assumed you knew."

"Course I did. It's almost as big-time as Scotland, Georgia."

"And how big is that vast city?" I asked.

"Depends on whether you count the farm animals. Doubles the number."

I laughed at this and he grinned. But then the humor slid away from his face. "Robbed," he said. "You all right?"

I shrugged. "She took all our money, but no one got hurt or anything."

"*She?*"

He stood next to the now-empty trunk with his hands in his pockets. There were two chairs in the room. The stain was worn right down to the wood on the arms, but they worked, and I would've liked an invitation to sit down. But he just stood there waiting for my story.

So I told him about that conniving Sissy Salloway, happy as a fool just to be in the same room, entertaining him with impressions of the squawking singer and stone-faced banjo player.

But why didn't he ask me to sit, as any gentleman would? It irritated me almost as much as my own silly bliss at his attention. The idea that he was being disrespectful by making me stand grew until I came to the part about Billy.

"He was so handsome—turns out he was rich, too!—and he practically begged me just to take a walk. And of course, that's not all he wanted." I let a little smile play on my lips, as if this had been a secret pleasure instead of the nightmare it actually was. I suppose I just wanted Tip to know that other men found me fascinating, even if he wouldn't do so much as offer me a seat.

His eyes, which had been latched onto me like I was the latest Mary Pickford movie, suddenly wandered around the room as if he could no longer look at me.

"Well, best not to get into all that," I said. "Anyway, I hope Mother learned her lesson, and she'll take a little more care with her choice of friends."

He didn't respond for a moment, but his eyes were back on me. "Ought to be careful, Mizz Gert," he said finally. "There's a whole lotta bad out there most folks never see coming."

I had only meant to flirt with him a little, and here he was unknowingly reminding me of my stupidity with that damned phony cowboy. I felt like a fool. I made some silly excuse about wanting to see the flicker Ohmann was running at the beginning of the show, and it was all I could do to make myself walk calmly down the hallway, and not gallop like a spooked horse. I was confused. And I rarely found men confusing.

Winnie and Kit were in the wings with a couple of other performers watching the movie. It was Mabel Normand in *Mabel's Blunder*, all about a misunderstanding she has with her fiancé. It was nonsense, of course. The problems people have in movies could be sorted out or avoided altogether by a nine-year-old with half a lick of sense.

When the movie reel ran out, the stage lights came up and Willie "Watermelon" Lee took to the boards, waving his arms around with that crooked branch of a cane. Since I had nothing better to do, I stayed to watch. He started off singing "All I Wants Is Ma Chickens," and then went on to "Mammy's Little Pickaninny Boy" and "Coon, Coon, Coon."

Although it's not my color, I'm feeling mighty blue;
I've got a lot of trouble, I'll tell it all to you;
I'm cert'nly clean disgusted with life, and that's a fact,
Because my hair is wooly, and because my color's black.
My gal she took a notion against the colored race.
She said if I would win her I'd have to change my face;
She said if she would wed me, that she'd regret it soon,
And now I'm shook, yes, good and hard,
Because I am a coon.
Coon! Coon! Coon! I wish my color would fade;
Coon! Coon! Coon! I'd like a different shade,
Coon! Coon! Coon! Morning, night, and noon,
I wish I was a white man, 'stead of a Coon! Coon! Coon!

I'd heard these songs before, of course, but they'd never made me feel like I'd swallowed a glass of spoiled milk. Everyone was laughing, but it wasn't funny anymore. Not to me.

Then Tip walked by.

I froze as if I'd been caught with my hand in the box office till. He looked at me and strode past, never even glancing to the performance onstage.

Lee took his bows; the audience clapped and cheered.

It was just another day in vaudeville.

CHAPTER
19

WINNIE

I was a thirteen-year-old boy for thirty years.
—Mickey Rooney, singer, dancer, and actor

As thrilling as a dressing room is, it has one major drawback. You're expected to stay in it! After that first rush of excitement, the shine wore off fairly quickly as Nell nursed Harry in the only chair, and we all stood around staring at one another. Backstage there was the constant buzz of stagehands bustling about, and new friends to meet. Of course, my mind kept spooling back to one certain face that I felt inexplicably drawn to.

I went out into the hallway and saw Gert leaning against the doorjamb by Tip's dressing room. As I passed, she let her hand slide out behind her into the hallway and made a little flicking motion at me. I did as she indicated and scooted past her toward the stage.

We were friendly with Tip, and it was natural that we'd want to catch up after his hasty departure the last time we'd seen him. Yet passing behind Gert, I felt a certain heat to the situation, as if she were crossing a rickety bridge over a flow of molten lava. We'd already seen the trouble that could come just from accidental contact. I didn't want that to happen to him again. And I certainly didn't want it to happen because of us.

Backstage, Joe and Lucy Cole sat side by side on their trunk, backs against the wall, looking lost as they watched the stagehands run back and forth preparing for the first show. Lucy looked up. "Winnie!" she said, grinning broadly. "Joe, get Winnie a chair."

Joe looked around, and I did, too. If I didn't have anything to sit on, I would have to hover above them, and the conversation would be curtailed by the temporary quality of our positions. I found a three-legged stool, likely used by the stagehands to reach the higher curtain ropes cinched to large wooden cleats. "This'll do," I said, and set it near them. As casually as I could, I lowered myself onto it, crossing my legs out in front of me, and then seeing how unladylike that appeared, sliding them to one side, bending my knees and trying desperately not to let my costume ride up my thighs. It's a delicate thing to try to behave properly with new friends when you're wearing only a black satin tumbling dress and flesh-toned stockings.

"How old are you?" Lucy asked brightly.

"Lucy," murmured Joe. "Not polite."

"That's all right," I said. "I don't mind. I'm older than I look, so I'd rather have you ask and know the truth. I'm seventeen."

Lucy studied me. "Really? That old?"

"I'll be eighteen this summer."

This was the wrong answer for Lucy Cole. She held her hand out to Joe, palm down, and he flicked the back of her hand with his index finger.

"Ow!" She seemed more annoyed than hurt.

"It wasn't that hard," he scoffed. To me he explained, "I guessed sixteen, she said thirteen."

"How old do you think *we* are?" said Lucy.

I took the opportunity to fully invade them with my eyes, Lucy first, of course, so as not to appear forward with Joe. She was small and dressed like a little girl, but her mind was quick and I suspected that, like me, she was older than she looked. To flatter her, I added one year to my guess. "Eleven?"

She stuck out her chin triumphantly. "Sixteen."

"You are not," Joe muttered, eyes flitting around the area. "Don't lie to her."

"You told me to say that," Lucy insisted. "You said I shouldn't tell anyone that the birth certificate the agent gave me was a fake."

"Winnie's not going to turn you in to the Gerrymen." He looked at me, a hint of doubt in his eye. "You wouldn't, would you?"

"Of course not. Why would I do that?"

"Our agent says sometimes acts stir up trouble for each other to cut the competition."

I thought of the Peppers getting Tip fired. Then I thought of what I'd done to their pigeon cage, and a wave of shame came over me. I'll admit, however, that it passed quickly.

"Well, that's true," I conceded. "Sometimes it can get a little . . . underhanded. But I won't tell. Besides, my sister Kit doesn't even have a fake—she's so tall no one would guess she's only thirteen. There. Now if I tattle on you, you can tattle on Kit, and both our acts will be ruined."

Joe let out a little chuckle, and Lucy said, "I'm twelve. But I don't get to flick your hand because you were almost right. What about Joe? He's easy, I think."

This was my chance to really study him, though I was distracted by his eyes gazing back at me. I judged him to be fully grown, with his closely shaved whiskers, man-sized shoulders, and large, strong hands, though I could imagine the cute little boy he once was. He had no wrinkles, of course, but there were dark crescents under his eyes that even a month of sleep might not bleach away. As they had before, those beautiful brown eyes drew me in, as if I might have been the only kind soul he'd met in a year.

"Twenty-three," I guessed.

Lucy looked at Joe and grinned. "Hold out your hand," she told me.

"Nineteen," said Joe, and flicked his finger against my knuckle.

"Didn't hurt," I teased.

He laughed, and for a brief moment the dark circles were compressed almost to nothing by his rounded cheeks. "Next time I'll try harder," he teased back, and I felt wonderfully accomplished to have made those eyes crinkle in humor.

As we sat and chatted, my stomach began to rumble. It was embarrassing, of course, but worse, like a dinner bell it announced the end of our little getting-to-know-you party.

"I think we'd better get some lunch before the one o'clock show," said Joe, rising and stretching his legs from his low perch on the trunk. "Also, we haven't found a hotel yet."

"We're staying at the Congress Hall, just a few blocks down. They still had a vacancy a couple of hours ago. It's just down the street, past the little park."

Joe thanked me for the suggestion, and the two of them left with the trunk. I went to find Mother, wondering why she hadn't gone out for sandwiches yet. I expected that she was taking orders from the other acts, as she liked to do. As I headed to our dressing room, or "dressing closet" as we would soon joke, Mother's voice drifted toward me before I was even in the back hall.

"Aren't they sweet!" she was saying. "Jackie, you're just wonderful with them."

I stopped in front of the first dressing room and peeked in through the partly opened door. Mother was sitting on the little chair by the kidney-shaped table. Mr. O'Sullivan was on the love seat, sandwiched between Mike and Mary, who were nibbling on crackers, their short legs bent up at the knees in front of them. Mary reached across for one of Mike's crackers, though she still had a small pile on the arm of the love seat next to her. Mike slapped her hand away.

"Play nice, you two, or you're back in the crate," said Jackie, flashing an apologetic smile at Mother. His teeth were distractingly straight and white, and I wondered if they might be dentures. In the far corner was a cage, about three feet square. It seemed barely big enough for one ape, much less two.

"Excuse me, Mother," I said. "Should I go out and get sandwiches?"

I expected her to insist on doing it herself, but she said, "Certainly, dear. Have you met Mr. O'Sullivan? Jackie, my daughter Winnie would be happy to pick up some lunch for you, too, if you'd rather not go out."

"Why, yes." He smiled coyly at Mother as he reached into his pocket for a couple of coins. "I'm quite happy to stay right here."

Mother gave me a dollar and change, and said, "There's a place we passed down on Water Street. Miss Bell's, I believe it's called."

I raised my eyebrows at her. I'd seen Miss Bell's, too, and it was a far cry from the drugstore lunch counters we generally patronized.

Mother raised her eyebrows back, a *don't-challenge-me* look, and said, "Go on, now."

I hesitated in the doorway. Since she seemed to be feeling flush, I thought it might be a good time to make a request. "Could I please buy a few small things at the drugstore? I'd like to make a first aid kit like the one recommended in the manual."

"Well, my goodness, Winnie," Mother clucked, with a little eye roll toward Mr. O'Sullivan. "What kind of accidents are we preparing for?"

Mr. O'Sullivan took his cue from her. "Vaudeville can be dangerous, I'll grant you that," he said, making clear that he was granting me no such thing, "but it *is* a mite safer than, say . . . *coal mining*."

Mother laughed girlishly. "Or building one of those new skyscrapers hundreds of feet off the ground!"

"Where do you think we are?" added Mr. O'Sullivan. "Chicago?"

The two of them grinned wider than the monkeys, showing off for each other at my expense. "She's got a new first aid book," Mother explained. "And she's just as eager as a Girl Scout to help people. Isn't that sweet?"

"Sweet as pie," he said. Except he wasn't looking at me. He was looking at Mother.

I left without another word, cheeks aflame in humiliation.

I bought sandwiches at Miss Bell's at a luxurious twenty-five cents apiece. For myself I bought a cheese sandwich at Dobbins Drugs, and used the rest to buy an Esmarch bandage, like the one in my first aid manual. It was a triangular piece of muslin four feet long on the diagonal side, and had pictures of six half-naked men modeling the thirty-two different ways the bandage could be used as a tourniquet, wound covering, sling, or splint tie. It was thrilling. And a bit titillating, to be honest. I had never seen the male figure with so little left to the imagination, and I took a few stolen moments to study the bandage, wondering how true to life it might be.

I had thus far had very little interaction with the male form, never having succumbed to anything more than a wholly unfulfilled crush or two. I had been kissed exactly four times, the first by surprise in the eighth grade. Luigi O'Malley pulled me into the shade of a lilac hedge one May evening, took my shoulders in his meaty hands, and said, "May I kiss you?"

"What?" I said, stunned. He apparently took this to mean that I wasn't completely opposed to the idea, and pressed his warm, garlicky lips against mine. I gasped in shock, but with my mouth sealed by his, the air rushed in through my nose, and the sweet, hopeful smell of blooming lilac filled my lungs.

When it was over, he scurried off as fast as his freckled legs would carry him, and we never spoke of it again. The other three kisses occurred in darkened basements during the few parties I'd been invited to, and I was always disappointed when there was no lilac scent to improve the experience.

You could never find Kit, except when you couldn't get rid of her.

I had handed out all the sandwiches but hers. Mother and Mr. O'Sullivan were still in his dressing room, cozy as you please, and I felt a wave of concern. *She's just making new friends,* I told myself. *Like we all are.*

Nell and Gert were in our dressing room. This time Tip was the one standing in the doorway, and I felt bad that I hadn't gotten him a sandwich, too.

"I'll share," said Gert. "This is too much for me anyway."

"That's mighty kind of you, but I should get back to my own dressing room," said Tip. Then he chuckled. "My own dressing room. Never thought I'd get the chance to say that."

"We never did, either," said Nell, tearing off nibbles of her sandwich to feed little Harry, seated on her lap. He snapped his wet gums together, mashing each piece, eyes bright at the surprise of this new taste. "It's not quite what we expected, is it, Gert?"

"Well, for one thing, I thought there would be more than one chair!" Gert sat on the overturned packing crate, her shapely legs draped to the side. "Please, Tip." She offered the sandwich half, held out in her long white arm. "Help me out."

He reached for it and for the briefest possible moment, his dark fingers and her pale ones nearly touched. I believe everyone in the room watched that homely bit of bread and meat pass from Gert to Tip, her face turned up toward his, his gaze decidedly not meeting it, concentrating on the sandwich as if it were something sharp, on which he might cut himself.

"I . . . I'd better find Kit before this goes stale." I held up the last butcher-papered package and forced a smile, anxious to leave the disquiet of the suddenly silent room.

I found Kit on my stool, of all places, talking with Joe and Lucy. They had found some old crates to sit on, having taken their trunk to the hotel.

"Here, sit next to me!" Lucy insisted, squeezing over on her crate. "We're small enough to share. Kit was telling us all about the different kinds of stage curtains."

"Here's your lunch." I handed her the wrapped sandwich, and hoped that the prospect of a meal that involved meat might distract her from a lecture on theatre operations. No such luck. She unwrapped the paper, took a sniff, said, "Ham?" incredulously, and kept talking.

"Those front curtains are travelers; they go back and forth on an operating line that the stagehands pull. I hear that in the big-time theatres they run on a motor, and all you have to do is push a button! These skinny little curtains there"—Kit gestured toward the side of the stage—"they're called legs and they hide what's happening in the wings, but leave an opening for performers to get off and on." She took a bite of the sandwich and chewed a moment, her face a picture of bliss. Before I could change the subject, she said, "Then you have your guillotine curtain midstage. It goes up on ropes into the fly space up above the stage, and when it comes down . . ." She drew a finger across her neck with a ghoulish look.

Lucy laughed and Joe smiled indulgently. Kit finished chewing and drew a breath to blab on about curtains and ropes, but I cut her off. "Where are you from?" I asked.

"We're from Boston," Joe said quietly. The laughter ebbed from Lucy's face.

"Boston!" Kit said, licking her fingers like a half-starved street waif. "That's a big city."

"It's big, yes," said Joe.

"We're from Johnson City, New York," I said quickly, to move the conversation away from their obvious reticence, "next to Binghamton. It's only a couple of hours from here by train."

"It's nowhere near as big as Boston." Kit picked a stray crumb off the butcher paper and popped it into her mouth. "Did you ever play at the Boston Theatre? I hear it's huge—three thousand seats! One of the stagehands in Fredonia said the stage is so big you practically need roller skates to get from one side to the other in a hurry."

"We never played there, but we've been to a lot of theatres in Boston," said Lucy. "Joe took me all the time after . . ." Her voice trailed off and she glanced at Joe.

Joe looked down at his hands. He laced his fingers and unlaced them, then spread them out on his thighs. It reminded me of little Harry, watching his toes wiggle as if they weren't a part of his own body.

"Well, where did you start?" asked Kit.

Joe gave a polite but pale smile. "I used to play in a bar called Jack's Lighthouse. They have entertainment"—he shrugged—"but not the family kind. Lucy would come after school and sit at the piano with me and sing between shows. Then they let her up onstage a couple of times, and word got around, so we started going to other bars, too."

"That's how Mr. Birnbaum found us," Lucy added.

"*Morty* Birnbaum?" I said.

"You know him?" said Joe. "He's our agent."

"He's our agent, too!"

"That's some coincidence," said Joe. "What do you make of him?"

"I can't really say. He seems nice enough, and he got us all these bookings . . ."

Joe nodded. "You worry, though," he said. "He's got our lives in his hands."

I hadn't thought of it quite like that, but it was true. If Birnbaum cut us loose tomorrow—and there was nothing to ensure that he wouldn't—we'd be right back in the soup kettle.

At intermission Kit took Lucy back to see our dressing room. Joe and I sat on our crates, and I tapped my knuckles, searching anxiously for a polite way to ask about his accent. Before I could come up with anything, he said, "Do you play?"

"Play?"

"The piano. You were playing your knuckles. I think I even saw some chords in there."

"No." I laughed, embarrassed that he'd noticed my nervous habit. "I was just thinking."

"I see." He smiled that lovely smile. "And what were you thinking about?"

"Well, to be truthful, I was trying to think of a way to ask about your accent."

His smile faded slightly. "What kind of name is Turner?" he asked. "What nationality?"

"It's English, but it's an old name. The Turners have been in America for a long time."

He stiffened. "I'm American, too."

"I didn't mean to insinuate that you weren't," I said, wondering how things had gone from pleasant to uncomfortable so quickly. "Only that you have an interesting lilt to your voice."

He looked away. "In Boston, it's not even an accent," he muttered.

"Well, I've never been to Boston. I don't know how people there sound."

"We don't all sound alike. Not everyone has been here as long as the Turners."

His defensiveness was starting to concern me. "I wasn't implying—"

"We're Italian." His chin rose just a little, daring me to impugn his country of origin.

"How nice."

My response seemed to calm him and he added quickly, "What I mean to say is that my family is from Italy, but Lucy and I are American. We were born here." When he said *Italy*, the first syllable sounded slightly more like *eat* than *it*.

I was afraid to say another word, but then I thought of Mrs. Califano, our neighbor back in Johnson City, who always had a pot of tomato gravy on the stove.

"I . . . I bet your mother is a good cook," I said.

His chin descended from its testy angle, and I could see the thought of her warm his memory. "She is. She's wonderful."

Grateful to have stumbled upon the right response, I asked, "What does she make?"

"Pasta e fagioli, of course, and pasta puttanesca, biscotti—she can make anything."

I had never heard of any of these dishes. He might have been telling me that his mother boiled old fish in dirty dishwater and I would've been none the wiser. "Delicious!" I said.

Disaster had been averted. At least for the time being.

CHAPTER

20

GERT

Success in show business depends on
your ability to make and keep friends.
—Sophie Tucker, singer

We'd traveled as a pack our whole lives, squabbling and pushing all the way, maybe, but together just the same. But in Lyons, a strange thing happened. The Turners finally separated.

Kit and dainty Lucy, a foot apart in height, explored every nook and hidey-hole of the theatre. They even got the stagehands to let them climb up the rickety wooden ladders to the fly loft where the lights and backdrops hung. Winnie stuck to that piano player like he had the keys to the Library of Congress, and though Nell was in the dressing room with little Harry while he nursed or slept, often as not I'd peek in to find the place empty.

"Where've you been?" I asked when she returned with the baby tucked into her jacket.

"Out for a walk. It's so balmy, and the mint fields smell so nice." Lyons, as it turned out, was the peppermint capital of the world, shipping its product all over the globe. "Then I went into a little café for a cup of tea and met another mother with a baby. We had the nicest chat." Even Nell was making friends!

Mother was in Jackie O'Sullivan's dressing room anytime I passed it, darning his socks or mending Mike and Mary's tacky little costumes, her high-pitched laughter practically cracking plaster. I didn't like it one bit, especially with poor Dad home alone with no one to talk to. Not that he talked all that much. In fact, maybe he didn't mind a little peace and quiet so he actually could hear his records for once. I didn't think anything would come of Mother's little flirtation. Still, all that giggling was enough to make you stick cotton in your ears.

Frankly, I should've thanked O'Sullivan for distracting Mother while I was with Tip. I could practically have spent the afternoon locked in his dressing room alone with him and she wouldn't have noticed. Not that it mattered. Tip always left the door wide open.

He was sitting in one of the chairs with his long legs stretched out in front of him the next day, relaxing after his first performance. He sat up when I peeked my head in the doorway.

"Did you ever send that postcard to your aunt?" I asked.

"I did." He shook his head. "Shouldn't have, though, seeing as I got cut the next day."

"I disagree."

He smiled at this. "Oh, you do, do you?"

"Yes, I do. You laid them out that night, and that doesn't go away just because some lousy manager fired you for no good reason."

"He said the reason was decorum."

I crossed my arms. "Well, if anyone was being indecorous, it was me. I'm the one who barreled into you."

"It wasn't you, Gert." His eyes caught mine, making his point. "It was just . . . people."

"Awful people," I said. "Not everyone's that awful."

"No," he said. "It's not always easy to tell which is which, though."

"You're smart. I bet you figure it out pretty quick."

"I bet you do, too."

I thought of Billy, and how I'd pegged him as just a dope with a silly crush. "Oh, I get fooled every once in a while."

"We all do," he said gently.

I could've fallen right into the arms of such sweetness right then and there.

"Would you like to sit?" he asked.

I took the seat across from him, our two chairs separated by his huge trunk like the Wall of China. "Why didn't you invite me to sit down when I was telling you about getting robbed?"

"I didn't want to make you uncomfortable."

"The only thing I was uncomfortable about was standing that whole time," I said. "I think you were the one who was uncomfortable."

He smiled and nodded. "I was a bit."

"And now?"

"I guess I'm getting used to it."

We talked all afternoon. The door was open, but no one passed by. We might as well have been on the moon.

"Five minutes, Turners!" Albert, the stage manager, called.

I got up to go and paused to check my makeup. Tip's mirror was a rusted disgrace. "How do I look?" I asked, hoping I wasn't too smudged.

He smiled. "You look just right."

And that's how I felt. Just right.

I didn't feel just right onstage, though. I felt light-headed, my mind wandering back to Tip as I botched a line or missed a step. I felt so *real* with him, Gert Turner in all my glory, no more, no less. *I've spent my whole life being too much or too little for people,* I thought as I dropped Winnie. I wasn't too torn up about it, though, because Winnie was even worse. She was practically dropping herself!

Mother and O'Sullivan watched from the wings, and as we limped offstage to faint applause, Mother's face was pink with embarrassment. "Girls!" she hissed. "Everyone to the dressing room right now." She handed little Harry to Kit, turned, and marched toward the backstage hallway, knowing we would follow her like ducklings after the mother duck.

We crowded into the stuffy little room, and Mother's finger flew out in front of her. "What is the reason for this sloppiness? Gert, your head is in the clouds! You nearly missed the punch line of that last bit altogether. Winnie, your timing is like a broken clock. I should keep your ice bag from you so the pain of that lump will keep you wide awake for the next show!"

"Sorry, Mother," she mumbled. "I'll try harder."

"You won't just *try*, Winnie Turner," Mother warned. "You'll succeed. Is that clear?"

All eyes were on me; my turn to grovel. But I wasn't in the mood to give a fake apology, no matter how it would smooth my way. I wanted to feel real. I wanted to be with Tip.

"It was an off day," I said. "Everyone has them."

"Off day, my foot!" Mother yelled. I cringed, knowing the sound would carry down the tiny hallway. I wondered if Tip was sitting in his dressing room next door, grateful there was no one to snarl at him after a bad performance. Not that he ever had one.

"You nearly broke your sister's arm, dropping her like that! Then where would we be?" Mother had never shown such concern over Winnie's injuries in the past. She just felt humiliated in front of her new friend—the headliner, no less.

Nell nudged me. Time to make nice. "Sorry, Mother," I mumbled.

Harry rubbed a chubby fist into his eye.

Mother snapped, "Now leave poor Nell in peace so she can give this child a nap."

I didn't need to be told twice. But Tip's door was closed for the first time since we'd arrived. Winnie slowed a step to eye me as I wavered, deciding whether to knock.

I wheeled around and plowed past her, right out the stage door toward those minty fields, to breathe and think and figure out what in the world I was up to.

CHAPTER
21

WINNIE

Curiosity may have killed the cat,
but it did all right by me.
—Helen Hayes, actress

The stage door slammed behind her and I stood there a moment. Gert angry—I was used to that, I would barely have blinked. This was different. This was Gert in a jumble.

I headed for backstage, as much to get away from Mother as to see if the Coles—one Cole in particular, if I was being honest—might like some company. Kit had gotten there ahead of me, of course, and she and Lucy ran off exploring. I sank down onto one of the old crates by Joe. "Not our best performance," I sighed, examining the bruise rising like a dirigible on my arm.

"Are you okay?" he asked. "You took some tough spills."

"Before vaudeville this would have made me cry," I said. "Now I barely notice. Except that this one is an interesting shape. Do you see it? The blood vessels must have broken from the impact of Gert's curved hand, and the surrounding tissue absorbed it in that distinct pattern."

I've been studying that first aid book too long, I thought. *I'm blathering on like a walking textbook.*

Joe's eyebrows went halfway up his forehead, and I cringed, knowing that girls usually try to act dumber than boys, not smarter. But then he smiled. "I'll bet you got all A's in science." I gave the tiniest shrug of admission. "Good for you!" he said. "Brains are what America is all about, after all. That's where the opportunities come from."

I felt my throat tighten with a sudden surge of emotion. He liked my brains! I didn't know there were any boys on the planet who felt that way, much less that I'd find one backstage at a vaudeville show. The only reply I could manage was a slightly strangled, "Thanks."

"Just don't fall and hit your head," he teased. "You have to protect all those smarts."

I certainly would try.

As we resumed our conversation, Joe's eyes followed Lucy, his face a kaleidoscope that rotated from concern to relief. "Are they supposed to be up there?" he fretted when she and Kit leaned from the catwalk and waved. And once he murmured, "She's so happy," as if this were unexpected, almost perplexing.

"Where did she learn to sing like that?" I asked, to distract him.

He stared into middle space, as if he couldn't remember, or perhaps didn't want to, and then said, "My father loved to sing."

Past tense.

There are only two reasons a person who once loved to do a particular thing doesn't do it anymore: something has made him stop loving it, or something has forced him to stop doing it. In either case, the reason is likely an unhappy one. I angled my response to spare him an explanation. "She has a beautiful voice. So strong for a young girl. It must come from her toes!"

"She's always been like that," he said. "When she was little and didn't get her way, she was as loud as a grown woman yelling at street urchins stealing from her clothesline."

"And you took piano lessons, so she would use those lungs for singing instead," I joked.

He smiled back, but it was a smile that makes you want to put your hand on the smiler's arm, or bring them a cup of tea. "I never took lessons," he said. "My father taught me."

His father is dead, I thought, *and it looks to be recent.*

"Was it the Spanish flu?" It wasn't something people talked about, but the loss seemed so freshly painful, I wondered if saying a few words about his father might help, like letting the blood flow from a wound for a moment or two, to sluice the dirt out before you bound it up tight.

Joe shook his head. "He drowned." His eyes caught on mine, and I couldn't look away.

"When?"

"January."

It had only been three months. "I'm so sorry," I murmured.

"What about your father—why isn't he with you?" asked Joe, and I told him about Dad's accident, our dire financial circumstances, and even about Harry's death. His warm gaze took in every word and gesture, inspiring me to reveal far more of our family's misfortune than was considered polite. But I didn't care. I wanted him to know.

"So you perform to pay your rent, not because you love the stage so much."

"Well, yes, I suppose that's true," I said. "But we've grown to like it."

"You've got a taste for the sound of applause now."

I smiled. "There are worse sounds."

"Like the sound of the landlord coming for the rent money," he said ruefully, and I guessed that he knew all too well what that sounded like.

"Yes," I said. "That's definitely worse."

CHAPTER

22

GERT

Just don't give up trying to do what you really want to do.
Where there is love and inspiration,
I don't think you can go wrong.
—Ella Fitzgerald, singer

"Where did you go when you left Wellsville?" I asked him. There was a grassy abandoned lot out behind the theatre, and we sat on an old stone wall eating dinner before the last show of the evening. His sandwich was made from thick slices of hard bread, a few pieces of cheese, and a couple of leaves of a dark green vegetable I couldn't place. Mine was whatever Winnie had handed me.

"I almost went back to Georgia. Almost gave up altogether."

"Because you were fired?"

He thought for a moment and shook his head. "'Cause I was angry."

"Angry enough to quit the business?"

"Just about."

"Would have been a shame," I said. "With all that talent."

"It was already a shame. A damn shame." He glanced over at me. "Beg your pardon."

I laughed. "Don't worry, I've heard worse."

He gave that little slow smile of his. "Is that right? And where's a girl like you hear such gutter talk, I'd like to know."

"J. J. Wiley's Pub and Café, Binghamton, New York, is where. The bar is about thirty feet long. Very popular with the after-work crowd. Also popular with the last-call crowd."

"You eat there a lot, do you?"

"No, I waitress there a lot."

"Oh." He dropped his eyes. "I'm sorry. I guess I . . . I guess I'm still working out . . . who you are exactly."

"No need to apologize. I'm still working out who I am exactly, too."

He chuckled. "I reckon we all are, in one way or another."

A silence came over us as we gazed at each other. A stillness. His eyes on mine.

Then after a moment he looked away. "I just went on to the next town," he said. "After Wellsville."

"What made you decide not to give up and go back to Georgia?"

"Couple things, I guess." I waited. I knew he would tell me if I just left room for the answer. "First, I got no home to go home to anymore. My aunt and uncle live on the road." He leaned back in his chair. "Second, all I know is tapping. What am I gonna do, start sharecropping? Can't even grow a weed.

"Third . . ." He looked over at me, checking to see if he could say what he was about to say next. "Third, the hell with him. The hell with all of them that just wants to put me down, keep me from doing what I know how to do."

I nodded. "The hell with every last one of them."

He laughed and shook his head. "And last of all. Last of all, I said to myself, I just need to keep finding the good people. I just need to meet one good person every place I go, and then I'll keep going. Like the Turner sisters, I told myself. If I keep finding Turners everywhere I go, I'm gonna be all right."

CHAPTER
23

WINNIE

People who throw kisses are hopelessly lazy.
—Bob Hope, actor and comedian

The next morning we came down to breakfast in the hotel dining room, which was mostly empty, it being late for breakfast and early for lunch. The windows were hung with heavy rose-colored curtains with gold satin cords. Midmorning sun poured in, and dust motes swirled lazily through the air as we waited for the sullen waitress to bring coffee. I held little Harry on my lap, leaning over every few moments to retrieve the spoon he liked to throw onto the floor.

"Sit with us!" Kit suddenly called out, and we turned to see Joe and Lucy Cole enter from the foyer. There was one unused chair between Kit and me, and she jumped up to purloin another from a nearby table. Lucy started to sit in the chair next to mine, but I saw Joe's hand slide to her shoulder and nudge her toward the one closer to Kit.

He wants to sit by me! I had to bite the inside of my cheek to keep from grinning.

Good mornings were said all around. Then Lucy said, "You all look so different!" It was true—we had never been in such close proximity without full stage makeup before. Surreptitiously I studied Joe's true skin color: olive toned, rather than the heavy orange of the pancake foundation we all used. He turned toward me, and seemed strangely startled, as if I'd said *boo!*

Then little Harry threw a spoon at him.

"Oh, Harry!" said Nell.

"No, it's all right," Joe insisted. Turning to Harry he said, "I'll make a little toy for you, sir, and then maybe you won't be so quick to throw things at me." He took a cloth napkin and knotted it twice, once in the middle, and once again over that knot, so the two remaining corners stuck up like rabbit ears. Harry reached for the little bunny, but Joe hopped it up Harry's arm until one of the "ears" tickled his cheek, making him squeal and bat his hand to try and grasp it. He finally got hold of it and let out a crow of victory. This set the whole table to laughing.

Joe let out a hearty laugh, too, and my heart nearly burst to see his sad face glow with humor. It was the best breakfast I could ever remember, and I hadn't had a thing to eat.

As we came offstage after the first show, I asked Mother if I should get the sandwiches again. "Yes, that's perfect," she said. "I'm about to land the last stitches in these new costumes, so I'd rather just buckle down and do it." She headed off with her sewing basket.

Gert gave me a look. We knew where she was going to "buckle down," and it wasn't our dressing room, a place she only visited to keep an eye on Harry when we were onstage.

"Hope those monkeys don't end up with our costumes," Gert muttered.

"Hope Mr. O'Sullivan doesn't ask her to make him a tuxedo," I said. Gert gave a smirk of accord, and headed back toward our dressing room. Or *someone's* dressing room, anyway.

Much as I wanted to leave Mother's friendship with Mr. O'Sullivan in the realm of snickering humor with Gert, it pestered me like a mosquito by my ear. What exactly did she *want* with him, anyway? I hoped it was merely adult companionship, new conversational subject matter, and mutual assistance (though he seemed to offer nothing as he reaped the benefit of her sewing skills and my sandwich runs). Actual infidelity was unthinkable. Wasn't it?

I needed to get away from the stuffy backstage and the ring of her girlish laughter. "I'm going out for sandwiches," I told Joe. "Can I get anything for you and Lucy?"

"I wouldn't want you to carry all that by yourself. Why don't I tag along and help?"

It was exactly what I'd hoped he'd say.

When we entered Miss Bell's, Joe looked at the prices on the tasseled menu and cut a look toward me that mirrored my own thoughts. "It's a little rich for my budget," he said quietly.

"It's a little rich for ours, too. But I'm ordering for Mr. O'Sullivan, and he gets a bigger paycheck than we do. Mother doesn't want to embarrass us by going somewhere cheaper."

"Would you mind if I stopped at the drugstore?" he asked.

"As it so happens, I'm going there myself."

At Dobbins Drugs, I bought myself a cheese sandwich and used the remaining few coins to purchase a small tube of tincture of iodine.

"Have you cut yourself?" Joe asked.

"No, I'm just putting together a little first aid kit, in case of emergency." As we headed back to the theatre, I told him about my job at Lourdes Hospital and my new first aid book.

"You'd make a good nurse," he said. He slowed in front of the park, which fairly glowed with budding trees and greenery. "Do we have a few minutes to sit in the sun?"

"We had such a nice big breakfast, I'm sure no one's starving yet." I certainly hoped that was true. But even if it wasn't—even if my sisters, Mother, and Mr. O'Sullivan were staggering around in a near faint from malnutrition—I don't think anything could have stopped me from accepting an invitation to sit on a park bench with Joe Cole.

He tipped his face upward, eyes half lidded in the sunshine. "This reminds me of home."

"You have a park like this?"

"Well, Boston has a lot of parks. But it doesn't remind me of that so much as how the old ladies pull their kitchen chairs out onto the sidewalks on the first warm days of spring. Or they put a pillow on the windowsill for a soft place to rest their arms."

It sounded like the North Side of Binghamton, the Seventh Ward, with the ladies in their windows, and the smell of onions and peppers wafting out. "Can I ask you a question?"

He turned his face from the late-afternoon light to look at me. "Sure," he said.

"I don't mean for you to take this as anything other than idle curiosity."

There was an echo of wariness in his "All right . . ."

"If your family is from Italy, why is your last name Cole?"

He laughed. "You had me worried for a minute!" He explained that the name had been Colella, but his father had changed it after he'd immigrated. "He couldn't get hired by anyone except other Italians, and they didn't always have the best business prospects themselves."

"What did your father do for work?" I expected that he must have been a fisherman since he'd surely been in water when he'd drowned.

"He was a delivery man for the Messina Fruit Company. He drove his cart all over Boston, taking produce to the markets." Joe's gaze settled on the middle space between us, remembering. "They always let him take his favorite horse from the company stalls. Her name was Cindy or Sandy—something silly like that, but he called her Dolcezza. It means 'sweetness'."

I felt the wave hit him. A longing that would never find relief.

He turned his head, jaw clenching against emotion. My throat tightened in vicarious sorrow, and I didn't trust myself to speak. All we could do was sit in the silent sunlight and wait for it to pass, knowing it would never truly pass completely.

We returned to the theatre, and Joe went off in search of Lucy and Kit to hand out their sandwiches. I found Mother with Mr. O'Sullivan, of course. As I gave them their meal I noticed that Mike and Mary were hunched over in the cramped cage, eating crackers and peanuts. "Have they been bad?" I asked.

"Your mother's more comfortable without them roaming around," Mr. O'Sullivan said, clearly more invested in Mother's comfort than that of his meal ticket. Just then, one of the orangutans let out an aggravated screech, and Mother flinched.

"Pipe down!" O'Sullivan yelled.

"You must have nerves of steel, Jackie," Mother said. "It takes a strong constitution to deal with jungle animals!" He smiled proudly, revealing those strangely too-white teeth.

I excused myself and headed for our dressing room, expecting to see both of my older sisters. But only Nell was there, cuddling little Harry against her shoulder as he slept.

"Want me to hold him so you can eat?"

"No, he's just fallen off," she whispered. "I don't want to risk waking him."

I took the sandwich from the paper wrapping and held it up. Nell nodded, and I put it to her lips so she could take a bite.

"Where's Gert?" I asked.

Nell lifted her free shoulder, a half shrug that said she didn't know.

"But you have an idea," I said.

Nell only held my gaze as she finished chewing.

"I just don't want anything bad to happen," I said.

She swallowed and whispered, "Gert isn't stupid."

"No. But you can lose your head about these things."

Nell raised an eyebrow as I gave her another bite of sandwich. I felt my cheeks go warm.

"I mean, *anyone* . . . a person could find themselves . . . ," I stammered.

She tried to hide her smile behind her chewing, but I could see her amusement.

I sighed. "He's very nice."

"Yes, he seems so," she said. "He seems responsible and gentlemanly and he certainly seems to enjoy your company."

"Really? Do you think so?"

"Winnie." Her tone was measured. "I know you're enjoying his company, too—which is lovely. But you understand it can only be short-lived. Sunday, we'll move on, and so will he."

I felt as if she'd struck me. I'd been so caught up in the excitement of getting to know him, I hadn't thought to consider the hand of time.

"Oh dear," Nell sighed. "I didn't mean to ruin your good mood. You'll just have to enjoy his friendship in the time you have left."

I nodded and smiled, a pathetic attempt at cheerfulness as dread overtook me. It was only after I left that I realized the emphasis she'd put on the word *friendship*.

"Are you going to Minty Millie's?" Joe asked me during intermission.

"I think so. Are you?" Willie "Watermelon" Lee had organized a group outing to a local watering hole to celebrate the halfway point in the show's run. Nell, Gert, and I had little interest, but then Mr. Lee had said, "I reckon your dear mother'll have to represent the family. She's bound and determined to be there." He shuffled off, and we cut our eyes to one another.

Tip happened to be there as we discussed whether one of us should go. "Why are y'all so worried about your mother?" he asked. "She's a grown woman. And I'm sure one of the menfolk will walk her back to your hotel."

There was really no way to answer this without blatantly impugning Mother's sense of decorum. After a moment of awkward silence, Tip raised his hands in surrender. "All right, y'all know the situation better than I do, 'specially since I never had a mother to speak of myself."

The change in Gert's face was imperceptible. Not a muscle shifted. Perhaps it's only because as sisters we share a common infinitesimal thread in the vast tapestry of humanity. Perhaps it's because we're so close in age, and her face has been in front of mine more than almost any other image. Either way, I knew as clearly as if she'd broken down and wept: her heart was stabbed with pain at the thought of Tip's motherlessness.

As for Minty Millie's, Nell had little Harry to look after, and Gert flatly refused. That left me as the lucky winner. But once I knew Joe was interested in going, I quickly revised my view.

"I'd like to go," he said, eyes flicking toward mine and then away again. "But I can't bring Lucy, and I don't want to leave her alone."

My pulse quickened at the thought of being out with him late at night. "Kit will be at the hotel," I said, the plan hatching in my mind only a step ahead of my words. "Lucy could stay in our room with Kit. And Nell will be right next door if they need anything."

"She would love that," he said.

And she did. "It'll be like a slumber party!" she said. I didn't have the heart to tell her that the party would likely only last about fifteen minutes before Kit fell into a snoring stupor.

Minty Millie's was ramshackle in a homely sort of way, rather than dirty or disreputable. The wooden booths were worn smooth, but clean. The rafters were lined with blue and lavender bottles that had once contained peppermint extract, adding a soft dusk-like color to the room.

Willie Lee insisted we go straight there from the theatre, and so we did our best to scrub up in the theatre restrooms, and trooped into Minty Millie's with vestiges of black liner around our eyes. Of all of us assembled there—Willie, O'Sullivan, Grayson, the tenor, Joe, Mother, and me—only Mother looked normal. The rest of us, caught between full stage makeup and clean faces, looked like escapees from a silent film.

"Didn't think you'd join us," Willie said to Mr. Grayson as the latter settled his wide bottom onto the end of the booth next to Joe and me. "Night air and all." He winked at O'Sullivan, who reciprocated with a low *heh, heh, heh.*

"I find this backwater town dreadfully boring," said Grayson. "Even the hotel bar is tedious. I can't wait to get back to the city."

"What city, Rochester?" said Willie.

Grayson gave a shudder of disgust in response, raised his finger and called, "Miss!"

Thus began the rounds of drinking.

Grayson took his Madeira from a tiny glass, as if sipping from a teacup. Yet he seemed to go through them rather quickly, shooting a finger skyward with a little circling motion over and over. Willie and O'Sullivan drank rye straight up, slamming their short glasses onto the table to indicate another round was in order. Joe would take a swig of his beer and then leave the mug on the table for a while before lifting it for another gulp.

Mother ordered sherry, and though she didn't drink quickly, I knew even a little could exacerbate the real source of potential indiscretion—her unquenchable desire for attention.

"Now where are those adorable monkeys of yours, Jackie?" she said, her lips pouty. "You didn't leave them at the theatre, did you?"

"Aw, they'll be all right. I'll just give the cage an extra good cleaning in the morning."

I winced at the thought of those poor creatures crammed into the tiny cage, trapped with their own refuse. I'd heard that stage animals were often abused and neglected, but it sickened me to learn of it personally.

"That's not right," Joe murmured. He was wedged rather close to me, Grayson taking up more than his share of the bench, and I could feel the warmth of his breath by my ear.

"I don't think he cares about them at all," I whispered back.

"What are you drinking?" he asked.

"Sarsaparilla." I might have liked to try a glass of sherry, just to feel more adult and womanly, but I didn't dare jeopardize my mission of keeping an eye on Mother by dulling my faculties. "Why?" I asked.

"No reason," he said. "It's just . . . your breath smells sweet."

Oh my goodness. The flip-flop my stomach did at that comment!

The night wore on. We learned that Grayson was from Manhattan. "Well, perhaps a tad outside."

"How far outside?" asked O'Sullivan.

"A bit."

"What's a bit?"

Grayson drained his latest glass of Madeira and let out a high-pitched giggle. "Jersey City!"

O'Sullivan slammed his hand on the table. "I'm from Brooklyn—we're neighbors!" This sent the two of them into gales of laughter.

Willie was from South Carolina, and though he'd been heckled in the north for his act, he insisted that "the darkies down south love it.

They *love* it. Now that's the best proof that there's nothing more than fun and entertainment to coon shoutin'. Them darkie-lovers up in Boston can kiss my hindquarters!" He quaffed down some rye and looked at Joe. "Where you from, kid?"

"Boston."

"Hell of a town," he said. "Wait a minute. You live anywhere near the flood?"

I felt Joe flinch beside me, and a prickle ran up my neck.

"Yeah."

"How close?"

Joe took a big swallow of his beer. "North End."

"Damn, son. You were right there, right where it happened!"

"Why, what happened?" said Mother, her voice overly enthusiastic and bright.

"Mother!" I muttered.

"Now don't you 'Mother' me, young lady! Let the boy answer!"

Joe took another swig.

Willie was too excited to wait for Joe's reply. "Damn anarchists blew up a huge molasses tank! Big ol' tower of molasses come roaring down the street like a tidal wave. Killed a bunch of people and horses. Terrible!"

I knew then.

Desperate to offer some sign of support, I reached for Joe's hand under the table. His hand was large and warm, and it locked onto mine.

"You know anyone who died?" Willie pressed on, too drunk to read the pain on Joe's face. "You musta knowed someone, living close like you did."

Joe squeezed my hand so hard he nearly broke my little finger.

"I need to use the restroom!" People at other tables turned to look at me.

"Well, my goodness, Winnie," said Mother. "You don't need to shout." Suddenly she was the proper one, and I was the one lacking in decorum.

Joe gave Grayson a shove, and the portly man nearly fell out of the booth.

"I'm heading back," Joe said. He tossed a couple of coins onto the table.

"I'll go back, too." Joe clearly needed a friend, and I told myself Mother would be fine.

Mother squinted at me. "I thought you had to use the powder room."

"Not *here*," I said, as if it had always been my intention to use the one at the hotel.

We were out the door in no time, and Joe strode so quickly I had to jog to keep up. In a few minutes we came to an intersection and I could see trees a few blocks down. "There's the park," I said, and tugged the sleeve of his jacket in that direction.

We collapsed onto the same bench that had been so sunny only a few hours earlier and let our lungs rest, the nighttime air cooling us.

"Thanks for getting me out of there," he said.

"He's an idiot."

"He didn't know."

"He's still an idiot," I said.

"True."

We were quiet for a while then, and it seemed perfectly natural, the two of us sitting in the darkened park in the middle of the night.

"I feel so good with you," he said finally. "I've been feeling so bad, feeling good is . . . I don't know. Confusing, I guess."

"Life is full of good and bad, all mixed up together."

By the light of the streetlamp, I could see his face relax. "You're pretty young for a philosopher."

I smiled. "I guess I should wait until I'm an old coot of nineteen, like you."

He turned to look at me, his face sad and happy, all mixed up together. "Mind if I put my arm around you?" he said. I moved into the crook of his shoulder, and he wrapped his arm behind me, resting his hand on my ribs.

If I die now, I thought, *if the Lord takes me right this minute, I will go to my reward feeling as good as any girl has ever felt in the history of the world.*

"I've been trying not to like you too much," he murmured.

"Why?"

"Because three days from now, I may never see you again."

There was a physical pain in my chest at his words, like someone clamping it in a vise. "I've been trying not to like you too much either," I said, "but not because of that."

"Why then?"

"Because I wasn't sure if you liked me."

I felt a little snort of laughter in his chest ripple into my back. "Trust me," he said. "I like you. Lucy's been teasing me for days."

"She has? How?"

"Yesterday when we came down to breakfast and I saw you up close for the first time without your makeup, Lucy kept pecking at me afterward. 'Why were you startled? What did you see?'"

"What *did* you see?"

"It's a little embarrassing."

"Tell me!"

"I said . . . well, without all the paint, your eyes are so green. They're like sea glass."

A tiny gasp of joy filled my lungs. He must have felt it, because he held me a little closer and murmured, "She keeps saying *'sea glass, sea glass'* at me whenever she thinks no one's listening."

My heart knocked against my chest like it might break right through my ribs.

"Winnie," he whispered. "Would it . . . would it be okay if I kissed you?"

I turned toward him, and he loosened his grip, only to tighten it again when I faced him. His lips brushed my cheek and landed gently on my mouth. My hand went up to his chest and I could feel the pounding of his own heart. I pressed my lips against his and then they seemed to part of their own accord. His lungs filled suddenly under my hand, a little gasp of pleasure.

No, I thought, this *is the best any girl has ever felt in the history of the world.*

And there wasn't a blooming lilac bush within miles.

CHAPTER
24

GERT

Perfect love is the most beautiful of all frustrations
because it is more than one can express.
—Charlie Chaplin, actor, writer, and director

That awful coon shouter had rounded up Mother, Winnie, and the others and made off for Minty Molly's or whatever the damn place was called. Little Harry wailed for his bedtime as Nell hustled Kit and Lucy along to the hotel.

Tip's dressing room door was almost closed, but not quite. I'd only meant to say good night, needed one last look at him, one last word between us, like some sort of silly schoolgirl mooning over the star basketball player. *You're being ridiculous*, I told myself. But I needed the sight of him like I needed air.

When I peeked through the narrow opening into his room he was standing in front of the rusty old mirror, staring into his muddled reflection. I could almost hear the words in his head. *What are you doing with that girl?*

What was he doing? And what was I doing?

In my own head, I called the whole thing off right then and there. There were a hundred different ways things could go bad, and it wasn't fair to him. It wasn't fair to either of us. I did not want to feel this way about a man I could never have, even if vaudeville would've torn us apart in three days anyway. I did not want to long for him when he was gone.

I stood there another moment, just long enough to take a breath and let it out, a silent ending to the whole hopeless thing.

That's when he turned and caught me.

"Gert." His voice was a murmur, almost a prayer. I couldn't help but put a finger to the door and nudge it open just a few more inches.

When he stepped back to let me in, his heel hit that monster of a trunk, and he went spilling backward, arms flying out behind him to try and stop his crashing fall. His cheek hit the arm of the chair as he went down, and blood bubbled up from the small gash. I was beside him in a heartbeat, clutching his thick muscular arm, helping him up as he muttered at himself.

"Are you all right?"

"Course I am." He pulled himself up to sit on the trunk. "Just clumsy."

"You're the least clumsy person I ever met. Let me see what I can find for that cut." I dashed next door to our dressing room, grabbed a little undershirt of Harry's, and went back to sit in the chair by him.

"Bring your face over here." I took his chin in my hand and dabbed at the cut. "It's not too big, but you might end up with a scar." A scar on that beautiful brown cheek. I hated the thought of it. "Let me just press it for a minute to make the blood stop."

My chair being higher than the trunk he sat on, our faces were at an even level and I'll admit I took the opportunity to really look at him. It was over, after all. This would be my last chance.

Slowly his hand rose to my arm that held his chin. His long fingers gently circled my wrist. His eyes watched me for any hint of hesitation.

Hesitation? It was all I could do not to slide into his lap and put my arms around him. This man who seemed to know me better than anyone—who loved my fearlessness but also saw my hidden softness. For whom I would've done anything, given anything.

"Tip," I breathed.

He closed his eyes for a moment, as if he were memorizing me.

Then he opened them and looked away. "It's late," he said. "I better walk you back to your hotel."

CHAPTER
25

WINNIE

By and large, jazz has always been like the kind of a man you wouldn't want your daughter to associate with.
—Duke Ellington, musician and bandleader

When Joe and I got back to the hotel, I waited until I was safely in my own room to lay both hands over my mouth and contain a silent squeal of happiness. His kisses—oh my! As my eyes adjusted to the dark, I saw Kit sprawled out as usual, both feet and one hand hanging from various edges of the bed. Dainty Little Lucy, true to her billing, was curled sweetly into a crescent around her pillow.

Further into the dimness was the bed I shared with Gert. It was as smooth and freshly made as we'd left it that morning, and Gert was nowhere to be found!

I had no idea of what to do, but I most certainly could not lie down and go to sleep. I headed back out into the hallway and down the stairs, with faint hope that she might be in the first-floor sitting room reading a book. Except Gert didn't generally like to read.

The sitting room was empty. My next hope was that if she was with Tip, they were tucked quietly into some corner of the hotel, hidden from the world, but findable by me. I moved silently through the downstairs, grateful that the hotel clerk had closed up the front desk and gone to bed himself. I searched and searched, but there was no sign of them.

Gert! I sent my thoughts out like rockets into the night, hoping they would land on her careless self. *Gertie, come back here right now. You're starting up a world of trouble!*

I went upstairs, in hopes of waking Nell without alerting Mother. I turned the knob and slid through the smallest possible opening of the door into the pitch-dark room.

"Mother?" Nell's voice was thick with sleep.

I slipped over toward the sound of Nell's voice. "No, it's only me," I whispered.

"Is Mother with you?"

I stared hard into the darkness to the bed where Mother should've been. "Isn't she here?"

Nell sat up. "I thought you were keeping an eye on her!"

"Well, I was, but then I left, and when I got back, Gert wasn't here, so I went to look for her, but I can't find her."

"Mother and Gert are *both* missing?"

I told Nell that I had searched the hotel. "I'll have to go out and look for them."

"Should we call the police?" she asked.

We both knew we couldn't do that unless we were willing to risk Tip going to jail. Or far worse. "You can't go out into the night alone," said Nell. "Who knows who's out there."

"I'll get Joe." Nell raised her eyebrows at me.

"You have another idea?" I said sharply.

"I'm just glad you two have become such good *friends* that you feel you can ask a favor as big as this. Now, when did you last see Mother?"

"At the bar with Jackie O'Sullivan." I winced at the thought. "She'd been drinking."

"*Why on earth did you leave?*" Nell had never spoken so harshly to me, and my face went warm with shame.

"It was a bit of an emergency."

"An emergency involving Joe Cole?" she said pointedly.

"I'll tell you all about it tomorrow. Right now, I'm going to get Joe and try to find Gert."

"I'll look for Mother," said Nell.

"She isn't in the hotel," I said. "I've searched all the public areas."

The thought struck us both at the same time. Nell's shoulders slumped. "I'll check O'Sullivan's room."

CHAPTER

26

GERT

There are three kinds of men. The one that learns by reading.
The few who learn by observation. The rest of them have to
pee on the electric fence for themselves.
—Will Rogers, actor, singer, comedian, and social commentator

We left through the stage door and out into the cool of midnight, my wrist still warm where his fingers had held it. He turned left toward Williams Street, but I turned right toward a little alley in back of the theatre.

"Hotel's this way, isn't it?" he said.

"Let's go a different route."

He stood there, broad chest rising and falling. "Gertie . . . ," he murmured, and shook his head.

Gertie. Only Winnie had ever called me that.

I turned and walked down the alley, praying—knowing—he would follow. In a moment he was in step next to me. The alley brought us out to another street behind the town. We walked in silence down the empty sidewalk past darkened houses.

We came to another street. "Your hotel's in the other direction," he said, but he kept walking beside me, as the houses got farther and farther apart with no streetlamps to light the way. We came to a baseball diamond, and I wanted to go and sit on the players' bench and maybe just talk for a while. Just be with him, away from prying eyes and peoples' opinions of what might or might not be right.

Tip stopped. "Gert," he said. "Where are we going?"

"Away," I said. "Can't we just go *away*, even for a little bit?"

He sighed. "Aw, Gertie. There's no such thing as 'away' enough for us."

He was right, of course. If word got out, we'd never work again, my family would be shamed and shunned, I'd be branded as some sort of deviant.

Tip, of course, would face far worse.

We might as well write our suicide notes right now, I thought. *That, or wait for Mother to save us the trouble and do the job herself.*

But there he was. Tip, the most beautiful man—the most beautiful soul—I'd ever known.

I took his hand in mine and pressed it up to my cheek. "I want there to be. I never wanted anything so much in my life."

"Lord, I want that, too," he breathed, his thumb stroking my cheek. "You are something, Gert Turner. Since you stood up for me back in Wellsville, I can't stop thinking about you. Can't stop wanting you by my side. But you got to understand. There is nothing in this for you. Nothing but trouble."

I took his hand from my face and let it drop. "Is that what you think? That I'm here with you in a strange little town in the middle of the goddamned night because I think there's something *in this* for me?"

"Well, why are you here, I'd like to know!" His voice was hard with doubt.

"You *know* why. And you know how you know? Because you're here for the same fool reason. There isn't anything *in it* for either of us, and yet here we are."

We stood there staring each other down, breath rising into the blackened sky.

Then he took my hand.

"Come on," he said softly, almost regretfully, as if he couldn't keep his body from rebelling against his mind's better judgment. "Let's go find 'away.'"

CHAPTER
27

WINNIE

Love is like playing checkers.
You have to know which man to move.
—Moms Mabley, comedian and singer

When Joe opened his door, his eyes flicked up and down the hall. "Winnie, what are you—?"

"Gert's missing," I whispered. "I'm so sorry to bother you, but I really can't go out looking for her in the dark by myself."

"You should call the police."

"I can't."

"Why can't—"

"I can't say why. If we find her, you'll know, but I can't tell you. Can you just trust me?"

In another moment we were hurrying down the hotel stairs and back out into the night. We headed to the theatre. The front doors were locked, as was the stage door. We picked our way through the weeds and old bottles along the back of the building, listening for voices in the dressing rooms. All we heard were the plaintive whines of Mike and Mary.

"O'Sullivan should be put in a cage himself," muttered Joe.

"And shipped to Africa," I added.

We searched the park and the few taverns that were still open, little by little making our way toward the outskirts of town. There was a baseball diamond, and I thought maybe they'd gone to sit on the players' bench, but it was empty. I sat down, wobbly with fatigue, nearly hopeless that we'd find her, and scared about what we might see if we did.

"Are you ready to call the police now?" asked Joe as he slumped down onto the rough wooden bench beside me.

I was ready to call out the National Guard, except that I couldn't. If she was with Tip—and where else would she be?—I couldn't jeopardize him by alerting the authorities.

"Winnie, I don't mean to pry, and maybe I'm all wrong . . . but I've noticed your sister has struck up a . . . a friendship with the tap dancer."

I nodded. "We met him a couple of weeks ago in another town. He was very nice to us."

"Is it possible . . . I mean, are you worried that he might have . . . ?"

"No! Tip's not like that." I sighed. "If anything, it's Gert."

His face fell. "Has she been known to . . . ?"

"No. I mean, she likes men, and men certainly like her. But she's a good girl." *As far as I know,* I thought, because now I wondered how far she might go to have something she wanted.

"Sometimes a man will take a woman's attention the wrong way," said Joe, "and assume she's thinking things she isn't thinking."

I looked up at him. Was he thinking things *I* wasn't thinking? After all, here I was alone in the middle of the night with a man I'd met only three days ago. Who could say what that might lead him to assume?

"I don't mean me," he said quickly.

"I believe you're honorable, Joe." I did believe it, but I also dearly hoped I was right to.

"I am," he said. "More than ever. I'm the man of the family now." His words were filled with anxiety and pride in equal measure. "Lucy and my mother are my responsibility. Everything I do, I have to think of them first, just like my father always did."

I thought of my own father, who went to a job he disliked every day (until, of course, he couldn't) and put up with Mother's schemes and our bickering, and any number of other aggravations, to try and give us a decent home and a chance at happiness. It made me wonder what kind of life he would have chosen if he hadn't had us to consider.

"Were there things your father might have liked to do that he couldn't?" I asked.

Joe sighed. "He wanted to be a farmer. He grew up on a farm in Sala Consilina, and loved growing things. But my mother was from Salerno, and she had heard stories of women going to live on the plains and being so bored and lonely and exhausted from all the hard work. She only agreed to marry him and move to America if he promised she could live in a city."

"That must have been a disappointment for him."

He smiled. "Not really. He found a way to keep his word and have his farm, too. He put some money down on a piece of land west of Boston, in a little town called Belham. He took the train out there every Sunday and tended his garden. He hoped that someday she might be willing to live there, and he would build her any kind of house she liked."

Sadness swept over him, and me, too. "Did you have to sell it when he died?"

"I should have. Everyone told me to. My mother wouldn't think of going there now, and there's still money owed on it." He pulled in a heavy breath and let it out slowly. "I couldn't, though. I just couldn't. I went with him most Sundays to help with the garden, and he taught me all he knew. At first I loved it because I was with him, but I suppose over time I came to love growing things, too. When I'm there, it feels like he's with me." He shook his head. "Vaudeville was the only way I could think of to pay for it. But of course, it broke my mother's heart all over again that we had to leave her to save his dream—and mine. " He'd been pulled in more directions and known more tragedy than anyone his age should have to face. I squeezed his hand in sympathy.

Off in the trees I heard a soft murmuring, and at first I thought there might be a stream nearby. I stood up and walked a few yards toward the sound. Voices. A flash of blond in the trees beyond left field. A tinkle of laughter.

Joe stood beside me, his face suddenly hard. "I'm going to leave now. You can walk back with your sister."

"Why?"

"So I won't have to lie if anyone asks what I know." There was a chill to his voice, and he left without another word.

I headed toward the edge of the field, disconcerted by his reaction. True, it was almost unheard of for whites and coloreds to pursue a romantic involvement—even friendships weren't all that common. But was it truly wrong?

When I crossed into the cool darkness of the pines, I saw them. They were about fifty feet away, too far to hear their words, but close enough to see the gibbous moon outlining their features. I pressed against a tree trunk to give myself a moment to come up with what to say.

I should be angry, I thought. *I should yell at her and say she'd had us all worried and she should come back to the hotel right now and apologize.*

But I wasn't angry. I was strangely sympathetic, and in my confusion over what I should have felt and what I did feel, I stood motionless and simply watched them.

Gert stood with her back against a tree, her chin tipped up to look squarely into Tip's face. Then she reached out and took Tip's hand in hers, holding it loosely, their fingers slowly entwining. The flat plane of his high-boned cheek rounded into a smile.

I must have seen black skin touch white skin sometime in the course of my seventeen years, but I couldn't have told you when. I might have seen a white man shake a colored man's hand, or I might not. But I'll say one thing with utmost certainty: I had never seen a colored man lace his fingers with a white woman's. Ever.

With her other hand, Gert reached up and cupped that round, brown cheek. Tip shook his head just a little, but not hard enough to dislodge her. His chest rose and fell more quickly as she slipped her fingers around to the nape of his neck and seemed to pull him closer.

They looked at each other for a long time then, bodies swaying slightly. He began to say something, shaking his head again in that slow, sorrowful way. And quick as a lightning strike, she pulled him toward her, his lips against hers. His hand shot out to the tree trunk to brace himself against the forward motion of his own impulses, but he didn't pull back.

That kiss was infinitely tender. I'd certainly never seen my parents kiss like that, nor had I seen anything quite like it in the movies, where the hero always seemed to slam his lips against the heroine's in a conquering fashion. This was no conquest.

If anything it was like a slow, sweet dance, two people drifting, unaware of the dance floor or the music or possibly the entire world. I'd seen Gert flirt and dance and kiss boys before, but I had never witnessed anything like the softness she offered up under the branches of that pine.

Tip's bracing arm loosened and his body moved toward hers until he was holding her. A colored man's arms around my sister's very white shoulders, her arms around the back of his very black neck. And no matter what I'd been given to believe about how wrong this should be—how vile and punishable—I could find nothing but sweetness in it.

An engine hummed and rattled, headlights flickering along the road that ran behind the stand of pines. They tensed stock-still for a moment, then he pressed himself against her, covering her blond hair with his large black hands, his coloring far better camouflage than hers.

My heart pounded with anxiety at the enormity of it. Strangely, it wasn't my own sister I worried about. Gert's reputation would be ruined if their attachment were ever revealed, of course. But in my experience Gert could handle just about anything that was thrown at her.

It was Tip my soul quaked for. Because no matter how tender the scene I had just witnessed, there was no way this could go on. A colored man's hands on a white woman's body was intolerable to a great many people, and grounds for any number of hideous, unthinkable acts.

It could very quickly and easily be the death of him.

CHAPTER
28

GERT

I ain't afraid to love a man. I ain't afraid to shoot him, either.
—Annie Oakley, sharpshooter

I never knew a kiss could feel like that. It was all give. No take. From either of us. I suppose when there's no future and nothing to gain, the only reason to kiss another person is simply because you want to. Need to.

His lips. His arms around me. His body pressed against mine to shield me from those headlights.

"Gert."

I heard her voice a ways off and I knew. We both did.

He kissed me again, and said, "Go on now. I'll see you tomorrow."

He slipped away in the opposite direction. I stood there a moment, watching him go, then turned and walked toward her.

"You won't say anything," I said as we trudged across the outfield toward the road.

"Of course not."

"But you're scandalized." Good-girl Winnie. I was certain she was.

"Not really."

I eyed her, looking for the lie, but she kept walking.

"Mother must be in fits," I said.

"Mother has no idea."

"Thanks for keeping it from her, then."

"She wasn't there to hear about it," said Winnie. "With any luck, Nell's found her by now, and gotten her back to their room."

"*Found* her?"

"We think she may have gone off with O'Sullivan."

"Weren't you supposed to be watching her?"

She stopped and turned to face me. "Are *you* criticizing *me*? Because last I looked, no one had to stay up half the night searching over hill and dale for *me*."

I glared back, but she was right and we both knew it. She started walking again, and I had to hurry to catch up. "Thanks for not calling the police."

"I would never do that to him."

We were walking quickly now, turning onto Water Street, and I hoped she didn't hear the hitch in my voice when I murmured, "Thank you."

Upstairs, Winnie tapped on Nell's door. It opened quickly and we slid inside. Mother was asleep in her bed, snoring like a half-strangled tuba. The collar of her shirtwaist peeked out from under the blanket; she was still in her street clothes.

"Where was she?" I asked.

"Where were *you*?" Nell retorted. She was sharper these days, now that she wasn't quite so sad. I almost liked her better before.

"She was out, Nell," said Winnie. "Let's leave it at that. Where did you find Mother?"

"Mr. O'Sullivan's room. They were sound asleep, he on his bed, she in the chair."

I let out a sigh, but Nell didn't look as relieved as I felt. "What?" I asked.

"Her shoes were off." This seemed harmless enough until Nell added, "Her chair was pulled up next to the bed, and her feet were on his lap, as if he'd been . . . rubbing them."

My stomach turned. "That's disgusting."

Winnie winced and shook her head. "At least it's not adultery."

"No, it's not," said Nell. "Though I suppose it could have progressed to that if they hadn't had so much to drink."

Mother inhaled a huge snort, and let it out with a whoosh. I wanted to slap her—she was a married woman, for cripes' sake! But who was I to judge? I was doing something far more despicable in many peoples' eyes.

"She's just lonely," Nell sighed. "And having your feet rubbed is nice."

We stared at Nell. Clearly there was a whole world of bodily contact we single girls could only begin to imagine.

"Listen," said Nell. "You two are becoming women. It's all terribly important in the moment. I remember. I remember very well." She crossed her arms over her nightdress. "But you're taking risks we can't afford."

She was right, of course, and I'd known it long before she said so. Which doesn't mean I felt regret. I didn't. But I nodded all the same.

We went back to our own room, undressed, and slid quietly into our bed. I couldn't sleep, though. I couldn't stop thinking about Tip, and the absolute rightness of his arms around me, in the face of everyone else in the world thinking it was so wrong.

And Winnie—she could do whatever she wanted with that piano player! She could run off with him when she was supposed to be watching Mother, and no one scolded her. He could be a Bolshevik for all we knew, and it didn't matter one bit. His skin wasn't as pale as ours, but it was light enough to make him A-okay. The unfairness of it, the loss I could see barreling down on me like an avalanche, it made me lash out.

"It's so easy for you," I hissed into the darkness. "You can sit in the park and canoodle all day long, and everyone thinks it's cute—not an attack on all that's holy."

"I know."

"Yes, but you don't care, do you!"

I knew it wasn't true. It was hardly even the point.

"Gert," she said. "I let the pigeons out."

"What?"

"Pepper's pigeons. After they got him fired, I opened the cage and let their birds loose."

"You didn't!"

"They deserved it after what they did."

"Won't Tip smile when he hears!" I could barely wait to tell him. Little Winnie—doing something so dastardly! "Wish I'd done it myself."

"You would've if you'd had the chance."

She was right about that, of course. I would've done anything to even the score. But I hadn't. And Winnie had.

I don't cry much, and I certainly don't weep and wail like other girls do. I kept it quiet, but I suppose she could feel the tremors in the mattress.

"Oh, Gertie."

"There's nothing I can do for him," I whispered. "Nothing at all."

"Hey, sleepyheads!" Kit's voice roared above us. I blinked and my eyeballs felt as if they'd been dragged through sand. Winnie waved her arm like she was fending off an intruder.

"What's with you two?" boomed Kit. "It's almost noon!"

We dragged ourselves out of bed and splashed water on our faces, still speckled with yesterday's makeup. "Go on down and eat without us," I grumbled at Kit.

"Lucy and I had breakfast hours ago, all by ourselves!" Her glee was like a tin horn in my ear. "Joe didn't get up, either—Lucy called him Rip Van Winkle."

No one said much as we hurried through breakfast. Mother didn't even come down, saying Harry needed a bit more sleep, and she'd meet us at the theatre. Joe joined us briefly, but only drank coffee and tucked a roll into his pocket as he left.

"What's with him?" I murmured to Nell.

"He was out late with Winnie, looking for you."

Winnie looked like she'd been socked in the stomach. He'd been cold, but he'd sat with us, which he wouldn't have done if he'd been disgusted with me and hated Winnie for dragging him into it. "He'll be back," I said to Winnie, and Nell nodded.

"How do you know?"

How did I know? I just knew. "He doesn't seem . . . done."

"He sure *looks* done," Winnie muttered, voice quavering from holding back tears.

"No, he looks unsettled," I said. "Unsettled is good. Just don't go running after him."

We went upstairs to change. In all the previous night's distractions, Winnie and I hadn't rinsed and hung up our costumes, as we did every night. They were wrinkled and smelled like we'd worn them on an expedition to find the Northwest Passage.

"Mother said we're to wear the new costumes she made," said Nell, handing them out, and I felt a feeble thrill at the idea of new clothes. But when I put it on, it was clear Mother had made a mistake cutting the fabric. The skirts were well above our knees.

But that wasn't the only problem. Winnie's costume barely fit at all.

"I've gained weight," she said miserably.

"Only in certain places," I said. Her breasts were still small, but pressed into the new outfit, it was easy to see that they had bloomed. She nudged me away from the mirror over the washstand and stared in horrified wonder.

Nell came in wearing her new costume. "It's practically indecent!" she said, tugging down the skirt. "Mr. Ohmann might very well throw us out. He's not running a burlesque show."

I'd never noticed just how long Kit's legs were before I'd seen them with so little coverage. Surprisingly, she was the least bothered by it. "The stagehands always say if we showed more leg, we'd get a bigger reaction."

That silenced our complaints in a hurry. "My goodness," said Nell, chuckling. "We've become applause hounds. Maybe we should just go out in our corsets."

"Eva Tanguay doesn't wear much more than that," said Kit, "and she makes over three thousand a week!"

We headed to the theatre, coats tightly buttoned. Mother soon arrived and explained she'd run short on fabric. "You look fine," she said, waving us away, anxious to take up her spot with O'Sullivan, I supposed. "They're only a few inches shorter."

"Mother, look at my seams!" Winnie said. "They're pulling apart like zipper teeth!"

Mother squinted at Winne's torso as if it were an acquaintance she couldn't quite place. "Winnie," she said, "I do believe the Good Lord has finally seen fit to grant you some bosoms!"

Kit burst into cackling laughter. Nell smiled at the baby as if he'd just made a joke of some kind. I crossed my arms and put a hand up to my chin, fingers over my lips to cover the wicked grin behind them. Then that foot-rubbing O'Sullivan stuck his head in our doorway. "What's all the giggling and carrying on about?" he said, grinning. "I can hear it clear down the hall!"

Winnie bolted.

CHAPTER 29

WINNIE

I do not like vaudeville, but what can I do? It likes me.
—Anna Held, actress and singer

Just then, Joe entered at the far end of the hallway, and I was not about to face him in my current state of humiliation. I ducked into the nearest open door: Tip's dressing room.

The room was empty and I slipped behind the door to hide. Everyone laughing at me like I was some sort of freak in a circus! I felt hot tears slip from my eyes, and it made me even angrier!

I stood there heaving and snuffling and trying to get hold of myself. My eye caught on Tip's enormous battered trunk, pocked and scarred with years of wear.

Tip. He knew how I felt. People looked at Negroes and snickered or told coarse jokes all the time.

All the time.

And here I'd only had to put up with it once in all my seventeen years.

I calmed myself with a deep, shuddering breath, and ran my fingertips under my eyes to wipe away my tears and indignation.

When I went back to our dressing room, only Nell and Gert were there, and I glared at them a moment until Nell said, "Oh, Winnie, I'm sorry. Mother can be so . . ." We all knew how Mother could be.

"I told her she's got to find some fabric scraps and put panels in along your seams," Gert said. "How can you work like that, for cripes' sake?" It wasn't like Gert to take up my cause, and I didn't know what to make of it at first. But after a moment it came to me: pigeons.

"Joe came by looking for you," said Nell.

"Should I—?"

"No!" said Gert. "He can work a little harder than that."

"What if he came by to say that he never wants to speak to me again?"

They looked at each other. "First of all," said Gert, "if that's what he's after, he can *definitely* work a little harder. Second of all, that's not what he's after."

"Well, what *is* he after then?"

Gert shrugged. "Who knows? Let him hunt for you and say so himself. For now, you just sit here with us."

The day took a turn for the better, then, as my sisters told me stories and mishaps of their early romantic careers. These included such scandalous episodes as necking behind the cigar factory and coming home reeking of freshly rolled tobacco; riding in Bobby McDonough's jalopy at breakneck speed from the top of the Park Avenue hill, hitting a bump in the road and nearly being pitched from the car; and late-night swimming in drawers and corset in Quaker Lake. These were Gert's tales, of course, but Nell told one about smoking her first cigarette with Harry and throwing up in his mother's primrose hedge, which shocked and delighted us.

It felt wonderful to say Harry's name with smiles on our faces rather than tears for once.

When the stage manager gave us the five-minute warning, we made our way to the wings, passing Joe and Lucy backstage. "Chin high," whispered Gert, and I sent mine skyward.

Buoyed by good spirits, and by the cheers and hoots I could only attribute to our newly abbreviated skirts, we gave one of our best performances yet. Despite the difficulties of the past twelve hours, I felt happy and proud to be a Tumbling Turner.

Until my costume exploded.

It was our last stunt, the tree of sisters, and I climbed onto Kit's shoulders as I had countless times before. Only this time, when I shot my arms into the air, I felt a sudden release from the compression of the tight costume. The left seam had split all the way down my ribs, and the top of the outfit flapped open, completely exposing my left breast.

The roar of approval from the gallery gods, those young men who inhabit the cheap seats in every theatre in America, was deafening. You would've thought that one lone tea saucer's worth of skin was an entire chorus line of burlesque showgirls, for all the libido it stirred. Ladies in the front rows gasped in horror, as did a few gentlemen, though I saw some grins, too.

I grabbed up the front of my costume, teetering wildly, and Kit groaned with the effort of keeping us all upright. My sisters had no idea of the reason for the audience's wildly opposing reactions, and I had to yell, "Get me down, *get me down*!" above the wall of noise before they understood that something had gone terribly wrong.

I leapt to the boards, holding up my costume, and ran for the wings. Standing squarely in my way was Joe, his face wide with surprise. I tried to bolt past him, but he whipped off his suit jacket and caught me in it. He wrapped it around me like a blanket and hustled me back toward the dressing room, past the smirking stagehands, his arm tight around my shoulders.

Once we got there, of course, we had no idea what to do. He stood there, fist bunched around the front of the jacket, holding it closed. We looked at each other. His face went red and he looked away. But then his eyes came back to mine, a sheepish grin blooming on his face. "That was some showstopper," he chuckled.

"It's not funny!" I said, but I had already begun to laugh, too.

In another moment, my sisters and mother were upon us, and Gert said, "Thanks, Joe. We'll take it from here." They crowded around me, the jacket was slipped from my shoulders, and when the door closed, he was no longer in the room.

During intermission, Kit ran back to get Mother's sewing basket and a skirt and shirtwaist for me to wear. After I was properly attired, Nell and I took Harry for a walk to the park and let him scramble about in the grass. He was almost nine months old now and loved hanging on to the park bench where we sat, working his way from one end to the other, our hands at the ready to catch him if he fell.

"He'll be walking before we know it!" I said, and testing the strength of our newfound willingness to say his name, I added, "Wish Harry could see him."

I watched carefully, but Nell's breath didn't catch in her chest. "I like to think he can," she said. "I like to think he's helping me." Her soft brown eyes pierced my own. "I'm beginning to see that the love's still there, Winnie. Even when everything else is gone."

She glanced past my shoulder, a little smile crossed her lips, and she patted my hand.

A shadow passed over us and I looked up to see curly hair in silhouette.

"Hello, Joe," said Nell. "That was a nice bit of swashbuckling you did, saving Winnie from the gaping masses. Douglas Fairbanks would've been impressed." She stood and pulled the baby up into her arms. "Nap time for you, my little traveler."

My heart pounded as she walked away, but then I remembered Gert's words: *Unsettled is good.* And I tried to imagine that perhaps Joe was even more nervous than I was.

"Uh, mind if I . . ." He gestured to the empty end of the bench.

"Go right ahead." I tried to affect an offhanded, yet not entirely inhospitable tone.

"So." He kneaded the palm of one hand with the thumb of the other. "Last night . . ."

"I can't be held responsible for who my sister cares for!" I blurted out.

He blinked at me, startled. "She *cares* for him?"

"Of course she cares for him. Why else would she be out in a forest in the middle of night with him?"

"Well, I . . ." His thumb dug deep into that palm, mining for understanding. "But he's . . ."

"Colored. Yes, I'm aware."

"Winnie," he said slowly. "They can't be together. It's not even legal in a lot of places. Do you have any idea of what will happen to him if—"

"Of course I do. But what can you do when you can't stop caring for someone, even if you know there's no future in it—not even next week?"

That brought us both up short.

He stopped his palm-kneading, and his hands dropped between his knees. I bit the inside of my cheek, the pain distracting me from the anguish of my own words.

Not even next week.

"I guess you make the best of the time you have," he said quietly. "And try not to get killed."

The warm nights had given confined spaces no time to air out or cool off, and performers were less inclined to remain in the claustrophobic little dressing rooms. Mother and Mr. O'Sullivan started taking walks, as she said the intensifying smell of orangutans made her woozy. Even Mr. Grayson, the tenor, had thrown caution to the balmy breeze, returning with only minutes to spare before his last performance of the night. A silly little half smile had replaced his usual sour expression. I was sitting with Joe backstage and we glanced to each other.

"Hello there, children," Grayson said, and gave a jaunty two-fingered salute.

"There you are!" said Albert, the stage manager. "Two minutes, Mr. Grayson."

Grayson gave his shirt cuffs a tug, then placed his fingers to his throat. "La-la-la, lo-lo-lo, lu-lu-luuuuuu. Ha!" he chortled. "That's a lulu!"

"Is he . . . ?" I murmured to Joe.

"He's definitely had a few." We went to hide behind one of the leg curtains to watch Grayson's performance. He stood a little closer to the footlights than was entirely safe, and belted out his first few songs with less technique and more volume than usual. The audience, however, seemed to appreciate the sheer muscularity of his voice, and he got more applause than he had all week. This caused him to sing with even greater abandon, arms flung wide and high.

His last song was "I Wonder Who's Kissing Her Now," and in prior performances he'd enunciated the words far too crisply to convey any believable sadness that the girl he loved was canoodling with another. That night, however, you might have believed that she'd been kidnapped and beaten into performing unspeakable acts. Grayson clenched his hands in front of his chest and sang with a cry in his voice we'd never heard before.

I wonder who's kissing her now, I wonder who's teaching her how,
Wonder who's looking into her eyes, breathing sighs, telling lies;
I wonder who's buying the wine, for lips that I used to call mine.
I wonder if she ever tells him of me, I wonder who's kissing her now.

As the song went on, we noticed that the guillotine curtain behind him was billowing erratically. "What is that?" I said, and we took a few steps toward the back to peek behind it.

To our dismay, Mike and Mary, the orangutans, were the cause of the disturbance! Mike had on his little shirt, but no pants, and Mary's dress hung from one shoulder. She'd evidently gotten into the tasty lipstick she liked so well, because her mouth was smeared with it.

"We'd better round them up," said Joe.

It was precisely the wrong thing to do. As soon as we approached, they ran, skittering around the far end of the curtain and right out onstage. Grayson had no idea why the audience gasped in surprise, as the apes began to toddle around behind him. Joe and I whispered their names from stage left, and of course they headed away from us, making for the front of the stage.

Grayson's eyes were closed as he strained to project up into the farthest rafters. "*I wonder who's kissing her now. I wonder who's teaching her how!*" Mary sat down next to him, dress askew, and proceeded to lick hungrily at her lipstick, pink tongue lapping around her protruding reddened mouth. It looked like a lecherous enactment of the song, and the howls of laughter from the audience were nearly deafening.

Mike stood on Grayson's other side waving his long, hairy arms around, which seemed to mimic Grayson's grand gesturing, and the audience screamed even louder with hilarity. Joe and I could hardly keep from laughing ourselves, and the stagehands were completely doubled over.

"*I wonder who's kissing her*—" Grayson sucked in a bellyful of air for the last note, and flung his arms wide, hitting Mike squarely in the face with the back of his hand. The orangutan let out an aggrieved yell and batted at Grayson, who finally opened his eyes and realized that he was sharing the stage with two half-clothed apes.

Grayson let out a shriek that could have shattered glass. Mr. O'Sullivan, just back from a stroll with Mother, ran onstage to corral his animals, causing them to jump off the stage into the orchestra pit, knock over music stands, and head for the theatre aisles. Patrons began to hurry for the doors, leaving them open for Mike and Mary's final escape.

Grayson, meanwhile, had collapsed onstage in a half-drunken faint, and Joe and I ran to his aid. "Turn him on his side!" I yelled above the commotion that continued around us.

"What? Why?" Joe yelled back.

Assume command of the situation, my first aid book had said in the section titled "The First Thing to Do." *There can be only one chief.*

"Just do it!" I said.

We heaved the rotund man onto his side and turned his cheek to the floor just in time for him to vomit voluminously all over the boards. The stagehands heading toward us stopped in their tracks and sent up a chorus of disgusted groans, while down in the seating area, Mr. Ohmann implored exiting patrons to, "Remain calm! Please take your seats and *remain calm!*"

I generally don't curse, but there's really no other way this can be adequately expressed: it was one hell of a night.

"Do you think he's okay?" I asked Joe. We were back at Minty Millie's, this time blissfully alone.

"If being drunk and frightened were a medical condition, they'd run out of hospital beds in no time at all. Geneva General's just keeping an eye on him for a few days."

"I wish he were nearby so I could check on him."

Joe smiled and took a sip of his beer.

"What's so funny?" I asked.

"You act like he's your patient."

"Well, I did keep him from suffocating in his own vomit."

"Probably saved his life."

"Do you really think so?"

"You know it even better than I do! All I can say is you better make your money and get back to school. The world needs quick-thinking nurses like you." I had told him about my hopes of going to college only that afternoon.

"I'm not sure if I want to be a nurse, though."

"Whatever you want to be, Winnie, you'll be swell." His gaze shifted to the wooden clock over the bar. "Will your mother worry that you're out this late?"

After the police had shown up, most of us had headed back to the hotel. Except for Mr. Grayson, of course, who'd begged to be taken straight to Mount Sinai Hospital in New York City. And except for Mr. O'Sullivan, who was charged with some sort of crime involving the mishandling of wild and vicious animals. Mother had gone directly to bed with a cool cloth over her eyes. Gert said she was going out. Neither Nell nor I bothered to ask where or with whom.

"No," I told Joe, "Mother won't worry at all."

CHAPTER
30

GERT

It is no disgrace to be a Negro, but it is very inconvenient.
—Bert Williams, comedian, actor, pantomimist, and singer

Bert Williams was the funniest man I ever saw
and the saddest man I ever knew.
—W. C. Fields, comedian and actor

"How old are you?" I asked Tip. We sat in a buggy in an old cart shed we'd happened upon at the edge of town. An almost-full moon shined in through one of the windows.

Age wasn't something I generally cared about, because it often didn't mean anything. Sometimes I felt ageless altogether.

But it was Thursday—actually it was the wee hours of Friday—and our time was quickly coming to an end. I found myself wanting to know everything I could about him.

"Twenty-four," he said. "You?"

"Eighteen."

I could see his eyes trace over me, considering. "You seem older."

"I am older," I said. His cheeks rounded into that slow smile, and he squeezed my hand a little tighter. "When's your birthday?" Another useless question I needed the answer to.

"October fourteenth. Least that's what my aunt says."

"You have reason to doubt her?"

He chuckled. "Oh no. I'd never risk my life by doubting a woman as strong-minded as my aunt." He shifted and tucked me into the crook of his broad shoulder, and I suddenly felt safer and happier than I could ever remember feeling.

"My mother died when I was born. They were young, just teenagers, and she was the only girl my father ever loved. It was the worst day of his life, and he didn't dignify it by wishing me a happy birthday, so I was never quite sure when it was."

"But your aunt knew."

"I reckon she guessed. Said she was digging peanuts for extra money when she heard, so it woulda been September, October, thereabouts. She picked out the fourteenth herself, so she'd know when to bake a cake."

October 14. I tucked this little shred of information away like it might somehow be useful, although I knew it never would be. How could it?

"How did he die?" I whispered.

He shook his head. "You don't want to know 'bout that."

"I want to know everything about you."

He looked down at me. Put a hand up to my cheek and stroked it with his thumb. "It's a sad story," he said. "Too sad."

"Tip," I murmured. "We're right in the middle of a sad story of our own, aren't we? If I can handle this, I can handle anything."

He pulled in a long breath and let it out.

"He had a still, you know, to make liquor. Used to sell it to the local bars and such. He got an order to make a delivery for a party in one of the big houses, which he never done before. He thought it might be the start of a better line of business. That's what he said to me 'fore he left. '*A better line of business.*'"

Tip's voice was thick with bitterness, and he didn't say anything for a moment or two. I waited, bracing myself.

"He got there, and it was a bunch of white boys, young bulls, no parents around. And they didn't have no money, or if they did, they weren't of a mind to pay. They took the liquor, and he . . . well I guess he wanted his money."

"But they didn't give it to him."

"No."

I had to know the end. I had to know this about Tip. "What did they do?"

His breathing was hard, I could feel it by my ear and against my body as he held me.

"They tied him up to the back of his own cart and drug him through the dirt till he died."

"Oh, Tip," I breathed. "Oh, honey, I'm so sorry. How did you find out?"

"They drug him home. Cut the rope and took off in the cart. Laughing. I was eight years old, my father's body lying in front of me, all broken and bloody. And they were laughing. I heard them."

I curled myself into his lap and held him so tight, and I would've given myself to him right there in the dusty old carriage if he'd wanted. But I'd reopened the deepest kind of wound with my prying, one he'd likely never spoken of in all the years since it happened, and it was all he could do to just keep breathing.

After a while, when the worst of it had passed, he surprised me with his own prying question. "Gertie," he whispered. "What is it you want most in this world?"

"Everything," I said, gazing up at him. "I want everything."

He chuckled and gave me a little squeeze. "Specifically. You want to be a star? You want to be a rich lady with a big house? What?"

I didn't care about stardom, though I'd come to like performing more than I ever thought I would. And fancy things didn't excite me that much. "I want the same things you want—to be able to go wherever I like, and do whatever it is I'm good at. And I want to meet interesting people, and stay up all night if I feel like it, without anyone telling me it's time to go to bed. I want the freedom to make my own choices."

"Money helps with that."

"Money helps with everything." My gaze shot up to him. "Almost."

"Almost." He smoothed a curl away from my eye.

"I want to love whoever I want to love," I whispered.

His gaze, so sweet and sad, wrapped its tender arms around my soul. "I already do love who I love," he said. "Just can't do nothing about it."

CHAPTER
31

WINNIE

I never approved of talkies. Silent movies were well on their
way to developing an entirely new art form.
—Lillian Gish, actress

The next morning Mr. Ohmann sat in the front row staring up at us, pale and weary. "In all my years in the business," he said, "I have never seen such a calamitous series of events as were visited upon me yesterday." He took a puff of his cigar, and we waited to hear if he'd shut down the show and send us all home with half our pay.

"With the headliner in jail, his act on the way to a zoo, and another act in the hospital, we're down to about half a show. I've decided to put you all in the first half, and run a full-length flicker after intermission." He shook his head in disgust. "Of course, the only film I have on hand is one I personally find distasteful. But it's a few years old, and I'd guess most people have already seen it. Damn thing's over three hours long, so if they haven't, most won't stay after the first half. But I have to offer them some reason to pay for a whole show, even if they choose not to partake of all of it."

"All I want to know is will we get paid," said Willie "Watermelon" Lee. "Doesn't matter to me if'n you fill out the show with the Ziegfeld Follies or a bunch of cross-eyed milkmaids."

Mr. Ohmann glared. "You'll get paid. Whether you've earned it or not."

The first show was almost empty, as if half the town was terrified to step foot in the place, and the other half was disappointed all the fun was over. It was disheartening to perform for such an empty house, and out of pity, Albert told us we could sneak into the back of the theatre and watch the movie after intermission.

"I've never seen it," I said to Joe. "Have you?"

"No. Some places in Boston wouldn't play it. Said it wasn't fair to the Negroes."

Well, coon shouting didn't seem fair to the Negroes, either, I thought, but people did it all the time. "Let's see what it's like," I said.

The Birth of a Nation is about two families: one from the South and one from the North, around the time of the Civil War. There's a grand cast of characters and each scene—from happy family life, to soldiers fighting and dying on enormous battlefields, to the burning of whole cities—was amazingly realistic. The camera must have been right in the middle of everything! I felt like I myself was that mother up in the hills with children clinging to me, while in the valley below Union soldiers burned my home to the ground.

At the end of the first half, I didn't see anything terribly offensive about it. Lillian Gish, the leading lady, was sympathetic and beautiful. Most of the Negroes were played by blacked-up white people, but that didn't seem so remarkable—it was an everyday affair in vaudeville.

The second part, after the war, begins with quotes from President Woodrow Wilson: "The policy of the congressional leaders wrought . . . a veritable overthrow of civilization in the South . . . in their determination to 'put the white South under the heel of the black South.' "

From then on, the bad colored people stop working and take all the free supplies denied the now poverty-stricken whites. When Election Day arrives, the title card explains: "All blacks are given the ballot, while the leading whites are disenfranchised." Negro soldiers shove stately white gentlemen away from the ballot box. The state legislature is now comprised of Negroes drinking and taking off their shoes on their desks. They vote "Passage of a bill, providing for the intermarriage of blacks and whites," as they ogle the white women in the gallery above.

The leading man, Colonel Cameron, is inspired to solve this problem when he sees two white children hide under a sheet and scare off superstitious colored children. "The result. The Ku Klux Klan, the organization that saved the South from the anarchy of black rule . . ."

Things go from bad to worse for another hour or so until the mulatto lieutenant governor insists on marrying Lillian Gish's character. Her blue eyes go wide with shock as he says, "I will build a Black Empire and you as a Queen shall sit by my side." Then he tells his colored henchmen to prepare for a forced wedding.

All is general mayhem. But then the KKK comes to Lillian Gish's rescue and parades through the streets, and all the Negroes drop their guns and run away. At the next election, the Klansmen keep all the colored people from voting.

The last scene is that of Jesus looking down over all the happy white people. There are no colored people, happy or otherwise.

I'd heard the KKK had enjoyed a sudden upsurge since the movie came out in 1915, and now I could see why. I had always thought the Klan was a bunch of rednecks with nothing better to do than cause trouble for coloreds. But maybe there was more to the story. The movie, with its remarkable realism, had been very convincing that the Klan had good reason for their activities.

Afterward as we walked to Dobbins Drugs through the rain to get sandwiches, I learned that Joe was of an entirely different opinion: he was spitting mad.

"It's the kind of lie people tell about anyone who isn't like them," he muttered venomously. "We're savages, we're devils, we want their women."

I was astounded! "But, Joe . . . ," I stammered stupidly. "You're white."

"Yes, but in some people's eyes, I'm not. In some people's eyes, I'm *Italian*—greasy and stupid and only fit for dirty work, like sweeping horseshit out of the street!" He was immediately apologetic. "Forgive me," he muttered. "I didn't mean to disrespect you."

"It's okay, I've heard curse words before." I didn't mention that my own mother and sister were often the culprits.

"I suppose I feel comfortable enough with you to say how I truly feel." He shook his head bitterly. "And I do not feel polite about lies that can ruin people."

As we walked through the misting rain, I did something rather bold. I took his hand and laced my fingers in his. I wouldn't usually be so forward, but I was frankly flabbergasted. I consider myself a reasonably intelligent and informed person, but in a matter of moments, Joe had made me see with clarity an important issue about which I had been woefully unenlightened.

At Dobbins Drugs, Joe and I were just tucking into our sandwiches when Gert came in and ordered two lunches. "Who's the other one for?" I asked.

She gave me an annoyed look but didn't answer.

"Is he afraid of a little rain?" I joked. It wasn't like Gert to fetch anything for anyone, much less a man who was interested in her.

"He won't leave the theatre," she murmured. "Not after Ohmann showed that movie. He saw how it incited people to violence down south."

"But this is New York," I said.

"That's what I said, but he won't budge."

"You know, the Klan's not only down south," said Joe. "A chapter just got started at Harvard this year."

I found that pretty shocking. Maybe Tip was right. If educated young men in the cradle of the abolitionist movement could sign up with such an anti-Negro organization, it could certainly happen anywhere. As we walked back to the theatre, however, we saw nothing but umbrellas, their owners more intent on getting somewhere dry than causing trouble for a traveling tap dancer who happened to have an unusual skin color for the neighborhood.

·   ·   ·

After the last show, all the performers scurried back to the hotel, collars up around our chins, hats pulled tight over our heads to keep the driving rain from finding the chinks in our woolen armor. Even Gert came, but she soon went out again. Joe and I dallied in the hotel lobby, talking and holding hands until the mole-faced hotel clerk informed us that he was "closing up" and it was high time "children" should be in their rooms.

"We just want to sit and talk without bothering our families," said Joe.

"I'm sure this little girl's mother is wondering where she is," said the clerk, his words thick with disdain. "And you should find someone your own age."

Joe stood up, his stance menacing. "She's seventeen," he growled.

The clerk raised his hands in false conciliation. "I'm sure that's what she told you—"

"I'll be eighteen in July!" I insisted.

He might have been intimidated by Joe, but he certainly wasn't by me. "Why don't I call the authorities to come and check your birth certificate?" he sneered. "The Gerrymen would be happy to confirm that a vaudeville performer of your *stature* is within the bounds of the law."

"Go right ahead!" said Joe.

"Never mind," I said quickly. "I'm tired anyway. I'll see you in the morning, Joe." I pecked him on the cheek and headed up the stairs.

He caught up with me on the second-floor landing, where I was waiting for him. "Why didn't you call his bluff?" he asked.

"Because if he called the Gerrymen, I'd be fine, but what if they started snooping around Kit and Lucy, and figured out that they're both underage? It wasn't worth opening that can of worms."

Joe slid his arms around my waist and gave me a sly smile.

"What are you grinning about?" I asked.

"My father always said, '*Whatever you do, don't fall for a smart girl. They're always one step ahead of you.*'"

"That's a terrible thing to say!"

"It would've been. Except he only ever said it in front of my mother.

And then she would pinch his cheek and say, '*Ah*, poverino. *Poor thing. Everybody feel-a sorry for you.*' "

The love I felt for him in that moment surged through every vein in my body. I put my arms around his neck and tipped my chin up to his. "So, you'll never fall for a smart girl."

"It's too late for that," he murmured.

"*Poverino*," I whispered, and kissed him so hard I nearly knocked him over.

Daylight was softly sifting in around the curtains when I heard the knob turn. I let my eyes open only to slits, and saw Gert slipping into our room. She took off her coat and slid into bed with me. "I know you're awake," she said.

"We both need sleep."

"We'll need a lot more than that tomorrow when everyone goes their separate ways."

"Let's not think about it."

"No," she said. "What would be the point."

I didn't go back to sleep, though, just lay there thinking of Joe. How he looked at me, the way he smelled when I buried my nose in his neck. How he'd stood to defend our being together against that mole-faced hotel clerk. About his mother, and how devastated she must be to have lost her husband. About losing Joe to the relentless locomotion of our current employment.

I dressed quietly and went down to breakfast. Joe was there, and he slid his hand into mine under the table. "Our last full day together," he said, as if reading my mind.

The rain had let up, and wind had whipped the moisture from the sidewalks and park benches, though it lurked in the grass and gutters; the weather remained strangely unstable, breezy and cool one moment, warm and heavy the next.

That night, our last performance in Lyons, Willie "Watermelon" Lee went on first, as usual. The crowd, however, was anything but usual. They were rowdy and loud, stomping their feet, singing along with the refrains.

"Coon, coon, coon!" they hollered, as if it were the best tune they'd
ever heard.

"Saturday night," Joe said to me as he and Lucy waited in the wings
for Willie to finish. "People like to have a drink or two before the show."
But there was more to it than just the rosy glow of libation. They were
riled. They applauded for Lucy, but her brand of adorableness was less
appealing to them than the bawdiness of Willie's blackened face shouting about how every coon looked the same to him.

As Lucy launched into her last song, Tip came up beside me to
wait for his entrance. From the shadow of a leg curtain, he stared out
like a Christian eyeing lions in the coliseum. His hands clenched and
loosened, and he bounced on his knees a bit.

"You'll do great," I said lamely, as if it were stage jitters that worried
him.

He turned to me and held my gaze. "Thank you." I knew it wasn't
for the halfhearted encouragement I'd just given him. "I think highly of
your family," he added solemnly.

I doubt if I'll ever truly know what possessed me to do what I did
next. Perhaps it was curiosity. Perhaps it was the only thing I could
think of. Whatever the reason, I slipped my hand into his. "We think
very highly of you, too," I said, and squeezed the first black skin I had
ever touched. It didn't feel like anything special. It was just a hand,
after all.

I heard boos scattered in with the applause when Tip went on.
Gert came up behind Joe and me. "He's worried," she murmured.

We stood there watching Tip move as fast as he ever had, as if by
sheer force of talent he could keep them appeased. But the applause
was losing ground to the heckling.

"Get off the stage, boy!" someone called out.

"Go pick some cotton!" yelled another.

Gert grabbed my arm. "He needs to get out of here."

"I'm going to get his pay," Joe said, and strode quickly away.

Tip kept tapping.

A burly man in the audience stood up. "You like that movie, boy?"

He pulled his white handkerchief from his pocket and draped it over his head. "You scared now?"

People called for the man to sit down, but he remained standing. "Did I see you walking with a white girl, over by Cutler's shed last night?" A gasp went up in the crowd. The piano player missed some notes and had to play quickly to get back in concert with the other musicians.

"You like white girls, boy?" It was another man this time.

Then another called out, "Probably more than he likes drowning in canal muck!"

Suddenly the front curtain began to close. I looked to the opposite wing, and there was skinny Albert, pulling the cords with all his might. "Go!" he hissed to Tip.

Gert and I ran onto the stage to help Tip collect his springboard and table. As we hauled them offstage, Mr. Ohmann met us in the wings. He handed Tip some money.

"Extra in there for your trouble," he said, shaking his head. "Damn flicker. Never should've shown it. Most people in town are decent folks, but there's a few . . ."

"When's the next train?" said Tip, mopping the sweat from his face with his hand.

"Not for a while," said Ohmann. "Go on down to the canal and see if someone will take you onboard."

"I'll go with you," said Joe. "I'll find someone."

In another moment, the table and springboard were loaded in his trunk.

"Don't go out the stage door," said Ohmann. "If anyone's waiting, that's where they'll be. There's a door from my office. Follow me."

Tip looked at Gert. She met his gaze.

And then he was gone.

She stood staring after him, at the space he'd so recently warmed with his presence, and an emptiness came over me—over all of us, I suspect—a hopeless, faithless bitterness that made me want to lie down and never get up.

"You have to go on," Albert told us. "Best thing you can do for him now is keep the audience in their seats."

The curtain went up and the Tumbling Turners tumbled and leapt and told jokes with vaudeville-size smiles on our faces. We entertained as we never had before. We entertained like our lives—or the life of someone we loved—depended on it.

CHAPTER
32

GERT

The sweetest joy, the wildest woe is love.
What the world really needs is more love and less paperwork.
—Pearl Bailey, singer and actress

I'm not quite sure how I got back to the hotel after that. I remember an arm around my waist, small but strong, guiding me like I was blind.

We sat in the lobby and waited for Joe. It was years. I could feel myself aging.

"Breathe, Gertie," Winnie said, and for once I did as I was told.

Nell came down. "Harry and the girls are asleep," she murmured. "Any word?"

Winnie shook her head. Nell sat beside me and took my other hand.

Finally the wind blew the door open with a *thunk*. Made us all jump as if it were gunfire. Joe's hair was stuck with leaves. "He's okay. Should be well on his way to Rochester by now."

He looked at me and said softly, "He asked me to tell you he's sorry."

I stared at him. *Sorry?* I thought. *Sorry for having black skin?* But that wasn't what it meant. Tip wasn't apologizing for himself. He was apologizing for the world.

I wanted to thank Joe. *Thank you for keeping him safe,* I wanted to say. Until the next time someone feels like killing him, of course. For all

I knew he was dead already. But I couldn't get the words out. I covered my face and wept.

When I quieted, they took me upstairs. "Do you want to talk?" Nell whispered. Black eye makeup striped down her cheeks. Winnie's, too.

What good would talking do? What good would anything do?

"I'm just so tired," I said.

Lucy and Kit were fast asleep. We washed our faces, changed into our nightdresses, and got into bed. As I lay there, my loss grew to include Winnie's.

She would lose Joe. He was a good man. I saw that now.

"You love Joe, don't you?" I said into the darkness.

"I . . . I think so."

"You should go to him."

"Right now?"

"We're leaving in the morning. You can't waste even a minute."

"But that's not . . . it's not . . . ," she stammered. Winnie the word lover. She only came up with, ". . . ladylike."

"When did you ever care about being *ladylike*?" I shot back. "You want to go to college, for godsake."

I heard a little gasp. "How did you know that?"

"It's obvious. You were practically born for it. Now stop talking and go."

"But what if he thinks I'm some kind of harlot?"

"Are you?"

"No, of course not!"

"Listen to me," I said. "The only thing you are is Winnie Turner. After that, you make your own terms."

CHAPTER
33

WINNIE

I used to be Snow White, but I drifted.
—Mae West, actress and comedian

Joe opened the door wearing an undershirt and pants, unbuckled belt dangling from the loops. His brow furrowed with concern. "Are you going out again?"

I had my coat on and even my shoes. I didn't want anyone to think I was traipsing around in only a nightdress, which was precisely what I was doing. "No, I . . . I just wanted to talk."

He ushered me in, closing the door behind me. "About what?"

"Anything, really. But if you're tired, I could go."

"I'm exhausted," he said, smiling wearily, "but I definitely don't want you to go."

"I should start by saying that I'm not here to—"

"No, that's fine," he said quickly. "I mean, of course not. I'll sit in the chair and you can sit on the bed. Or maybe you should sit in the chair . . ."

I took off my boots and curled my feet under me in the overstuffed chair, but I kept my coat on. "Tell me what happened with Tip."

Joe said they had run down to the canal as fast as any two men dragging an oversized trunk could. Then they followed the mule path beside the canal out of town for about a mile until they came to some trees that Tip could hide in.

"I waited until I saw a colored barge captain and flagged him down. The canal is so narrow there you can practically walk along and talk in a normal voice to someone onboard. I told him what happened, and he agreed to take Tip the forty miles or so to Rochester."

I could picture it all clearly. But one thing wasn't so clear, at least not to me.

"Joe, why did you want to help him like that? I know you weren't enthusiastic about his relationship with Gert."

"*Madonne!*" he snapped. "I should have let that bunch of thugs string him up?"

"Now, don't be like that," I said softly. "You're not friendly with Tip. You didn't owe him anything. I only wondered."

This seemed to defuse him. "I don't know what he was up to with your sister, and I really don't want to know. The only thing that was clear to me was that it was mutual between them. And you think he's a decent fellow—I trust your judgment." He looked down at his hand, thumb and pinky wide across the chenille bedspread. Then he sighed and shook his head. "When that guy threatened to drown him in canal muck . . . I thought of my father drowning in molasses, and I wished someone had been there to help him."

We talked on through the night, and by degrees I pulled my chair over to the bed, and then got into the bed next to him so we could hold hands.

"You could take off your coat, you know."

"I only have my nightdress on."

"I'd like to see you in that."

To me he was the most beautiful thing in the world. I loved him with every molecule of my girlish heart, and wanted nothing more than to lie in his arms.

Your own terms, Gert had said.

"I'd like to take off my coat," I said. "And I'd like to lie in this bed next to you and know what it feels like to sleep with your arms around me." I gave him a hard look. "But that's all. I'm trusting you to respect my wishes."

His gaze was serious. "I respect your wishes and every single other thing about you."

It was our first night together. Even now, the thought of it fills me with joy.

The train to Sackets Harbor the next day took us north along Lake Ontario. By then Kit's crying had slowed to the occasional sniffle, but even that got under Mother's skin. "If I hear so much as another hiccup out of you," she muttered, "I won't be responsible for my actions!"

"But she was the best friend I ever had!"

"You only knew her for a week!"

"Yes, but . . ." Kit turned away to hide the newly formed tears threatening to spill.

The problem was not that Mother didn't understand; it was that she understood all too well, and didn't want to be reminded. A week in the company of a like-minded soul, under circumstances that could produce anything from ecstasy to misery, forms a sort of kinship that might take years under normal conditions. Kit had never fit in—quite literally—with girls her own age in Johnson City. Nor had I. Nor, for that matter, had Mother. We had always been just a beat off from our contemporaries.

Gert would've had an easy time fitting in, if only she'd cared to. Instead she'd always preferred to fly above the crowd and find excitement a little closer to the sun. Only Nell had ever had easy relationships with girlfriends, but those had been eclipsed years ago, first by her all-encompassing love for Harry, and then by her grief over his loss.

In Sackets Harbor we played the International Order of Odd Fellows Hall, and the name of the theatre is really all I remember, perhaps because it seemed to fit our mood so perfectly. We felt odd. Out of sorts. We were friendly, but made no actual friends.

We collected our pay and traveled north to Clayton, New York, gateway to the Thousand Islands of the St. Lawrence River. The only memorable part of that week was tasting a salad dressing named for the area. I didn't find it all that enticing. Probably just a passing fad.

We played the Sheldon Opera House in Hamilton, New York, home to Colgate University. It was our first experience with "rah-rah boys"—college men who wait at the stage door and try to get female performers to come out with them. Gert was the main object of their efforts, of course, but even Kit and I had a few tagging after us as we made our way to the hotel each night.

For the first time in my career as a vaudevillian, I found myself bored. The hours between performances seemed to lengthen at each stop, until I was glad when we had to play five shows instead of four. I studied my first aid book and surreptitiously collected more supplies: gauze pads, a small penknife, and a pack of matches for sterilizing. I also returned to *Little Women*.

When I'd first read it years before, I'd been annoyed with Jo for turning down Laurie's offer of marriage. He seemed so completely devoted to her, and generally beloved by all the family. He was their version of Harry. But this time, I saw what Miss Alcott had in mind. Laurie wasn't enough—maybe for Amy, but not for Jo. Jo needed something different.

I became a more reliable postcard writer, keeping Dad apprised of our successes, saying nothing of what had happened in Lyons with Gert. Nor with me. And certainly not with Mother and Mr. O'Sullivan. I still didn't know what exactly to make of that. Perhaps it was naive of me, but I chose to believe it was an innocent flirtation taken half a step too far. When Dad's postcards found us, they were upbeat, too, though I could read his loneliness seeping between the lines, and it made me feel even worse about Mother's indelicate behavior.

I sent cards almost daily to Joe. We'd exchanged schedules before parting, and I tried to keep myself fresh in his mind. Of course, I never knew if they would reach him, and was only certain when he responded with a reference to something I'd said many days before. It paled to ghostlike in contrast to the immediacy and intimacy of our constant companionship in Lyons.

In the first week of May the Tumbling Turners traveled to Oneonta, the largest city on our tour, and then on to Walton, New York, one of the smallest. We were at the end of our nine-week run and there'd been no word from Birnbaum. For all we knew, our time as vaudevillians was over.

On the train ride home, the last stop before Binghamton was Nineveh. Gert sat next to me, looking out the dirty train car windows at the tiny town. I knew that she, more than any of us, dreaded returning to our old lives.

"In the Bible," I said to distract her, "Nineveh's a terribly wicked place, and God sends Jonah there to tell them to be good."

We stared at the tidy little houses. An old man drove a rickety cart down the dusty street. "Doesn't look wicked to me," she muttered. "Looks dull as dishwater."

"Apparently they listened to Jonah," I joked.

She looked away. "And look where that got them."

CHAPTER 34

GERT

*Dancing in Tijuana when I was thirteen—that was my
"summer camp." How else do you think I could keep up with
Fred Astaire when I was nineteen?*
—Rita Hayworth, actress and dancer

Dad was waiting on the platform, thinning hair whipping in the breeze, looking so hopeful it gave me guilt pangs. *My* hope was to leave him again as soon as possible. We stepped off the train, and he pulled us into his arms, saying, "Oh, my girls!" with a catch in his voice. Then he looked at Mother, taking her measure. "How are you, Ethel?" he said.

She gazed back at him. "I'm all right, Frank. And you?"

"Better now that you're home." He stepped toward her, and she leaned into his arms like she'd been waiting to fall into them since we left. After a brief embrace, they separated. Dad tugged his jacket straight, and Mother adjusted her hat. If I live to be a hundred, I swear I'll never understand the bond between those two. But what I think isn't worth the breath it would take to say so, is it? It's only what *they* think that matters. I get that now.

"How's your hand, Dad?" Winnie asked.

He held it out in front of us, and the scars and twists of his fingers were still godawful to look at. Then he clenched his fist. We all gasped. "It works!" said Kit.

"It's not nearly as good as it was, but I squeeze a rubber ball each day to strengthen it."

"I'm so happy for you, Dad!" Winnie said, and I'll be darned if she didn't get a little teary, too.

"Last week I went back to work," he told us. "I don't make as much money as I used to, but with what you've earned, if we're thrifty we'll be set for a while to come." He smiled at Kit, Winnie, and me. "I already reregistered you for school. You're set to go back tomorrow."

School, for cripes' sake—as if I wasn't miserable enough already.

"Damn it, Frank!" Mother fumed, tossing cold water onto their rare moment of marital bliss. Business as usual. "For all you know, they're going back on the road again next week!"

"Are they?" he said.

"Not at the moment, but if Birnbaum calls . . ."

He gave her a little pat on the shoulder. "Yes, dear," he said gently. It's a funny thing about him. When he gets his way, it's generally by *not* fighting her.

The trolley ride to Johnson City was quiet, and it occurred to me that maybe I wasn't the only miserable sister. Maybe we were all thinking the same thing. With Dad working, and no help from Birnbaum, our vaudeville career was breathing its last.

The house looked even smaller than when we'd left it, if that was possible. We went upstairs to unpack. The baby needed a nap, so I went across the hall to Kit and Winnie's room, feeling so low I was ready to jump out the window. Of course, it was only one floor up. Probably only break my legs, and then where would I be?

Kit slumped on the bed. "I hate school. Everyone's so mean." Her eyes filled. "My muscles are bigger now from the act, and I think I might even be"—she inhaled a sniffle—"taller!"

Winnie sat down, put an arm around her waist, and looked up at her. "But you have a secret now. You're a vaudevillian, and no one could ever take that away, no matter how mean they are."

"But what if Mr. Birnbaum never calls and we never get to go back?" she wailed.

Poor kid. I hadn't really thought about it before, but Kit had it the worst of all of us. At thirteen, she had five long years till she could claim her freedom. I sat down on the other side of her and hooked my arm in hers. The two of them looked at me like I'd suddenly started speaking Swedish or something. "What?" I demanded.

Winnie smiled. "Nothing," she said, and I felt the hand she'd curled around Kit's waist reach out to gently pat my back.

It was painful—by which I mean it actually hurt!—to wake up so early in the morning after months of rising at ten or eleven. The three of us trudged to school. Maybe she was just tired or missing Joe, but even Winnie seemed unenthusiastic.

When we walked home that afternoon I told her I wasn't going back. "I was so bored I was practically ready to take my own life. I'm going to start waitressing full-time."

"Gert, that's ridiculous! You're only a month away from graduating!"

"More like three months away, with all I missed when we were on the road. I'll never be able to make it all up, so why even try?"

For some reason this made her scorching mad, and she didn't even speak to me for a couple of blocks. I felt like screaming, *There's nothing I want to do in this world that requires a high school diploma!*

But she knew that. It was something else. Something she wanted for her.

"I'll do it," she said.

"Do what?"

"All your papers and homework, and I'll prep you for tests. But you have to promise you'll go to class and take some notes."

"What's in it for you?"

"It just galls me—you're almost there! I'd do anything to have my graduation in such easy reach." Her eyes flicked away, the gears of her overactive little mind turning. "Give me half of what you make waitressing, and I'll get you to graduation if I have to carry you piggyback."

"Half! Are you out of your mind? I don't even care about graduating."

She said nothing, only stared stubbornly at me. And I thought of one thing.

Pigeons.

"One quarter," I said. "Take it or leave it."

I admit, the arrangement worked out pretty well. Winnie did her schoolwork and mine, she helped Kit with hers, and got back her job at Lourdes Hospital. I didn't go back to J. J. Wiley's—I didn't want to see Roy—but I did get a job in the dining room of the fancy Arlington Hotel, and took every shift they offered. The two of us were busier than we'd ever been before, which left fewer hours for mooning about our losses.

I wasn't one to moon anyway. It was more like the ache of a gut wound that wouldn't quite heal. I wasn't one to pray, either, but I prayed for him every hour of every day. Looked for him on every street corner. Dreamed or had nightmares about him every night.

My beautiful Tip.

Mother held out a full twenty-four hours before storming over to Mrs. Califano's to call Birnbaum. When she returned she was spitting nails, and I thought she might punch Dad right in the snoot. "Why in hell didn't you tell me!" she screeched. "He said he left messages several times!"

"Well, I . . . I wasn't absolutely certain . . . ," Dad stammered.

"*Of what*?"

"If it was him. Mrs. Califano said a man called but she couldn't remember his name."

"Oh, Dad!" I groaned. "Who *else* could it be?"

"I figured, even if it was him, it was just as likely that it was bad news as good," he sputtered. "Besides, I'm working! You don't have to do that . . . performing anymore!"

"We like performing!" I said, and looked around at the rest of them. "Don't we? Is there anyone who wouldn't go back out on the road right this minute?"

"I would!" said Kit.

"I did enjoy it," said Nell. She gave Dad an apologetic look. "But I like being home, too."

All eyes turned to Winnie. "I loved it," she admitted. "But since we're here now, I just want to finish out the school year." She fixed me with a hard look. "I want *all* of us to finish out the school year."

"Well, it looks like you'll have your way," said Mother. "He couldn't reach us, so he didn't book us." A cry went up from Kit, and even Nell looked unhappy. "He'll see what he can do, but as he was quick to say, there are no guarantees in life, and in vaudeville, even fewer."

CHAPTER
35

WINNIE

Art is an elastic sort of love.
—Josephine Baker, exotic dancer and singer

I don't know how much longer I can keep doing this.

Joe wrote letters instead of postcards, now that he could be sure they'd reach me.

Lucy hasn't met any friends like Kit, so she gets fussy and irritable. Last week she had a cold, and I had no idea what to do for her. I'm no parent.

Mama is so lonely. In her letters she never complains, and she says she's proud of me for stepping into Papa's shoes to take care of the family. But I can feel her sadness. She lost her husband, and now her children are gone, too. What kind of life have I left her with? My father's garden never got planted because I was on the road. I'm failing at everything.

Only the money keeps me going. I figure if we get small-time gigs for another two years, I can pay off the land and put a little aside so I can go back to playing in local bars for a living. Lucy can finish her schooling. Mama will be happy again, once we're with her.

Two years. It makes me sick inside to think about it.

If only you could be with me, Winnie. If only I could put my arms around you, and kiss you and talk to you, I could hold on. I could do it forever.

About a week after we got home, I went downstairs in the middle of the night to use the bathroom and smelled smoke.

Fire! I thought, and my mind flashed to the Binghamton Clothing Factory fire, and all those poor girls sewing overalls. I was about to scream for everyone to get out of the house, when I realized it had a very particular odor: not of worldly possessions in flames, but the earthy scent of burning plant matter. I followed it out to the front porch, where Gert sat on one of our traveling trunks, a cigarette dangling from her fingers.

"Where did you get that?" I said, rubbing my eyes. "You don't smoke."

She only shrugged. In all likelihood, some young man had offered them as a love token—maybe the better word for it is *bait*—and she had simply walked off with them.

I should have gone back up to bed: the faintly lightening sky announced the approach of dawn. But instead I nudged her over and sat down. She offered me the cigarette, and though I'd never smoked before, I accepted it and took a hesitant drag. It tasted as I always suspected it would—like eating soot—but also something more. Acceptance. Maybe even friendship.

"How's Joe?"

"Fine." I handed her back the cigarette. "Bored."

She shot me a sideways smile. "Lovelorn."

I smiled back and shrugged. "You ever hear from Tip?"

She shook her head. "He left too fast. Never got a chance to give him our address." She took a deep drag and blew it high to the wainscoted porch ceiling.

"Wherever he is, he misses you."

"I'm too busy being mad at the world to miss him." She stared off over the neighborhood toward Floral Park Cemetery. Then a little smile came to her lips. "I still can't believe you let those pigeons loose."

"It kind of surprised me, too."

"It's a good thing you did."

"Why?"

"Because if somebody hadn't done something like that, I might have had to." She took another drag. "And it might've been a lot worse than setting some stupid birds free."

She handed me back the cigarette and I puffed inexpertly at it. It wasn't as bad the second time, though it wasn't good, either. But it was Gert's, and I wanted to be part of it.

I blew the smoke into the darkness. "How come you didn't go back to J. J. Wiley's?"

She lifted the cigarette from my fingers. "There's a guy there I don't want to see." She took another drag and I could see her deciding how much to tell. "We were together . . . but he got mad when I went on the road."

"How could he be mad about that? Did he want us to get evicted?"

"He didn't see it that way. He wanted control." Her eyes slid toward mine. "Most of them do, you know."

On Monday, June 2, we'd been home for two weeks and I was feeling very accomplished. Gert's graduation was on the twenty-second, and I was up to date with all of her assignments, as well as my own. I had even gotten an A-plus-plus on my women's suffrage paper, though that probably had more to do with my history teacher Miss Darlington's passion for the movement. She and I had both worn suffrage-white to school the day after the House of Representatives passed the Nineteenth Amendment. If approved by the Senate and ratified by two-thirds of the states, it would ensure that "the right of citizens of the United States to vote shall not be denied or abridged by the United States or by any state on account of sex." It was thrilling!

Secretly, Gert and I opened bank accounts. With all our schoolwork to consider, I could only take a few shifts per week at the hospital, so her balance was four times the size of mine. But my $11.37 put a smile on my face every time I thought of it. I was a long way from putting myself through college, but it was a start.

Even more than that, my anemic little account symbolized the greater goal of my own self-governance, which I had barely considered when we'd begun this vaudeville odyssey. Mother seemed to believe she could exercise her control in perpetuity, and the thought of wresting it from her gave me a shiver of excitement. Maybe I was turning into Gert!

On that Monday morning, however, all our plans for gradually increasing our accounts were upended when Mother came to school.

The principal appeared at Miss Cartery's classroom door, beckoned her over, and whispered something. Then they looked at me, faces solemn. I had seen grave expressions all too often during the Spanish flu, when news of death arrived almost daily for some poor student.

Oh, God, I prayed. *Oh, dear Lord, no* . . .

"Winnie, would you gather your things, please?" said Miss Cartery.

With broken glass in my veins I made my way through the maze of desks to the doorway. Someone patted my arm as I went by.

"I'm so sorry, but your grandmother has passed," the principal murmured. "Your mother is waiting for you in the main office."

"My grandmother?"

"Yes, dear. You'll be leaving for Albany right away for the wake and funeral."

It was all I could do not to laugh. Mother's parents had been dead for years! This had to be something else—something she needed to lie about. It could only be one thing.

Gert was already in the office and we had to suffer through several more rounds of condolences before we could get out of the building and Mother could tell us the truth. "Someone canceled and we're the disappointment act in Geneva this week! Two hundred dollars! Nell's home packing. We have a nine thirty train to catch!"

I stopped in my tracks. "Geneva?" I let out a mad whoop and grabbed Gert by the arms. They were rightly puzzled, until I sang out, "Joe's in Geneva!"

*The Saturday matinee was in full swing when I arrived backstage,
and there I suddenly found my inarticulate self in a dazzling land
of smiling, jostling people wearing and not wearing all sorts of
costumes and doing all sorts of clever things. And that's when I
knew! What other life could there be but that of an actor?"*

—Cary Grant, actor (the former Archie Leach, acrobat)

"Mother, Winnie and I have been talking."

We hadn't actually been talking. I'd talked, but I could tell
Winnie wasn't really listening. Too busy daydreaming about seeing Joe.

"I've noticed you two have been getting along better." Mother
didn't even glance up from the newspaper swaying in her hand as the
train rocked its way toward Geneva.

"We've been talking about the money we get paid for performing.
Or I should say, the *family* gets paid."

This caught her attention; she put aside the newspaper to eye me.

"We girls performed for nine weeks and never saw a cent, which
is fine, seeing as Dad couldn't work. But he is working now, and I'm
guessing you banked roughly . . . four hundred dollars?"

I watched Mother carefully. If it had been less than that, she would
have jumped to correct me, but she just kept glaring.

"That's quite a cushion," I said. "And if we keep working, we'll make even more."

"What are you getting at?" Mother growled.

"We have a proposal. From now on, you keep half our earnings, pay the travel expenses from it, and bank the rest. We girls split the other half four ways." I had already done the math, of course. Birnbaum had negotiated a whopping two hundred dollars for the week. Half of that divided by four was twenty-five dollars. It was more than I made at the Arlington in a month.

"Absolutely not," Mother scoffed. "Gert, you think you're smart enough to handle that kind of money? This isn't a few dollars you get from waitressing. This is serious dough, and I'm not going to let you fritter it away."

I felt my blood boil. "First of all, I *am* smart enough. And second of all—"

"The discussion is over." She picked up the newspaper and stared at it, though her eyes weren't tracking the text. I was prepared for this. And for the first time in my life, I truly understood it. Despite the gilded cage the world puts you in as a wife and mother—for just being female, for cripes' sake—she finally had a little say-so, and she wanted to keep it.

But my new sympathy didn't make me stupid. If anything, it spurred me on. Time for the big guns. "Winnie and I won't perform unless we get our share."

Mother turned on Winnie. "You're conspiring against me."

To her everlasting credit, the girl said nothing. I had dragged her into my mutiny without a warning, but she didn't abandon me. Besides, she knew I was right.

"It doesn't matter," Mother said coolly. "I won't give you the money, and that is final."

The rest of the train ride was silent, and Winnie shot me angry looks. But not that angry. She was still with me. When we stood on the platform in Geneva, I took her arm. "Winnie and I will take the next train back to Binghamton if you won't give us part of our pay."

Winnie stiffened till she nearly broke in half. *I know — Joe is a short walk away*, I wanted to tell her. *But you have to stick with me, or we'll never get any of it.*

Mother looked to Nell for reinforcement. She stunned us all by tucking little Harry onto her hip and taking a step toward Winnie and me. "It's only fair, Mother," she said gently.

Kit scrambled over beside us before anyone could even look at her.

Mother was fit to be tied. "You can't go back to Binghamton," she hissed. "You don't even have the train fare!"

"Maybe not," I said, "but we won't perform. What are you going to do? Leave us all here?"

Mother shot eye daggers at me while she calculated her options. "Fine!" she said suddenly, and stalked off toward town.

The victory improved my dark mood, at least for the moment.

Geneva, New York, was the biggest city we'd played so far, and with summer people starting to arrive, the "drawing population" (in theatre lingo) was even bigger. When you've only played small time, nothing really prepares you for the luxury of a place like the Smith Opera House: three stories of red brick with enormous bay windows, and glass globes on pedestals all along the roofline. With eighteen hundred seats and the biggest stage we'd ever performed on, the size alone was a step up.

Monday-morning rehearsal was in full swing, and there was a herd of young men in acrobat tights and sleeveless shirts wandering around, so I knew competition would be stiff for choice spots on the bill. I didn't see Joe — Winnie's head practically spun on her neck like a top searching for him — but there was one familiar face we hadn't expected to see: Fred Delorme, from our very first show in Earlville. He was in his tails and top hat, muttering at his dance partner, April. Her face was flat with boredom, as if she'd heard it all too many times.

"Fred?" said Nell.

He glanced over and took a moment to recognize her. "Nell? Nell Turner! Well, haven't we all come up in the world," he teased. "It's a far cry from Earlville, isn't it?"

Nell gave him a warm smile. "How've you been, Fred?"

"Fine, fine. And look at this young man—he's as big as a bear cub now." He gave Harry a little chuck under the chin, and the baby offered up a toothy grin. "With chompers, too!"

"Hello, April," said Nell. "How are you?"

"Just swell." April crossed her arms and looked away.

Fred greeted us all with smiles and handshakes. Winnie was the only one who didn't chatter along, her eyes scanning the crowd. I felt my own eyes wander for a moment, too.

Don't be an idiot, I told myself. But I wondered if I'd ever really stop looking for him.

"Dainty Little Lucy!" called the stage manager, and suddenly there they were, parting the crowd to get to the stage.

"Joe!" Winnie headed toward him on a dead run.

"Winnie! What—?" He grabbed her up in a huge hug and kissed her, and I felt my chest clench in envy. What I wouldn't have given just to have Tip near, never mind a public embrace. The boy acrobats sent up a little round of applause and a couple of snickers of "Atta boy!"

"Dainty Little Lucy, you're on!"

"Don't go anywhere!" Joe called back.

"Where would I go?" Winnie bubbled like a fountain. I had to look away from all that sticky sweetness.

I wasn't the only one cringing. "Winnie Turner!" Mother hissed.

Winnie knew that tone, though I couldn't remember it being aimed specifically in her direction before—it was generally reserved for me. Her face fell as she faced Mother's wrath.

"I turned a blind eye to your little friendship with that *Italian* boy back in Lyons." Mother said it like *Eye-talian*. And her eye had certainly been blind all right—blinded by monkey man O'Sullivan. She'd barely even noticed how Joe and Winnie had carried on right under her nose. I had taken full advantage of her "blindness" myself, of course.

Mother went on. "But I won't tolerate this kind of canoodling. Especially with a . . . a person of that sort."

"Mother!" Winnie spat back. "The *sort of person* Joe is . . . is . . .

well, he's wonderful! And if you think . . . if you don't . . . ," she stammered. Good-girl Winnie had it bad if she was back-talking like that!

"Winnie, Mother's right." I tipped my head toward Mother and made an *I'm-with-you* face. "Don't worry," I said to Mother. "It's just calf love. Besides, it can't amount to much. They've only got a week."

Mother cut her eyes toward me and huffed an aggravated sigh. "All right. But keep an eye on her, will you, Gert? I can't be everywhere." I nodded solemnly, clenching my molars to keep a straight face.

Winnie looked like she might slap me, but I wrapped a firm arm around her shoulder and steered her away. "Just keep it down in public, for cripes' sake," I murmured in her ear.

She gasped in surprise and whispered, "I love you, Gertie."

I gave her a shove, and we went to the wings to watch lover boy.

You could tell Joe was flustered. He played so many wrong notes it's a wonder Lucy could follow him at all. A true professional, she just sang louder to drown out his mistakes. When they were done, they both came off at a trot, Lucy into the crowd to find Kit, and Joe straight to Winnie, of course. "Are you in the show?"

"Somebody canceled—we're the disappointment act."

"How've you been?" He kissed her before she could answer. She pulled away quickly and whispered something in his ear, which I imagine was along the lines of, *Not here.*

"The Tumbling Turner Sisters!" called the stage manager, thankfully putting an end to the mush.

It was such a thrill to be back onstage again—to be *anywhere* again. Out in the world without an apron around my waist. Apron—I didn't even have a corset on!

When we heard the lineup, I felt bad for Joe and Lucy. Joe's poor performance landed them in the closing spot. Dainty Little Lucy wasn't a dumb act, which made the insult even worse. It should have gone to the fellow who drew huge charcoal pictures of famous buildings blindfolded, but he got the opener instead.

We got the third spot, after Fred and April in the deuce. Given the competition and the fact that we weren't originally on the bill at all, it was a nice surprise. We were followed by a singer called Marie Dubois, a French girl with big blue eyes and bright blond hair.

She had four male dancers in tight black pants, striped shirts, and berets, who carried her around on their shoulders or lay at her feet in rapt attention to her beauty and talent. Her voice was good, but not as strong as Lucy's. Her face and figure were attractive, but you couldn't actually call her beautiful. Her brittle hair had been dyed so often it looked like hay.

But Marie lacked nothing in the confidence department. Her chin was always high and she had a little sashay to her walk. When we finished our act, she started onstage before we were completely off, heading right for me, and I had to skip out of the way to avoid a collision.

"What's with her?" I said.

"Maybe she thought you were a mirror—you're practically twins!" Kit giggled. She went off to explore the theatre with Lucy, and Mother and Nell went to find our dressing room. There were fourteen of them below stage, so every act got one. Some of the bigger acts even got two.

"Don't give her the satisfaction," Winnie said after I told her I was staying to watch that French floozy Marie Dubois.

I shrugged. "Nothing better to do, and maybe I can pick up a trick or two."

Then she and Joe practically sprinted to his dressing room. Oh, the envy I felt.

I concentrated on Marie. What she lacked in talent she made up for in allure. There was this move she did . . . I stood there in the leg curtain and studied it.

Kit and Lucy scurried up. They had made friends with the acrobat boys. "One of them said he'd help me learn a few of their stunts," said Kit. "His name is Archie, and he's even taller than me!"

After intermission, Kit dragged Joe and Winnie upstairs with Nell and the baby to watch the Bob Pender Acrobat Troupe. I'll admit they were quite a sight. Their act was more muscular than ours, of course, and didn't include any jokes—the humor was in the knockabout bits, one pretending to punch another and the other guy handspringing backward from the blow.

When they came off, wiping their faces with the frayed handker-chiefs Mrs. Pender doled out, Kit called to her new friend: "Archie! Come meet my sisters."

His big brown eyes and black hair resembled Joe's, though Archie greased his hair down, rather than left it curly, as Joe did. He was taller by half a foot, and wider across the shoulders. He was handsome in a dopey-kid kind of way.

"How'd y'do." His English accent was so thick I could barely understand him!

"Um . . . how do you do," I said extending my hand.

"You've got quite an act," said Winnie. "It's like a barrel of monkeys!"

He blinked his long eyelashes at her, uncertain what to make of it.

"It's very entertaining," Nell said.

He nodded, relieved. "Yours is crackin'!"

We assumed this was a good thing.

"How long have you been in America?" asked Joe.

"We came over last year and played The Hippodrome in New York City," he said with a hint of pride. With over five thousand seats, it was the biggest theatre in the world, and could host an entire circus. "Been traveling around since."

"The Hippodrome!" said Kit. "What did you see?"

"We saw Houdini make an entire bloody elephant disappear. That was a sight!"

"Awright, now," Mrs. Pender chided, nudging at him and the other boys as if they were overgrown toddlers. "Don't dally about backstage. Off with you. Go on and get some fresh air while you can." She herded them toward the stage door, with Kit and Lucy tagging after.

"Looks like Kit has a crush," Winnie murmured to Nell and me.

"Well, don't bother her about it." Nell smiled wryly. "After all, we didn't bother you."

For the last show that evening, I added a little move I'd "borrowed" from Marie Dubois. I didn't feel bad about it—like Nat and Benny said, stealing is a way of life in vaudeville. After my handsprings onto the stage, I wagged my outstretched arms and shoulders just slightly, which caused a little jiggle across my chest—not so much as to earn a blue envelope, but enough to make the young men hoot and stomp their feet. Hobart College was only a couple of blocks away, and every audience was peppered with rah-rah boys. The later the shows, the more of them there were. I did the arm jiggle a few more times; then every time I held out my arms, they cheered in anticipation. When we took our bows, the applause was like thunder.

Marie Dubois glared murder at me and bumped my shoulder as she took the stage after us. Her costume was pretty: a flapper-style sleeveless dress with little flags of taffeta hanging from the waist that floated around when she danced and vamped. But it wasn't as scant as our tumbling costumes, so the arm jiggle didn't come off as nearly so enticing—all the worse because they'd just seen me do it. It made Marie seem like the thief.

"I think you may need a bodyguard after this," Nell whispered as we watched.

"She was already gunning for me," I said. "All I did was give her a good reason."

"The stage-door johnnies will all be waiting for you now."

"They're a dime a dozen, and she can have every last one of them." I crossed my arms. "The only thing I care about is making our act the best it can be so I never have to go back to waiting tables in Johnson City. If that means cribbing a move here or there, then so be it."

We stayed at the Seneca Hotel a few blocks away. Of course, Lucy wanted to sleep with Kit in our room again, which was fine by Mother—once Joe agreed to chip in fifty cents per night. Now that she pocketed less of our wages, she penny-pinched more than ever. It's a wonder she didn't add a fee for babysitting. But he didn't hesitate; it was worth it to have Lucy happy, he said. The fact that he and Winnie could sneak out and walk by Seneca Lake in the moonlight didn't hurt, either, I suppose.

The next day, Mother homed in on the headliner, Isadora the

Incredible Impersonator. Her act involved lightning-quick clothing changes from male to female, and mimicking everyone from President Wilson to Mary Pickford. It occurred to me that at every stop, Mother always befriended the headliner—male or female, it didn't seem to matter. Maybe it wasn't romance she was after at all; maybe it was just rubbing shoulders with fame and success. Father was no headliner, of course—how could a dear old lump of coal carry a show? I wondered if that might be the key to their unhappiness. Neither of them held quite the right spot on the bill for the other.

None of the performers interested me in the least, of course. Who could hold a candle to Tip? I preferred the quiet cave of our dressing room. I was with Nell, feeding the baby pea-sized bits of my corned beef sandwich, when Winnie suddenly poked her head in the door. I hoped we might have a little time free from her all-consuming obsession, and from talk of men in general.

No such luck.

"Do you mind if Joe sits with us for a while after his act is over?" she asked.

"Why? Are you getting tired of being alone with him?" I tried not to sound hopeful.

"Not at all! I guess I . . . I just want you both to get to know him a little."

Nell raised her eyebrows. "I didn't think you were getting so serious already."

Winnie looked confused. "That's serious?"

"Why, sure, honey," said Nell. "At first you want him all to yourself—and you certainly don't want your family's quirks ruining it for you." She laughed. "But then you feel comfortable and solid, so you start wanting him to know the people who are important to you."

I had never wanted Roy to spend time with my family, didn't even want them to know about him. Mother might've forbidden me from seeing someone ten years older. Or she might not. You never could tell what might send her, and I couldn't chance it.

But maybe it was something else, too. Maybe I just hadn't felt solid enough, as Nell said.

"Is that what it was like with Harry?" Winnie asked.

"Why do you think I kept bringing him to dinner? I held my breath every time, never knowing if Mother might swear, or Kit might eat all the meat loaf, or Dad might wander off without a word to listen to his Victrola."

I thought of Harry sitting there so politely through all those noisy dinners. "Poor fella."

"Oh, he loved you all, but he certainly knew what he was getting himself into when he asked me to marry him."

"What did he think of me?" Winnie asked shyly.

Nell smiled. "I believe the first thing he said about you was, '*Well, she certainly has quite a vocabulary!*'"

We all laughed—he'd hit the nail on the head—but the humor soon shifted to sadness. Oh, Harry. I thought we'd eventually stop missing him, but now I saw we never would. Nell's eyes went shiny and Winnie's did, too.

The baby reached up to grab Nell's cheek and she took his sticky little hand and blew a kiss against his palm, which made him giggle. Sweetness and sorrow all mixed up.

Joe appeared in the doorway. "There you are! Oh . . . should I come back later?"

"No, please," said Nell, patting away a stray tear. "We were just being silly."

Joe looked uncertainly to Winnie. "We were talking about Nell's husband, Harry," she said, "and how he thought I had a big vocabulary."

Joe chuckled. "He had that right. Sometimes I think I should carry a dictionary." He sat down next to Nell. "I don't think I ever said how sorry I am."

"I'm sorry for the loss of your father, too, Joe."

Suddenly there were footsteps in the hallway.

"April! You can't!"

"See for yourself if I can." Our dressing room door was partly open, and she came into view in the hallway just as a black-suited arm reached to grab her elbow. She wore a plain brown dress with a little cloche hat. A battered tapestry bag hung from her hand. "Let *go*!" She yanked her elbow free and nearly fell over.

"They won't take you back," he warned, just out of view. "You broke their hearts too many times."

"Oh, they will," she said with a tired smile. "Just like you. They say they won't but they always do."

"April, please. If you just hang on, we can make enough money for a hospital."

"A *sanitarium*, you mean. They'll lock me up and I'll never get out."

"Better than jail!"

"You should've just left me there."

A humorless snort. "Which time?"

She stared in his direction for a moment, her face fallen with hurt.

"I'm sorry," he muttered. "That was mean."

"No," she said softly. "*I'm* mean. You've spent your whole life watching out for me. You're the best brother anyone could ask for, Freddie, and over and over I let you down."

He was her brother! Now it made sense that he hadn't just left her by the side of the road somewhere.

"If you could just stay away from it . . ." His voice was pleading but hopeless.

"You know I can't. And you'll never understand why. Maybe if I could find someone who understands . . . but no one admits to it. No one just says, 'I have a problem.'" She let out a weary sigh. "Well, Freddie. I have a problem. And I'll be damned if I'm going to keep making it *your* problem."

He took one of her hands and put some bills into it. "It's all I have," he said, his voice beaten with sadness. "Promise you'll use it for train fare home."

She held his hand in hers for a moment. "You know what my promises are worth." Then she strode quickly away.

He took a step after her and came into view. He glanced into our dressing room. "I'm sorry you had to hear that," he muttered, and turned away.

"Fred, don't go!" Winnie jumped up and went to the door. "Come sit with us. Please."

"I should tell the manager to find a disappointment act," he said, but he allowed her to guide him to a chair.

"Where can you go with no money?" said Joe. "You have to stay in the show and get your pay. Can you do it alone?"

Fred thought for a moment, but shook his head.

"I could do April's part," Winnie offered. "You could teach me the steps and the jokes."

He looked up at her quickly, then an uncomfortable smile crossed his lips. "That's very kind of you," he said. "But I think it's best to let it go."

"Winnie'd be great!" said Joe. "At least you'd have some money in your pocket."

But Fred's uneasiness remained. "You have to understand," he said. "I'm thirty years old."

She clearly didn't know what that had to do with the price of tea in China, and Joe seemed confused, too. "Winnie," I said, "all the jokes are courtship gags. You look young for your age. It would seem as if Fred were . . ."

Joe nodded at the realization. ". . . an old man going after a little girl."

I was about to offer to do April's bit myself, though I hated their silly soft-shoe routine, and was in absolutely no mood to act coy and amorous. But Nell surprised us all and beat me to the punch. "I could do it," she said.

Fred blinked at her. "I couldn't ask you to."

"Oh well." Nell shrugged. "It probably wouldn't work anyway. Who'd believe you'd want to court me? I'm an old mother, after all." She was only twenty-two, and rather pretty now that she'd put a little weight back on. I stifled a smile at the way she'd made it impossible for him to turn her down.

"No, of course not!" Fred said. "You're so . . . I'd be thrillighted . . . I mean, thrilled . . . and delighted!"

Nell handed little Harry to me and stood up. "I guess we'd better get practicing, then."

They didn't have long. The next show began in half an hour. Fred simplified some of the dance steps, and taught her most of the gags.

April had left her blue ball gown behind, which would've been loose on Nell, except that she had to wear her tumbling costume underneath. The Turner Sisters followed right after on the bill, so she didn't have time to change.

She was nervous as we waited in the wings for the old blindfolded fellow to finish his wobbly sketches of the White House and the Eiffel Tower. "What have I gotten myself into?" she murmured in my ear.

"Break a leg!" I whispered back.

"He'll be lucky if I don't break his!"

They didn't exactly bring down the house. Even drunk, April knew the act and was a better dancer. But Nell was better at delivering lines, if only because she didn't slur her speech.

They twirled onto the boards and did an easy waltz around the stage, then went into a little side-by-side soft shoe. Fred started the patter by saying, "I'd like to take you out. You're one in a million!"

"That's quite a coincidence!" said Nell.

"It is? Why?"

She cocked her head coyly. "Because so are your chances."

The audience chuckled at this, and Fred waited a beat before clutching his hands to his chest and exclaiming, "But my heart burns like a blazing fire!"

Nell waved him away and said, "Aw, now don't be a fuel."

Bigger laughter this time, which was encouraging. Nell missed a step here or there when they danced between gags, but Fred held her tight and kept her on course. When it was time to deliver their next set of jokes, they soft-shoed back and forth again.

"I have a record of all our good times together," said Fred.

"Oh, that's nice!" said Nell brightly. "Is it a diary?"

Fred rolled his eyes. "No, it's my checkbook!" He paused again for laughter, then added, "Since I met you I can't eat or drink!"

"That's so sweet! Why not?"

He pulled the lining out of his pockets. "I'm broke!"

They danced again and Fred attempted the low dip he always did with April. But Nell was caught off guard and tried to keep herself from falling backward. They teetered wildly until he was able to pull her up to standing. I heard a boo or two, and hoped Fred and Nell were too busy getting back in step to notice.

In the next series of gags, he grinned suggestively at her. "Now that our date is over, wanna neck, honey?"

Nell brought her fingers to her throat and said, "No, thanks, I have one of my own."

"May I at least hold your hand?" Fred pleaded.

Nell mimed weighing one hand in the other. "No need," she said. "It's not that heavy."

When they took their bows, the applause was polite, but not overly enthusiastic. At least they hadn't been heckled off the stage.

"I'm so sorry, Fred," Nell said when they made it back to the wings. "I'll remember the dip next time."

He laughed and shook his head. "I've had worse shows, believe me. *Far* worse."

As they talked, Winnie and I stripped the blue ball gown off Nell, and she wiggled to get it down over her hips. "Can we practice some more after I come off again?" she asked Fred.

"Yes, of course." His face flushed slightly and he looked away. "Anytime you like."

As the dress hit the floor in a puddle, the stage manager hustled over. "Where's April?"

"She's . . . uh . . . she's not here," stammered Fred.

"Well, you tell her she'd better stay off the sauce for the next performance. You looked like you were dancing with a clubfooted rag doll out there!"

Early the next morning, Kit was a foghorn in our ears. "Get up! We have to go to the theatre—Archie's going to teach us some tricks!"

"Leave us alone," Winnie groaned.

"Gert, you want to add some fancy new tricks to the act, don't you? Archie knows a million of 'em!"

"Archie's an idiot," I said from under my pillow. "He'll be slopping pigs for a living by the time he's twenty."

Kit wouldn't quit. She'd already blasted Nell out of bed with her badgering, and soon we were all trudging through the stabbing mid-morning light to the Opera House. Archie met us at the stage door, black hair slicked back, dark eyes shining.

"It's so nice of you to help us like this," said Nell, stifling a yawn.

"Happy to, missus," he murmured shyly. "Truly, I am."

Some of Archie's stunts seemed likely to end in multiple broken limbs or necks, but eventually he came up with a couple that we could pull off without risk of death. In the first, Winnie ran toward Kit from stage left and bounced on the springboard. Kit stood stage right and threw an old dancer's cane Archie had found backstage. Winnie was supposed to catch it midair, then Kit would catch her and twirl her around with the cane held out in her arms.

"That bouncy board is bloody brilliant!" said Archie after they'd missed the catch and crumpled to the floor for the sixth or eighth time.

Bouncy board, for cripes' sake. He didn't even know the right name. And he had his eye on it, I could tell. The girls kept blowing the stunt, and he just kept grinning like a Limey jack-o'-lantern, tickled pink over Tip's springboard.

"You'd better not steal it," I warned. "If I find out you have one of these at your next gig, I'll hunt you down and beat you with it."

Archie flinched, like I was a dog who might bite him. He was twice my size, the big baby!

"Gert," said Nell. "He won't."

"Tip gave it to *us*," I said, and for a brief moment I'll admit I did feel wild enough to do violence over it. "He didn't want every act in vaudeville to have one."

"Gertie," Winnie soothed. "We won't let him steal it."

"What can Gert do?" Kit pleaded to Archie. "Don't you have a great trick for her?"

He eyed me warily, making no sudden moves.

As the flash of rage passed, I felt foolish. He was just a stupid teen-age boy. I took a breath and let it out. "Yes, I'd like that," I said, still shaken by my own reaction. "Please."

His next idea was a rolling human ball. I lay on my back, Nell stood with her feet by my hands, then leaned over and grasped my ankles. She tumbled forward, and I held on to her ankles and rose up. Then Nell was on the floor with me above her, and it was my turn to roll forward.

"The trick of it is, you relax into the fall," said Archie. "Your instinct is to stiffen up, but if you do, you get banged up and it's a real dog's dinner."

"A mess." Kit had evidently been hanging around him enough to pick up his slang.

We practiced our rolling and got the hang of it after a while. Kit and Winnie worked on the jump-and-throw, but the timing was tricky, and they weren't reliable enough by showtime. Anyway, we had bigger problems than adding new stunts.

The French floozy was on the warpath.

After the first show, Winnie dragged me out with Joe to find some lunch, though of course I had absolutely no interest in tagging along with the lovebirds. I could tell she was worried about me after that silly scene I made with Archie, and the thought of it only made me feel more bitter. But I went, just to get her off my back. There was a little sandwich place on Exchange Street that had corned beef "sliced very thin," as our old friends Nat and Benny would say. It reminded me of them with every bite I took, and made me miss the old guys. *Stop it!* I told myself. It was more missing than I could take.

On our way back, we turned down the little alley by the theatre and saw Marie standing at the stage door with a couple of fellows. When she saw us, she waved the boys away. They came down the alley toward us, eyes darting sideways at us as they passed.

"What's with them?" said Joe.

"Marie's rah-rah boys. She was probably giving them rotten fruit to throw at us," Winnie joked.

"I wouldn't put it past her," I said.

So we shouldn't have been surprised when the booing started during our next performance. It seemed halfhearted, though, and stopped completely when our comedy gags made the audience burst out laughing. The human rolling ball was a big hit, too.

We were in the middle of our snew sketch—Winnie had just

announced that she had a bad case of snew—when something came flying onstage! A biscuit, flung by one of the two boys who'd been in the alley. I could see them plain as day, sitting in the front row. It hit me on the shoulder and dropped to the boards at my feet.

The nerve of those two snot-nosed college boys, thinking they could humiliate me like that. I felt the rage boil up again in my blood . . .

I bent down and picked up that damned biscuit. Then I wound up and pelted it right at them. It hit one of them squarely in the chest. I booed back! Nat and Benny would've been so proud. But to make it truly work, I had to finish the sketch.

I turned to Winnie and demanded, "*What's snew?*"

"Uh . . . nothing," she stammered. "What's new with you?"

The audience went utterly demented with laughter. We finished the rest of the act and took our curtsies, but applause and cheers kept us on the boards for almost a full minute.

That conniving Marie started onstage before we were off, as usual. This time I dawdled, and when she barreled straight toward me, I didn't sidestep.

I slapped her across the face.

A gasp went up from the audience, but Marie made no sound, as if being hit were not all that surprising. She raised her arm to return the favor, but I ducked and strode offstage.

Mother was watching from the wings with little Harry in her arms, and she pointed a finger at me, as the others stood there in shock. "You showed her!" she said. "The Turners don't take any guff!"

I knew I shouldn't smile. I'd just struck a stranger—onstage of all places! But I couldn't help it. After the biscuit, she deserved it. We watched her act, and I'll give her this: she performed as if it were just another day in vaudeville.

That night, instead of sneaking off with Joe, Winnie slid into bed beside me.

"You and Scott Joplin have a fight?" I said as snores drifted from Lucy's and Kit's bed.

"I'm just tired." She forced a yawn. "We got up so early."

"Too tired for the man of your dreams? Sounds like trouble in the tunnel of love to me."

"We're fine," she insisted

"Then there's only one other explanation." My pride flared up. "Babysitting."

She sighed. "Well, you have to admit, your temper's been hotter than usual."

"With good reason!"

"Not this morning with Archie. That boy was afraid for his life."

"He looked like he might faint." I chuckled. "It was kind of funny."

She tried to stay stern, but couldn't keep it up. "He almost wet himself," she snickered.

"If he can't handle tough talk, he's not long for vaudeville. Probably won't amount to much anyway. He's too polite. And that cleft in his chin is so big you could park a car in it."

Winnie burst out laughing. "He could be a chauffeur! Comes with his own parking spot!"

We laughed so loudly the girls woke up.

"Go back to sleep," I hissed. "It's the middle of the night, for goodness' sake!"

We waited for them to drift off again. Winnie was quiet, but I knew she wasn't asleep.

"Know what really makes me mad?" It was hard to say out loud, but I had to get it off my chest somehow. "That I'll never know if he's okay. He's somewhere out in this wide, Negro-hating world, and he could be dead already. But I'll never know. I'll worry the rest of my life about a man who may or may not even be alive."

"If anyone can take care of himself, it's Tip. He knows how to stay away from trouble."

"He didn't stay away from me, and I'm probably the biggest trouble he ever met."

"You listen to *me*, this time," she said. "You didn't do anything wrong. You just loved him, and he'll carry that with him forever. People's hatred put him in danger, not your love."

It was the sweetest, truest thing anyone could have said, and it eased the burden of my guilt just enough to make it almost bearable.

"I asked him once if he was the jealous type," I told her. "You know what he said? He said, 'Gertie, I'm like a little brown bear in the Arctic—an easy target. I can't afford the luxury of jealousy. I can barely afford the luxury of keeping my black hide squarely covering my bones. It's no time for acting large.'"

"But he didn't act small, either," Winnie insisted. "Remember how he wouldn't black up in Wellsville? And he made friends with us, even though he knew the risk."

"That's true," I murmured.

"And when those men were saying terrible things in Lyons, he just kept dancing. He wouldn't stop until the curtains were pulled. He's about the bravest man I've ever met," she said. "He may not be entirely free to do as he pleases, but no one can say he acts small, Gert. No one."

She was right, and I felt the flicker of courage in my own heart burn a little brighter. "Maybe I could live large enough for two," I said.

She gazed at me, her little face serious as a judge. "If anyone can, Gertie, it's you."

CHAPTER
37

WINNIE

*I'll make a prediction with my eyes open: that a woman can
and will be elected if she is qualified and gets enough votes.*
—Gracie Allen, actress and comedian

"Will you look at this?" said Joe at breakfast the next morning, flicking the back of his hand against the *Geneva Daily News*. "There's an article about Gert!" He handed me the folded paper and pointed to the bottom-right corner. Nell and Gert peered over my shoulder.

FIGHT BETWEEN LADY PERFORMERS
CAUSED BY BISCUIT

The article was a bit silly, making Gert and Marie out to be longtime rivals attempting to end each other's careers. It said Marie had engaged the assistance of an "ardent fan" to pelt Gert with eggs. However, the young man in question, purportedly a fine upstanding member of the Hobart College Glee Club, felt eggs would be "ungentlemanly" and brought along a biscuit from his noon meal instead.

**Miss Gertrude Turner, a member of the lively and
well-received Tumbling Turner Sisters, responded**

to the biscuit assault by returning it at high speed to its rightful owner. She later applied the palm of her hand at a similar velocity to Miss Dubois's cheek when the two passed each other onstage. This is hardly the kind of genteel activity that is expected of well-mannered ladies at the Opera House.

"I hope we won't be fired," Nell murmured.

"I should've held my temper." Gert shook her head, but the regret seemed to be aimed at the potential consequences rather than her actions.

"Let's wait and see," I said, and flipped the paper over to hide the offending article from further consideration. That's when I saw the headline:

SUFFRAGE WINS IN SENATE: NOW GOES TO STATES

"It passed!" I said, half in shock.

"What did?" said Joe.

"Women's right to vote! It passed in the House a couple of weeks ago, but the Senate vote had been too close to call." I turned to my sisters. "If the states ratify, we'll be voters!"

"That's wonderful," said Nell, but she was clearly still distracted by the prospect of our future unemployment. "We should get to the theatre." She and Gert stood up from the table and headed for the dining room door.

"I'll be right there," I said, wanting to read the full article.

"I wouldn't get too excited." Joe was buttoning his jacket.

"For goodness' sake, why not?" I said. "It's history in the making!"

"It isn't history unless two-thirds of the states agree. And they won't." I stared up at him. "How can you be so sure?"

"Massachusetts already passed a law *against* the women's vote just four years ago," he said matter-of-factly. "And if we're not for it, it's not likely many others will be."

"Massachusetts isn't the center of the whole solar system!" I stood and tossed my napkin onto the table.

His eyebrows shot upward. "I didn't know you were such a radical."

"Radical? It's been before the legislature every session for decades! It's not exactly a newfangled idea."

"No, just an unnecessary one. There's no need for women to vote, Winnie. They've got enough to do just taking care of their families. My mother doesn't want the bother of voting."

"Then let her stay home and make meatballs!" I yelled. "*I* want to vote!"

People from other tables were looking over to see what the ruckus was. We certainly didn't need another Turner sister ending up in the paper for unseemly behavior, so I walked with as much speed as dignity would allow out the door of the dining room and up the sidewalk toward the theatre.

I soon caught up with my sisters. "He's antisuffrage!" I fumed.

"The hell with him, then," said Gert.

"Gert!" Nell scolded. "Winnie, give him some time to come around to the idea. And try to put it out of your mind—we've got more pressing concerns at the moment."

We braced ourselves as we entered the theatre. Kit had gone over early, as she often did, and we found her kneeling on the stage apron, changing a burned-out incandescent bulb in one of the footlights. Distracted by our unexpected approach, her hand banged into the fixture. There must have been some loose wires because a spray of sparks flew out and onto the wooden boards. She slapped at them with her hands, and we could only hope that none of them fell between the cracks to smolder below the stage.

Annoyed, she snapped at us, "What's wrong now? You all look like you're about to face a firing squad."

"Has anyone said anything about the article in the paper?" asked Nell. Evidently no one had, because Kit knew nothing about it, and returned to her bulb-changing before the explanation was fully completed.

We gathered in our dressing room to apply makeup and sat tight, hoping that outrage over the article would blow over before there were any further consequences.

This was not to be the case, but the consequences were certainly not what we expected. We all went up when Fred and Nell were called for their act, and were shocked to see the house completely full. The first show of the day was generally sparse, often older women or young mothers with children looking for an activity to pass the afternoon. But the house was standing room only, and there were plenty of gentlemen in the seats, as well.

Fred and Nell had taken every opportunity to practice, and enjoyed a much better reception. Not only was their dancing smoother, but they had settled into a new rhythm with the jokes. Nell played her part with a perky quirkiness that added punch to the corny gags, a feat that April with her flat, bored expression had never achieved.

They took their bows to enthusiastic applause, and we tore the blue gown off Nell in the wings. "Break a leg!" we all whispered to one another, and began our act.

Even from inside the suitcase, I sensed the audience's anticipation. They cheered for Nell's cartwheels, but the volume rose when Gert entered with her handsprings. By the time I rolled out onto the proscenium, the audience was like a pack of hungry dogs, ready to devour any scraps of entertainment we threw them. Gert's arm jiggles sent them into paroxysms, and the human rolling ball, with skirts flapping up as they spun, caused a wild round of boot stomping.

At the end, the applause went on and on, even after we'd headed for the wings. The stage manager, who had a restraining hand on Marie's arm, waved us back onto the stage for an encore. Of course, we were entirely unprepared, never having been obliged to reprise our act before. It was Kit who saved us. She produced the cane, which she'd apparently hidden behind one of the curtain pulls, and gave me the eye.

"No!" I whispered.

"Go!" she said. And there I was, an almost fully grown woman, ordered by my thirteen-year-old stage brat of a sister to perform a stunt I hadn't mastered. I ran to stage left while she positioned the springboard.

Please, Lord, don't let me break anything or anyone, I prayed, and ran full speed toward my doom.

I did not catch the cane. It bounced off my fingertips and flew into the wings behind me. Kit did, however, catch *me* and swung around with such force I almost went sailing off into the orchestra pit. The audience seemed to think we'd done what we'd set out to do, because they were on their feet applauding and calling, "Brava! Brava!"

After another round of curtsies, we trotted off. The stage manager had apparently let go of Marie a couple of beats early, and she and Gert came face-to-face at the edge of the stage, shooting eye daggers at each other.

An *oooooh* rose from the audience, and then tapered off as Gert continued offstage.

The applause surged for Marie. In the places where she had previously done the stolen arm jiggle, she instead stroked her fingers up her long satin gloves, leaning forward slightly, which enticed the audiences into hoots of approval.

"Not too low, Marie," the stage manager murmured nervously, "Not too low . . ."

In the end, she, too, was called back for an encore, for which she was clearly prepared.

We headed to our dressing room, anxious to discuss this surprising turn of events.

"I can't believe all those people," said Nell. "On a Thursday afternoon, no less!"

"I don't think the theatre manager can be too mad at us now," I said.

"Are you kidding?" said Kit. "They love this stuff. Barney said they were bracing for an invasion."

"Who in the world is Barney?" said Gert.

"The stage manager!" said Kit. "Gee, you people don't pay any attention at all."

We were soon graced with unexpected company. Marie Dubois tapped her gloved fingertips on our open door. "May I enter?" she said.

"No, you may not," said Mother. "You've caused enough trouble."

Marie ignored this and aimed her icy blue eyes at Gert. "We have done well, no?"

Gert scrutinized her. "Done well?"

"Our *antipithie* has filled ze house. Now we must . . . *quel est le mot* . . . capitalize."

"What are you suggesting?"

"Simply zat we continue to show our discord. It is"—she drew out the *s* as she searched for the phrase—"big news?"

"Okay," said Gert hesitantly.

"A warning. If you ever touch my face again"—at this she smiled coldly—"I will scar you."

"Understood," said Gert, affecting an arctic aplomb. "The same rules apply to us both."

Marie gave a regal nod and left us.

"Do you think she cooked up the whole thing on purpose?" said Kit.

"She's not that bright," said Mother. "Besides, Gert started it when she stole that move."

"She's smart enough to come down here and *capitalize*," I said. "That took guts."

"I still don't like her," said Gert.

"It seems the feeling is mutual," said Nell with a wry smile. "And it's probably best for business if you keep it that way."

Joe did not come and find me as he usually did, and this began to eat a hole in my fury toward him over women's suffrage like a moth in a sweater factory. I was no less firm in my belief that women should vote, but I did worry that it might cause a permanent rift. I wondered if I could turn down the volume on my opinions without giving them up altogether. How much bending of oneself was necessary to nurture one's love for someone with differing views? And was Joe wondering the same things—or did he think that because I was the woman, I would do all the bending?

There was only one thing I truly regretted, and that was the crack about his mother's meatballs. It wasn't nice. The poor woman had been through enough.

But he didn't come for me. I took a walk with Nell and the baby, went out for sandwiches with Gert, and between shows Kit dragged me onstage to practice our jump-and-throw. Archie helped her time the cane toss, declaring us "the cat's pajamas" even when we failed. He really was a sweet boy, and I hoped luck (in combination with those lovely dark eyes) might one day land him an even better job than chauffeur. Or at least better than pig slopper.

By the last show, our jump-and-throw was fairly reliable, if not an absolute sure thing. Kit did drop me once, but the audience seemed to appreciate the effort and clapped all the same.

Gert and Marie made sure to pass each other onstage with a sneer or threat of a slap. For the last show, Marie gave the back of Gert's hair a tug, and Gert shook her fist as Marie smiled victoriously and took her place downstage.

After that, we headed straight for the hotel instead of waiting for Joe and Lucy to close.

"But I always wait for Lucy!" said Kit.

"You're not hanging around a theatre full of randy stagehands till all hours of the night without one of us there," said Mother in a burst of random maternal protectiveness. Of course, there had been countless hours when she had no inkling as to Kit's whereabouts, probably assuming that her size and sass would keep her safe.

"Have you talked to him?" Nell murmured as we entered the hotel lobby.

"No. I'm not sure if I want to."

She gave me a little pat on the shoulder that said she didn't believe that for one minute. "Why don't you sit down here where it's quiet and think about what you do want."

It was after midnight and the hotel clerk had closed up for the night. The lobby was hushed except for the soft clicking of the grandfather clock pendulum. I looked out the tall windows to Seneca Lake, its satiny darkness bejeweled with the twinkling lights from moored boats. In the quiet, I could hear the lapping of the waves against the stony shore.

What did I want?

Gert had dedicated herself to "living large"—large enough for two, even. But that wasn't me. Fame, money, adventure. I didn't crave any of these things.

In all that I'd learned during my time in vaudeville, the most important was the realization that, even beyond going to college, what I truly wanted was to be taken seriously: to be able to form my own opinions—ones that might be challenged, certainly, but not utterly discounted; to dream my own dreams, and not have them limited by the happenstance of my gender or social standing. I wanted to be Winnie Turner, and as small and poor and female as that made me, I wanted the right to forge my own future.

I also wanted love.

Greedy girl, I thought. But who isn't greedy in the secret shimmering fairyland of their own wishes?

The front door to the hotel opened and closed with a heavy *thunk*.

"Go on up," I heard Joe say, and Lucy's steps, *kip kip kip*, on the stairs.

I tipped my head to one side, giving his wary expression a moment to soften. "I shouldn't have said that about your mother's meatballs."

He broke into a reluctant smile and strode toward me. I could feel him wanting to slide his arms around my waist as he always did, but he clasped his hands behind his back instead. "So," he said, weighing his words. "You're one of those political types?"

"Not especially. But I do like to talk about it sometimes. Are you one of those *women-aren't-smart-enough-to-have-political-opinions* types?"

"*Madonne*, Winnie. You're one of the smartest people I know."

"But I shouldn't vote."

My words hung in the air, and I could practically see the battle being waged in his head between what he'd always presumed about a woman's place, and the woman he now knew standing before him. He threw his hands up in the air. "I don't know!"

It's a start, I thought. And though I was fairly certain he'd eventually see that women voting would not cause the devastation of society, I did wonder about his own secret fairyland of wishes, and whether I would ultimately be able to grant any of them.

The next day was Friday, and Kit was determined to make the jump-and-throw a reliable success before we left Geneva. She dragged me off to practice anytime the stage was free, which impeded my time with Joe. But a little part of me didn't mind so much. I loved Joe, and was certain he had strong feelings for me, as well. But there was a new note to our tune, maybe even a whole minor chord. Women's suffrage hadn't so much come between us as alerted us to the fact that as deep as our feelings might be, there was still so much we didn't know about each other. Who could predict what far more contentious matters might loom in the future?

During intermission of the six o'clock show, Archie came to help Kit and me practice. The teeter-totter of their friendship seemed to have tipped in Kit's favor, and now he was the one following her around like a colt after the feedbag.

We had time for only a couple of run-throughs before Archie had to go on with the Pender Troupe after intermission. In our hurry, the springboard was incorrectly placed and instead of catching the cane, I batted it away as it flew toward me too soon. Archie tried to catch it before it impaled him, and the metal tip of the cane made an inch-long gash in the heel of his palm.

"Crikey, that smarts!" he said, as blood pooled around it.

"Kit—quick! Run and get my little first aid bag. It's on the table in our dressing room!"

I guided him to the wings and sat him in a chair, holding his hand above his head and pressing two fingers against the wound, as the first aid book had instructed. "Get a doctor," I urged a stagehand. "He's going to need stitches."

"Stiches!" said one of the acrobat boys. "We go on soon!"

"I've got to do the act," Archie insisted. "My mates need me."

Kit came with my first aid bag and I used the gauze pads to wipe away the blood. The cut wasn't deep, but if he was to go on, I had to find a way to stabilize it. "This has alcohol in it," I warned, pouring tincture of iodine onto a piece of gauze. "It's going to hurt."

He clenched his teeth and muttered, "Bloody hell!" but he didn't pull his hand away from the pain. The blood bubbled up, but it didn't spurt, and the more I pressed on the iodine-soaked gauze, the less it leaked. "You missed a vein, at least," I told him. "Only just a capillary."

"They're on in ten minutes," said Barney, the stage manager. "Will he be okay to go?"

At first I didn't know to whom this question was aimed—Mr. Pender, possibly, or even Archie himself. But when no one answered, I glanced up and saw the eyes of the troupe, stagehands, and my mother and sisters, who had followed Kit up with the first aid supplies, all trained on me. I had taken charge of the situation, as the book instructed, and they all waited on my word!

"It'll hurt," I warned Archie, "but if you want, I can try and put a few stitches in and then bandage it up to get you through the act."

Archie blanched, and his eyes darted to Kit. She nodded encouragingly and said, "You can do it, Archie!"

"Yes, but can *she* do it?" he murmured, tipping his head toward me.

Kit smiled. "Oh, don't worry—she's read all about it."

I felt my confidence plummet. With a total lack of experience, what business did I have offering to perform this procedure? Like a child anxiously contemplating her first steps, I instinctively glanced to my mother.

"I'll get my sewing kit," she said. "Big needle or small?"

Gratitude surged through me. Mother could be many things: temperamental, ornery, fickle, controlling . . . but she had brought me into this world and guided me safely through seventeen years of it, and her confidence in my ability—whether to quickly learn how to fly through the air, or to stitch human skin—meant the world to me.

I thought for a moment. "Big enough for your strongest thread."

She returned with a needle already threaded, and I wiped it down with iodine before taking Archie's hand in mine. "Kit, stick out your pointer finger. Now, Archie you squeeze that as hard as you can with your good hand, and try not to move."

I stared down into the wound for a moment and took a deep breath. *Five quick stitches*, I told myself. *Pretend it's just a popped seam.*

I tried to recall the old doctor who had mended my father's hand to replicate his actions, but with less quaking of my fingers—a tall order, given the anxiety coursing through me! But then I forced myself to replace his image with that of the competent and unflappable Dr. Lodge, and this helped to calm me. I soon became fascinated by the texture of the skin, how easily it took the needle and seemed to want to reconnect with its opposite shore.

Archie let out an occasional muffled groan through gritted teeth, but I'll say one thing for him: that boy did not budge. He was made of stronger stuff than any of us would have guessed.

In just a few minutes, I had completed the stitching, then applied a new round of iodine-soaked gauze. I wound my prized Esmarch triangular bandage, with the figures of half-naked men, around his hand and wrist to cushion and stabilize it.

"Thank you, miss!" said Mrs. Pender as the boys all ran out onto the stage. I didn't need her thanks; my own veins and capillaries bubbled with the thrill of stitching my first wound!

Gert leaned over and whispered in my ear, "Living large, I see."

On Saturday, our final day in Geneva, there was a surprise visitor waiting for us just before the last show that night.

"Hello, Turners," said Morty Birnbaum, his form as stooped and his suit as brown as ever. He shook hands all around, but when he came to me he squinted his eyes of innominate color. "You've grown," he said.

"A little," I said self-consciously.

He studied me a moment longer and then moved on to Gert. "Yankees pitching scout's been sniffing around, but I said, no, I think she's sticking with vaudeville. Am I right, or should I call him back?" He let out his little barking laugh. "You've caused quite a stir, missy."

"Did you come to see us?" said Gert.

"Course I did," said Birnbaum. "Word is, you've tumbled yourselves right into a high-class act. I hear you've added a springboard, bigger stunts, and even some comedy routines. That's a far cry from the few splits and somersaults you started out with. Barney says you're keeping the crowds rolling in, feuding with one of the other acts. Priceless. I'll tell you what. I got a booking agent from the Keith-Albee circuit to come up and give you a look-see, so give it your all, girls."

"Keith-Albee?" Kit's jaw was agape. "You mean it? That's big-time."

"The biggest," said Birnbaum. "They got the best theatre in every major city east of the Mississippi."

"The Palace!" She practically went into a swoon just saying the name.

"Let's not get ahead of ourselves. I'd be tickled just to get you booked in Poughkeepsie."

The show was about to start. Birnbaum went to take his seat, and we went to freshen our makeup and try to ward off fits of anxiety as we waited to perform for a big-time booking agent.

"We have to do the jump-and-throw," insisted Kit.

"I'm so nervous, I'm afraid I'll miss the cane and break my neck!"

"Even if you break every bone in your body, just get up and bow. They'll love it."

Gert stood up. "I have to find Marie." It was the last we saw of her until showtime.

Nell and Fred had their act down, and the applause was respectable, even delighted. As I hid in one of the leg curtains, I spotted Birnbaum in the second row, and the man sitting next to him said something that my limited lip-reading skills interpreted as "Charming!"

They *were* charming, and it wrenched me to realize that our success would likely mean Fred's misfortune. If we got into the big time, he'd have to find another partner and start all over again. I clapped hard when they finished, amplifying the ovation as best I could.

In the next moment, they were done, Nell shimmied out of the gown, and I got into my suitcase. Blood thrummed like crashing waves in my chest as I waited in the cramped space. Then I was rolling out onto the stage, smiling as if it were my birthday, Christmas, and the Fourth of July, directly into the face of the Keith-Albee booking agent.

We punched every punch line, landed every jump, and I even caught the cane. But the thing that made the audience roar like a pride full of lions at a kill was when Marie Dubois entered too early, as usual. She and Gert came to a dead stop glaring at each other, and patrons waited to see if another world war might begin right on the stage of the Smith Opera House.

Gert did something completely unexpected: she held out her hand to shake. Marie eyed her warily for a moment, and then nodded and shook Gert's hand. The audience applauded this act of diplomacy, of course, but only because it was the civilized thing to do.

When Gert turned to go, she pulled her hand back and tugged Marie's long black glove right off! She flipped it over her shoulder as she sashayed toward the wings, and Marie gave a look of pure spite before grabbing it back. The audience exploded with delight at the feud's second life, and Marie used the opportunity to pull her glove back on in a darkly sensual fashion.

"Gert, that was brilliant!" I said.

"It was half Marie's idea."

"And it was half yours."

Her gaze flicked appreciatively at me. "Big time," she murmured, "or die trying."

I found Joe in his dressing room. Birnbaum was his agent, too. "Have you seen him?" I asked when I got to the door.

"We saw him," said Joe. I followed his gaze into the corner of the small room, and there was Lucy, hunched over on a chair, her face damp with recent tears.

"What's wrong?" I said, and went to sit by her, stroking the hair off her forehead.

"Joe won't do the song, and Mr. Birnbaum said we've got no zing, and I don't want to go back to Boston!" She began to wail all over again.

Joe rolled his eyes. "That's not what he said. He said he was disappointed to see us closing, and it didn't look good for big time if we're only good enough to close in small time."

"We have to do the song!" she cried.

"*Lucia*, you know we cannot do that song." He seemed tired, as if this particular disagreement had gone on for ages.

"What song?" I asked. "Why not?"

He shook his head. "It doesn't matter. I probably can't even get through it." He glanced at Lucy. "And neither can you."

She stood up and glared at him. "*Vigliacco*!" she sneered, shaking a finger at him. "Just because you're too cowardly doesn't mean *I* am!"

"*Basta!*" he yelled. "That's enough of your disrespect!"

She put her knuckles on her hips, palms out like I'd seen the women in the Seventh Ward of Binghamton do. Then she closed her eyes and began to sing.

Oh, Papa, my papa,
I was born to the sound of your voice,
Singing the joy of the day, serenading my way
To a life of happiness.

I looked at Joe, and all the anger seemed to seep out of him, leaving only sorrow as he watched her. Tears formed in Lucy's eyes, but her voice never faltered. If anything it grew more resonant.

And when the winds of sadness blew,
You taught me to be strong, so strong,
But I could never be as strong as you,
Oh, Papa.

She stopped and glared at him. "Should I go on? Or do you admit I can do it?"

We both waited for his answer. His eyes were shiny, and he seemed unable to respond.

"Joe," I said gently. "It's beautiful. Did you write it?" He nodded.

"It's the best song we have," insisted Lucy. "It's a showstopper."

She was right. If they could get through it without falling apart, it would bring down the house.

"Joe, I have a question, and maybe you don't know the answer, but I'm going to ask anyway." He gazed down at me, beautiful brown eyes so full of pain. "How would your father feel about it? Would he be proud?"

At that he put his chin down and cried, shoulders shaking, hand across his face. I put my arms around him and held him. He was a good man, this Joe Cole, and I was grateful to be allowed into his most profound sadness.

His crying slowed, and he reached into his pocket for a handkerchief to wipe his face. "Yes," he said finally. "I think he would be very proud."

"Can you get through it?"

He cut his eyes toward his sister. "If she can, I can."

"It's so beautiful, people in the audience who've lost their own fathers might really appreciate it."

He gazed at me, grateful, full of love. "I never thought of it that way."

I smiled. "It made me miss my dad, and we've only been apart five days."

When the stage manager called, we went up to wait for their entrance. Isadora the Incredible Impersonator was doing President Wilson. Onstage she'd set up a folding screen for costume changes. She could go from Abraham Lincoln to a baby in diapers in ten seconds. As President Wilson, she looked over her pince-nez glasses and spoke in stentorian tones about the coming Prohibition, garnering laughs about being a nation with the shakes.

"Is that really how President Wilson sounds?" I asked Joe, to get his mind off his nerves.

"Who knows? Unless you've seen him in person, how could you tell?" Apparently being an impersonator was more about the costumes and gags than actual mimicry.

I could feel their anxiety rising as Isadora wrapped up her stint; when she was called back for two encores, the three of us almost went mad with anticipation. But finally it was their turn, and though a few people headed up the aisles to leave, the house remained mostly full.

Lucy gave it her all with "Pretty Baby," "By the Light of the Silvery

Moon," and "In the Good Old Summertime," inviting the audience to sing along with her at the refrains. For a "haircuts" act, she was doing well, keeping the audience happy enough to stay. I wondered if they'd need the song about their father after all.

Then a few more patrons got up to leave, and Joe began to play some soft and wistful chords I hadn't heard before. The audience stilled itself to catch the tune. Lucy gestured back to Joe and said demurely, "This is a song my brother wrote for our father." Then she began to sing.

An audience is a living organism, in constant motion, producing constant sound. A finger scratches an arm, a fist covers a cough, lips move to say, "Oh, excuse me," when a coat falls. But that audience was as close to still and silent as any group of eighteen hundred people could possibly be. The final lines were even more heartrending than the ones she'd sung in the dressing room.

> Oh, Papa, my papa,
> You sheltered me against the storm
> You kept me safe, you kept me warm
> This hard, cold world I never knew
> Until God said, "Come home," to you.

A little gasp rose in the house, a collective, sympathetic *ohhhh*. That simple, primal sigh of compassion was for all the little girls who'd lost fathers, for all the sorrow of all the children in the world. Her voice was strong and sweet even as tears pooled in her lids, and the audience began to sniffle and dab their own eyes in response.

When she hit the last refrain, Lucy dropped down onto her knees, hands clasped in front of her, and lifted her gaze to the vaulted ceiling.

> Oh, Papa, my papa,
> I love you—I'll always love you,
> And miss . . . you . . . so!

For a moment after the last notes drifted away, the only sound was of people openly weeping. Then the audience rose to their feet and sent up applause that echoed through the chamber in an outpouring of love and sympathy.

Joe came forward, his eyes full, and reached down to help Lucy stand, which set off another round of applause and calls of "Bravo!" It seemed as if their bows might never end.

After another few moments they left the stage, but the applause surged again. They looked so utterly exhausted I hated to tell them: "You have to do an encore!"

"*Porca vacca!*" Joe muttered to himself. "I can't."

I looked at Lucy. "It just means 'pig cow,'" she said. "But not in a nice way." Her face brightened. "I know—'Stella Stellina'! Joe, that's so easy."

She pulled him back onstage and he slumped down onto the piano bench. Lucy told the audience, "This is an Italian lullaby our papa used to sing to us."

She sang it first in Italian, then in English.

Star, little star,
The night is coming, the flame is flickering.
The cow is in the stable. The sheep and the lamb,
The cow with her calf, the hen with her chicks,
The cat with her kittens; and all are sleeping
In the mother's heart!

Afterward, we all waited backstage for our wages, and while I was thrilled at the prospect of the biggest paycheck I'd ever known—a walloping twenty-five dollars!—my mind was overrun with pride for Joe and Lucy. As we say in the business, they laid 'em out in the aisles (and in a few overly emotional cases, almost literally). I couldn't wait to see Mr. Birnbaum's reaction.

But he was nowhere to be found, and we had no idea if he had gone back to New York, or was staying at one of the handful of local hotels.

"He can't just go without a word!" said Gert as we left the theatre.

"I've a mind to start contacting other agents," Mother warned, as if saying so would make Birnbaum appear from out of the mists that drifted in off Seneca Lake.

Joe walked a few paces behind, his arm around Lucy, guiding her as if her vision were impaired. The performance had exhausted her, and her head lolled against his shoulder, little eyelids blinking back sleep. Up in the hotel room, he tucked her tenderly into bed next to Kit and went to wash his face and change into civilian clothes, while Gert and I did the same.

"Want to come out with Joe and me?" I asked as we wiggled out of the tight costumes and into shirtwaists and skirts, ringlets of hair sticking to our freshly scrubbed cheeks. Gert gave a deadpan *don't-be-ridiculous* look. She had taken to going out on her own since the Biscuit Incident—where I couldn't be sure—and much as I wanted to be alone with Joe for our last night together, I worried about the potential danger to her person as well as her reputation.

Mother was strangely silent on the matter of Gert's nighttime solo jaunts. There seemed to be an unspoken deal struck between them, or if it was spoken, I hadn't been privy to that particular battle of titans. The outcome, however, was clear. Gert would do what was necessary to keep the act's trajectory moving skyward, and in return she could . . . well, she could do just about anything. The Biscuit Incident was her own personal moment of emancipation, and she was, in a word, free.

I benefited from this new policy, and sailed along in the slipstream of Gert's carte blanche. But it wasn't just that. After she'd seen my command of the situation with Archie's hand, Mother seemed to have a new appreciation for my own ability to navigate in the world. Not that wound stitching necessarily translated to self-preservation skills, but nevertheless, her expressions of concern over my wanderings with Joe took on a pro forma quality.

"Are you girls going out again tonight?" Mother said, peeking her head in our door.

"Just for a bit," said Gert. She had recently taken to applying a touch of powder and lipstick. Not enough to be unseemly, but it did make her look like a woman of the world.

"Well . . . all right," said Mother, as if we'd asked for her permission and she was granting us provisional assent. "But not too late."

"Where are *you* going?" Gert asked. "I see you've got your best brooch on." It was a little gold-plated clover with a green glass bead at its center, a gift from Dad on their twentieth anniversary.

"Oh, this," said Mother offhandedly. "Isadora is having a few of us up to her room." She couldn't help adding, "She's on the top floor. It's a two-room suite."

"Headliners can afford that sort of thing, I suppose," said Gert, dabbing the excess lipstick away with a piece of tissue.

All the while, I kept still and silent, hoping that Mother's eagerness to take up her spot as Isadora's best girlfriend of the week would outweigh her maternal concerns. And in fact, she did leave within moments, but not without one last meaningful glance meant to convey some sort of general message about being careful and not embarrassing the family. Gert held her eye rolling until Mother had closed the door behind her.

The two of us went down to the lobby, and Gert proceeded on out the door, toward what assignation or adventure I had no idea. There was murmuring back toward the windows that overlooked the lake, and framed between the velveteen curtains I saw Nell and Fred Delorme, their heads bent toward each other. I nearly tripped over a potted plant, taken aback at the prospect of Nell's face that near any man's.

"I won't stand for it!" Fred said, his voice suddenly loud enough for me to hear. "That's not the kind of man I am."

"No one's asking you to be that kind of man," said Nell angrily, "only to be practical!"

Fred turned away from her, and his gaze caught on mine, standing stock-still as I was, afraid to go forward or retreat. "I'm sorry . . . ," I stammered. "I didn't mean to . . ."

"That's all right, Winnie," said Fred. "The conversation was over anyway." He strode past me and up the stairs.

Nell shook her head. "They say *we're* the irrational sex."

"Is everything okay?"

"No," she said. "But there's only so much I can do about that."

Joe came down then. "Oh, hello, Nell," he said, slipping his hand to the small of my back. "Join us for a drink?"

"You're kind to ask," she said with a hint of a smile. "But I wouldn't dream of it. Besides, my little scalawag doesn't care if I've had ten hours of sleep or two. He'll demand breakfast at the break of dawn all the same."

Joe and I went to a bar on Castle Street called Pinky's and prepared to part once again. Birnbaum had booked him and Lucy in a few small towns in Rhode Island and Connecticut, and then they would be back in Boston for the rest of the summer.

"I want you to come for a visit," he said. "Mama wants to meet this Winnie she's been hearing about."

"You told her about me?"

He took a sip of his beer, buying time to compose his answer. "Truthfully? Lucy blabbed about you in a letter home when we were in Lyons, and then I got a letter from Mama full of question marks." He affected a thick Italian accent. "'Giuseppe, who's this-a Winnie? Is she *italiana*? Is she one of those-a loose vaudeville girls with the skimpy costumes?'"

"So, she doesn't really want to meet me, so much as make sure I'm not a . . . a . . ."

"*Puttana.*"

I raised my eyebrows in question, and he said, "It means what you think it means."

His mother knew about me! Of course, my mother had known about him all along, but that wasn't remotely as fascinating as the idea of a woman I'd never met demanding to know if I was good enough for her son. It felt grand and also a little terrifying that my name was being spoken somewhere I'd never even been.

"What did you tell her about me?"

He reached across the table and took my fingers, studying them, running his thumb across the nails. Then he looked up. "I told her the truth. That you are smart and beautiful and everything good. And that I love you and I need to find a way for us to be together."

I brought his hand up to my cheek. "What did she say?" I whispered.

He raised his other hand to my face, cupping my cheeks, his long fingers slipping into my hair. "She said, 'Well you better bring her to Boston, then.'"

CHAPTER
38

GERT

The secret of life is honesty and fair dealing.
If you can fake that, you've got it made.
—Groucho Marx, actor and comedian

Sunday morning, we had breakfast in the hotel dining room with Joe and Lucy, as usual. Then Fred Delorme came toward the table eyeing Nell as if she might bite him. Winnie told me she'd seen them arguing. But Nell slid her chair away from mine and made space for him anyway, saint that she is. As he pulled a seat over from another table, he murmured, "I'm sorry, Nell. I was harsh last night, and I had no right to be."

"You have a right to your opinion, Fred. I just don't share it."

"I can't let you carry me," he insisted. "A man doesn't lean on a woman like that."

I shot a look to Winnie, but she didn't seem to know anything, either.

"This is vaudeville," Nell whispered, just as insistent. "We help each other because it's the only way we get by sometimes. And besides, as a dear old friend once told me, whether you're in the business or not, it's the only way to live."

I was so focused on Nell and Fred I didn't notice a familiar brown suit approach. "Room for one more?" he asked.

We scrambled like the Keystone Kops to get Birnbaum a chair and rearrange ourselves around him.

"That was some show last night, wasn't it?" he said, tucking his napkin onto his lap and shaking his head. "Some show, all right!"

Wasting no time on subtlety, Mother asked, "What did the booking agent think?"

"Well, he was mighty impressed—with all of you!" He smiled and looked around until his eyes caught on Fred, and his brow furrowed. Then he went back to smiling. "He was definitely interested."

The waitress took his order, poured him coffee, and got him a clean spoon because the first one had something stuck to it. All the while I felt as if my head was about to pop off! What would be our future? Only God and Birnbaum knew.

Kit crumbled to curiosity first. "Are we going back on the road? In the big time?"

Birnbaum took a sip of his coffee. "Well, now, let's not get ahead of ourselves. The booker will report back, he'll make some inquiries, see what spots he's got to fill. These things don't happen overnight. It's a work in progress, but I expect good news."

Nell spoke up. "Mr. Birnbaum, I'm sure you noticed that I'm in two acts now—the Tumbling Turners, of course, and Delorme and Delorme."

"Yes, I did indeed." He cut his eyes to Fred. "The dance-and-patter act."

"Would it be possible . . . ," she said, "is there a way that I could . . ."

"You want your gentleman friend to travel with you so you can do both acts."

"Oh, he's not my gentleman friend," said Nell quickly. "That is, he's a gentleman and we're friends, but we aren't . . . attached."

"Are you related in any way? Because if he were, for instance, a *cousin*, I could make the argument that you should perform together for the sake of the family." He put a finger up. "However, adding that kind of a clause to a contract generally means less pay. It's the price of your convenience. And if big-time bookers want the Tumbling Turners more than the dance-and-patter, you'll all play smaller houses."

"And if the situation is reversed," said Nell, "Delorme and Delorme would be the one held back." Either way, someone got the short end.

"Nell," I said. "Fred has to find someone else. It's best for everyone." I turned to Fred. "You understand, don't you?"

"Of course I do. I didn't like the idea to begin with—no sense hobbling you all with my problems." He ran a hand over little Harry's downy blond head. "Nell, you're the only one he has now. You could make a boodle, and I won't stand in the way of that."

Nell said nothing, only gazed down at the baby sitting on her lap.

I don't fancy myself a mind reader, but I do know my sisters. And if I were a gambler, I would've bet all my earnings that Nell was thinking of Nat's kindness, Tip's courage, and of her own Harry, whose heart had been bigger than any of ours.

"I won't go without Fred," she said quietly. "I'll stay home with Dad and take in laundry if I have to, but I won't perform."

"Nell Turner," Mother hissed, "you'll do what is best for this family!"

Nell smiled at Mother as if she were soothing a cranky toddler. "I know you want so much for all of us, Mother. But I have to do what's best for *my* family. How can I teach him to stand up for his friends if I don't stand up for mine?"

Atta girl! I thought. The awful sadness of Harry's death had kept her from busting out of Mother's control, but now she was taking the reins. Nell was going to be okay. By the peaceful look on her face, I knew she felt it, too.

I turned to Birnbaum. "Fred's in."

Fred looked as if he didn't know whether to spit or go blind. "Nell . . . ," he said.

"You're in, Fred," said Winnie. And that was that.

Breakfast arrived and we all began to eat, but I could see Winnie eyeing Birnbaum, waiting till he'd gobbled down most of his poached eggs and corned beef hash before asking, "What did you think of Joe and Lucy?"

"Stupendous," he said. "Brought down the house."

"I'll bet the booking agent was impressed."

"Had to give him my handkerchief. The guy blubbered all the way to the train station." He stopped loading hash onto his fork and looked at Joe. "I was worried, I don't mind saying. But I gotta hand it to you, you pulled it off. I got a meeting with him next week to nail down a schedule for the Turners, and Dainty Little Lucy is on my list of topics."

Lucy chimed in, "I knew you'd like that song!"

"Little girl, I loved it. But what's more important is the audience loved it. And if the audience loved the sound of a chicken clucking 'My Country 'Tis of Thee,' I'd love that, too."

"Mr. Birnbaum," said Joe suddenly. "I'd like to make a request."

Oh, for cripes' sake, I thought. *Not you, too.*

Birnbaum gave him a warning look, but Joe went on. "Lucy and I have become close friends with the Turners, and on the road you need friends. Well, I suppose you don't absolutely need them, but they certainly make it more pleasant. I'd like to ask that, if it's in your power, we'd like to be booked with the Turners."

Birnbaum dropped his fork with a clatter onto his plate, and his glare scanned the table. "Now listen. Are you people in this for business or pleasure? Because if it's just a Sunday jaunt in the countryside for you, we should go our own ways."

"Business!" Winnie blurted out. "He's in it for business—we all are."

"All right, then," said Birnbaum. "Can we just eat now?"

We sat in silence watching his fork move from his plate to his mouth like a conveyor belt. When he was done, he got up, tossed some coins onto the table, and said, "I've got a train to catch. All I can say is, I'll do my best."

We all had trains to catch, all heading in different directions. Winnie and Joe didn't have much time to talk before we had to be on our way.

"*Business?*" I heard him murmur. "How could you think money is more important than being together? I never thought of you as that kind of person, Winnie, the kind who values the weight of your purse over the people you care for. If you even care for me!"

Winnie must have whispered some sort of assurance to him as we parted because he looked a little less like a bear who'd been poked with a stick.

"He sounds like a girl," I said as we waited on the train platform.

"Gert, really."

"Prove your love! Be poor! Let *me* be poor! We can be poor and unsuccessful *together*!"

She laughed despite my meanness to the man she loved. "I told him I didn't do it for the money," she said. "I did it for us. If he lowers his prospects for me and doesn't make enough to keep his father's land, he'll regret it. And eventually he'll resent me."

She was one step ahead of him. She was one step ahead of *me*, too, but instead of envy, I felt proud of her. "You're getting kind of good at this."

She shrugged, but she liked the compliment, I could tell. "You'll always be better at it, though."

"I don't think so," I said. "I would have done it for the money."

Back in Johnson City, as we waited to hear from Birnbaum, Winnie settled in like a hen warming a nest full of eggs, happily pecking away at her schoolwork. I didn't even go back to school. I just picked up more shifts at the Arlington, and flashed my vaudeville smile for the big tippers.

"If you don't go to school, how will I know what papers to write?" Winnie whined. "How will you take your tests?"

"I'm not taking them."

"Then you won't graduate!"

"I never cared about that—you did."

"You're this close! What's the harm of going to your last two weeks of school?"

"The harm is in doing something *I absolutely don't care about*. Winnie, get this through your head: there is no acceptable future for me that requires a high school diploma."

"For cripes' sake, Gert!" she yelled, and my eyebrows nearly hit my hairline at the sound of saucy language coming out of her mouth. "If there's anything we've learned this year with this whole"—she waved her arms around in frustration—"Dad's hand and vaudeville and Tip and just . . . *everything*, it's that we can't possibly *know* what the future will bring! Maybe you're right, and you'll never need it. But what if things don't go as planned—because *they almost never do*—and it comes in handy? Would it be the worst thing in the world to have it in your back pocket, just for insurance?"

I stared at her, dumbstruck—more because of her yelling and sassing and waving her arms around than by what she'd said. It was a whole new side of her!

"Oh, forget it!" she huffed, and stormed out of the room.

Once I got over the shock of it, I did think about what she said. I still didn't agree with her, but I was impressed by how much she wanted me to have "insurance," the kind only she could offer.

The next morning as I dozed in my bed while she and Kit got ready for school, she suddenly stomped into my room. "Okay, *I'll* pay *you*."

I opened my eyes. "You won't, either."

"Will, too. I'll buy you a graduation dress. Don't you want to wear a pretty dress and parade around in front of all those snotty girls you hate?"

Oh, I really had her—or she had me, I'm not sure which. The idea of showing up all those gossiping ninnies was like a pack of Necco wafers I couldn't stop eating. I pursed my lips, pretending to consider. "And shoes," I said finally.

I failed all my tests. Technically I didn't pass history class at all, even with the good grades on the papers Winnie wrote for me, but I sweet-talked that pigeon-toed Mr. Finkhausen into giving me a D-minus instead of an F.

And so on June 22, 1919, despite all my best intentions, I graduated from high school. I crossed the dais and collected my little piece of paper, and when I walked back to my family afterward, Winnie was grinning like she'd just won the Kentucky Derby. I handed her the diploma and whispered in her ear, "Congratulations."

Birnbaum called the next day.

"It's summer," he told Mother over the phone while Mrs. Califano stirred her tomato gravy and eavesdropped. "A lot of big-time acts don't like to play in hot theatres. People go to the beach instead of shows. I got you and the Delorme act booked in some pretty high-class houses. But don't expect it to last," he warned. "Come September, you'll probably only get closing at the shabby end of big time."

"What about Lucy and Joe?" asked Kit, when Mother returned and told us what he'd said.

"He didn't mention them."

"Did you ask?"

She drilled Kit with a dark look and said simply, "No." Kit was only thirteen. It would be years before Mother would give up her right to fire warning shots.

A week later we left for Altoona, Pennsylvania.

The Mishler Theatre had big time written all over it, from the long row of huge doors lining the front, to the four paintings of fancy old-time women above them. The lobby had thick marble columns and gold-painted carved trim all around the ceiling. Inside the theatre there was red carpet and silk drapes, and a crystal chandelier that dropped down from a painting of the sky dotted with half-naked angels. The best part was the green leather seats—there were almost two thousand of them! The building was pretty, but in my short time in the business, I'd learned that it was the size of the crowd that made for success, not gilded babies and curlicues on the ceiling. With all those seats, the Turner Sisters were on our way.

Now that we were in the big time, the cities we played had two, three, even five theatres, often within a few blocks of one another. Keith-Albee was a "two-a-day" circuit, so we only performed matinee and evening shows instead of the small-time "continuous" shows that might require up to six performances daily. We were working less and getting paid much more. In Columbus, Ohio, we made $650, and that was after Birnbaum got his 10 percent!

To my mind, this required a renegotiation of our percentages. But first I had to soften Mother up.

"Isn't it lovely?" I said to her as we stood gazing up at the Southern Theatre, with its attached hotel. "And so safe! With all that brick and tile, they say it's completely fireproof."

Mother gave a predictable shudder, and I expected her to mention those poor girls in the Binghamton Clothing Factory fire, as she often did. "That's what they said about the Iroquois in Chicago. 'Absolutely fireproof!'" She shook her head. "Went up like a haystack, and six hundred souls right along with it."

I had to wait until she had her feet up on the upholstered chaise longue in her room, free of her new toe-pinching, French-heeled oxford pumps, sighing at the luxury of it all. I decided to get right to the point this time. "It's not fair for you to make $325 minus expenses, and for each of us to make only $81.25."

She lifted her head to eye me. "Expenses have gone up, too."

They had—but only a little. In small towns, we'd paid anywhere from one to two dollars a room each night for lodging. Here at the high-class Southern Hotel we paid $2.50. The train fare was higher because of the longer distances we traveled, and we did eat better. No more drugstore sandwiches—we went to actual restaurants. Kit's love of Delmonico steak and German chocolate cake added to the bill, but Mother still banked far more than we did.

She had already seen that I could rally my sisters behind me, so it wasn't hard to negotiate a flat 20 percent for each family member, with everyone kicking into a kitty for the expenses. Extras like new clothes or going out at night were on the spender. "If you want a new hat," I told them, "that's your business."

And we wanted new hats. Oh, we certainly did. We tried to go on a shopping spree at the Lazarus department store in Columbus. Every floor had a thing called an escalator—moving stairs—all you had to do was stand there and not fall over! We only had an hour before the show, and we were so overwhelmed by six floors of choices we didn't buy a thing.

"I'm going back tomorrow." Nell held little Harry's fingers and let him practice his walking backstage. "And I'm not leaving until I have three new dresses."

"Why three?" I asked.

"Because then I can get rid of all my long skirts and shirtwaists. I'm done wearing those old-lady fashions like some secretary in a stuffy office building."

The next day we all trouped back to Lazarus, and Nell didn't let us leave the store until we each had our three dresses. What a shock it was, tossing our tight corsets, high collars, and pinched waists for the flowing lightness of the new fashions. Sleeveless, low necked, and dropped-waist, with shamelessly flimsy undergarments beneath, they made me feel like I was wearing a summer nightgown instead of a dress. On a whim, we all got bobbed haircuts at the salon on the third floor, too. Kit wanted bangs, Nell's was parted on the side, mine tickled at the nape of my neck, and Winnie's was the shortest of all, with little crescent curls at the ears.

We all felt lighter than air, but somehow it was Nell who shone the brightest in her new clothes and hairdo. Maybe it was being in two acts instead of one, doubling her vaudeville status; maybe it was the extra money she made as a result. But I'd wager that it was little Harry, growing like a weed, rising up onto two feet and eyeing the world from new heights that made Nell do the same. Her partnership with Fred Delorme had blossomed into an easy friendship. They laughed and talked and worked on their act like lifelong chums. Little by little, the trenches between Fred's brows seemed to iron themselves out, too.

"It took him a few weeks to trust that I was really going to show up ready to work every time," Nell told me. "He's just happy to have a partner he doesn't have to carry—literally."

"Doesn't it wear you out, performing twice as much as everyone else?"

"Not at all," she said. "It's good for me. I'm too busy remembering my lines and too tired from all the stunts and dancing to worry like I used to. Traveling and meeting new people all the time brought me out of myself. To be honest, I think vaudeville might have saved my life."

As it turned out, Birnbaum had booked Dainty Little Lucy at three of the same theatres we played, and one at a different theatre in the same city. This made Winnie and Joe nauseatingly happy, of course, but it also was nice for Kit to have Lucy again.

Though we now had enough dough to get our own rooms, Winnie and I still shared with Kit and Lucy. Maybe this was just habit, or protectiveness over the young girls. But it was also about freedom. Mother had practically given up pestering us altogether. We could go anywhere, do anything we pleased, and we took full advantage. But after an evening out on my own, there was something nice about coming back to a room with my sisters in it. I might've been willing to do that for the rest of my life if I'd had the chance.

Winnie went off with lover boy, of course. Whatever direction they headed in, I went the opposite. Out of jealousy, of course—why subject myself to their billing and cooing. But then I began to love the daring of being out in the night, a woman alone. I had always looked and acted older, and now with my new fashionable dresses and a bit of makeup, people took me for twenty-five at least. Occasionally I had to raise my voice, a lady in distress, or once even throw an elbow into some cad's breastbone. But the greater the risks, the more alive I felt.

Living large enough for two. It was the best medicine for a heart that felt like it would always be just a little bit broken.

CHAPTER
39

WINNIE

Fire has always been and, seemingly, will always remain,
the most terrible of the elements.
—Harry Houdini, magician and escape artist

"*D io mio . . . ,*" Joe muttered when he saw me. "Your hair! What did you do?"

"Thanks a lot!"

"No, I . . . I think I like it, it's just so short. And modern."

I took that as a compliment, though I knew Joe didn't necessarily mean it that way. I wanted to be a more modern version of myself. I would turn eighteen on Friday, and it seemed the perfect time to make adjustments, inside and out.

My net worth was growing. Each week, Nell, Gert, and I wired money to our bank accounts. When we learned we'd be going back on the road, Nell had helped Kit set up an account with Nell as the trustee. Mother hadn't liked that one bit, but Nell played it off as something they'd done on a whim one afternoon. I think we all just wanted Kit to have a little something of her own, without Mother's interference.

Though I did occasionally splurge on new clothes and books, I didn't spend any of my hard-earned savings on July 25. It was my birthday and Joe insisted on taking me to a fancy restaurant called The

Maramor after the evening show. The windows must have been ten feet high along the front wall, and delicate chandeliers lit the room with cottony warmth. There were upholstered chairs and thick cloth napkins, and the waitress was so attentive you would have thought we were royalty instead of teenagers on our first real date.

"We'll have a couple of Singapore Slings, please," Joe said to the waitress, who smiled and nodded at his good taste. I did see her consult with the restaurant manager a few moments later, however, the two of them eyeing us suspiciously. Then the manager simply shrugged. Prohibition was breathing down the necks of every restaurant owner in the country. With the prospects of lost income from the sale of alcohol, they were apparently willing to take in every penny they could before the well went dry.

"What's a Singapore Sling?" I asked Joe.

"It's this new drink from the Orient. Gin, cherry brandy, pineapple juice, and soda water. You'll like it, it's sweet."

It was very sweet and very pink and just bubbly enough to taste like a sort of fruity Dr Pepper. I liked them a little too well, and so did Joe. I had never seen him order anything other than beer, which he generally drank at an unhurried, disinterested pace. But these frothy, candied cocktails went down quickly.

We were all smiles by the time our plate of mixed pickles came, giggly when the imperial baked ham with champagne sauce arrived, and lacked all caution as our spoons did battle over the English apple cake à la mode that we were too full for, but witless enough to order anyway.

We should have ordered coffee and poured some bitter black sense into us.

Instead we went back to Joe's room, took off our street clothes, and got into bed, as we had done any number of times before. But with my new fashionable dresses, I no longer wore voluminous drawers. Instead I wore step-in panties with a little camisole on top. There was just so much more bare skin involved, and what wasn't bare was readily identifiable under such gossamer coverings.

We began to neck and pet, our senses brought to entirely new levels of hot pink frothy ardor, fueled as it was by gin and cherry brandy. We pressed against each other as if our sanity could only be found in the skin of the other person. Our hands roamed to previously unexplored places. There were things I learned about a man's body that I hadn't fully understood before, no matter how many half-naked figures were displayed on my prized Esmarch bandage. There were things I learned about my own body, as well.

While most of me was clutched in the arms of love and lust, another little part of my brain took notes. *Gosh, would you look at that*, I thought, or *Holy smokes, I had no idea!* I found myself heartily impressed by the design of the human body, male and female perfectly suited and aligned—and so devilishly inspired!—to re-create itself.

I knew about sex. I had worked in a maternity ward; the mechanics were fairly unmistakable. What I had never learned, or even guessed at, were the feelings, the desperate inexorable draw of one body toward another, of how my lips and hands and hips would act as if detonated, speeding toward Joe just as his rocketed toward me.

I thought I would faint. Or he would. Or we would both die right there, victims of our own passion. And then, breathless and spent, it was over.

Suddenly all the other knowledge I had, which my brain (or whatever organ had wielded its mighty control) had conveniently hidden from view, came flooding back. Insemination. Conception. Implantation. Cell division. Cervical dilation. Delivery.

Motherhood.

I burst into tears.

"Winnie! Are you in pain? *Carissima*, did I hurt you?"

"I don't want to be a mother!" I wailed.

As silly and carefree as the evening of my birthday had been, the wee hours were spent making contingency plans and regretting our carelessness. Actually, I sensed less actual remorse on Joe's part than his words indicated. He was sorry and he took responsibility and said he would marry me and stand by our family, if in fact that was what we would become. But he dozed off once or twice, something the high-pitched screech of my anxiety would not allow me to do. And his comforting hugs and kisses sometimes veered back toward amorousness.

"Stop!" I muttered at him once when his reinflated desire became particularly evident. "Can't you turn that thing off?"

He chuckled. "Yes, of course. There's a little switch right underneath. Just feel around and I'm sure you'll find it."

I punched him in the stomach. That flipped the switch, all right.

Eventually I did sleep, a fitful torpor barraged with dreams that I couldn't quite remember, but left me reverberating with fear and self-loathing as I woke. Joe was staring at the ceiling, dark lashes flicking up and down in the dove-gray light of early morning. After a moment he sensed my consciousness and turned toward me without touching me.

We gazed at each other for several minutes. It was the first near-peace I'd felt in hours.

"I would never abandon you," he whispered.

Altoona, Pennsylvania; Dayton and Toledo, Ohio; Terre Haute, Indiana; Columbus, Ohio; Bay City, Michigan; Lexington, Kentucky; Knoxville, Tennessee; Augusta, Georgia; Lynchburg and Norfolk, Virginia; Wheeling, West Virginia. It was September and our twelve weeks on the Keith-Albee circuit was up.

I was not pregnant. Nor was I foolish enough to provoke fate by chancing it again, thanks to nurse Margaret Sanger's tireless campaign to promote "birth control," as she termed it. Though she'd once gone to jail for it, Mrs. Sanger's efforts made barriers to pregnancy far more readily available, and Joe acquired the necessary supplies.

"You're not being stupid, right?" whispered Gert as I slid into our bed early one morning. "Because you can't depend on men not to be stupid. You have to be the smart one."

"I'm not stupid, and neither is Joe."

"You can't let down your guard, not even for a minute."

"I won't. I promise." Of course, I didn't mention that I already had. But one night of tearful regret was enough to teach me that particular lesson.

●　　●　　●

Birnbaum didn't like Keith-Albee's terms for another run on their circuit. "It's time we twist the arm of fate," he said. "If Albee won't bring you to New York, we'll see what Martin Beck can do for us." While Keith-Albee was the major eastern circuit, Beck's Orpheum circuit controlled the big-time theatres in the West. Our tour would take us across the northern states and then down the West Coast to California.

"Hollywood!" said Kit. "That's where all the new film studios are. Paramount, United Artists . . . I want to see how they make movies." As always, Kit was more interested in what happened offstage than on.

Fred Delorme would once again travel with us, but Birnbaum made them change the name of the act to Delorme and Herkimer. "Your jokes are all about courtship," he said. "Delorme and Delorme sounds like you're already hitched."

Mother got it into her head to update the name of our act, too. "Turner has got to be the most boring name on the face of the earth," she said. "I almost didn't marry your father, knowing I'd have to be boring old Mrs. Turner for the rest of my days."

This was highly unlikely. We'd never heard her disdain her married name before, and it was the kind of thing Mother would've enjoyed saying all these years, if only she'd thought of it.

The foreign acts had "cachet" she said, and spent the better part of an afternoon in the Wheeling, West Virginia, library one day, poring over a French-English dictionary. The verb *trinquer* means "to toast, to drink to," and she decided it meant we'd be the toast of the town. She lopped off the final *r* and added the accented *e* to make it look more French.

"The Tumbling Trinqué Sisters!" she announced triumphantly. "The perfect name to get us to The Palace." To her surprise and disgust, no store in Wheeling, West Virginia, sold berets. She had to wait until we began our Orpheum tour in St. Louis to complete the picture of Frenchness she was so anxious to present. Funny how a word and a hat can change your ancestry in the blink of an eye.

The western circuit was known to be a bit more forgiving, as audiences on that side of the continent weren't as likely to have seen big-time acts. This made it easier for Birnbaum to book Joe and Lucy at the same houses we played. We all settled into an easy rhythm, with the occasional fracas here and there. We were Turners after all, no matter what name was listed on the playbill, and each had streaks of contentiousness of varying widths, set off with a regularity that our traveling companions seemed to get used to after weeks together on the road.

St. Louis, Missouri; Champaign and Galesburg, Illinois; St. Paul, Minnesota.

Mid-October found us in Seattle, Washington, and there was something about the city I liked right away. Twenty years before, the Great Fire of Seattle had taken a good portion of the city to the ground, but it had been quickly rebuilt with an eye toward the future. The Smith Tower had gone up in 1914, and at thirty-eight floors it was the tallest building west of the Mississippi. The city sat on the shore of Puget Sound, which was both bustling with activity—shipbuilding, commerce, and traveling—and also quite lovely. On the second day the cloud cover cleared and we saw the towering snow-tipped Olympic Mountains in the distance across the sound.

"Are those the Alps?" Kit asked.

"No, and you need to go back to school," I chided her. "Specifically geography class."

The Lincoln Hotel was an extravagant choice for lodging, but with our wages at eight hundred dollars per week, we were now paid more than our father had ever made in an entire year. The rooms were large and comfortable, with two big soft double beds piled with coverlets and down-filled pillows, and there were actual closets for our clothes. Heavy red damask curtains hung at the windows, and burgundy patterned carpets covered the floors. As much as I enjoyed the luxuriousness of the room, I loved the rooftop garden even more, with its delicate greenery and panoramic views of the city.

In the morning, Joe and I strolled from the hotel on Fourth and Madison down to Pike Place Market.

"It reminds me of Haymarket in Boston," he said. "The people, too. So many languages spoken. It's a different mix, of course—there are definitely more Orientals here than in Massachusetts. But still, it feels familiar."

He traded quips with an Italian fishmonger in one of the stalls at the market.

"What did he say?" I asked.

"He said he'd trade his biggest salmon for you. He thought you'd weigh about the same."

"What an offer! Thanks for turning him down."

Joe grinned. "Who says I turned him down? That was a beautiful piece of fish he had!"

I fell in love with that city. Not only with the buildings and the views and the variation of people, but with the pioneer spirit Seattle-ites seemed to have in their very marrow. The city was the jumping-off spot for gold prospectors headed for the Klondike, purchasing tools and supplies before chancing everything in the wilds of Alaska. They were risk takers, willing to adjust the boundaries of tradition in order to reach for something more, something bigger. The University of Washington admitted women, and I daydreamed about taking classes there someday.

"Could you ever see yourself living here?" We were eating grilled Alaskan halibut and Dungeness crab legs at the Athenian luncheonette in Pike Place Market, with its grand view of the sound and the boats twinkling like pearls on the dark water.

"I could live here in a minute," he said. "But I'd have to convince Mama and Lucy to come. They're my responsibility—I could never move so far away without them."

"Would they agree to it?"

He considered this as he gazed out over the water. "I think they might. Mama writes that Boston stinks of molasses, even after ten months, and it gives her nightmares of drowning."

A prickle ran up my spine, as it often did when I thought of such a gruesome death, the tarry substance clogging the poor man's nose and mouth, the terror he must have felt. I wondered if there could be any worse way to die.

• • •

We played the Moore Theatre, which was relatively plain on the out-side, but filled with marble, onyx, gleaming wood, and stained glass inside. We had the coveted last-before-intermission spot, right after Lucy and Joe, and audiences were very enthusiastic. The headliner was a buxom woman named Trixie Friganza, who sang and told jokes about her ample size.

"The way for a fat woman to do the shimmy," she told the audience on the first night, "is to walk fast and stop short." They loved her.

Unfortunately for her—and wildly fortunate for us—by Thursday, she'd caught a terrible cold and could barely be heard from three feet away, much less from up in the gallery. The theatre manager, Mr. Cort, didn't waste a moment fretting about his lost headliner. "Trinket Sis-ters!" he yelled. (That name didn't always work out quite as Mother had planned.) "Trinkets, you're headlining!"

Headlining—at a big-time vaudeville house!

And as if that weren't enough, Birnbaum called the next day to say that Keith-Albee wanted us back on the East Coast, "in the city." There was only one city to vaudevillians, and that was New York. "You've got a shot at The Palace," he said. "You're laying them out in Seattle. If you can do as well in other theatres in the city, they'll get you in. Maybe you'll open, or even close. But once you can say you played The Palace, you can play anywhere, ladies. Anywhere. It's the keys to the kingdom."

That Thursday night we tumbled like we were invincible.

In the middle of the night, a city clothes itself in secrecy. The daytime people in their beds never know about the lovers, the criminals, the homeless, or the hopeless who move through the streets or crouch in doorways or under bridges. The daytime buzz of industry and industri-ousness downshifts to a wandering, desultory hum, and you can imag-ine things you might not have considered in the noise of the day.

"So it's settled, then. When we make all the money we need, we'll move to Seattle." Joe and I walked along Alaskan Way, listening to the waves slap against the wharf pilings. I was still enjoying the intoxicating bliss of having headlined my first show.

"Absolutely." His big, warm hand clasped mine a little tighter, a squeeze that meant he knew it was a fantasy, but one that might some-day come true. "You say the word, and Seattle's our home."

I squeezed back. "Don't make fun. It could happen."

He stopped and pulled me into a loose embrace, head tipped down to look at me. "Winnie, *tesoro*, if you make up your mind for it to hap-pen, I have no doubt that it will." *Tesoro*. I was his treasure.

Suddenly a siren sounded, a low groan that quickly accelerated to a worrisome wail.

"Hope it's nothing serious," said Joe.

"Maybe one of the canneries," I said. "Fish oil is pretty flammable."

We listened as another siren started up. "It's not down here on the waterfront," he said. "It's coming from up the hill."

We looked at each other for a beat and, without another word, we began walking and then running up Madison, the screeching sirens growing louder and more insistent as we crossed First Avenue, then Second, terror rising as we saw the smoke billowing up just a few blocks farther where the Lincoln Hotel stood.

The sidewalks were filling with dazed lodgers in nightgowns and nightshirts, and Joe and I scanned them desperately. "Lucy!" Joe began to bellow, and I called my mother's and sisters' names, too, but no one responded to allay our worst fears.

Firefighters were trying to keep the crowd away from the building, but in the confusion we were able to make our way to one of the side doors of the hotel. We saw no flames, only smoke. "I'm going in," said Joe.

"They won't let you!"

"No one's here to stop me," he said. "Stay right here, I'll get them all." He ran up the short steps and into the building.

How could he get them all? But what if they needed help? I saw their faces in my mind: Lucy, Gert, Kit, Nell, Harry, Mother . . . What if they couldn't make it out on their own? He couldn't carry them all.

Panic will make a person do any number of instinctive things: scream, faint, run away.

I ran into the building.

People rushed toward me through the smoke, almost knocking me back down the stairs several times, and it felt like it took forever to reach the third floor. I had to feel for the room doors and could barely make out the numbers as I made my way down the hallway against the tide of the terrified running for their lives.

"Lucy!"

I followed Joe's voice into the next open doorway. He was crouched over the first bed, screaming her name. Kit was sitting on the floor next to her, blinking against the smoke filling the room.

"Kit! Get up!" I yelled, tugging at her. She was dazed, and I slapped her cheek to get her to look at me.

"I tried to carry her," she mumbled as I got her to her feet. "I didn't want to leave her."

"Where's Gert?" I pushed Kit toward the hallway. I hadn't been able to see far enough into the room to know if Gert was in the bed by the window. "Did she come back to the room?"

"I don't know."

"Follow the people out," I told her. "Don't stop until you get outside! Do you hear me?"

"Yes." I guided her into the exodus and then she was gone.

The pounding of running steps and cries of distress were joined by another sound, a sort of rumble, as if the building itself were quaking in fear.

I turned back into the room. Joe had Lucy in his arms. "She won't wake up!" he wailed.

"Get her out! I'm going to check for Gert, and then Nell and Mother. Go—I'll be right behind you!"

"Come with me!"

"No, I have to make sure about the others!"

The smoke grew thicker as I felt my way across the room. "Gert!" I screamed. "Gert!" But no one answered. My knees hit the bed and I leaned over to sweep my arms across it.

Empty, thank God.

I turned to make my way back to the door, and the rumbling sound suddenly burst into an angry roar. Flames shot through the doorway, and a blast of heat hit my face. I stumbled back toward the window, tugged the heavy drapes apart, and struggled as the sash resisted my efforts to open it. I was about to break the glass, desperate for fresh air, when the wood relented and the window went up with a bang.

The scene below was mayhem, people scattering, calling for one another, the fire brigade in their heavy coats and helmets running here and there, a swarm of them holding out a round net below someone else's window.

"*Winnie!*"

I heard her thundering scream, and it was like cool water on my baking nerves.

Another boom of destruction behind me and I could feel the heat crawl closer. I looked back to see Kit's and Lucy's bed erupt in flames.

"*Winnie, jump!*"

It was three tall floors. My addled brain began to calculate . . . if I lived . . . if I lived I would break my legs . . . there would be internal injuries . . . hemorrhaging . . .

"*Winnie, I'll catch you!*"

The fire was closing in, crawling toward me, voraciously swallowing everything in its path: the plush carpet, the upholstered chairs, the wardrobe trunks where we'd hurriedly tossed our satin costumes after the show, my first aid book on the bedside table . . .

She screamed my name again, a banshee's wail slicing through the cacophony of sounds.

Fire climbed the heavy curtain to my right, leapt to my shoulder, and sunk its teeth in.

I focused on her face, and jumped.

CHAPTER
40
GERT

If a thing is worth doing, it is worth doing slowly . . . very slowly.
—Gypsy Rose Lee, dancer, actress, novelist, and stripper

The night I met Nils Magnusson, I was utterly exhausted and completely happy for the first time in months.

Headlining!

For one glittering night, the Tumbling Turner Sisters (it's how I'll always think of us) were the stars of the show. I can still feel the Moore Theatre's dusty boards beneath my hands as I sprang out onto the stage that night, can still see my sisters' jittery brightness as we did our joke sketches, lines firing back and forth like a game of tag, you're it.

We were "it," all right. The most "it" we'd ever been.

Applause roared toward us like an oncoming locomotive.

Afterward I could barely stand up, I was so wrung out from effort and nerves and happiness. I never knew how exhausting happiness could be. Come to think of it, at the time I didn't know just how exhausting unhappiness could be, either.

After the show, Nell took Harry and the younger girls back to the Lincoln, and Joe and Winnie wandered away without a word, as usual. Mother said she was taking "soup" to Trixie Friganza at her hotel, but where she might have found soup at midnight, I won't even bother to guess. Mother was always tagging after the headliner, even one who wasn't actually headlining at the moment.

After changing my clothes, washing the heavy greasepaint from my face, and applying a light coat of evening makeup, I headed down the block to the Virginia Inn, a little tavern where I could get someone to buy me a drink without much effort in return. The men there were regular fellows, not the types to press for too much attention.

It wasn't that I couldn't pay for my own drinks. I could have bought a round for everyone in the place if I'd wanted. But where was the fun in that, if I could get them for free?

"What'll you have, miss?" The bartender was so skinny he looked as if a stiff breeze through his handlebar mustache might knock him over.

"I haven't quite decided yet," I said. Sometimes it took a couple of minutes for one of the fellows to get up the gumption to offer. I bided my time, gazing at the shiny oak bar, replaying our star turn in my head.

We're on the rise, I thought, smiling secretly to myself. *We can go anywhere!* Visions of headlining bigger and better theatres, meeting fascinating people, and traveling to high-flying places like New York City or maybe even London twirled in my brain.

Suddenly a flute of champagne slid in front of me. "Compliments of Mr. Magnusson," said the bartender, tipping his handlebars toward a group of men seated at a small table across the room. I raised the flute in their direction and aimed a smile of surprised and innocent gratitude, happy that I wouldn't even have to talk to them.

When I ordered for myself, I generally had a Manhattan. I liked the clash of muscular whiskey and girlish maraschino cherry, which also served as a terribly wicked prop. Holding it high by the stem and lowering it to your lips put a burst of color in even the soberest man's cheeks. The champagne was delicious, though, strangely smooth, yet pulsing with bubbles, and I felt my eyes brighten and weariness fade.

"Like that, do you?" said the bartender. "You oughta. It's a Bollinger. Most expensive bottle in the house."

Before I took the last sip, another flute appeared, and shortly after that, so did Nils. The bartender glared at the man seated next to me. Without a word, he slid off the bar stool and disappeared to some other corner of the tavern. Then Nils was there, his smooth gray pinstriped sleeve an inch away from my bare arm.

"Actress?" he said, voice as smooth as his sleeve.

"Acrobat," I said.

"Vaudeville?"

I smiled. "Headliner."

"Ah." He nodded. "I might have guessed."

We flirted and drank. His eyes lit with interest. I thought of Nat and Benny saying Swedes were so quiet and hardworking they were like shovels. Nils was no shovel.

He was a businessman, he said. Later it came out that he owned the Gaiety Theatre a few blocks from my hotel. "It's burlesque," he said simply, with neither pride nor shame.

"I've never seen burlesque."

He took a pocket watch the size of a beer coaster from his vest pocket. "We're just in time for the last show." He laid crisp bills from his money clip onto the bar, stepped to the tile floor, and held out his elbow to me.

It was the most interesting thing that had happened in months, so I took it.

"Thank you, Mr. Magnusson!" the barman called as we reached the door. "Thank you kindly!"

The Gaiety was huge but without the luxury of big-time vaudeville. The carpets were worn, the walls had no decoration. Once we stepped inside the darkened theatre, though, it looked like any opera house, and the show seemed like just another vaudeville bill, with singers and comedians and the like.

I'll admit the jokes were bawdier. Apparently burlesque doesn't have blue envelopes. "In India, when a man dies, forty girls dance nude around him for forty days. If he doesn't get up, they know damn well he's dead!"

It wasn't until the headliner that the show went for the truly risqué.

When the curtain pulled back, ten chorus girls in long red satin skirts and high-collared red blouses stood swaying in time to the music.

They had little red caps with devil horns sticking out of them, and when they turned around, there were red feather tails attached to their backsides. They swished those tails, hips popping back and forth, and the audience clapped and stomped their feet like in vaudeville. But there was another sound, too, one I'd never heard in a theatre before, a low sort of growl like a pack of dogs all wanting the same bone.

The band struck up a familiar song: "On the Level, You're a Little Devil, but I'll Soon Make an Angel Out of You." The featured singer made her entrance and swooped among the she-devils in a shimmering long white dress with gauzy white wings attached to her arms.

Her voice was awful, but then the devils began to take off their blouses and long skirts, opening them coyly, lowering them slowly, swinging their hips and jiggling their shoulders, revealing red bras and tight shorts. The growl got louder, punctuated by hoots and wolf whistles. It was clear that the mostly male audience wasn't there for the music.

I'll admit I was fascinated. I'd always heard burlesque was a dirty business, but this didn't seem so bad, and the hunger of the men around me had a thrilling dangerousness about it.

The singer wound around the chorus girls, gliding her wings in front of each one's chest, and when she moved on, the girl had undone her bra and dropped it to the floor, bare breasts right there for all to see! The ripple of sound around me swelled, and from the corners of my eyes, I could see a flutter of motion. Some of the men had newspapers across their laps, but the papers were moving, jumping up and down . . . They were . . . In public, for godsake!

"I have to leave," I told Nils as I got up and pushed past him to the aisle. "It's late and my mother will have the police out after me if I don't get back to the hotel."

"Gert, don't go—"

I practically sprinted for the theatre doors, out to the street, where the night was cool and fairly quiet, and I could try and put the sound of those rattling newspapers out of my mind.

Suddenly the blare of a different sound made the hair go up on the back of my neck: sirens. Fire engines rattled past me, blowing street dust into my dress and face. I shielded my eyes and began to walk the few blocks to our hotel. I couldn't wait to get back to our room and slip into bed with Winnie, hoping by morning the burlesque show would seem like just a very strange dream.

Then I realized that the trucks clogged the street right in front of the Lincoln.

I began to run—away from the Gaiety, toward the far more alarming sight of people streaming out of the hotel in their nightclothes and the sounds of screams above the sirens. By the time I got there, firemen had herded people away from the building. I tried to slip by them, but a thick hand caught my arm. "Where do you think you're going?"

"My mother and sisters are in there!"

"They're probably out by now." His helmet was low over his brow, and I couldn't see his eyes to know if he was lying. "Besides, you can't go in—the building's about to go."

I ran through the crowd, desperate to catch sight of my family through the smoke and terror-struck faces. "Nell!" I screamed. "Winnie! Kit!"

"Gert!" It was Nell, holding the baby inside her coat. Mother stood with her in just a shirtwaist and skirt, without a coat, hat, or even any shoes on.

"Where are the others?" I asked.

"I don't know!" cried Nell. "The baby was croupy and I came out to walk him in the cool air—"

"I was in Trixie's hotel room down the block," said Mother, looking pale and shaken. "I ran up here when I heard the sirens. Sweet Jesus, Gert, if they're not with you . . ."

"Stay here," I told her. "Stay right here by the street so I can find you again. I'll go look for them."

I ran like some sort of devil myself, calling their names, trying to scream louder than everyone else calling out for their loved ones.

And then I looked up.

There in the window.

Winnie.

CHAPTER
41

WINNIE

We could never learn to be brave and patient,
if there were only joy in the world.
—Helen Keller, deaf and blind author, educator and activist

Across the endless, burning desert, I heard a voice that sounded like Kit's, though I couldn't be sure. It was rasping, and she kept taking little sips of air after every few words. "Winnie," *breath*, "you're in a," *breath*, "hospital for," *breath*, "Swedish people."

Am I in Sweden? Then pain slammed into me like a wall of molten lava, and I dove back down into the balm of unconsciousness.

Hours, or possibly days later, I opened my eyes and saw a chubby pink leg dangling and bobbing, a sturdy white ankle-high shoe kicking around looking for something to land on.

Harry. You must be walking now.

Later it was Mother's voice, unmistakably shrill and annoyed. "And how am I supposed to pay for all of this?"

Sometime after that, soothing words found me, the girl I was, behind my animal screams. "Hang on, Winnie. Please, darling, stay with us. You fell off a cliff, but you haven't fallen onto rocks."

I let out a guttural growl, desperate to locate the space outside my universe of pain. "Where . . . is . . . Gert?"

"She's on another floor. The doctors are taking good care of her. She'll be right as rain in no time."

But I won't, and I never will be. Rain is freedom, but I will always be trapped in fire.

"Joe."

A suspicious silence.

"Joe!"

The voice grew firm. "He's taken Lucy back to Boston."

The Great War probably saved my life, which is ironic when you think of how many lives it took. The care of all those burned and wounded soldiers precipitated great strides in medical treatment. I tried to focus on that, and on all the things I could learn from my extended stay at Swedish Hospital in Seattle, rather than the only other thing in my world: excruciating pain. Doctors used silver nitrate as a corrosive agent on the burns and then debrided the dead skin to create eschars, or scabs. In effect, they had to torture me to save me.

What truly saved my life, of course, was Gert. After all the times she dropped me—by accident or on purpose—the last and most important time I jumped into her arms, she stood firm and made the catch. Because of her I didn't die right there on the sidewalk . . . though in truth, there were many long days and weeks afterward when I wished I had.

"Why doesn't he write to me?" I asked, three weeks after the fire. Gert sat in my room, her casted arm in a sling, the bruises on her face and neck yellowed to splattered tea stains.

"Because he's a coward."

"He's not! He went in to save you!"

"But he left you there, didn't he? He should never have left you in that room, Winnie."

"I *told* him to."

"A man doesn't leave a woman in a burning building, no matter what she says. And now he doesn't want to deal with the consequence of his stupidity." She let out a snort of disgust and looked away. "Coward."

The consequence. That was me. No longer a desirable young woman, I was burned from below my right elbow up to my ear and halfway down my back, and still unable to care for myself. A consequence, indeed.

Yet, even in such a state, physically and emotionally scorched, I was almost certain the connection between Joe and me was stronger than that. Maybe we would never be lovers again, but he would at least want to extend his comfort and friendship, wouldn't he? He was a better man than to simply walk away. Wasn't he?

"Should I write to him?" I asked Nell a week later.

She didn't answer for a minute, just sat there staring down the length of the hospital ward with its rows of white metal beds, and biting the inside of her lip until I was sure she must be tasting blood. "I think he may need some time," was all she said. "Maybe it's best to wait until he contacts you."

"Now, Winnie," Mother said after I'd been in the hospital for a month and a half, taking my left hand in hers. She always positioned herself on my left; true to her squeamish nature, she couldn't stand the sight of the wounds on my right side, which doctors left open for the purpose of drying.

I could feel some sort of announcement coming, and the first crazy thing that popped into my mind was that Joe hadn't made it out of the fire at all. That he was dead. I braced myself for the kind of pain no medicine could dull.

"Oh, it's not so bad," she soothed. "We'll all be together again soon."

"What? You're leaving?"

"Now, dear," she started, and that's how I knew for certain she was leaving. Only Dad ever called us "dear." "We've . . . well, we've run out of money."

"Run out?" I said. "But there was so much! How could it all be gone?"

Her eyes shifted around the ward. "This is a very good hospital," she said. "You likely would've died if we'd been in some podunk little backwater instead of a real city. Even still, in those first few days, we thought we'd lost you." I saw her bite down to still the emotion the very mention of this raised. She forced a smile. "We're all very grateful to have you with us, and happy to give what we had."

She was so careful with her words. My mother, who generally shot her mouth off any which way she pleased, had somehow learned to be tactful in the last six weeks.

"*Everyone's* money is gone?"

"Well, not yours. You're not a minor anymore, so I had no way to get at it. But we'll need it to pay the hospital until you get out. You'll have to wire for it."

Dread hit me in wave after wave, as I realized the far-reaching repercussions of this simple fact. "What about the house?"

"Dad paid December's rent yesterday, but he can't cover January's unless we get some real dough, not just the few dollars he makes at the factory."

"But how? We can't perform . . ."

"Nell can." She waited while I put the puzzle pieces together. Nell and Fred could earn good money on the road, but Nell wouldn't go without little Harry, and as a toddler who now loved to run off any chance he got, little Harry couldn't go without someone to watch him while Nell and Fred were onstage.

"I'll take care of Harry," said Mother. "Birnbaum was all broken up over what happened, so he called in every favor he had and got us a good run. Kit's going home to Dad. Lourdes Hospital is right there if her breathing takes a turn for the worse. Gert will stay here with you. She's already got a room at a boardinghouse nearby and a spot in a local chorus line."

I tried so hard not to cry—hadn't I caused enough trouble? But the tears leaked down my face and into the scars on my neck anyway.

"Now, now." Mother patted my hand. "At least we're all alive to tell the tale. It can only get better from here."

In a matter of days they were gone.

Gert visited every day, and I looked forward to her arrival like a prisoner in a maximum-security jail. But she had to work, and could never stay long. The nurses became my friends, and over the next few weeks, I learned their schedules, mannerisms, likes and dislikes: one was hoping her boyfriend would pop the question on Christmas Eve; one liked to stay out too late and irritated the other nurses by being tardy for her shift; some were truly interested in medicine, and some only biding their time until something better came along.

My favorite was Lisette D'Orsay. She took my questions seriously, explaining procedures and finding answers when she didn't know them herself.

"You're not really French," she said one day, as she changed the dressing on my right elbow. "At least, you certainly don't speak the language."

I smiled—more of a grimace as she tugged at a stuck bandage. "What gave it away?"

"Trinqué."

"It means to give a toast, doesn't it? Mother wanted us to be the toast of the town."

"Yes, but that spelling, it has another meaning."

"What?"

"Damaged."

How appropriate, I thought.

The days went by; I got stronger.

And Joe never wrote.

I had healed well enough to travel back to Johnson City just in time for the holidays. The only thing I can say for Christmas 1919 was that it was better than Christmas 1918. Dad and Kit made us a nice meal, but we decided not to exchange presents. It would've been too strange without all the others there, and we were still watching our budget.

I missed Gert. She'd found a job with a traveling revue. Even if she hadn't, she would never have gone back to Johnson City. "I may not be living large, but at least I'm working on it," she wrote. To her, home meant giving up, and Gert was no quitter.

Kit's breathing was much better, but she never quite lost the rasp in her voice, and now sounded like she'd smoked a pack a day since she was born. Combined with her height, she routinely passed for twenty, though she was only fourteen. The Stone Opera House in Binghamton hired her on as a stagehand, and she spent almost every waking hour there, when she wasn't in school.

"You need new clothes," she said to me a few weeks after Christmas had passed.

I'd been wearing my old high-necked shirtwaists to cover my back, right arm and shoulder, and the side of my neck. "I can't wear those new fashions anymore," I said. "I'd scare people. Besides, we can't afford it."

"I'm making good money at the Stone," she said. "And I should pay you back for all the help you give me on schoolwork."

"You don't have to pay me to help you, Kit. Besides, what else have I got to do?"

"Go to school yourself."

I'd thought of this, of course, but had decided to wait until the following fall. By then I hoped my scars would have turned from a red that seemed to rage against the twisted seams of skin to a more resigned pinkish-white.

That wasn't the only reason, of course. The real reason, the one I could barely admit even to myself, was that I was scared. Standing at that open window, facing a choice between death by fire and death by impact, a near paralysis had set in that hadn't completely left me. I had to force myself to get out of bed in the morning, and rarely left the house. I was also terribly, painfully sad. I had lost my livelihood, all my money for college tuition, the company of Nell and Gert, to whom I'd grown so close. And Joe. In the thick fog of fear and sorrow, I couldn't even begin to make sense of why he hadn't written.

"It's too late in the school year to start now," I told Kit.

"You could catch up."

"It's too much work."

She studied me.

"What?" I said.

"Nothing. It's just not like you."

•   •   •

A couple of weeks later, I lay dozing on the couch, and my eye caught on something glinting through the lace curtains. The previous night a ferocious ice storm had whistled around the house, but now sunlight shone through the icicles hanging from the tree branches like tiny sparkling crystal chandeliers. I smiled and thought, *How lovely!*

It was the first bit of beauty I'd noticed in the three months since the fire. I looked down at the graying shirtwaist I wore, and the raveled hem of my ankle-length skirt, and I began to feel the stirrings of anger—at myself! Why was I living this way? I knew better. Vaudeville had taught me better: Life is hard sometimes. So what.

It was time to start booing back.

My first small step forward was to let Kit take me clothes shopping. A kind and discreet saleslady helped me choose two dresses. One had a shawl collar that rose high enough at the sides and back to cover my scars. The other had a bow that tied at the throat. Both had long sleeves, of course, but they were otherwise not too terribly unfashionable.

When I thanked Kit for my new purchases, she said simply, "Tomorrow, school."

And so I went. I had planned just to visit Miss Cartery, my favorite English teacher, and Miss Darlington, the history teacher who'd joined me in wearing white for women's suffrage. School was over for the day—I wasn't up to facing crowds of students, many of whom I knew—and I felt a wave of longing just walking down the empty hallways. The faint smell of chalk dust filtered around me, and I could almost hear the clang of the bell announcing the start of the school day. It was as if my senses were finally reawakening after months of catatonia.

My teachers were delighted to see me again and pressed me to return, promising to do anything in their power to help me catch up. What could I do in the face of such kindness but agree?

I studied and wrote papers almost around the clock. I took makeup exams after school. It was a crazy business, but the path I'd been on was a far worse threat to my sanity. Having something to occupy my mind and a goal to achieve helped immeasurably.

Despite my gradually lifting spirits, however, one thing continued to darken my thoughts.

I waited for my brain to tire of wondering about Joe, but it never quite did. Why hadn't he contacted me? Did he know if I was alive or dead? Did he care? Or was it as Gert had said, that he didn't want to face a horribly scarred former girlfriend? The longer I waited for a letter, the more I started to believe she might be right. The more I started to wonder if our love had ever been real at all, or something I had just wanted to feel in the moment.

At times I still longed for him, but other times I felt my fury rise. Had he duped me into believing in a love he hadn't really felt, so that he could gain physical satisfaction? Or had he truly loved me only to abandon me at my darkest hour? Either way, I now questioned whether Joe Cole was the man he had presented himself to be.

It's for the best, I told myself when my anger abated and I felt the pain of his absence again. I was free to pursue any life I chose without deferring to the needs of another. Maybe I might become another Dr. Lodge, guiding new life into the world. With no husband to please, the horizon of my future broadened considerably.

The spring wore on, and Misses Darlington and Cartery pressed me to apply for college.

"I have no money for tuition," I told them.

"Just apply," said Miss Cartery. "Sometimes they give scholarships to good students."

Cornell was at the top of the list, of course, but they suggested a few other places, as well.

I sprinted to the end of the school year—mentally, not physically, of course. I still wasn't moving terribly quickly, though small improvements had gotten me from walking like a humpbacked crone to more like a middle-aged matron with back pain.

Nell, Mother, and Harry made it home for my graduation, and it almost felt like a real party. Fred came along, too. "We asked Mr. Birnbaum if he could get us some gigs in the area," he explained. "We're playing the Stone Opera House this week."

We all went to see them, of course. It was the first time I'd been in

a theatre since that last show in Seattle at The Moore, when we'd headlined. As I sat in the third row, surrounded by happy people settling in
for the first act, memories came flooding back: the sounds of the hall
filling with footsteps and voices, the smell of the leather seats and dusty
boards, the glow of the footlights against the velvet front curtain. I even
felt the jitter of preshow nerves.

But it was all backward. I longed to be experiencing it from the
other side of the curtain, whispering "break a leg" to the other performers, squeezing into my old trunk with the internal latch, and feeling the warm flood of applause as I rolled out of it onto the stage. I
dabbed at my tears in the darkness and pretended it was from laughing.

In the middle of the night I crept downstairs, past Fred snoring like a
one-man band, with his long legs hanging off the couch, and out to the
front porch.

I missed Gert. And Joe. Graduating from high school had been a far
greater challenge than I'd ever imagined it could be, and I was proud I
had made it. But without them, the joy of it was dulled.

The front door opened and Nell came outside to sit on the old
trunk next to me.

"I miss Gert," she said.

"Me, too. Never thought I'd say that."

"You two are more alike than anyone else in the family."

"We are not!"

Nell laughed. "I mean it in the best way. Hardworking, determined,
talented." She cut her eyes at me. "And a little big on yourselves. You
each think you're smarter than the other."

I had to admit, she was just a tiny bit right.

"I hope she's happy," I said. "That revue she's in sounds like a pretty
big deal, playing all up and down the West Coast."

Nell patted my knee. "And you're both secretly very generous to
each other."

I laughed. The things only sisters know.

I thought of Gert and me smoking out here together the last time we were home. "You don't happen to have a cigarette, do you?" I asked Nell.

"I certainly do not, and I hope you don't, either. Smoking is very unladylike."

"You're right," I said, and I meant it, but not about the cigarette.

We sat there in the silence of 3 a.m., listening to the wind blow through the weeping willows in the cemetery.

"Nell?"

"Yes."

"Fred's pretty nice, isn't he?"

A secret little smile lit her face, and I knew for sure that what I'd suspected was true. "Yes," she said, "he's very nice."'

"We all really like him," I said, and her smile brightened just that much more. I'm ashamed to say I felt a pinch of envy in the face of such happiness. The love of a good man had found Nell twice. I was no longer sure it had even found me once.

She must have sensed my turmoil. "Are you still thinking about Joe?" she asked.

I shrugged.

"I think you should go see him."

I nearly fell off the trunk. "*Go see him?* You were the one who told me not even to write!"

She lowered her eyes. "I may have been wrong about that."

"Oh, Nell," I snapped angrily. "How am I supposed to face him now? And what would I say? 'I know it's been eight long months, and you clearly don't care about me anymore, but I thought I'd travel several hundred miles to drop in and say hello anyway'?"

Her gaze flicked up to mine and held it. "I'm sorry if I gave the wrong advice. I truly thought it was best at the time, and he'd write to you when he was ready." She sighed. "People just don't always do what you expect them to do."

As if that wasn't the understatement of the year.

I let my temper cool a minute before responding. If excruciating pain had taught me anything, it was not to spew out all the vitriol in your head in the heat of the moment. Even a nurse who understands the nature of her work will take offense when you yell that she's a ham-handed incompetent after she removes a stuck dressing and peels open a newly formed scar. "Nell, he doesn't want to see me," I said evenly. "If he did, he could've gotten on a train any day of the week."

"That may be true," she said. "But I'm not concerned with what he does or doesn't want. I care about you, and what you want. I think you want—need—to find out why he never tried to contact you, and face-to-face is the best way to do it. We're playing the Orpheum in Boston in a couple of weeks. You could take the train and meet us there."

"You're actually advising me to confront him, when no good can come of it."

"Yes," she said, meeting my steely gaze with her own. "For your own peace of mind."

I let out a breath I didn't even know I'd been holding. "When."

"The week of July eighth."

My mind reeled at the thought of facing him. How would I even find him? He'd once named the street where he lived. A funny name for a road . . . a planet? Moon Street.

"If you're going to see him, there's something you should know."

He's married. He's dead. He moved back to Italy. The mind will come up with some pretty far-fetched ideas when faced with a comment like "There's something you should know."

"What?" I asked.

"Winnie . . . Lucy didn't make it."

"Home?"

"No." Nell took my hand and squeezed it. "She didn't live. It was the smoke. Even at the hospital, they couldn't revive her."

I clutched Nell's arm, gasping at the incomprehensibility of it. "Oh, God, no!" And then something else hit me, and my blood nearly boiled. *"Why in holy hell didn't any of you tell me?"*

Nell sighed, and I knew she was bearing the brunt of what was likely Mother's decision. Or Gert's. Or some consensus they'd all come to while I writhed in pain.

"It was too much," said Nell. "You were clinging to life. Joe was gone, the act was over. We didn't think you could take one more tragedy. And then you got better, and you didn't ask."

"Didn't ask? I didn't *know* to ask! In fact, you all lied about it! You said he'd taken her back to Boston."

"He did."

I felt my heart halt in my chest.

Her body. He'd taken her body back to Boston.

CHAPTER
42

GERT

I try to bring the audience's own drama—tears and laughter
they know about—to them.
—Judy Garland, singer and actress

The guilt. It was like a starving animal, gnawing at my gut. I should have been there instead of playing my little game of free drinks. Instead of watching girls take their clothes off while men rattled the newspapers in their laps. I would have gotten Kit and Lucy out.

Nell felt it, too, though unlike me, she'd had every good reason to be out of the building, with poor Harry wailing and coughing. Mother—who knows? I'm sure she felt bad that she was star-worshipping fat Trixie Friganza instead of dragging those poor girls from a burning building. But Mother is Mother. We all know remorse isn't one of her long suits. It'd be like wishing champagne flowed from the kitchen spigot. Go on and wish all you want. Won't make a lick of difference.

Besides, she was the one who got Nell and Fred back on the road. "You're not doing Winnie any good sitting around the hospital," she insisted, which was true. And she was the one who hounded Birnbaum until they had a nice long tour set up. Naturally, they'd need Mother to come along and watch the baby.

I saw her face when she looked at Winnie, though. She'd always been afraid of fire, and now her worst nightmare had come true. Or almost—at least Kit and Winnie were still with us. But seeing their pain was truly more than she could take.

We all wanted our version of freedom, every last one of us.

For me, it helped to sit there with Winnie as she endured the unendurable, squeezing her one good hand with my one good one. Together we made a whole person.

I caught her. And so did my collarbone, shoulder, and wrist, all of which broke. There was so much plaster, sometimes I wondered if there was still an arm underneath it all. Except of course when it itched, and I wanted to cut the damn thing off and be done with it. Then I'd look at Winnie, and hate myself all over again.

I often read *Variety* while she slept. A week after the fire, I saw the notice.

BENNY WHEELER DIES ONSTAGE

Benny Wheeler, of the comedy duo Case and Wheeler, suffered a heart attack at the Lotus Theatre in Sheridan, Wyoming, and was pronounced dead on the scene. His partner, Nat Case, said he hadn't been feeling well, but wanted to go on. He died while taking his bows. Mr. Case will conduct auditions for a replacement after an appropriate period of mourning.

I never told anyone. It would've been more than my sisters could bear. As it was, I had to go back to my hospital bed, bury my head under the covers, and pretend to sleep for hours after I read it. I didn't want them to see me weeping.

That's when I decided we wouldn't tell Winnie about Lucy.

"Oh, Gert," Nell said. "She'll be so angry when she finds out we didn't tell her."

"How will she ever know?"

"Joe will contact her eventually."

"Maybe he will and maybe he won't. Either way, she can't take one more piece of bad news. Not right now. Not while she's fighting for her life." I turned to Kit. "And you'd better not let it slip, either, not if you care about her."

Kit's eyes began to leak, of course, which they did anytime Lucy's name was mentioned. She hadn't been able to get Lucy out, either. We had all failed that poor girl — Joe most of all, which is why I was pretty sure he'd never contact Winnie. He was only at the hospital for a few hours when Lucy and Winnie were brought in, but it was long enough for me to see how deep his self-hatred ran.

Guilt and shame. The only one of us who didn't visibly stagger under that burden was Mother. Badgering Birnbaum, quibbling with the hospital about every bill, packing Kit off to Johnson City, and ordering Nell to pull herself together so she could work, Mother kept herself too busy to wallow in regret. To be honest, I'm thankful for that. Once again, Ethel Turner's grit and smarts saved the family from utter ruin.

"You'll stay here with her," Mother told me as she latched up her trunk and doled out ten dollars — probably her last — along with the name of a boardinghouse a couple of blocks away. "And you'll have to get a job." She eyed the sling around my shoulder. "Get rid of that thing or no one will hire you."

She didn't say it particularly nicely, but she was right. No one did hire me. The cast was off, but my arm was still too weak to wait tables, much less do a handspring. What kind of work could I do? I put on my best dress and went to The Gaiety.

"I'm looking for Nils Magnusson," I said to one of the stagehands.

"Isn't every girl?" His eyes crawled all over me like an octopus.

I drilled him with a cold glare. "What was your name? I'm sure he'd like to know."

Suddenly I was being politely escorted to the theatre manager's office. Nils was seated, squinting through a glass eyepiece at some sort of ledger, while the manager stood by, shifting his weight from foot to foot. Nils looked up. "Why, hello there. Bertha, was it?"

"Gert," I said. "Gert Turner. I'm here for a job."

He smiled the kind of smile I hate. The kind that says they have the upper hand. "What kind of job were you looking for?"

I kept my chin high so he wouldn't know how desperate I was. "Anything but onstage."

CHAPTER 43

WINNIE

Never place a period in your life where God only meant to place a comma.

—Gracie Allen, actress and comedian

I got off the train at North Union Station on Causeway Street with a pit the size of a granite quarry in my stomach. I had told myself over and over that I'd already lost him. The only thing I was here for was to express my condolences about Lucy.

Well, not quite the only thing.

"You have to *ask*," Nell had said about a dozen times before she'd left Johnson City two weeks before. "He's not going to offer up an explanation out of nowhere."

Why didn't you write to me?

I know you must have been overcome with grief.

I understand that I'm not the same girl you loved. I wouldn't have held you to anything.

But couldn't you have written to find out what had become of me? To offer your support and good wishes? Wasn't I important enough to you even for that courtesy?

That's what I'm here for, I reminded myself all the way down Causeway Street. An answer. Nothing more.

Moon Street wasn't hard to locate. I needed only to find someone who spoke English, and I was soon walking down Prince Street,
past four- and five-story brick apartment buildings, some with copper
bay windows jutting out over the narrow cobblestone street. I passed
St. Leonard's Church, with its full-sized statue of the saint pointing
toward the heavens, and Salem Street, where the Old North Church
ruled over the smaller buildings. I crossed Hanover Street, the main
thoroughfare, lights from countless shops, bars, and cafes flooding the
growing darkness.

Even after a year and a half, the smell of molasses was unmistakable
in the July heat. I found myself thinking of Joe's mother, wondering if
she still had dreams of drowning.

Prince Street ended at a little triangular area called North Square.
On the other side was Moon Street. I stood there, heart pounding, a
drop of sweat trickling down the unnatural streambeds carved into the
terrain of my back.

This is crazy, I thought. *And pointless.*

Nell and I had planned to meet at their hotel after the show. It was
nine o'clock. I could go a few hours early and wait in the lobby. I could
leave this place and never come back.

A figure sat on a stoop nearby, his back hunched, face as pock-
marked as the surface of the moon. "*Ti sei perso?*" he called, his voice so
cracked with age I could barely tell if he was speaking or clearing his
ancient throat. He awaited my answer, then tried again. "Lost?"

"I'm looking for Joe Cole."

"Ah." He nodded and pointed to one of the doors on Moon Street.
"He live there. But he's-a not there now. He play at the Trattoria
Pagliacci on Hanover." He pointed a crooked finger back the way I had
come.

"Thank you," I said, and he waved me away, anxious to have his
instructions followed.

I passed the Trattoria Pagliacci three times before I saw the small
sign on the wooden door, and then I just stood there staring at it. Joe
was on the other side of that door.

My fingers instinctively went to the knuckle of my opposite hand, and I must have played an entire symphony, trying to gather up enough courage to enter.

But I couldn't do it. I turned and rushed up Hanover, quickly at first, strangely worried about being followed. But who would follow me? No one. In a couple of blocks my heart rate slowed and so did my stride. When I came to the end of Hanover I turned left and walked along the wharves, gazing out to Boston Harbor, where lights from a hundred ships of all sizes and uses made the darkness seem like only twilight.

This was Joe's neighborhood. He had an ocean for a backyard.

Shortly I came to an open area, so unexpected on the crowded waterfront, as if some giant hand had wiped away the buildings and warehouses. The site of a cataclysm of some sort.

Molasses. The tank had exploded right here. This was where Joe's father had drawn his last breath. Then, ten short months later, his sister had drawn hers. They had both suffocated, and Joe had been unable to save either of them. For all he knew, I was dead, too.

I sat down on an old crate and thought for a long time. I didn't want to face him, didn't want to ask hard questions. But maybe he deserved at least to know that I was alive.

I gathered up my courage and walked back to Hanover Street and opened the old wooden door. The room was cavernous and dark, much larger than its humble exterior hinted. As my eyes adjusted, I could see the upright piano against the wall by the bar. The round stool was empty. Maybe the old man had been wrong.

It was late, and I was suddenly so tired, and wanted only to sit down, sip something cool, and consider my options. A plump waitress with silver threads running through her black hair led me to a small table on the other side of the dining area. I ordered sarsaparilla, and she pecked at me to get some food, more from motherly pity at my small size, I suspected, than from a desire to run up the bill. "I can't read Italian," I told her, pointing to the smudged menu.

She swatted her thick hand in the air. "I'll get you something."

Sitting back in my chair, I felt relief settle on me for the first time since Nell had proposed this crazy plan. Maybe I wouldn't have to face him after all. At least I could say I had tried.

Then I heard the first few notes of "In the Good Old Summertime."

Panic set the blood coursing through my veins. He was there at the piano, his back bent toward the keys, his black hair curling in its familiar way.

Joe. I wanted to sprint across the dim room and throw my arms around him, to yell and unleash my anger, and to run away, all at the same time. But I only sat watching him until the waitress brought a plate of linguini with meatballs.

At first I couldn't eat, my stomach clenched in nerves. But eventually I took a bite, and the savory spiciness of the sauce distracted and calmed me. The waitress came by scoffing at my pathetic attempts to eat the long strands of pasta and showed me how to twirl it around my fork.

I ate slowly as I listened to Joe play, and remembered: the moment I first saw him at the train depot in Cuba, and how drawn to him I'd been from that moment. The night we searched for Gert, how first our friendship and then our romance had grown and bloomed. The fights we had. The passion we felt.

I really had nowhere to go, and he was the only reason I'd come, and so I finished eating, paid my bill, and sat with a glass of sarsaparilla until after eleven when he pulled the fallboard over the keys, stood and stretched, said good-bye to the bartender, and left.

I followed him down Hanover to quieter, narrower Prince Street, finally marshaling the courage to say his name.

"Joe."

He turned immediately, eyes wide with shock, almost fearful, as if I were a spectral presence calling him to the afterworld instead of the girl he'd once loved.

"*Dio mio* . . . ," he breathed.

As I came toward him I studied his familiar face in the streetlight— the sadness that had been etched around his eyes when we'd met seemed to have taken over the entire landscape of his face.

No time for sentimentality, I told myself. *Get down to business.*

I straightened myself and felt the warped skin on my back pull tight. "I wanted to tell you how sorry I am about Lucy." I'd practiced the words so many times it felt like reciting an assigned poem in English class. "I only heard the news a few weeks ago, or I would have contacted you sooner."

Halfway there, I thought.

He put a hand out and steadied himself on the brick wall of the building beside him. "Winnie, *dio mio* . . . you're alive. I heard the doctors talking about you at the hospital . . . they said you were so burned, you probably wouldn't . . . And then I had to bring . . . I had to go back . . ."

I took a deep breath. *Part two*, I told myself. *That's why you're here.*

"Why didn't you write and find out? I was there for months. Didn't I mean at least that much to you? Enough to offer some expression of friendship and concern for my well-being?" I felt the ire in my voice, and took a breath to calm myself. I'd never get a straight answer if he felt attacked. "I have no expectations, if that's what you were worried about. I know I'm not what . . . what a man might . . . want . . . anymore."

Not as smooth as I'd practiced, but the words were finally out, and I felt a sense of relief at having accomplished the task I'd come so far to complete. The relief was short-lived, however, as Joe crumpled against the side of the building and gasped in misery.

"You must hate me," he said, squeezing the words from his half-strangled throat. "You must wish I died, too."

"No, of course not! Why in the world would you say such a thing?"

"I left you there—"

"I told you to!"

"But I should have made you come. I wanted to make you come with me, but I . . ." He gasped as if he could barely breathe. "I only had two hands . . . and I . . . I chose her. And she died anyway. I didn't save either of you. I only saved myself. " He inhaled a little sob, and tears filled his eyes. "I was sure I would never see you again. The doctors said . . . and anyway I didn't deserve to. Your family must hate me. It's unforgivable, what I did."

"Joe." I stepped toward him and almost reached out to comfort him, but stopped myself. He wasn't mine to touch anymore. "You weren't trying to save yourself, you wanted to save everyone, remember? That's what you said before you went into a burning building while everyone else was running out. You were brave even to try!"

He shook his head, face hard with self-loathing. "She's dead, and you were as good as dead. I failed the two people I loved most. That's all that matters."

"No, you're wrong. You did your best under horrifying circumstances. *That's* what matters. The fire was not your fault, and neither was the outcome. Lucy wouldn't have blamed you. I certainly don't."

He blinked at me, taking in my words. "I've imagined talking to you so many times, begging your forgiveness."

"If you need my forgiveness, then it's yours. I only wish you would've written, and we could have talked about it sooner."

"I think of you every single day, Winnie. But I was certain that even if you were alive, you would despise me."

"I don't." To the contrary, in the face of his profound suffering and remorse, the last vestiges of my anger dissipated. It was all I could do to keep from putting my arms around him and kissing him. Love flooded through me like water over a broken dam. It was time to leave before I started crying, too. "I wish you all the best, Joe. Sincerely, I do." I put my hand out for him to shake. He only stared at it.

"You're leaving?"

"Well, I . . . I'm supposed to meet Nell. She and Fred are playing Keith's."

"You'll come back tomorrow, then?"

I blinked at him; my lips parted but no words came out. What was I supposed to say? Were we to be friends now? Would I soon be congratulating him on his marriage to some other, unscarred woman? I could live my life alone, I was sure of it, but I couldn't play the kindly, slightly misshapen maiden aunt to his children.

Before I could answer, he said, "Don't go. We'll send word to the hotel that you're staying with me. Mama's asleep by now, but she'll want to meet you in the morning." He took my hand, and it was the best I'd felt in almost a year, since the last time he'd held it in Seattle.

His apartment was only a few blocks away, and we were soon climbing the stairs and entering a small hallway. He led me into a parlor crowded with dark-legged furniture: a settee with faded green velvet fabric, a rocking chair with wide arms and a padded leather seat, a high buffet and mirror carved with scrolling woodwork. It smelled faintly of cooked meat and furniture wax, and there wasn't a speck of dust anywhere. "She cleans," he said. "It helps." He gestured for me to join him on the settee, but I chose the rocking chair instead.

"Did you ever pay off the land?" I asked. "Where was it—not far from here, right?"

"Yes, it's all mine. It's about twenty miles west, in a little town called Belham. I take the train every Sunday to work in the garden and check on the building. I bought a house from Sears. The kit came a couple of weeks ago, and some carpenters are putting it together for me."

"A house! Will you live there? What about your mother?"

"She's sick of it here. 'The memories exhaust me,' she says. And what about you?" He seemed to be treading lightly. "What have you been doing?"

I told him about going back to school, working hard to graduate. He smiled broadly and said, "I'm so proud of you, Winnie." It nearly broke my heart, that smile, and I tried to steel myself against it, to keep the avalanche of feelings from burying me. *I'll go to Nell's hotel tomorrow and have a good hard cry*, I told myself.

We sat in silence for a moment, and he said quietly, "Your dress, it's very . . ."

Dowdy, I thought. *Like someone's mother.*

". . . warm for July," he said.

"It hides my scars."

"I want to see them."

I almost laughed at the ridiculousness of it. No one wanted to see my scars. My own family could barely stand the sight of them. "Trust me, you don't," I said.

He rolled up his long sleeves and raised his arms as if he were cradling someone in front of him. In fact, he *had* been cradling someone in front of him, but he hadn't known at the time that she was already past saving. His forearms were mottled with a patchwork of melted skin.

"Oh, Joe," I whispered.

"Now you."

I tugged at the left side of my high collar and pulled back my hair, which I grew to my shoulders now, no longer cutely bobbed as when he'd last seen me. The scars ran from the hairline behind my ear into the secrecy of my dress, down my shoulder to my elbow.

"Come sit beside me," he said.

If he touches me, my heart will break into a thousand pieces, I thought, but I went anyway, like Anne Boleyn to the guillotine.

"I want to see them all."

"No," I said.

"Winnie, *tesoro*, I need to see what happened to you." Slowly, he undid the buttons and pulled the dress down until it was around my waist with only my thin camisole to cover me.

"Oh," he breathed as he studied my shoulder and back. "Oh, Winnie, the pain must have been terrible!" He traced a finger down my arm. "Can you feel this?"

"A little, but not very well."

He cupped my cheeks in his hands. "I wish I had been there to comfort you."

"I missed you so much," I whispered, and my tears leaked down over his thumbs.

"I missed *you*, my beautiful Winnie."

"Not so beautiful anymore."

He leaned forward and kissed my cheeks and lips, and then gently, tenderly, he kissed my scarred shoulder. He raised his gaze to mine, firm and serious. "To me, even more beautiful."

He went briefly to a neighbor's house to use their phone and leave word at Nell's hotel that I would meet her in the morning. We stayed up all night talking, shedding tears when the wrenching pain of the past year reared up through our words. We understood each other's devastation like no one else could, and the very fact of releasing it from the dark and broken corners of our hearts provided a relief neither of us had thought possible. As we nestled on the settee with the faded green velvet cushions, I felt myself healing.

I left Boston with promises to write and visit soon.

When I got home, a letter awaited me, but this one wasn't from Joe.

Mother was the only one who was surprised that I was accepted into college—mainly because she was the only one who was surprised to learn that I had any interest in it to begin with. "Winnie Turner, you are no more going to college than I am going to ride in an airplane."

It was the heart of the summer, when many big-time acts avoided the stiflingly hot theatres, so Nell and Fred had a week off between tours. He'd gone back to Buffalo to see his family, including April, who after a year of unexplained wandering had eventually made her way home. She had been right; they had taken her back.

Nell, Mother, and little Harry had come to visit us in Johnson City.

"Mother, she has to go," Nell said, passing the plate of meat loaf across the kitchen table at dinner that night. "This is Winnie's dream."

"Dream, my foot! It's the biggest waste of time and money I can think of, even if she were a boy, which she isn't. What's next," she scoffed, "letting her run for *mayor*?"

"I got a partial scholarship," I said. "We wouldn't have to pay the entire tuition."

"No, no, and no." Mother spread a knife-load of butter over her bread. "We've all worked so hard to get this family back on track, and I won't let you derail us with this little flight of fancy. Now that's an end to it."

With help from Nell and Gert, I had cobbled together the money for the first semester. But at nineteen years old, I had never before set out to do anything my mother had explicitly forbidden me to do. Could she stop me? Might it splinter the family if I were to disregard her wishes so completely?

"She's going." Dad's voice was quiet but clear.

Mother let out a derisive snort. "Well, I like that! The person with the least means to send her says it's just fine and dandy if she goes."

"She's got the money, and she's going."

Mother put her hands flat on the table, eyes narrowed at Dad. "She's not."

The air fairly crackled with her fury, and my mind darted to devise a solution, some way I could convince her, or possibly go without her knowing . . .

Dad suddenly stood, the feet of his chair screeching in protest against the floorboards. He picked up his plate, and I thought he might take it out to the porch to finish his meal in peace. The plate hovered a moment in the air, and then he simply let it fall so that it crashed down onto the table, breaking into pieces, mashed potatoes splattering across our place settings.

"She's going, Ethel. And neither you nor anyone else will stop her."

CHAPTER
44

GERT

I am not sorry. I will tell anybody that, and it is the truth.
I lived the way I wanted and never did what people said
I should do or advised me to do.
—Fanny Brice, comedian and singer

I lied about the money, but I knew Winnie would've turned it down flat if she knew it took three months to make enough for her tuition instead of three weeks. Leg shows don't pay like vaudeville, even if you are the featured girl.

I didn't start out like that. I'd asked Nils for anything but onstage, and that's just what I did for two months, until well after Winnie went back to Johnson City last December. So I never lied to her face, only to the paper I wrote my letters on after she left.

The funny thing was, the first question Nils asked me was whether I had a high school diploma, because if I did, he'd give me a job in his secretarial pool.

Oh, this is rich, I thought. Someday I'll tell Winnie and we'll have a good laugh over it.

There were three of us girls in the "pool," but we didn't have time to talk or be friendly. It turns out running a string of burlesque houses takes an awful lot of paperwork. We never had a moment to breathe. It was my worst nightmare, showing daily. I even had to go out and buy a high-collar shirtwaist and long skirt with my first paycheck—no new fashions allowed!

On top of everything, the money was peanuts. I was never going to get out of that filthy boardinghouse if I stayed in the pool. Every night I sat in my cramped little room and lifted a dictionary over and over with my bad arm, working the muscles, gaining my strength back.

I tried to get in with a new vaudeville act, but I couldn't find any acrobats who needed another girl, and tumbling is really all I know. I can't sing or eat fire. I can't do impressions or regurgitate a fish. All that time I would've given anything to get away from my family, and now I'd give anything to be working with them again instead of shaking for a living.

I hate burlesque. I started in February and swore to myself I'd bank up some dough and be out in six months. But then Winnie got into college, and I couldn't let her down. I shudder to imagine what Tip would think. He wouldn't even black up, for cripes' sake.

With any luck it won't be long, though. Last week the craziest thing happened.

We'd closed the show, put our clothes back on, and were all filing out into the alley as usual. I ignored the stage-door johnnies—I wasn't interested in free drinks anymore. It was cold for October, even in Fresno, and I just wanted to go back to my shabby little hotel room and sleep. But at the far end of the alley by the street, a small man with wispy hair leaned against the brick wall. In a brown suit.

I stopped dead in my tracks, mortified at being found out.

"Hungry?" he said.

I wasn't, but I knew he was. Birnbaum was *always* hungry.

"Now don't be embarrassed," he said. "You ain't the first girl to get her paycheck however she can. Let's get a bite and see what we can work out."

"How'd you find me?"

"I know people." He took my arm and steered me to a little diner down the street. "Besides, your mother was worried that maybe your chorus line was no Ziegfeld Follies. When that woman gets an idea in her head she's like a dog with a bone. She gets a look, and I don't care if you're Geronimo himself, your knees start knocking. You know that look?"

"Oh yes," I said with a chuckle. "I'm familiar."

The waitress came by, slow and slack-eyed. It was 2 a.m., and I knew how tired she must be. "Reubens and coffee for both of us," he told her. "And get yourself a cup while you're at it."

He turned back to me. "Now, listen. What do you want to do? You want to stay in burlesque, fine by me, it's our little secret. You want to go back to vaudeville, I'll see what I can find. But I gotta warn you, it's starting to get scarce out there. Flickers are getting better all the time, and they say it won't be long before they have sound, too. Someday soon you'll be able to see a whole vaudeville show just by running a film projector. Radio stations are starting to play music and entertainment. Why would people go out and pay for a show when they can stay home and listen for free?" The waitress brought over the coffee, and he took a giant slurp.

"What about you?" I said. "What are you going to do if vaudeville goes belly-up?"

"It's already in the works. I'm going to go to Hollywood and be an agent for all those flicker actors. I got the skills and contacts. Just need to get things nailed down."

I had to smile. He and Mother had one thing in common: they always had an eye out for the next scheme.

He wagged a finger at me. "That's where you should be."

I'd thought of this, of course. But it was a dicey game. Burlesque was jam-packed with girls who'd tried and failed. "You think I could make it?"

He gazed at me a moment. "I'll tell you what I think. I think I'm looking at a girl whose act stunk when I first took it on. And in less than a year, it was high class and headlining in the big time. I'm looking at a girl who's smart enough to spot an opportunity when it comes her way and make the most of it. So yes, if I had to lay money, I'd say you could make it."

It was the most hopeful I'd felt in a year, since the fire. I could have kissed the man. "You want to be my agent?" I said with a smile. "Again?"

"I do, but let's not get ahead of ourselves. I gotta get out to Holly-wood and set up shop. Can you hang in there a month or two more, till I can get some traction? Even then it's not a sure thing, of course. There's no guarantees in life, and in showbiz even fewer."

I nodded and tried not to burst with gratitude. "For you, Mr. Birn-baum, I can wait."

His pale cheeks colored, and his grin went sheepish. "Ah, call me Morty."

EPILOGUE

WINNIE

You ain't heard nothin' yet.
—Al Jolson, actor, singer, and minstrel

NOVEMBER 1920

Tower Court is the nicest place I've ever lived for more than a week.
The great room is two stories high, and there are floor-to-ceiling
lead glass windows that look out over the pond. I like to sit on the high-
backed cushioned benches by the fireplace and do my homework. My
roommate, Miss Olive Ann Greenbridge of the Huntington Bay Green-
bridges, can't study with anyone else around. She's easily distracted, and
she isn't used to sharing a room, which she announced quite matter-of-
factly when I met her on my first day here at Wellesley College.

Lucky me, I thought.

Actually, I *am* lucky. I can read a book in the midst of people
rehearsing their songs or knockabout routines, with wild animals or
drunken performers wandering by. And I definitely know how to share.

On Saturday mornings I get up early and take a trolley west to
Natick and another north into Belham to see Joe and Signora Cole. She
didn't like me at first, no matter how hard I tried.

"An Italian mother never thinks any woman is good enough for her son. The fact that you're not *italiana* only makes it worse," Joe explained as he helped me move into my dorm room in September. "The way Mama sees it, if she accepts you right away, it means I'm not worth very much, which would be an insult to her mother-hood."

"So if I understand correctly," I said, "to like me is to insult herself."

Joe laughed. "Exactly. But she's a reasonable person—"

"Oh yes, that sounds *entirely* reasonable."

"You can't see it now, but you will. She's smart and independent herself, and even though she doesn't like you, she respects you, which bothers her, and makes her like you less. But if you don't try so hard to make her like you, she will respect you even more, and the respect will win out, and she'll like you despite herself."

"I can only imagine what she thinks about my going to college."

"Oh, she hates it! But—"

"Don't tell me." I put up my hand. "She hates it, but she respects me because it's smart and independent, and because I continue to go even though she disapproves."

He threw his head back and laughed. "Ah, Winnie, *tesoro*! I love you so much."

"I suppose I must love you, too," I said. "Otherwise I'd run scream-ing from the premises."

Strangely, Signora Cole's dislike is proving be a wonderful gift. The only way I can even hope to make her like me is to stop trying to make her like me, and to go on being smart and independent. So that's what I'm doing. It isn't even very hard.

In fact, I enjoy it.

Today the sky hangs heavy with pewter gray clouds as the trolley car shudders along the tracks. *Snow's coming*, I think, and it's about time. In Upstate New York they've got half a foot already. I tug my cloche down over my ears and reach a mittened hand into the pocket of my coat. I reread Nell's letter so I can get all the details right when I tell the story to Joe.

November 12, 1920

Winnie Dear,

I've been thinking of you and hoping everything's going well at school. I'm sure you'll make the most of your classes, and not get too distracted by Joe living only two towns away. There's plenty of time for all of that.

I have a funny story to tell you. A couple of nights ago, Fred and I were in the middle of our act, and who comes toddling out onto the stage but your naughty nephew. Apparently Mother was chatting with the ventriloquist and took her eye off Harry for a moment.

He hit the boards calling, "Mama! Mama!" And what could I do? I scooped him up, turned to Fred, and said, "I guess there's something I should tell you." Fred made a great show of shock, and the audience howled with laughter. Then my little scalawag reached out, saying, "Fed!" That's what he calls Fred because he can't say his Rs yet.

That scoundrel took the baby into his arms, got down on one knee, and said, "Well then, I guess there's something I should ask you. Will you marry me?" A gasp went up in the house as they waited for my answer.

Well, I was more than a little caught off guard. But the answer I felt in my heart was yes. Yes! He's a good, kind man, he loves my boy, and we've gotten so close traveling together these past eighteen months. He's been patient enough to let our bond grow over time.

But this is vaudeville and we were in the middle of a show. I made my eyes go wide with surprise (which was hardly an act) and then broke into a big smile. "I guess I'd better!" I said, and the roof nearly came off the place, with all the hollering and clapping and foot stomping.

We've had to change the act, of course. It's a marriage gag now, and at the right moment, Mother sends little Harry running onstage. It slays them every time.

We'll take our vows in the city at Christmastime, and I hope *you'll be there with Joe and his mother, if she wishes to come. New York is so beautiful all dressed up for the holidays.*

I'm glad to hear Joe was able to pay off his father's land and build a little house there. That must be nice for him, knowing his father would be happy. And how wonderful that he's kept up his piano playing, too—at a little speakeasy called The Palace, no less! Lucy must be smiling down from heaven, knowing her big brother finally got to "play The Palace."

It's funny how much we care about what the dead might say if they could see us now. Harry would be so surprised to see me onstage. That's not at all who I was when I was married to him. But I think he would be glad for my happiness. He was so generous that way.

Yes, don't worry, I voted and I wore white. I'm just sorry you weren't old enough to join me. Two more years, and you'll be making full use of the Nineteenth Amendment, too.

All my love,
Nell

I tuck the letter back into my pocket and smile all over again, happiness for her warming me against the bitter gusts that blow through the trolley when the doors open at each stop. It certainly is a different life than she would've had with dear Harry, but a good one, if a bit out of the ordinary. I ponder this as the trolley makes its way through the village of Cochituate, past the churches and shops and the neat little houses. An ordinary life.

My parents began their marriage in the usual way, living under the same roof, my father going off to work each day, my mother cleaning and cooking and wagging her finger at us girls. They never seemed to suffer from an excess of happiness. And now Dad still goes to work, but he takes more time to fuss over Kit, and he can play his Enrico Caruso records as loudly as he likes. Mother is in as near a blissful state as I've ever known her to be, living in the larger-than-life world of big-time vaudeville. Her letters always include boasts and complaints about one thing and another, but that's just Mother, finally content.

Someday soon, Joe and I will have a conversation about life and its variations on "ordinary." I can sense that he wants to get on with things. The thought of it fills me with hope and dread in equal measure, as I try to imagine how his dreams might coexist with mine.

Gert's letter came the day after Nell's, but I don't carry it with me. I don't want Joe to see it—he wouldn't be able to read between the lines, to understand how much she cares for us both. Besides it's short and I know it by heart.

November 14, 1920

Winnie,

You're really beginning to annoy me. Stop fussing about whether I can afford your tuition! Like the old guys taught us, vaudevillians help vaudevillians. No matter where we go or what we become, that will always be a part of who we are. Besides, I like thinking about you sitting in some viney old building, using three-dollar words with people who actually understand them. Or care.

Just do me one favor. I like Joe, you know I do. But don't let him get in the way of your future. Maybe he'll be part of it, or maybe he won't. Either way, don't black up for other people's comfort.

Tell Nell I'm sorry I can't make it to the wedding. She'll under-stand. She knows the business.

Gert

PS: Miss you, too.

Joe waits for me at the trolley stop on Old Connecticut Path, as he does every Saturday morning. I notice that his coat is getting a little tight around the shoulders, now that he spends his days working the land instead of sitting around dim backstage areas, waiting to tickle the ivories for twelve minutes.

He pulls me into a snug embrace, kisses me, and says, "Mama says to tell you she made biscotti with the pistachios, the way you like it."

I raise my eyebrows. "That's very sweet of her."

"Just as you deserve. Now, how did you do on that biology test?"

I smile coyly.

"You aced it!" He grins. "I knew you would."

As we walk down the road, the treetops sway in a little soft shoe, and the weak morning sun illuminates a velvet curtain of clouds like a footlight.

AUTHOR'S NOTE

Vaudeville is dead, but it's always had a mighty lively corpse.
—Unknown

One of the criteria I used for where the Turner Sisters would perform was that the vaudeville houses had to remain in existence today. This proved quite a challenge, since the vast majority of theatres, no matter how opulent, fell into disuse and were demolished. Of those mentioned in this novel, some have been turned into movie theatres, but many have been restored to their original grandeur, and now host music, plays, and comedy acts. Please visit them! If not currently known by the name used in 1919, I've listed them below to make them easier to find:

- Cuba, New York—The Keller Opera House is now known by its original name, the Palmer Opera House. The original owner, Mr. Palmer, lost it in a poker game to Mr. H. E. Keller sometime in the early 1900s.
- Hamilton, New York—The Sheldon Opera House is now the Hamilton Movie Theatre.
- Sackets Harbor, New York—The International Order of Odd Fellows Hall is now the Lake Ontario Playhouse.
- Walton, New York—The Walton Opera House is now the Walton Theatre.

Opera houses only occasionally hosted actual operas. It was just another word for theatre. The cities listed on the Tumbling Turners' big-time tours also have vaudeville houses that exist today. The hotels and restaurants all existed, as well, though most are now long gone.

The Cahn-Leighton Official Theatrical Guide of 1913–14 was my bible of details about each theatre. Unfortunately no edition was published for 1919, so I operated under the assumption that information regarding stage dimensions, number of seats, dressing rooms, etc., was likely to remain stable. They have often changed dramatically since then, however. For instance, the Ohmann Theatre in Lyons, New York, was listed as having four dressing rooms, but they've somehow disappeared. The current manager suspects they were along the back of the house and later removed. For each location, I used the actual name of the theatre manager listed in the guide, and invented personal traits.

In the spirit of theft that permeated vaudeville, all of the comedy sketches in the novel are based on those of real vaudeville acts. Yes, they were that corny!

The quotes at the beginning of each chapter are from vaudeville performers, though readers today may know them from subsequent work in radio, TV, and movies. The one exception is Lillian Gish, who was a stage and film actress. Helen Keller, along with her teacher, Annie Sullivan, began her vaudeville career at The Palace in New York City in 1920. Her act, "The Star of Happiness," displayed her ability to understand spoken language by putting her hand on her teacher's lips, and respond to questions from the audience, showcasing her extraordinary intelligence and wit. Her act was instrumental in changing the prevailing sentiment that blind and deaf children should be institutionalized rather than taught.

The three-hour silent film *The Birth of a Nation* was hugely successful and horrifyingly racist (it was hard to sit through), and did in fact spark a major resurgence of the Ku Klux Klan. Harvard's chapter of the KKK began in 1921, not 1919 as stated in the story, but I thought the fact was so interesting and appalling that I moved up the date so I could include it. The film's writer/director/producer, D. W. Griffith, was the son of a Confederate Army general, and believed deeply in the story.

It's said that leading lady Lillian Gish denied the film's racism to her death in 1993 at the age of ninety-nine.

Archie Leach was fifteen years old in 1919, and was a member of the Bob Pender Troupe, as indicated in the novel. However, the troupe didn't come to America until 1920. In 1932, he changed his name to Cary Grant, and though he often used his acrobatic skills and performed many of his own stunts in movies, he was better known for his charm and sophistication than for his ability to do a pratfall. As he later became one of the most successful actors of all time, Gert's estimation that he would never amount to much certainly proved incorrect.

Women's suffrage, the right of all women to vote in federal elections, was ratified by three quarters of the state legislatures, and was thus encoded in federal law on August 26, 1920. It almost didn't happen. After a summer of intense debate, Tennessee, the last state needed to ratify, took its vote on August 18, and passed by only a one-vote margin. The surprise aye vote was twenty-four-year-old Harry Burn, who had been squarely in the antisuffrage camp. That morning he'd received a note from his mother imploring him to "be a good boy" and vote in favor. He enraged his antisuffrage colleagues by changing his vote—and history. He later defended himself by stating, "I know that a mother's advice is always safest for her boy to follow."

Margaret Sanger was a nurse who worked with the teeming immigrant population in New York City's Lower East Side. After watching her own mother die from the strain of eighteen pregnancies, she dedicated her life to the legalization of birth control, a term she coined in 1914. She opened the country's first pregnancy prevention clinic in 1916, for which she was promptly arrested.

On January 15, 1919, a five-story, 2.3-million-gallon metal tank on the shore of Boston's North End split open. A wave of molasses reported to be 15 feet high and 160 feet wide came crashing down Commercial Street, destroying everything in its path, killing 21 people and injuring about 150 others. At first it was thought to be an act of sabotage by anarchists, but it was eventually determined that shoddy construction was the cause, and years later the owners were made to pay compensation to the victims' families.

Why was there such an enormous tank of molasses on the Boston waterfront, you may ask? Molasses can be fermented to create ethanol, or drinking alcohol—most commonly in the form of rum—and in the last days before Prohibition, companies were anxious to make and sell as much alcohol as possible. It can also be used to make industrial alcohol, a necessary ingredient for certain kinds of explosives, which was particularly important during the recently concluded Great War.

The fire that broke out at the luxurious Lincoln Hotel in Seattle, Washington, actually happened on April 7, 1920, six months later than in the novel. It began in the basement a little after midnight and spread rapidly up through the building. The elevators stopped working, and over three hundred guests fled by means of stairs, external fire escapes, and fire engine ladders, and some were even lowered by ropes. Four people—a father and daughter, a young woman, and a firefighter—lost their lives in the blaze. The man and his daughter jumped to their deaths from the sixth floor. Afterward, the fire marshal said his department had considered the place a firetrap since its construction in 1899, "a lumber yard with four brick walls around it." This inspired closer scrutiny of the city's hotels to make sure they complied with the fire code.

Ethel Turner's fear of fire is spurred by the Binghamton Clothing Factory conflagration that occurred on July 22, 1913, killing thirty-one people, mostly young women. Because of the July heat, all the windows were open in the four-story building, and a stiff breeze fanned the flames, destroying the building in less than twenty minutes. Later, Ethel refers to the 1903 fire at the Iroquois Theatre in Chicago, in which approximately six hundred people died, due to the fact that twenty-seven of the thirty-nine exits were locked. Touted as "absolutely fireproof," the Iroquois remains the deadliest single-building fire in U.S. history.

I own three primary sources that were invaluable to me as I wrote this novel. The first is the *Montgomery Ward Catalogue & Buyers Guide* from 1919. At over a thousand pages, it gave me pictures of everything from what the Turners might have worn, to products they might have used, to the toys that little Harry might have played with. Though the fashions were likely above their means at the beginning of the story, it offered helpful ideas of what they might have aspired to.

My copy of *Johnson's First Aid Manual, Eighth Edition*, was distributed in 1918 as a giveaway mainly to industrial businesses, such as mining companies, whose employees would be most at risk for accidents. It contains all manner of instruction about handling injuries, such as: "Assume command of the situation. There can be only one chief."

I have a January 1929 edition of *American Cookery*, published by The Boston Cooking School Magazine Company, at 221 Columbus Avenue (now luxury condos). I got the recipe for Lima Bean Sausages and Beef Shank and Kidney Pie from this volume, and while it was published a decade after the time of the story, I thought these budget-conscious meals would fit the Turner family dinner table quite well.

Our Lady of Lourdes Hospital, where Winnie works in the maternity ward, did not actually open until 1925, founded by the Daughters of Charity. However, as I was born in that maternity ward, I decided to apply a bit of authorial license and use it anyway.

A final note of interest to those who may have read my earlier novels: The Palace in the fictitious town of Belham, where Joe plays piano at the end of the story, is the same tavern—affectionately known as The Pal—from *Shelter Me* and *The Shortest Way Home*.

My great-grandfather Fred Delorme (right) performed in many local variety and vaudeville shows in the Johnson City–Binghamton area in the early 1900s.

COURTESY OF THE AUTHOR

Great-grandpa Fred's dancing shoes.

PHOTO CREDIT: N. GRACE

For more pictures of vaudevillians who inspired characters in
The Tumbling Turner Sisters *and the real-life theatres
where the sisters performed, please go to www.juliettefay.com.*

ACKNOWLEDGMENTS

My great-grandfather Fred Delorme was a vaudevillian. He never quite made it to the big time, but from the many newspaper clippings we have, he certainly claimed his share of success in small-time shows and revues. He married Nell Smith in 1908 and had six children, including my grandmother, Margaret Delorme Dacey, who sometimes danced with him in shows. To support his family, Great-grandpa Fred kept his day job at the Endicott-Johnson Shoe Company in Johnson City, New York.

I like to think that having his name used in a story about vaudeville would appeal to my great-grandfather's love of entertainment. For the record, Great-grandma Nell was not married previously nor did she have any children before marrying Great-grandpa Fred. I've used their names and a few details of their lives, but generally the fiction begins very early on. I learned only after I'd written the novel that Great-grandma Nell actually did have a sister named Gert.

I'd like to thank my father, John Dacey, for inadvertently reminding me about his grandfather's vaudeville career while trying to convince me to write a novel about Oliver Cromwell's violent domination of Ireland. This happened to include mention of how our ancestors fled Ireland and settled in the area of Binghamton, New York, where many years later, I was born. Sorry, Dad, but I'm still glad I went with the vaudeville idea, and not Cromwell.

The late Anne Delorme Castelli was Fred Delorme's only living child, and she told me about his dancing with her sister, Margaret, and how he used to give clog dancing lessons at their house on Floral Avenue. My cousin, the late Jim Stein, sent along photos and newspaper clippings, and his sister, Nancy Grace, located Great-grandpa Fred's dancing shoes for me! I'd like to thank them and all the descendants of Fred and Nell Delorme, particularly my Dacey uncles, aunts, and cousins. They are a wonderfully entertaining bunch, and it's easy to see where they get it.

Warmest thanks go to my writers' group, Nichole Bernier, Kathy Crowley, EB Moore and Randy Susan Meyers; my friends, Megan Lucier and Catherine Toro-McCue; and my sister, Kristen Dacey Iwai, who provided multiple early reads and great feedback. I am also fortunate to be a part of the Fiction Writer's Co-op, whose collective willingness to promote one another's books, discuss industry intel, and generate hilarious comment threads is seemingly boundless.

My agent, Stephanie Abou, was tireless in finding the right home for this book. Her efforts brought me to editor Lauren McKenna and assistant editor Elana Cohen, who offered great vision as to how to make this story richer and stronger. Heartfelt thanks to all of these wonderful, smart women for helping me get the Turner show on the road.

Jeri Wellman and Randy Susan Meyers made sure I got all those wonderful Yiddish words right. Tom Herendeen, manager of the Ohmann Theatre in Lyons, New York, gave me the "nickel tour" of the former vaudeville house, and put me in contact with Bob Ohmann, grandson of Burt, who was the owner/manager of the theatre when the Turner sisters would have performed there. He told me that Burt Ohmann was "kind of gruff and loved his stogies." Jessica Allen at the Smith Opera House in Geneva, New York, was also kind enough to let me wander around and gave me a brochure full of wonderful pictures and a history of the Smith.

I'd also like to send out a posthumous prayer of thanks to the great George Burns, whose several autobiographies on his life in vaudeville with his beloved wife, Gracie Allen, provided a fascinating perspective. A true entertainer to the end, his were the most fun to read of the countless books I consumed on the subject.

As of this writing, my children, Quinn, Nick, Liam, and Brianna Fay, are ages thirteen to twenty-two, just like the Turner sisters. As I wrote, it was fun (and slightly anxiety producing) to imagine my four taking their talent and wit on the road. I am grateful for their love and inspiration, and for their finely honed ability to crack up their father and me. And I really don't know how I would make my life work at all without the love, good humor, and co-parenting wisdom of my husband, Tom Fay.